In ROYAL
SERVICE
to the
QUEEN

In ROYAL SERVICE

to the QUEEN

A NOVEL OF THE QUEEN'S GOVERNESS

TESSA ARLEN

BERKLEY
NEW YORK

BERKLEY
An imprint of Penguin Random House LLC
penguinrandomhouse.com

Library of Congress Cataloging-in-Publication Data

Names: Arlen, Tessa, author.
Title: In royal service to the Queen: a novel of the Queen's governess /
Tessa Arlen.
Description: First edition. | New York: Berkley, 2021.
Identifiers: LCCN 2021008119 (print) | LCCN 2021008120 (ebook) |
ISBN 9780593102480 (trade paperback) | ISBN 9780593102497 (ebook)
Subjects: LCSH: Crawford, Marion, 1909-1988—Fiction. |
Elizabeth II, Queen
of Great Britain, 1926—Fiction. | GSAFD: Biographical fiction.
Classification: LCC PS3601.R5445 I5 2021 (print) |
LCC PS3601.R5445 (ebook) | DDC 813/.6—dc23
LC record available at https://lccn.loc.gov/2021008119
LC ebook record available at https://lccn.loc.gov/2021008120

First Edition: June 2021

Printed in the United States of America
1st Printing

Book design by Tiffany Estreicher

To my mother

PART ONE

1931–1936

CHAPTER ONE

June 18, 1931
Limekiln Cottage, Dunfermline, Scotland

Good Lord above, Marion, have you quite gone off your head?" My mother banged the oven door shut and straightened up. Her cheeks flushed, and not from baking bread on the warmest afternoon of summer.

She pushed back graying hair, leaving her palm clasped across her forehead, as if to hold on to reason. "I hope you didn't accept!" Her voice lifted in pitch and volume. "I hope you didn't say yes." Her eyes bored into mine from across the kitchen. "You did, didn't you?" She threw her hands up—her fingers stiff with anger. "Well, you'll just have to tell them you are not going. I won't let you ruin your future because someone plants a daft idea in your head. And that's final."

"Oh dear." I kept my voice light. "And I always wanted to know what it would be like for a maid to bring me my early-morning tea and a footman to clean my shoes."

It was like putting a match to brandy pudding: her cheeks flared crimson; her eyes flashed a warning. "There is no need for you to be so flippant, my girl. Not when you are about to jeopardize your career with this ridiculous jaunt down south." She threw her tea towel on the kitchen table. "I don't understand you: the things you come up with. Did Lady Elgin put you up to this nonsense? Of course she did. I knew looking after her children this summer would distract you from your studies."

I began to regret my first excited, heedless words. "I have been offered a job teaching the Duchess of York's little girl . . ." I reached out to her, my fingers curled lightly around her arm. She shook them off with a twist of her shoulder. "Ma, would you please stop—for a moment?"

"I am trying to stop you—from wrecking your life!"

"There's a lot more to this than my going to London just because I was offered a posh job."

She clasped my shoulder. A shake with each word. "All your life you have wanted to be a teacher." The intensity in her voice softened. "Isn't that what all this hard work has been for? The letters of recommendation. The Moray Training College agreeing to extend your scholarship for the autumn term. Most people would give their eyeteeth . . . So, why on earth would you want to throw it all away?" She drew in a breath to continue, her earnest gaze fastened on my face. "My dear girl, you know as well as I do that these people . . . they are different. Nothing like us. Nothing! Their way of life, their money . . . their . . . their . . ." She wrung her hands in her apron and stumbled into speech again. "Their place in the world. They are demanding and inconsiderate to the folk who work for them. You'd be little better than one of their servants."

I opened my mouth to say I would be nothing of the kind, but I shut it again. I understood her desperate need to save me from the sort of life my grandmother knew: a housekeeper to a wealthy land-owning family. "I haven't said yes to the job. Because I wanted to thrash it out with you first. You know, the way we always do? Just like this." She huffed and turned away. "Come on, come outside and get a breath of air—it's stifling in here. I want to tell you everything that happened, and then you can tell me what you *really* think!"

A grunt of reluctant assent, but she allowed me to steer her through the door to our garden behind the cottage. I sat her down on an old oak bench under the kitchen window. She leaned back against the stone wall and flapped her hand in front of her face. "Oof, but it's hot in that kitchen—what a summer!"

She looked out across the vegetable garden. Two ducks glided in to land on the surface of the pond, braked with their wings, too late, and skidded into its far bank: a piece of clownery that always made her laugh, but not today. I watched her struggle for equanimity, or as she put it, to "get ahold of herself," a lifelong practice in the face of all the adversity and disappointment she had known in her fifty-six years. The rise and fall of her chest slowed its pace, her cheeks, still pink with distress, relaxed muscles tight with anxiety. I went back into the kitchen, worked the pump hard to bring up cold water from the well, and returned with two glasses.

She took a sip. "There, that's better." She turned to squint at me, her hand shielding her face from the sun slanting through the leaves of the mulberry tree that shaded the kitchen door. She took my hand in her lap and smoothed its palm with her thumb, as if trying to ease away my wayward thoughts.

"I didn't mean to lead off quite so . . ." Her mouth turned down. "You fairly caught me on the hop." She patted my hand to reassure herself that she had misunderstood. "You're not seriously thinking of taking up this offer, are you, Marion?"

I curled my fingers around her hand. "First of all, the job is only for three months. I will be back in Edinburgh at the end of September to start my psychology course. Nothing will—"

"Exhausted from overwork and completely unprepared."

I shook my head. "Not at all; this is a summer job. And I will have the afternoons free to study. There are only two girls in the family. The younger one will be looked after by her nanny. I am to teach the older one: Princess Elizabeth—Lilibet, they call her. She's five."

"A governess is *not* the same thing as a schoolteacher. One is a flunky; the other performs a public service—a vital one, and one sorely needed by the children of working families!"

"Yes, I know that, Ma. But you're all steamed up over nothing: this is a *short-term* job, and I'll be a schoolteacher for the rest of my working life. Anyway, I liked them. She is a nice woman: straightforward, kind, and, unlikely as it sounds, quite ordinary."

"There is nothing ordinary about a duchess, my darling girl, particularly a *royal* one."

I smiled, because the duchess, with her quick blue eyes, her unfashionable wispy fringe of fine brown hair, and her tinkly, girlish laugh, struck me, again, as commonplace. Not the sort of woman a king's son would marry, even if Prince Albert, the Duke of York, was second in line to the throne: the spare.

Be patient, I reminded myself as my mother said something about the arrogance of aristocrats, most of them with pea-size brains. *You know this is an amazing offer. Now, explain why to her— tactfully!*

"I didn't realize it until today, but I have never been out of Scotland before. A summer spent teaching the granddaughter to our king would be a chance to see a part of life that we only read about in history books . . . years later. It will be good for me: broadening, even!"

Her eyebrows arched high into her hairline, and one shoulder came up: "Who would want to see that? Weren't your grandmother's stories of working for Call-Me-God Lord Abercrombie and his family enough? The long, hard hours she endured, she had no life of her own—it was dedicated to making the Abercrombies' existence one of untroubled luxury." She snorted. "In those days there was little choice—you got work where you could—God help them."

I pretended not to see the dismissive shoulder. "They are offering me two pounds a week for teaching one little girl, five mornings a week. Hardly slave labor. Just think of the money I'll save." I could see interruptions forming in the impatient shake of her head and lifted a hand. "I think you would like the duchess. In fact, I know you would. She is unaffected, down-to-earth, with everyday manners. Her husband is not what I imagined a duke to be like at all."

I put my hand on her knee and slowed the urgency in my voice. "The duke reminds me of that man who rented Old Cottage, you remember him—years ago?"

She tilted an incredulous face up at me. "You don't mean that Mr. Whatsis—the retired postmaster from Glasgow who wanted to live in the country and then couldn't take the quiet?" Both hands came up to cover her mouth, and she giggled. "But he wasn't quite right—in the head."

"Yes, that's the one. No, I'm not saying that the duke doesn't have all his *marbles*. But he's nervy. Do you remember when Mr. Ross's cow chased Mr.—I wish I could remember his name—across the fields? He packed up and went back to the city."

"Came here to retire and lasted a week." Ma shook her head. "Poor wee chap." She laughed. "Fancy you remembering him—Mr. Thistle, was it? No, it was Twistleton." She raised the glass to her lips and took little pecking sips of water, laughing at the memory. "The duke reminded you of Mr. *Twistleton*?"

"A little bit. He's not as jumpy or as timid, but he is rather quiet and withdrawn, and he has that same watchful, awkward way about him with people or situations he is not familiar with."

"Inbreeding, that's their problem, the aristocracy."

I ignored her mistrust of the upper classes. "The duke has a nice sort of face; his eyes are probably his best feature when he actually lifts his head. He's a bit on the skinny side . . . I suppose, if anything, he's rather unprepossessing." I was putting it kindly, because he struck me as a diffident little man who had hung around in the background of Lady Elgin's impromptu elevenses party, smoking cigarettes as he gazed down at his impeccably polished brogues. "I mistook him for aloof: bored sitting with a bunch of women. Then it occurred to me that he's probably shy. He certainly let her do all the talking."

She stopped sipping her water to pounce. "Chatterbox, is she?"

"Lively. She referred to her Highland ancestry quite a bit. Her family are from Angus. She said how much she loved coming home to Scotland. But mostly she talked of her little girls—adorable, she called them."

A rousing harrumph from my mother at such affectations. A plainspoken Scotswoman who liked her children noisy and out from under her feet: catching tadpoles in the duckpond, scrumping for apples, and making tree forts. I looked down at her thin wrists and bowed shoulders. Her days as a mother of three young children were long gone. I am now her only child, and here I was breaking the news of a job nearly six hundred miles away.

I spread out the fingers of both hands. "This job is a small, cautious adventure before I return to Moray College," I explained. "The duchess completely understands about my returning to Edinburgh in September to finish my studies. She is really interested in my psychology course—asked me questions." *But no easily impressed fool either.* I remembered the way she watched me over the rim of her coffee cup, her cool blue gaze assessing, as she steered the conversation to my job teaching Lord and Lady Elgin's unruly gang of children for the summer.

"Lady Elgin tells me that you are instructing Andrew in history?" Her fluting, cultured voice held no hint that her family were from Angus. If I closed my eyes, I would have put the duchess's age at fourteen.

I glanced at Lady Elgin, sitting placidly in her comfortably shabby drawing room, smiling complacent approval at her son's accomplishments under my tutelage. "Yes, ma'am. Fifteenth century: the Wars of the Roses."

The duchess tilted her head, a playful smile on her round face. "I hope he is on the York side!" she said to laughter all round. "And the girls?"

"Martha and Jeanie are keeping a journal of the books they are reading this summer. Martha enjoys the Brontë sisters, and Jeanie"—I laughed—"Jeanie is a confirmed Scot: she is completely in love with the poetry of Robert Burns. Mary . . ."

But she wasn't interested in the Elgins' little cousin Mary, stumbling through her first reader. "Good for Jeanie. I was in love with Rabbie Burns too, when I was a girl." The duchess sat forward in her chair, her back straight, hands clasped in the lap of her powder blue dress in a parody of a schoolgirl called on to recite after tea. "Let me see if I can remember." She composed her face, eyes upward for inspiration. "Ah yes: 'My love is like a red, red rose That's newly sprung in June; My love is like the something-something'"—she rotated a hand in the air—"'That's . . . that's sweetly played in . . . tune'?" She lifted her hands and shrugged her shoulders in exaggerated apology.

"M-m-melody," her husband put in. "My l-l-love is like the . . . *melody*." His wide smile transformed him into a more vulnerable version of his pretty brother, the Prince of Wales.

"Of course, so silly of me. Thank you, Bertie." She beamed. "My love is like a melody!"

Her peel of self-deprecating laughter, her vitality, and her sense of the absurd warmed me to her. She might have been a girl of my own age and not daughter-in-law to the king, with two children in the nursery. Sometimes we serious Scots take life a bit too ponderously, but this little woman, with her bright smile and her rather ridiculous feathery hat, was fun!

I recounted all this to my mother—leaving out the poetry and the hat.

"And are you quite sure she understands that this is only for three months, that you will be returning to Edinburgh to continue your studies?"

"I will be back in Edinburgh to start my class on the twenty-ninth of September, and they are compensating me very generously, considering I have no experience—except for the Elgin children." I tried to keep my voice even and firm. My mother's protestations, coupled with the thought of traveling down to London alone to a strange and intimidatingly grand house owned by a duke, began to eat away at my excitement for adventure.

She sighed. "It isn't about money, Marion. You don't need to go all that way to earn a few extra pounds. We have always managed to squeak by on my savings and my war widow's pension. I am more concerned that you will end up a governess and not a teacher."

I knew there was another reason for her reluctance for this job, one she would never admit to. I am her only remaining child, and our family is a small one. Both my older brothers were killed in the Great War; my father died after it, his lungs weakened by mustard gas. My mother's two spinster sisters share a house in Aberdeen exclusively with the spirit of the Lord. A student in Edinburgh could catch the bus home every other weekend. I wouldn't be able to do that from London.

"And who was this duchess, anyway, before she married?"

"Lady Elizabeth Bowes-Lyon." I lapsed into the broad Highland dialect my grandmother had spoken, "Th' duchess is as Scawts as ye 'n' me, Ma, her fowk ur th' Strathmores o' Glamis."

She gave me a knowing look. "Thun her gerls wull be Princess

Elizabeth 'n' Princess Margaret Rose tae ye, Marion—Their Ryle Highnessus. Ah hawp ye git that straecht." She shook her head at my desire to work for southern royalty: soft from a life of privilege, and, if my description of the Duke of York was anything to go by, a man who wouldn't say boo to a cow.

"I liked the way she put it, Ma, when she offered me the job; she said, 'Why don't you come down to us at Royal Lodge for a month?'" She made it sound like an invitation to visit, not an offer of employment as an interim governess. "'And then you can see if you like us, and we like you. And if we get on, you can stay for the summer!'"

July 1, 1931
Royal Lodge, Home of the Duke of York
Windsor Great Park, Berkshire, England

I awoke to the cool, gray light of five o'clock in the morning leaking around the edges of the heavy curtains of my bedroom at Royal Lodge. I lay as I had gone to sleep, flat on my back with exhaustion and my arms by my sides. The only thing I could remember of my arrival was the car turning into the drive in the evening light and the large three-story house, as pretty as a bridal cake, glowing like a pink pearl in the last rays of the sun.

I watched the dark shadows in the room take on the commonplace shape of furniture as the light grew. A large wardrobe took up the wall by the door. Two small easy chairs with needlepoint cushions stood on either side of a fireplace. Books, organized by the height of their leather spines, were arranged in a library in the corner. Ebony-framed watercolors hung on green-and-white-striped papered walls. It was a comfortable and welcoming room, unlike the grand rose- and lily-scented apartments I had peered into as the butler escorted me up the graceful sweep of the marble staircase from the hall to the third floor on my arrival.

As the Daimler had drawn up in front of Royal Lodge, the Duke of York's country house, I had sat forward, my cold hands clasped tightly across my knees to stop them from shaking. The pristine grand façade, with its windows streaming light in the darkening night, like an oceangoing passenger liner putting out to sea, was intimidating. I felt grubby and untidy. I hesitated, reluctant to leave my refuge, when the duke's chauffeur opened the back door of the car. In our short journey the man who had rescued me from the confusing chaos of King's Cross station had become my only ally in an alien world. "Here we are, now, Miss Crawford. Your long journey is finally over." Mr. Hughes extended a large leather-clad hand to help me out of the car as a tall, gray-haired man came down the steps of the house to the drive. "Good evening, Miss Crawford, I am His Grace's butler, Mr. Ainslie. Welcome to Royal Lodge."

This sleek, well-pressed man with his quiet voice was nothing like the fat, patronizing majordomo, with soup stains on his tie, that the Elgins employed. "Such a long journey to make on your own. Your first visit to down south, isn't it?" He commiserated with my long hours in a third-class carriage, with four changes on drafty station platforms, with an empathetic nod.

I turned to look for my suitcase. "Not to worry about your luggage, Miss Crawford. James will bring it up to you." A young man emerged from the shadows of the portico and took my shabby suitcase from the chauffeur. I took three steps forward to stand blinking on the bright threshold as James disappeared through a door in the paneled wall.

A black-and-white marble-tiled hall stretched ahead of me. "The princesses are already in bed," Mr. Ainslie reassured me. "The duke and duchess are out for the evening and will stay the night in their London house, so you will have a chance to relax and get your bearings. Perhaps you would care for some supper?" He half turned as we started up the stairs. All I could think of was getting out of my tweed suit; the house felt incredibly hot after our drafty cottage and the windswept country stations I had waited in.

"Thank you, I'm not hungry, Mr. Ainslie, but I would love a cup of tea," I said as I stumbled on the top stair. I was too tired to eat and yearned to kick off my new shoes that pinched.

He opened a door in a wide corridor. "This is your room; there is a little sitting room through there." He waved to a door in the opposite wall. "The bathroom is across the corridor. Please tell James if there is anything you need when he brings up your luggage. Your tea will be with you directly." He twitched a curtain into place and looked around the room. "We are glad to have you with us, Miss Crawford. A good night's rest to you." He left me to the silence of my rooms, and I sank down onto the bed and kicked off my shoes. The door opened again: a maid brought in a tea tray, her eyes alert under lowered lids. She murmured something about bread and butter before she left.

I shed clothes as fast as I could, put on my nightgown, drank a cup of hot, sweet tea, and wolfed down the three slices of thinly cut bread and butter. I pulled back the coverlet and laid my tired body down between crisp linen sheets. Cramped limbs stretched out in gratitude. I pulled the blankets up around my ears and closed my eyes.

"Lilibet—she's sleeping." I awoke to full sunlight and a small, round-faced little girl in a white embroidered cotton nightgown standing at the side of my bed. She turned and lifted a finger to her lips.

A taller girl joined her as I struggled to sit up. "Hullo," she said. Large, clear blue eyes gazed down at me from a serious face. "We did knock, but I don't think you heard us. I'm Lilibet, and this is

Margaret Rose. We are awfully sorry to wake you, but we really wanted to see you before anyone else did." She frowned that she might have said the wrong thing. "What I really mean is, would you like to join us for breakfast?" Her gravity and self-assurance were endearing, as was the concern that she had intruded. The two sisters politely waited for my answer. They had their father's large eyes, but their gaze was as steady and direct as their mother's.

"Thank you, that would be lovely, and as I am sure you have already guessed, I'm Marion Crawford." I looked at the clock on the mantel. Dear God, it was nearly eight! In order to avoid an undignified scramble for my dressing gown, I asked, "And where do you eat your breakfast?"

Lilibet looked up at the clock too. "At nine o'clock in our day nursery, but you should be there just before. It's down the corridor to your right." She smiled; it was a polite, rather tentative smile, and showed missing front teeth.

"It's buttered eggs today, and they are slithery if they get cold." Her sister's candor widened Lilibet's smile, and she took her by the hand. "Come on, Margaret, we have to go now. Alah gets cross if we aren't dressed in time for breakfast."

"Alah is your nanny?"

Lilibet nodded. "She is Mrs. Knight, but we call her Alah."

Alah. In this orderly atmosphere of sunlit rooms and buttered eggs, I wasn't surprised that someone akin to God would be annoyed about little things like impunctuality.

CHAPTER TWO

August 1936
Royal Lodge, Windsor Great Park, Berkshire, England

I looked down at the curly head bobbing at my elbow. "Will you give me a boost, Crawfie? I can't see anything!" At just-turned six, Margaret Rose was still a short, round dot of a girl.

"There is nothing much to see." I put my hands on either side of her waist and lifted her up onto the base of the stone balustrade that ran along the front of the roof of Royal Lodge. "Better?" I took her hot hand in mine to steady her as she stood on tiptoe to peer down to the drive below. "Yes, a little bit, but it's mostly all gravel."

I inhaled the soft summer air: freshly cut grass with an undernote of summer flowers. "You can see the rose garden from here. Look, there's Mr. Carter cutting blooms for the dining room." I never tired of this serene view from this exquisite house with its peaceful gardens surrounded by ancient cedars of Lebanon. Neither could I imagine my life without the Yorks' little girls; they had become a part of me as much as I had become a part of their family.

The letter I had labored over to my mother at the end of that summer in 1931, informing her of my decision to stay on, had been the hardest one I had ever written. The immense distance between Dunfermline and Windsor had yawned greater with every line. Her swift reply, in return, had reassured me that she understood my decision. The York family offered great opportunities for me to experience a different and broader view of life—at least she had the grace to say so, but I knew that she was lonely for my company.

Margaret Rose scuffed the toes of her shoes against the stone as she levered herself up another inch, bringing me back to the present.

"Look, it's Papa and Mummy. They're coming out to wait for Uncle David and his girlfriend to arrive." We both stared down at the tops of two heads below us, one bare in the dull afternoon sun, the other crowned by a pale blue hat covered in mauve silk roses, as the duke and duchess awaited the arrival of England's new king for tea.

Now she had seen all there was to see, Margaret was ready to play. "Come on, Crawfie, Lilibet will be here in a minute—we've got to hide."

I held her still for a moment longer, as the duchess's light, clear voice lifted up to us, bell-like in the heavy August air. "He's going to marry her, Bertie. He probably asked her months ago, and of course you know she said yes."

I leaned forward to try to catch the hesitant, indistinct murmur of the duke's reply.

"No, Bertie darling, I *don't* think it is a passing thing," the duchess said through trilling laughter. "He's *completely* head over heels. It's serious this time."

The duke raised his voice. "She's . . . a nov . . . novelty."

"I only wish it were that simple." The duchess's voice had an edge to it, as if she found his hesitancy, his skepticism of what she was telling him, irritating. "But you know they'll never let him stay if he marries her."

I was eavesdropping, but I simply couldn't help myself. I craned out farther, straining to catch his reply. But there was no need; his voice was strong with conviction. "He would *never* do that." The duke was easily exasperated, but there was something else beneath his impatient and emphatic response. I watched the duchess reach out her hand to pat his forearm, the way I had seen her do countless times when her husband's temper began to fray. *She pats him as if he is a highly strung horse*, I realized.

The duke cleared his throat. "He would not do that to me—we've talked about it." Then, with the beginning of doubt: "H-h-he has given me h-h-his word."

"Let's pray that he keeps it; otherwise they'll be looking to us to fill the post, and it will be goodbye to our cozy life here," the duchess said. The blare of a horn, and long green car swooped up the drive toward the house. "Good heavens, what is he driving?"

The duke didn't answer, but I watched his head droop forward and knew he was gazing at his feet.

"Is that his new car?" She touched his elbow, bringing him back to the arrival of his brother. "It's green; what a strange idea!"

"Yes, he's very prou . . . proud of it; it's called a station wagon. It's American."

"Of course it is. Well, at least she will not be coming up to Balmoral next week!"

Margaret's hand slipped out of mine to pull on my arm. "Come on, Crawfie, let's hide behind the chimneys." I turned away from the roof's edge, but the duchess's earlier words were still hanging in the still air, as heavy with warning as the clouds gathering on the eastern horizon: *You know they'll never let him stay if he marries her.* What puzzled me most was that her tone had not expressed the anxiety and alarm I had heard in that of her husband. She spoke with the calm complacency of a woman who knew what the future held for her.

"Caught you, caught you both!" Lilibet's head appeared through the schoolroom sash window. "You aren't even hiding. Anyway, I always look here first because it's Margaret's favorite spot."

"That's not fair—you didn't give us enough time!" Margaret jumped down from the balustrade ledge.

"Yes, I did—more than enough, because Alah made me tidy up the mess you made of the toy cupboard."

Margaret Rose put her hands on her hips. "It was *not* a mess; you just like to tidy everything. And we've only just got here!"

Hair ribbon coming loose, my little urchin with her scuffed shoes and grubby hands lifted a chin at her freshly washed and brushed sister. Lilibet's appraising stare was derisive. "Have you seen the state of your dress—how did you manage to tear it? You've had ages to find a hiding spot. Now it's my turn."

"No, Lilibet, no! It's just not fair!" Margaret's continual cry if life threatened to thwart her plans. "Uncle David has just arrived for tea, and I haven't hidden yet!" Her lower lip jutted in protest.

Lilibet climbed out through the window onto the roof and sauntered past us to hang over the balustrade. "Papa and Mummy are getting into his new car. Where on earth are they going?"

Margaret stamped her foot, and tears rolled down her grubby cheeks. "And now he's leaving, and I haven't even said hullo or had tea!"

I crouched down in front of her and held out my handkerchief. "They are just off for a quick spin in His Majesty's new car. Come now, blow your nose, Margaret. So, tell me"—I lifted her wrist—"what time is it on your new watch?"

"It's five minutes to flippin' four." She giggled at the shocked gasp from Lilibet. Margaret had recently befriended a new page who muttered "flippin' heck" under his breath in times of stress.

"Just five minutes to four o'clock will do quite nicely, thank you. And what time is tea?"

"Five o'clock."

"Good girl, so you see we have time for one more round of hide-and-seek, and I do believe it's my turn to hide. Come on, in you get!" I helped Margaret Rose in through the window and ran down the back stairs to the utility cupboard between the bottom of the back stairs and the house's main staircase. I would have time for a private moment, or two, to ponder the scraps of conversation I had heard from the roof.

Surely the king has no intention of marrying Mrs. Simpson? All of his previous affairs were with women who had husbands, and he hadn't wanted to marry them.

The duke's stammered response to his wife's determination that the king was head over heels came back to me: *H-h-he has given me h-h-his word.* My heart went out to a man who adored and trusted his urbane and confident elder brother. But his trust had begun to unravel about the edges at his wife's insistence that the king intended to marry Mrs. Simpson. Her confident words made his own stick in his throat; he was incredulous that his beloved brother might let him down.

But it is time he married, now he's king—he's all of forty-two.

But to Mrs. Simpson? I tried to remember my constitutional history. Our monarch could not marry a Roman Catholic—of that I was quite clear. Britain's monarch was the head of the Church of England, so marriage to a Catholic was out of the question.

Perhaps the disapproval I had heard in Mr. Ainslie's and Alah's voices when Mrs. Simpson's name was mentioned was because she was a Catholic? No, it was because she was divorced, not from

Mr. Simpson, who was very much alive, and apparently also singularly active in London's hectic social scene. And didn't Mrs. Simpson have an ex-husband tucked away somewhere in America? I pondered the American's two husbands. It was unimaginable that our king, however progressive he thought he was, would even think of marrying a twice-divorced woman.

Divorce, such a tricky business in our country, might be legal, but it wasn't respectable, and the church would not sanction the king's marriage to this American divorcée while both her husbands were still alive.

As I crouched under the low ceiling of the utility cupboard among the mops and buckets in the dark, the next thought plinked into my head with stunning clarity. If our playboy king of seven meager months, whose coronation was still in the planning stages, insisted on marrying Mrs. Simpson—my head came up so sharply that it hit the ceiling of my hiding place—wouldn't it cause a crisis of such massive proportions that the only way he could marry would be to abdicate the throne? The fast-thinking Duchess of York obviously thought so. If I hadn't heard her confident assurances, minutes earlier, I would have laughed off the idea of Bertie as King of England as an impossibility.

I was fond of the duke: the kindest and most generous of fathers, a devoted husband, and a thoughtful and considerate employer. But his drawbacks as monarch were considerable. His reticence and his standoffish addiction to privacy were one thing, but dislike of public occasions and his stumbling and often stopped speech were not the stuff of which kings are made. *Poor man, he wouldn't have the inclination or the stamina for that awful job.*

Two pairs of feet thundered down the back stairs to my hiding place, and the crunch of car wheels on the gravel outside reminded me that the grown-ups had returned. Time to pull myself together.

It was a two-pronged attack: Lilibet threw open the door to my hiding place from the back stairs, and Margaret, with the flourish of a determined conjurer, opened the concealed door in the paneling of the main staircase, as the king, the duke and duchess, and Mrs. Simpson walked into the hall.

"Found you, I found you first!" Margaret yelled, fizzing excitement, as both Lilibet and I emerged from the between-stairs cupboard at a more dignified pace.

The duchess's laughing voice. "Good heavens, Margaret Rose, what have you done to your dress? Come and say good afternoon to His Majesty!"

"Uncle David, just in time for tea." Margaret threw herself toward him, followed by her sedate sister, who curtsied to the king and then, perhaps sensing her father's unease, went to his side and took his hand.

The king lifted Margaret up and whirled her in a shrieking circle. "Tea? How did yah know I'm starved?" He set his niece on her feet.

Was I mistaken? I glanced at the duchess and then at the duke. Surely His Majesty was playing some sort of joke: his accent was unmistakably transatlantic. "You haven't seen my noo car yet, have you, Lilibet? It's from the States; itsa station wagon."

"Yes, we have." Lilibet looked up at her father. "It's green!" She turned her mouth down, and her mother smiled.

"It certainly is." Cool in the muggy warmth of late summer, Mrs. Simpson bent down, in a waft of Guerlain, for Lilibet's dutiful peck, and Margaret Rose's exuberant smack, on her cheek. The duchess's spine grew taller at pushy Mrs. Simpson's vulgar demand of kisses from her daughters. Her eye caught mine, her thin brows raised a fraction before her expression turned to one of polite tolerance.

Standing in the shadow of the open door, I had my first good look at the king's mistress. Having always seen her from a distance—

strolling in the grounds or sipping a cocktail surrounded by friends on the terrace—I was surprised that she was neither beautiful nor even conventionally pretty. Her head was too large, her face too square, with a strong jaw and a bony nose. Her figure was fashionable: angular, almost boyish. She had the sort of shape that looked marvelous in clothes. There was no softness, no feminine curves, and her glance from the king to the duchess was assessing and shrewd. This was no hothouse flower from a long line of overprivileged aristocrats or some rich daddy's girl from America. Impeccably groomed, exquisitely and expensively dressed in a perfectly cut dress of emerald silk, Mrs. Simpson might not be a beauty, but she was languorous and wickedly chic. Her bare toes peeked out from heeled sandals and were lacquered a brilliant red in the same shade as her hard, lipsticked mouth: an impressive blend of Monte Carlo casinos and the shady Virginia verandahs I had read about in the society columns.

Next to this flawless elegance, the duchess, draped in cascades of pastel blue floral georgette with her hatful of roses, looked overdone and fussy in the August heat. As if she had just returned from opening a church fete. But she stood her ground in the center of her hall: legs, clad in silk stockings, planted firmly apart; handbag hanging from the crook of her arm; and two long strands of unimpeachable pearls around her neck. Elizabeth, the Duchess of York, gazed impassively at the American novelty. A glance that took in Mrs. Simpson's scarlet toes sharpened into a polite but thoughtful stare as if she wasn't quite sure what they were doing here in her gracious hall.

Mrs. Simpson tilted her chin in greeting to me. "Miss Crawford, isn't it? Whenever I visit Royal Lodge, you and the girls are always having so much fun!" Her voice was hard, metallic. I understood why the Yorks referred to her as the rusty saw.

"Hide-and-seek," I explained, feeling guilty about what I had overheard.

She turned to the king, her back to the Yorks and their children. Her jawbone jutted out on either side of her skinny neck like an adder. "Sounds like fun." She put her hand on the king's arm, her round, dark eyes fixed on his. "We should try it sometime." The look she gave him was the most consciously provocative I had ever seen in my life, and his smiling response so nakedly ardent that I had to look away.

This intoxicating blend of sex and brash sophistication was the king's married mistress! The moment this extraordinary-looking woman had spoken to the king, I could completely understand why he was standing there with that look of foolish yearning on his face.

Having established her ownership of the King of England, Mrs. Simpson returned her attention to the princesses. "And where were you hiding, in a coal cellar?"

"The roof," said Margaret Rose. "We watched you all from the roof!"

"So, that's why you are so sooty!" She was even flirtatious with Margaret. I glanced at the Yorks to see how they were taking Mrs. Simpson's teasing.

The king threw back his head and roared with laughter, but his brother was silent as he pulled his cigarette case out of his jacket pocket and lit up. I didn't know whether it was my imagination or not, but the look he cast his brother seemed assessing, with little of the puppylike adulation he usually demonstrated when they were together.

The duchess joined her brother-in-law in his laughter: a silvery tinkle of pure merriment, her smiling face affable but her back rigid with dislike.

"I thought it would be fun to have tea on the terrace; it won't be too chilly for you, will it, Wallis?" A quick glance at Mrs. Simpson's bare arms. "Now, girls, off you run to Alah to wash and change for tea." She dropped her voice as I walked toward her and took Margaret Rose by the hand. "Quite informal, Crawfie, no need for you to change; as you see Mrs. Simpson is perfectly dressed for the occasion."

Margaret caught her mother's mood. "Flippin' heck," she said under her breath.

"Well, quite," said the duchess.

If push figuratively comes to shove, I thought as we made our exit to the nursery floor, *my money is on the Duchess of York for queen.* The smiling duchess would make a far more acceptable consort than Wallis Simpson, even if the British people would be reluctant to lose their handsome king to his awkward, stammering brother.

December 9, 1936
Royal Lodge, Windsor Great Park, Berkshire, England

Dear Ma,

Well, it's over, the waiting and the worrying are finally, and at long last, over. The king came for dinner with the duke last night. He brought his adviser Mr. Monckton (practically rubbing his hands with delight—he must be making a packet out of advising the king through all this upheaval) and the prime minister—I could smell Mr. Baldwin's old pipe all the way up from my hiding place on the third floor of the stairwell!

The minute I saw the king's face, my worst suspicions were confirmed. He was bursting with good spirits: all hail-fellow-well-met and wreathed in smiles, especially for his brother.

They walked into the rose drawing room and shut the door, and I went to say good night to the girls.

Just before I turned in, I took the dogs out for their evening walk. When I came up the lawn, I saw there were no cars in the drive, and Mr. Ainslie was standing on the terrace, so I wandered over to say good evening.

"He's done it," he said as I came up the steps of the terrace. "What sort of a king would leave his people? His country?" And then he told me what had happened at dinner. The king was in top form: telling jokes and drinking glass after glass of wine, Mr. Baldwin was shoveling down his grouse, Monckton was watching the duke, and the duke was sitting there with his eyes on his brother's face, saying nothing. Mr. A. left them to their port, and when he returned, the duke was pleading with his brother not to do this to him, and Mr. A. realized it was over—the king was going to abandon the monarchy to marry Mrs. S.

It was terrible to see my dear friend so shaken, and the worst of it was I couldn't think of a thing to say—other than good riddance!

It's been an awful week: the duke picks at his food, chain-smokes through the day and probably most of the night too, going by how irritable he is. And the girls wander about, looking scared and trying to be good—even Margaret. I can't imagine how strange and odd it will be for them living in that barn of a palace after this beautiful house.

But all hats off to the duchess! She is coping admirably. I honestly think that without her common sense and quick wits, our new king would simply fold. I wouldn't say this to anyone but you, but our soon-to-be ex-king is a rubbishy little man, and our new one a decent and dutiful one who will do his best

*for his people and his country—once he has recovered from the
shock of his brother's dishonesty.*

*By the time you get this, you will have heard the news
because the day after tomorrow, our ex-king makes his abdication speech on the wireless.*

God save King George VI!

*All my love,
Marion*

PART TWO

1944–1948

CHAPTER THREE

December 1944
Windsor Castle, Windsor Great Park, Berkshire, England

W hat do you think? Isn't it gorgeous? I can't believe how well Bobo copied the photograph!"

The perennial wartime chill of Windsor Castle's formidable stone walls, where we had taken refuge from London's Blitz—and stayed for the duration—hardly seemed to touch the brilliant creature in front of me as she turned in a slow circle, her bare arms extended. The smooth, long line of the dress fell to the floor into graceful godets of gold silk. The dress gave her height, it emphasized her tiny waist, flattering her petite, hourglass figure, but my eyes couldn't help fixing themselves on the long V of the neckline. *Is it a wee bit too low?* I narrowed my eyes at Lilibet's white shoulders and bosom; this dress was a far-distant cry from the old blue silk net with its childish lace collar.

"I thought you were going to wear your blue," was all I could think of to say.

"That old dress? Oh, no, Crawfie, I can't possibly wear that—it hangs off me."

She spun faster, and the silk flared in a rippling circle. "I could dance all night in this." She came to an abrupt stop to look over her shoulder at the pier glass, and the skirt twisted in a voluptuous swirl around her legs. "I saw it in an American magazine. I know it's probably a bit out of date, but the style works so well with the silk that Bobo found."

I reassured myself that Bobo MacDonald, Lilibet's old nursemaid and a pillar of Scots rectitude, would never have made a dress that revealed too much of the heir presumptive's bosom.

"Has Alah seen you in it?" The royal nanny would have Bobo's guts for garters if she encouraged immodesty.

"She loves it." Lilibet opened the illustrated copy of the magazine she had brought with her. "Look, Bobo copied this photo." She tapped with her finger. "Didn't she do a splendid job?" An actress who looked like Ginger Rogers, her head thrown back with her eyes half-closed in ecstasy, was caught in the arms of a slender man with a large head and hair that looked as if it had been shellacked into place—his name escaped me for a moment.

If Ginger Rogers is an indication of Lilibet's present state of mind, the Windsor family's Christmas celebration is going to be a bit of an eye-opener for everyone.

With the magazine open on my lap, I looked up at her from my chair. She was wearing mascara, and her large, clear blue eyes jumped out of her pretty face. The full-lipped curve of her mouth, emphasized with red lipstick, was a sensuous bow in her flawless satin complexion. "This"—her hands fluttered down the front of her dress—"is the most beautiful thing I have ever owned."

"It is a sensational dress."

"Not too sensational?" The smile vanished.

"No, no," I reassured her. "Not in that way. You look lovely in it." I didn't want to take anything away from the joy Lilibet felt about her new dress. "But you'll certainly die of cold."

She shrugged off death from exposure. "I know it shows what they call décolleté, but it covers all of me—*completely.*" She turned to reveal the modest back and short, flounced sleeves.

Why did I feel as if she was the most seductive woman I had seen in years? Was it the makeup? No, even that was discreetly applied, emphasizing only what a beauty she had become. In the last year Lilibet had shed her last ounces of puppy fat and had emerged as the quintessential English rose. But in this dress, she glowed with health and glossy beauty: a bright light in the dimly lit room, a vivid patch of youthful loveliness in this cold, dismal old heap of a castle.

It is not the dress; it's her. She is feeling feminine and alluring, and so she is. Lilibet: serious, thoughtful Lilibet, who had played with her toy horses, frowned in concentration over her homework on constitutional law, and worried about being a good example to our Girl Guide troop, had grown up. I shook my head and laughed.

"Oh, Crawfie, now what's wrong? Is it not acceptable?"

"No, no, it is, it is." It was too easy to make her doubt herself. "You look just right, Lilibet. It's a gorgeous dress." *And you are utterly captivating without your fawn pleated wool skirt and white Viyella blouse with its Peter Pan collar.*

I had no idea why the queen had kept the eighteen-year-old Lilibet frozen in time: dressed in the same schoolgirl clothes that her sister, at fourteen, wore. *Is she reluctant to let her grow up?* Was she even aware that Lilibet and her younger sister both looked like two nicely-brought-up twelve-year-old girls? I caught my lower lip between my teeth. It was Her Majesty's apparent need to deny her daughter's physical maturity that made me anxious about the dress.

"I am glad you like it, Crawfie, really I am. So, now we can concentrate on everything else: our Christmas carols and rehearsing the Boxing Day pantomime." The serious princess emerged, the one preoccupied with schedules and punctuality.

She put her hand on my arm. "You would tell me if it was all wrong—the dress—wouldn't you? You know . . . too obvious?"

I nodded and patted her shoulder. "I really would . . ."

The door was thrown open, and in stalked my other charge, eyes flashing with outraged tears. "I won't . . ." she shouted, and threw down her sister's old evening gown. Lilibet's corgi, Susan, wandered over to sniff the heap of silk. Satisfied with the familiar scent, she curled up, cradled in stiff net embroidered with roses, and sank into puppy dreams.

"I don't care if there is a war on. I even don't care if shabby clothes are the thing. I won't wear this old hand-me-down. You have to talk to Nanny, Crawfie; otherwise I will look completely awful." She caught sight of her sister, and her bottom lip trembled. If she had been two years younger, Margaret Rose would have stamped her foot. "Look at Lilibet! She's got what she wanted. It's just not fair. She will be the glamour girl, and I'll look like an old frump."

Lilibet moved the puppy off of the dress and picked it up.

"Nanny doesn't expect you to wear the dress as it is. The only reason I'm not wearing it is because it doesn't fit me. We are only going to use the fabric from it. Look." She spread the skirt of the dress wide. "Forget about all the net. Look, the underskirt is such beautiful silk it will look lovely made into a dress for you. And then the lace collar will be used to cover the bodice. The blue is perfect; it's you. See . . . just like this." She turned the pages of the much-thumbed magazine to a pretty evening frock with a ruched bodice. "*That* will look heavenly on you. If you like it, Bobo will start work this afternoon."

Margaret blinked away tears as she studied the illustration. "Yes . . . but . . ."

"It is perfect, Margaret . . . and so pretty. Everyone will want to dance with you."

I had to stop myself from applauding Lilibet's deft tact as I looked over Margaret's shoulder at the picture. "The color brings out your eyes." I held the glossy silk up to her cheek. Lilibet, her eyebrows raised in encouragement, nodded agreement. Margaret took the dress and shook out its folds before tossing it over the arm of a chair.

"But I want it to be lower in front and fit me all the way down." Margaret's mouth was set. I felt nothing but pity for Bobo Mac-Donald, sitting in the nursery wing in the Lancaster Tower, threading up her sewing machine, completely oblivious of the tempest that was coming her way.

I caught Lilibet's eye and saw her falter for a second. At fourteen Margaret was as round-tummied as she had been at six. "Margaret." Lilibet's face was serious, deeply serious, as she gazed at her frowning sister. "Our Christmas party is not just for family but Mummy's friends too. You can't be . . . dressed like . . . well, dressed like *that*—Alah and Mummy wouldn't let you anyway. But this . . ." She fanned the pages back to the blue dress. "See how terrific the skirt of the dress will look? Come on—let's go and find Bobo now and show her this photo." She started toward the door. "Don't forget to bring the dress." She pointed to the heap of silk that Margaret had thrown on the chair. "We need to show her exactly what bits of it to use."

"I hope you've finished breakfast, Crawfie, because it snowed at least a foot in the night." Margaret burst into my sitting room in the Victoria Tower as I was finishing off my toast with a last cup of tea. "A white Christmas!"

Her round cheeks were pink with the exertion of running down long, drafty, unheated corridors from their rooms in the Lancaster Tower. Her restless eyes assessed my readiness for the frozen outdoors. "You will need this and this." She held out my scarf and my beret. "Come on, Crawfie, leave it. It's just toast. We're going to make a snow woman. She will be standing on guard at the entrance to the courtyard when Mummy and Papa arrive."

Lilibet followed her sister into the room. "Don't tell Crawfie what to do, Margaret. It's going to be a busy day, and she likes to take her time over breakfast." She picked up Susan and sat down to wait on the window seat. But I had already swallowed my tea and was looking round for my gloves. The moment I had opened my bedroom curtains to a white landscape, I had known what to expect.

"Are you sure you will be warm enough?" I asked Lilibet, who was looking out of the window, her chin resting on Susan's head. She was dressed in a cherry red wool dress: the only concession made to the frozen outdoors was a pair of old riding boots, with heavy socks turned down over their tops.

She turned from the window with such bright expectancy that a flash of alarm told me to pay attention. "Lilibet, will you be warm enough in that dress?"

"I'm sorry, Crawfie, I must have misunderstood you. My coat is downstairs." She got up from the window seat and put Susan on the floor, and when she lifted her face, all I saw was a mask of inscrutable politeness. *What on earth did you think I said?* I busied myself with tying my scarf. I knew how it felt when people intruded when you desperately wished they would just ignore you.

Lilibet brushed dog hair off the skirt of her dress. *Normally she doesn't give a hoot how much of Susan she is wearing.* I couldn't help myself. "You look remarkably bonny today."

Her eyebrows went up in surprise before her carefully schooled expression covered her thoughts. "And so do you, Crawfie. It's our Highland blood: bitterly cold weather agrees with us. And it's Christmas Eve!" She linked her arm through mine as if she were still a little girl, and it occurred to me that Lilibet was on the edge of making a discovery, not only about herself, but about her life as well. On this gray-skied winter morning, it was as if she was teetering on the edge of something enormous, something that was of great importance to her. *It isn't the happily anticipated arrival of her parents that's causing this distraction.*

"A snowy Christmas Eve—what a treat! We had better get a move on—everyone will be arriving soon," I said as I helped Margaret put on two pairs of gloves. Lilibet gave me a swift, almost triumphant look, and just like that, I understood the excitement of a new evening gown from a young woman who rarely glanced in the mirror twice. *Here is the reason for her changeable mood of the last week: dreamy one moment and all business the next.*

I put on my beret and started to button up my coat.

"Come on, Crawfie, don't drag your feet." Margaret took my hand and pulled me to the door. She was clutching a brown paper bag in her right hand.

"Crumbs for the birds?" I asked.

"No, a carrot and two pieces of coal. And we stole one of the Guards officers' caps too—she is going to be a military snow woman."

Lilibet left the world that was so demanding of her time and pushed her sister toward the door. "Come on, Margaret, we haven't got all day. They'll be here by half past eleven." She was laughing as we ran down the curved stairs of the tower.

Which one of our young officers is the reason why she is so excited about this particular morning?

There was no one outside, and the inner courtyard of the upper ward's lawn was covered in a foot of pristine snow. I hesitated, almost reluctant to walk on its perfect surface. But Margaret had no misgivings at all. She danced forward, leaving a trail of footprints across the snow, past the Guards standing sentry and out of the George Gate.

"She needs to be right there so they can see her when they arrive.

Let's start here and roll it all the way up to the top of the slope!" We barely noticed the cold as we bent to our task and started to roll up a ball of snow. Before we were halfway done, we were joined by a couple of Grenadier Guards officers and a visiting friend.

"Oi there, hold on. Your snowball's all lopsided!" Captain Lord Rupert Nevill, dressed in his uniform of the Life Guards, came out the terrace door.

"Roll it this way, where everyone will see her!" cried Margaret.

"Her? I think not; this chap looks as stout as our commanding officer." Nevill pulled on leather gloves and bent to help. I glanced at Lilibet. She was bent over too, her gloved hands smoothing and shaping the second snowball, which was to be the head. It was not Nevill who caused her to stare out the window at absolutely nothing for hours on end.

Margaret, ahead of her sister, stood at the top of the rise to the gate as three men labored behind a mammoth sphere of heavily packed snow. "Push it to the flat place, Teddy; otherwise she'll topple. Oh no, Lilibet, her head is far too small."

Lilibet rolled her eyes. "Don't just stand there bossing, Margaret. Help me! Oh no, it's rolling backward!" Her cheeks glowed from exertion, and her eyes were a deep penetrating blue from the cold. She braced herself against the giant ball of snow, her hat askew, breathless with laughter, and the three men pushed past one another to help.

"Not too quickly," Margaret instructed. "Otherwise it will fall apart." Panting with effort, we lifted the head up onto the body. "Now, that's quite perfect. Who says snow women can't be captains? Now, where's the coal for her eyes? Too wide apart, Crawfie; there, that's better. And the carrot!"

Lilibet stretched up on the toes of her boots and tried to balance the cap on the smooth surface of the head.

"Isn't that mine?" A tall young man with a long, straight nose and a perfectly trimmed mustache took the cap from her and turned it in his hands, smiling with pleasure. "It is mine! You swiped it—no wonder I couldn't find it. Of all the cheek, Lilibet!" He set the cap at the correct angle for an officer in the Grenadier Guards, stepped back, and saluted.

"Is it really yours, Hugh? I am sorry, I thought it was Teddy's. Anyway, it's just until everyone has arrived. Do say if you need it now."

Lilibet's apologetic tone sent Hugh into stammering reassurance. "Oh no, no, really . . . Don't need it at all. Not until church tomorrow." Scarlet to the roots of his dark hair, Hugh couldn't make Lilibet's taking his cap all right enough for her.

Hugh who? I tried to remember the officer's last name. *Euston! It has to be Lieutenant Viscount Hugh Euston, the Duke of Grafton's eldest son.* My eyes slewed over to see how Lilibet was taking his blushing, stammering delight, but she turned away, all interest in the snow woman and Hugh Euston gone. She was staring down the Long Walk past the sentries standing at the castle gates and beyond them to the drive that continued, straight as a die, to Windsor Great Park. A quick glance at her wristwatch and then back to the drive, as if she expected to see a car pull up at the gates.

"I'm freezing, and I've got hot ache." Margaret's wool gloves were heavy with melted snow.

There was no time to lose; her health was often precarious at this time of year, and that, combined with show nerves, would be a disaster for her part in the pantomime if she caught cold. "Inside with you, Margaret. It's time for hot cocoa." We left Lilibet standing by the snow woman, watching the drive.

"Yew know what 'er problem is, doncha?" Margaret imitated Mrs. Mundy, the head cook at the castle, who had a strong East London accent and a voice that could splinter glass. I raised my eyebrows. "Love," Margaret answered with conviction and in her own voice. "Know who, Crawfie?" I laughed; Margaret was a ruthless blurter of other people's secrets.

CHAPTER FOUR

Christmas Eve, 1944
Windsor Castle, Windsor Great Park, Berkshire, England

The damask walls glowed silky red in candle- and firelight. Men and women, cocktails in hand, chattered in small groups, broke away to greet old friends, to kiss cheeks and shake hands, to laugh and exclaim how long it had been.

"Pity we can't use the White Room. I simply can't get used to Windsor being half closed up." Lady Airlie, lady-in-waiting to Dowager Queen Mary, paused in her social round to say good evening. The old queen sat in state near the center of the room, back erect, her white wig crowned with the Vladimir tiara, and diamonds covering her large-bosomed front from neck to waist.

I preferred the family's private apartment at Windsor to the grandiose White Room. "Most of the staterooms are completely empty. Chandeliers, furniture, and paintings in storage, cabinets turned to the walls, and sandbags blocking up the windows."

She closed her eyes in mock martyrdom. "When will it ever end—this awful business? The war simply has to end soon, so we can enjoy visiting our dressmakers again. Look at us; we are getting shabbier by the year—almost threadbare!" Queen Mary turned in her chair, and the candelabra caught the lighthouse glare of diamonds. "Thank heavens we still have our jewels—even if they all need a good cleaning."

No one here tonight looks either threadbare or tatty. I thought of my mother in her old Shetland wool cardigan and her serviceable but worn boots. Lady Airlie needed to catch a crowded train from London to Birmingham in a third-class carriage if she wanted to see what shabby really looked like.

To my relief she drifted away—Lady Airlie's generation did not hobnob with the staff for longer than they needed to. The crowd parted, and there was the queen dressed in her favorite misty blue, her vivacious smile more brilliant than the thousands of carats that gleamed at her bosom and neck—not one of them needed cleaning, I noticed. Every so often the outer press around her would shift, and I would catch glimpses of her in a series of vignettes: head on one side as she listened with a grave face to Lord Wigram, the governor of the castle; her mouth half open in laughter the next; turning to bestow a friendly pat on the shoulder of Sir Gerald Kelly, who was still at work on the coronation portraits, and probably would be until the end of the war. But underneath the gay smile, when her face was composed, she looked tired and her face powder did not quite conceal the dark circles under her eyes.

I took a sip of champagne from my glass as I considered the woman I had worked for, for thirteen years. *Never underestimate her; never assume that the bright chatter is all there is to her.* I smiled at my own advice. A powerhouse of resolve and tenacity burned beneath the queen's deceptive exterior: light, sweet, and brittle as French meringue.

The war years have given her poise and greater dignity. I watched the queen nod a gracious welcome to a woman in beige silk who rose from a deep curtsy, the wife of an armaments industrialist, delighted to have finally breached the unscalable social divide of the castle walls. She lifted her chin in acknowledgment of the woman's husband: short, wide, and perspiring into his starched wing collar. Her gaze was serene, her gloved hand extended to him slowly, as if she were bestowing a blessing. She closed her eyes and smiled, accepting his gushing gratitude.

She lost her girlish manner when her brother-in-law abdicated, but not her ability to charm when something needs to be accomplished. I finished my champagne. *Now it is her approval they clamor for.*

Almost on cue there was a shout of laughter from the group standing around the queen. "Good evening, Crawfie." Lady Spencer's voice interrupted my thoughts. She followed my gaze to the queen and smiled her grim, thin-lipped smile. "Even when she's exhausted, she's always 'on.' Who would have thought that being our queen would suit her so well?" I turned my head in surprise as Lady Spencer echoed my own thoughts. "Anyway, how are you, Crawfie? It must be awfully difficult being shut up in this cold old fortress, year after year, and hard on the girls too."

"They seem to take everything in their stride, Lady Spencer; nothing seems to bother them," I said, rather too proudly.

She laughed. "Well, keep your eyes wide open. In my experience that's when young women like to put a spin on the ball—when everything appears to be going smoothly. I wonder how well Her Majesty will handle the domestic dramas of two young women in their teens who have been cooped up here for the last four years, without the distraction of war duties to fill her time." I bit my lip to stop myself from replying as I remembered Lilibet standing in front of the pier glass in her new dress. Lady Spencer bustled off to join her friends at the other end of the room, and I searched the crowd for the king.

Like me, he was standing on the edge of things, observing rather than participating. His newest best friend, Winston Churchill, talked steadily into his ear, his right hand jabbing his cigar in the air to punctuate his words. Over their heads hung a mingled cloud of cigarette and cigar smoke to keep the social mosquitoes at bay.

Surely, no one is as worn or as lined by these terrible years as our king. King George stubbed out his cigarette, and an equerry stepped forward, lighter at the ready. Without lifting his eyes or taking his attention away from Churchill, the king slipped his hand into his pocket and opened his cigarette case. At this distance the equerry's face wasn't easily recognizable. I frowned and narrowed my eyes to bring him into focus. He said something, evidently amusing, because the king's wide mouth broadened, and Churchill, renowned for his bawdy humor, clapped the young man on the shoulder, laughing at what had obviously been a risqué joke. The king responded and the three of them laughed.

"Lady Airlie, who is the king's new equerry?" She had circulated back to my side of the room to be near to the old queen, who was staring uncomprehendingly at someone in earnest conversation with her.

"She can't hear a word he is saying. Doesn't he know she's deaf?" she said in exasperation. "Who?" She followed my gaze to the man in the Royal Air Force uniform, who had stepped respectfully back so that Churchill and the king could continue their conversation. "Ah yes, he was temporary until this summer. Wing Commander Peter Townsend. Fighter pilot, a war hero. Drawerful of decorations, Her Majesty told me. Lost his nerve, apparently, poor chap—but they all do, those Spitfire and Hurricane boys. Good-looking, though, isn't he? And very personable! Watch out for that one, Crawfie. Pretty young women always end up marrying their father's equerries." She turned away, hailed by one of her gossipy friends.

How has Lilibet managed to get to know this handsome face? I paused for a moment to consider the idea that it was this new equerry who had brightened Lilibet's serious demeanor. It was a ridiculous one: Townsend was far too old for her. The king opened his cigarette case again; the lighter flashed as he bent his head. Churchill was still talking as the flame lit up the king's weary face.

Who would have thought, eight years ago, that this oversensitive, stammering younger brother would have stepped up to become our country's most loved and respected king? I set down my empty glass and took a full one from a passing tray. Champagne didn't come our way often at the castle, and this was the best there was.

He could never have done it without her, I thought as the king inhaled smoke and chased it down with a mouthful of scotch. *But what a price he's paid. Whereas she has* . . . I glanced back to the queen. It was almost as if Elizabeth had increased in majesty. She must have sensed my attention because she looked up, caught my eye, and half raised her hand in salute and flashed her brightest smile as she walked toward me.

"Crawfie, Merry Christmas." Her blue gaze swept over me, appraising and approving at the same time. "Such a pretty tartan sash—it's Campbell, isn't it? Of course, your mother's clan! And the lace jabot, such a graceful touch." She lifted her hand, and her empty glass was replaced immediately. "Well, the girls look so happy and pretty. You have done wonders with them, Crawfie. Now, how is your mother? And your aunts? We really must make time for you to go north to see your family." She put her hand on my arm briefly, the lightest touch and slightest pause, and she was off again. "Lord Scarborough told me that the trains are terrible at this time of year. Well, aren't they always? But if you can stand hours in a cold carriage clanking slowly north, then we will arrange something!"

She drew closer and lowered her voice. "Lilibet looks absolutely lovely in that dress. I had no idea Bobo had such a talent!"

My shoulders came down a notch or two at her reassurance that she had seen Lilibet in her new evening gown. She gave my arm a congratulatory pat and, turning back to her guests, called out, "Time for carols before we open presents!" in her bright, birdlike voice. She took a tiny sip from her glass and walked across the room toward the piano. Someone, it looked like Noël Coward, struck up the opening chords of "Once in Royal David's City," and a lump filled my throat as willing voices lifted to join in one of my most-loved carols.

"Here we all are, bright fires burning, the Christmas tree tow . . . towering over us and lit with candles. We only have each other, after all." It was the king at my side. "Merry Christmas, Crawfie." It was a hard phrase for him, bristling with *r*'s, but this evening he was relaxed in the company of old friends and his family, not the tense man who had arrived at Windsor this morning. "Did the queen tell you that . . . if you can get north in this horribly icy weather, you must go home to your mother to celebrate . . . the New Year?"

Hogmanay was more important to us Scots than Christmas, but of course he would know that; his wife was from the Highlands too. I allowed myself to think of my mother for a moment and said, "Merry Christmas, sir—and thank you; my mother will be delighted."

He nodded and looked around the room. The queen was standing close to the piano; she had a contented Margaret pulled close to her side. "Lilibet?" I could see the king looking for his eldest daughter. "Margaret is my joy," he always said when he and the queen arrived at Windsor for a rare weekend with their girls, "and Lilibet my pride."

But the king's pride was nowhere to be seen. He looked perplexed for a moment, eyebrows raised in question. "She was here a minute ago, sir. I'll go and find her." He nodded, walking back toward his guests and lifting his pleasant light baritone to join them in song. When the king sang, his words were clear and his consonants free from the stopped speech that had plagued him since early childhood.

. . .

Lilibet was in the anteroom surrounded by a group of young, laugh-ing faces. I looked for Hugh Euston, of the snow woman expedition, but he was off in a corner talking with such an intense expression to Ann Fortune that I felt just by noticing them together, I had in-truded. *So, definitely not him, then*, I thought as I tried to catch Lili-bet's eye. "Your Royal Highness, His Majesty asks . . ." She turned back to her friends, and I saw her radiant smile, so bright her pearly complexion looked lit from within. "Carols, everyone? I think Noël is playing. Sounds like him anyway." There was no trace of the hesi-tant young girl I had known since her sixth year. I had never seen Lilibet this self-assured, this vivid and alive. I searched the group for a new face and saw only cousins and the offspring of friends known to the Windsors for years. *Who is having this effect on her?* I asked myself as I walked ahead of the group back to the great room.

I wasn't the only one to notice.

"What on earth have you done to little Lilibet?" A smooth voice, too close to my ear, lifted the hair on the nape of my neck. The queen's younger brother, David Bowes-Lyon, stood at my elbow. *What on earth is he doing here? I thought he was in Washington, DC, attached to our embassy, part of the Political Warfare Executive.* A trumped-up job that gave David Bowes-Lyon the safety of living in America.

I turned a face that I hoped was empty of expression. "Done, sir?" I asked.

"Oh, come off it, Crawfie. Where's that chubby little schoolgirl with her badly cut hair and her dowdy skirtsh?" He was drunk. I felt the corner of my lip beginning to curl. "One of the Guards, is it?" he prompted.

The last thing in the world Lilibet needed was to be noticed by this scurrilous old gossip.

"Ten to one it's Lord Dalkeith!" Two deep-set, bloodshot eyes watched me closely. I kept my face impassive. "Not Dalkeith, then? Orright, so it's got to be Swinford. I've been on the case with Margaret and her little pals all evening, and her money is on Shwinford too." He lifted his cigarette to his mouth, inhaled, and enveloped me in a cloud of smoke. "Not him? Then it has to be old Porchey. Good strong rump on him, that chappie, should come in well ahead of the others—he's got staying power, has old Porchers."

I knew David Bowes-Lyon was a snake, but I had never heard him be crude before. I covered my distaste with what was safe to say. "I believe Sir Thomas Swinford's son was killed in North Africa, sir."

"Oh really? Poor bugger, so he was. Well, why don't *you* tell me who? We all know that you know." He blew more smoke and my eyes stung. "No, it's wrong of me to ask someone in the household to breach a confidence. I'll have to have another go at Margaret."

I tried to calm my breath, but the smoke caught in my throat and I coughed. Was this odious creature determined to dog the sisters' footsteps until he dug out Lilibet's closely guarded secret so that he could paw over the possibilities with his ghastly friends? The queen's younger brother was renowned for his gossip, his cruel gossip. Lady Spencer had told me that Elizabeth's little brother had run off scores of governesses in their nursery days with his mean practical jokes. No one in their right mind made an enemy of David Bowes-Lyon. *He must always be handled like fragile china*, I reminded myself, having made the mistake in my early days with the family of angering him and paying the price of being ragged on for months, until the queen had intervened.

The need to control my anger and panic brought a flush to my face. *Kind, considerate Lilibet the prey of this empty-headed, spiteful man? I would rather die!* I drew myself up with what Margaret called my "governess" look: eyebrows slightly raised, lips pressed firmly together.

"Touched on a nerve, eh, Crawfie?" He saw my reddening cheeks and laughed whiskey fumes in my face. *How dearly I would love to slap that stupid, leering smile off his face!*

I forced myself to feign incomprehension. I could do perplexity well after eight years of court life. I shook my head, eyes open wide in confusion.

Lilibet's Uncle David laughed. "The duenna doesn't know? Come on, be a sport, there is *someone*, isn't there? A dumpling doesn't turn into a swan overnight for no apparent reason."

I couldn't help myself. "It is cygnets that turn into swans, isn't it, sir?" I tried to smile, but my lips were trembling with fury.

He laughed, shrugging as he turned his back on me. "And sometimes little caterpillars turn into moths."

December 28, 1944
Windsor Castle, Windsor Great Park, Berkshire, England

The fog lay heavy in the park below our windows. The snow had melted, and our snow woman had shrunk to a pile of gray slush. Margaret fidgeted in her seat and rolled her eyes at her English grammar; Lilibet stared out of the window, her hand rhythmically stroking Susan's head, until the puppy's eyes closed in contented bliss.

"It was a lovely pantomime. What shall we choose for next year?" I asked, hoping to help them out of the doldrums.

"Whit shaa we choose fur next year?" Margaret mimicked the accent I had schooled myself to eradicate over the years, and the image of Uncle David with his sneering face peeked maliciously over Margaret's shoulder for a second. I blushed with embarrassment and looked down at the book on the table in front of me.

"Crawfie, I am so sorry. I didn't mean it to come out quite that way." Margaret was out of sorts—we had better beware. Lilibet, usually quick to correct selfish manners, didn't even look up.

"I think we should go for a walk before lunch. It will do us all good." I was determined not to be thrown off-balance by anything that might happen on this miserable day in our dark and drafty castle, now empty of Christmas guests. It was my job to keep royal morale up in the schoolroom.

"Keep up the good work, Crawfie," the king had said as he and the queen had prepared to leave, his mind already on the days ahead. And the queen had joined in. "Yes, Crawfie, well done. Important to keep them busy . . . and happy!"

Lilibet got up from her window seat and started the business of putting on the layers that kept us warm.

She was humming a tune as we ran down the stairs: "Heaven, I'm in heaven. And my heart beats so . . ." she sang under her breath. "We can stop off and see if the post has arrived."

Margaret shot me a wise look. "Papa and Mummy have already written to us since they left," she said with affected innocence.

Lilibet rounded on her. "Sometimes, Margaret, you imagine you are much cleverer than you actually are. I'll catch up with you two." And off she went, ahead of us out the door, with Susan trotting at her heels. I composed my face in a parody of the downright, sensible Scottish woman that I wished I was. It was going to be a long, cold winter at Windsor, and I would be hard put to keep these two isolated young women occupied, let alone happy. I was grateful that I had been given permission to visit my mother in Dunfermline for Hogmanay.

January 4, 1945
Limekiln Cottage, Dunferline, Scotland

I helped my mother stack wood outside the kitchen door. January in Scotland was an unforgiving time of year, and before I left, I wanted to make sure that she was prepared for a long winter.

"No need to carry any more wood. Ross McAlister's boy is home on leave, and I pay him to do the heavy work. And, yes, my dear, when the weather's bad, I have groceries delivered right to the front door. No need to worry. Why don't we walk over to say hullo to Betty? She would never forgive me if we didn't drop in so she could tell you all the news. Such a gossip is that woman, and you know how much she loves to see you."

We put on an extra layer of clothes. My mother's old friend Betty lived on what we called the cold side of the river in a gray stone cottage. No more than one room, it sat square on a promontory facing north and caught the worst of the weather. But on a clear day, no view could be finer than the one Betty had from her stone kitchen sink.

Betty was what we called a "pure tough 'n' brave lass." She towered over my mother and was ten years her junior. I often wondered how my mother would cope with her lonely life if there were no Betty.

"Ah yes, an' here ye are. Come on in—that wind'll cut ye in two. Now, Marion, let me take a guid look at yer. Such a bonny face, an nay mistake." Betty's cottage was simple, with a stone hearth on which she made her food. But she suffered from an incurable need to chatter, so our visit was limited by my mother to half an hour.

"Dear God," my mother said with a laugh when we were out of earshot of Betty's last exhortations to watch our footing on her stony lane. "Hind leg off a donkey, that one. To be sure, I heard everything she told us at least twice before you even arrived. No wonder no man ever pressed her into marriage. Poor Betty."

When I said goodbye the following morning, I felt no misgivings at leaving my mother standing in her kitchen doorway, her old Aran cardigan wrapped tight around her spare frame.

"Write when you get to Windsor, Marion, and give my love to your aunts." She waved me off down the path past the pond and into the lane. I was to stop overnight in Aberdeen to say hullo to my spinster aunts. "And tell Madge and Mary I'll be up to town in a week or two!"

I always turned at the bend in the lane for one last wave. And there she was, my resilient little ma, waving me off with all the goodwill in the world.

May 7, 1945
Windsor Castle, Windsor Great Park, Berkshire, England

"Come on—fresh air. Susan needs her evening walk before it gets too dark. Margaret, put on your coat, please." It was May, and it might as well have been March.

Margaret stood like a gloomy donkey with her nose pressed against the schoolroom window. "It's too cold to go out. Look, all the apple blossom is flying through the air—even the rain is blowing sideways. I thought this was supposed to be spring!" Her bottom lip was out as far as it could go. "And I hate this war—when will it end?"

The door opened and our page, Nigel, came into the room. "You are wanted on the telephone, Miss Crawford." He held the door open.

"Stop!" cried Lilibet. "Put on your coat. That room is arctic!" She draped my coat around my shoulders. Our eyes met briefly, and she nodded, a bright, eager, and expectant nod.

The queen half shouted down the receiver in a crackle of static, as if she was calling from the other side of the world: "Crawfie? Is that you? I can't hear you!"

"Yes, ma'am," I shouted. "Can you hear me now?"

"Yes, loud and clear!" A cloud of static. "Wonderful news!" Suddenly the line was as clear as if she was with me at Windsor. "Hitler took cyanide and then shot himself, and when it was all over, someone we have never heard of, a man called Karl Dönitz, surrendered Germany to the Allies. Apparently, Hitler poisoned his girlfriend and, for some horrid reason, his dog, but that's Nazis for you. Their General Jodl is signing a complete surrender at Allied headquarters in Reims, tomorrow." The queen's clear voice fluted down the telephone as if suicide by cyanide was the usual way wars were concluded. "I can barely bring myself to believe that, after all these years, we will be celebrating victory in Europe. But *don't* tell the girls yet—just have them ready to come up to the palace tomorrow after lunch." Her voice dropped to a conspiratorial whisper. "You never know, with these wretched people, what they might do at the last moment, so best to be oyster until we are quite sure." And with that she hung up.

My hands shook as I put down the receiver. It was over! I spun in a circle of joy, clapping my hands and mouthing silent hurrahs. It was finally over. No more air raids and the deathly silence of V-2 bombs before they dropped from above to obliterate us. No more hiding in the dark of night, praying that those we loved would survive to come home to us. Families would be together again—or at least what remained of them—and finally, after years of inadequate food and going without petrol and enough coal to warm our houses, we might now return to the life we had led before the war. I closed my eyes and conjured up deep, hot baths with scented soap and real shampoo.

Alone in the dusty, dark cave of the telephone room, I did a jig of absolute thankfulness before the second part of the queen's instructions repeated in my head. Keeping this exciting news from the princesses would be like trying to train Susan not to take an offered biscuit. Living on the edge of life as they did, Lilibet and Margaret were frighteningly intuitive where news of any kind was concerned.

I trotted two poorly lit corridors and three flights of stairs to the schoolroom. In the time it had taken to be told by a page that I was wanted on the phone to my return, it had been all of what—fifteen minutes? When I opened the door, Margaret and Lilibet jumped away from the wireless. Two guilty girls and the BBC Home Service. How on earth could I blame them?

"Don't worry, Crawfie, we'll pretend we don't know." Lilibet reached out to take my arm at my horrified expression. "That's what Mummy told you, wasn't it? 'Don't, whatever you do, tell the girls that the war is over—just yet!' We knew it was massively important news because Nigel was so secretive that it was Mummy on the phone. No one else calls and asks to speak to you, so we knew it was her." Lilibet's eyes were shining with laughter. "You do understand that we *had* to turn on the wireless . . . we simply couldn't resist. Crawfie, the war is truly over." And I had thought Germany's surrender was privy information? How could I be expected to keep the princesses in the dark with the BBC trumpeting the welcome news?

"The trouble with living away from the parents for so long," Margaret chimed in, in her "helpful" voice, "is that they think we are both babies. 'They must not, on any account ever, be dis-a-ppoin-ted. It is import-ant that they are always *heppy*.'" Her voice bore the unmistakable inflection and cadence of the one that I had just heard on the phone minutes ago. Margaret's ability to mimic was terrifyingly accurate, often unnerving, and always reduced us to helpless giggles.

"Well . . . certainly, you are far from being babies, but I think it would be a good idea if you were to let Nanny inform you she is packing to go to London, and not make announcements. I am sure Her Majesty will tell us exactly what the plan is when we go to the palace tomorrow."

Lilibet wasn't listening. She was singing what had become her favorite song since Boxing Day. She held her arms open as if she was waltzing with someone taller than herself and swayed to the melody in her head:

> *Heaven, I'm in heaven,*
> *And my heart beats so that I can hardly speak*

"Come on, Margaret, dance!"

"Blimey," said Margaret in her best Mrs. Mundy. "She's orff agin, in't she? Its lerve, lerve, lerve with our Lil." She danced across the room, caught Lilibet around the waist. In their headlong, giddy delight they abandoned all attempts to keep time and took off in a gallop, with Susan running after them in a tizzy of hysterical barking. They knocked over a side table and a wastepaper basket before they collapsed on a sofa, helpless with laughter.

Susan was so overwrought with delight that she nipped Nigel on the ankle when he came into the room. "Your Royal Highnesses." Fending the corgi off with one foot, he bowed his head to Lilibet. "Mrs. Knight has asked that you join her in your rooms when Miss Crawford can spare you."

At the mention of their nanny, there was immediate calm. "Well, girls, perhaps you had better pop up and see Alah now," I said as Lilibet ran over to the looking glass to smooth down her hair.

"Margaret, you had better do something to your's—it's all over the place." Lilibet handed her sister a comb.

But today Margaret didn't give a hoot for Alah. She ran her fingers through her hair until it was sticking up on end. "Alah wants to let us know that we are 'orff to the palace.' No more kicking our heels in this drafty old dump, Lilibet." She sailed through the door the page held open for her. "Because you see, Ni-gel, the war is *over!*"

CHAPTER FIVE

Victory in Europe, May 8, 1945
Windsor Castle to Buckingham Palace, London

Alah's habitual frown included everyone at the breakfast table, but our page caught the lash of her impatience. "Nigel, stop dithering and tune in to the Home Service now. I don't want to miss a word of His Majesty's Victory Day speech. *Yes*, that's it. Now, turn up the sound."

We shrank into our coffee cups as the announcer's voice blared, faded, and blared again. "This is the BBC Home Service . . . auspicious day . . . His Majesty . . . Buckingham Palace."

"Nigel, turn it down—we are not deaf!"

"Yes, Mrs. Knight, but it's not the sound; it's the reception." Nigel, his back to Alah, pulled a face. Margaret snickered. Lilibet frowned.

As clear as morning, the king joined us at the breakfast table. "Today we give thanks to Almighty God for a great . . . deliverance." His disciplined and measured tone, with only the slightest hesitancy, brought our shoulders down from around our ears. Alah glared at the lesser of her two nursemaids, Ruby MacDonald, sister to the more terrifying and very senior Bobo, as she scraped margarine onto her toast. Ruby caught Alah's disapproval and put down her knife.

"Speaking from our empire's oldest capital city, war-battered . . . but never for one moment daunted or dismayed . . ." A long pause; Lilibet's forehead creased with tension. "Speaking from London, I ask you . . . to join with me in the act of thanks . . . giving."

Thanksgiving! The king's brave, faltering voice had paused on the one word that I had heard in my head ever since the queen had told me the war was over. Our nation was giving thanks for the end of a nightmare. That simple word was more than I could bear. I stared down at the tablecloth and inhaled, blinking away at my coffee cup. *It doesn't matter if you cry,* I told myself. *We have pulled through. We made it through: there's no danger now.* Tears of relief and joy slid silently down my face as King George VI of the United Kingdom and the dominions of the British Commonwealth—a king of the free world, unvanquished by the Nazis with their dream of the Third Reich—gave us the best news we had heard since we won the Battle of Britain in 1940 and turned the tide of the Luftwaffe's Blitzkrieg.

"Germany, the enemy who drove all Europe into war, has been finally overcome." I brushed away the tears, and out of the corner of my eye, I saw Ruby and Bobo holding hands under the cover of the tablecloth. Alah, her back as straight as Queen Mary's, stared ahead of her, no doubt willing the king to control his stammer to the very end.

"Let us remember those who will not come back: their constancy and courage in battle, their sacrifice and endurance in the face of a merciless enemy; let us remember the men in all the services, and the women in all the services, who have laid down their lives. We have come to the end of our tribulation, and they are not with us at the moment of our rejoicing."

I thought of one man. A man I had known before the war when I had been a silly young thing at university. How enthralled I had been by his attention. How hopeful that this enigmatic soul was as fascinated by me as I had been by him. It had been nearly a year since I had last heard from George Buthlay—fighting with the Indian infantry somewhere near Imphal. I crossed my fingers on my lap that he was listening to this broadcast somewhere in northeast India. I prayed he was sitting back in a comfortable cane chair in the officers' mess, a glass of cold beer in his hand—safe from harm. We would all know soon enough who would be coming home—and who wouldn't.

The king's unemphatic, controlled voice went on to recognize the fight yet to come in East Asia. He halted twice, maybe three times. I lifted my head and saw the tension in Lilibet's eyes. The watchfulness in Margaret's. Their anxiety evident when their father spoke on the wireless or before large crowds.

"Let us thank Him for His mercies and in this hour of victory commit ourselves and our new task to the guidance of that same strong hand."

There was a moment of silence around the table as the king finished his speech.

Bobo was overcome; she had her hanky out and was sobbing into it, to Alah's disgust. I remembered that Bobo and Ruby Mac-Donald had lost a brother at the end of September in Arnhem.

Lilibet, with her usual equanimity, summed it up for us. "You know, I think he did really well. I thought he was going to come adrift in the middle, but he didn't." She reached out and took Bobo's hand in hers, holding it as her nursemaid's sobs receded. "No more crying," she said. "It's all over. Just one more round to go in the East."

"He should limit himself to just a couple of sentences, though," Margaret said. "Be kinder to us."

Alah's iron control vanished. "Yes, thank you, Margaret Rose, that will be quite enough. Bobo, have you and Ruby finished your packing? No, I didn't think so. We are leaving at half past ten. Please don't make us late."

The Daimler doors slammed shut, and two Guards, their faces stiff with trying to control their smiles, snapped off their best Victory Day salutes to send us on our way down the Long Walk and away from the castle.

"Goodbye!" Margaret Rose wound down the window and hung out to wave both hands as we drove toward the park.

"Home to Mummy and Papa." Lilibet smiled. My smile faltered as the image of the palace loomed: we were not going back to the simplicity of the Royal Lodge days, and Buckingham Palace wasn't my home. A small flint-stone cottage with a slate roof dwarfed by a large mulberry tree was where my mother lived. I saw her sharing a pot of tea with her old friend Betty at her kitchen table. A lump filled my throat, and I turned my head to look out of the window. From the moment we had arrived at Windsor Castle during the Blitz, I had rarely had a chance to spend any length of time with my mother. Would it be possible for me to leave the girls now? To return to my quiet backwater and find a teaching job at the local grammar school? Was there anything left for me in that tiny little village outside Dunfermline, other than my dear mother? And would I perhaps hear from old friends—and George Buthlay—again? I shook my shoulders: *You can think about all that tomorrow, Marion. Today the war is over!*

"Victory . . . victoreeeee!" Margaret Rose cried out to people walking their dogs in the park. I reached up and pulled her back into the car by the waist of her skirt, kissing her pink cheeks as she pretended to struggle back to her open window.

Our childlike delight lasted until we reached London's western suburbs. The sight of their broken appearance reduced both the princesses to silence.

"Have we really been away for five years?" Margaret asked me.

And I understood how hard the sight of this battered world must be for her. I had left Windsor to go to Scotland for holidays when I could be spared, and I had seen the wreckage wrought by the terrifying years of the Blitz and the V-2 bombs, and even Lilibet had had her time in the Auxiliary Territorial Service in Camberley, but Margaret's life had been lived exclusively at Windsor, with only a few trips to their aunt Marina at Coppins.

"I can't seem to recognize familiar landmarks we drove past countless times before the war." Lilibet's head was turned away from us as she frowned at the gaps where buildings had once been that were now mounds of dusty rubble. I tapped on the window that divided us from the front of the car. "Is this the way we usually came from Windsor to Buckingham Palace?" My old friend Mr. Hughes, who had met me at King's Cross station all those years ago, had driven down from the palace to collect us. He exchanged a look with our detective, Mr. Ellis. "Yes, Miss Crawford, it's the same route we always take."

"Oh no." Margaret tugged at her sister's arm. Lilibet turned and the two of them gazed out of the window as we passed a bombed-out church and what had once been a street of comfortable middle-class Edwardian villas and was now an uneven line of broken brick with an occasional brave house standing erect and miraculously whole. "Do you remember we saw that lady walking five Irish wolfhounds past this church when we were little?" Lilibet nodded and took Margaret's hand.

"It all looks so broken . . . so desolate." Lilibet cast an uncertain look back at a ruined steeple and searched street after street for a sign that London was not completely obliterated.

"It's not too bad here." Margaret craned her neck through the window as we came up the Cromwell Road. Lilibet, leaning away from us and toward the window on her side of the car, hadn't said a word since the bombed-out church.

"Look, most of it is still standing. Crawfie, do you remember when you took us on the bus to spend our pocket money at Woolworths?" Margaret looked apprehensive as we passed a mass of broken brick. "Oh no, what happened to Carstairs House? Look, Lilibet, it's gone, completely gone. Is it all like this?" she whispered. She badly wanted the end of the war to be just that: an end to the blackout, the pretended bravery, the nights spent in the castle bomb shelter in the cellars, and weeks without seeing her parents—not this dismal, dusty, and broken world.

"Poor old London, what a battering she has taken." Lilibet, overwhelmed by our entry into London's rubble-strewn inner suburbs, looked across to her sister and saw her tight, scared face. "I know it looks frightening, Margaret, but we will rebuild. Do you see? They have already started there." Lilibet's hands were locked tightly together as she searched for more signs of rebirth. "But where are the people living if their houses have been bombed?"

I was ashamed to say that I had no answer for her. "They have probably moved in with their friends . . . or their relatives," I said.

The window was still open between the back of the car and the front. "Mr. Ellis, do you happen to know how many homes were bombed here, in London?" Lilibet asked the man who had been our detective since 1939. He turned around and considered her for a moment. "An awful lot, I'm afraid, Your Royal Highness, and of course the final count isn't in yet—won't be for a while. But they say nearly two million houses were destroyed, and easily more than half of that number were in Greater London." He paused and glanced at me as if asking how far he should go with these depressing statistics. I nodded for him to continue. I wanted to know too, but more important, the heir to the crown should know what had happened to the capital city of our country. "The East End was very badly hit—especially around the London docks: streets, entire neighborhoods, are uninhabitable now. Gone." The scenes outside of our window were bad enough. I couldn't imagine what "gone" would look like.

Lilibet's eyes widened. "Entire neighborhoods," she said, grappling with the scope of how families who had lost everything could possibly continue. "But *where* are the people who have lost their homes living?" Mr. Ellis looked at me for help and shrugged. He had no idea either.

"We'll ask when we get to the palace. They have all that information," I said, knowing that this would be the first thing Lilibet would ask her father.

"Don't be sad, Lilibet." Margaret put her hand in her sister's—it was her turn to give sisterly comfort. "It's all over now. Be happy that it's all over."

"Yes, Your Highness, it's all over now. Time to celebrate!" Mr. Ellis said, but I could tell he knew far more than he was telling us.

All the excitement and enthusiasm for our return to the palace evaporated. "We were safely tucked up at Windsor while all this was going on. I mean, I knew it was bad when I was doing my ATS training in Camberley, but not like *this*. While we were knitting socks for soldiers and putting on pantomimes for the wool fund, this is what was happening to everyone else."

The car slowed down in the thick traffic of the Brompton Road, and Margaret turned back to her window, her face screwed up in tight anxiety, as she searched for a reason to celebrate. "Lilibet, do you see? Everything is normal here. Look!" I squeezed her small hand and felt its thankful clasp in mine.

"We are coming up to the palace; we'll see it any moment now," I said. The girls leaned forward, looking for familiar landmarks they hoped would still be there.

"Better cut across Green Park, Sid; you'll never make it down the Mall today. Everyone has come up to town to celebrate," Mr. Ellis said to Mr. Hughes. "Good Lord above, have you ever seen so many people?" We certainly hadn't since the king's coronation. The pavements were packed with flag wavers, standing shoulder to shoulder.

Lilibet put her arm around her sister, her smile radiant. "They are singing 'Rule, Britannia!'" she said.

"Rule, Britannia!" she sang, and Margaret joined in.

"Britannia rules the waves . . ."

Mr. Ellis turned in his seat, and with his hat in his hand sang out with us, and Mr. Hughes in a deep bashful baritone joined in the chorus.

Our song inside the car joined the revelers outside, infusing our tiny, protected world with hope.

We bowled through the open gates into Green Park, slowing so that the car with Alah, Bobo, and Ruby might catch up. "Why do our chauffeurs love to keep in procession formation?" I whispered to Margaret, and she giggled.

As we turned into the side entrance to Buckingham Palace, used by the family, both Margaret and Lilibet gasped. "Oh, Lilibet, look," cried Margaret, craning her neck. "Look down the Mall. Can you see? It's thick with people. I can't believe the crowds. Mr. Hughes, will you slow down? Look, Lil, they are all waving at us." A sea of fluttering paper Union Jacks, headscarves, hankies, and homemade banners filled our partial view of the Mall.

"How long have they been there?" Lilibet asked.

"As soon as peace was declared, Your Royal Highness. Most of them slept here last night, even through that heavy rain." Mr. Ellis smiled, no longer apologetic for what had happened to London. "No doubt they'll be here for days." He leaned over to Mr. Hughes and muttered inaudible instructions; he was on duty and now had little time for us. Crowds meant poor security. He had his hand on the door handle and was the first to alight as we drew to a halt.

A cordon of policemen was standing along the entrance to Constitution Hill, arms locked, as a mob of near-hysterical people swayed as they sang "Rule, Britannia!" I simply couldn't help it: my eyes filled, and I had to turn to wipe tears away.

"They are all here to celebrate!" Lilibet looked at me. "Look at them all. They are simply beside themselves." A sailor half collapsed into the arms of a policeman, who set him on his feet and gave him a pat on the shoulder.

"Even the policemen are celebrating!" said Margaret.

"The Victoria Memorial is thick with them. I can't see the statue of the old queen." Mr. Hughes was deeply impressed by the way scores of people had arranged themselves in, on, and around the great marble lap of England's longest-ruling monarch.

"Here we are! Here we *really* are!" Margaret cried as three foot-men came down the steps of the family's entrance to the palace.

When they opened the car doors, the noise from the crowds was deafening. Trumpets blared, hunting horns tantivvied, klaxons hooted, but above it all rose the human voice: it shouted, cheered, and sang snatches of whatever song it had heard from its singing neighbors. Its dizzy elation was overpowering.

Lilibet climbed out of the car and stood there for a moment to take it all in. "I want to go out there and be with them," she shouted over the din to me. "Do you think I might? Do you think Mummy and Papa would let me?"

"And me," said Margaret as we walked into the part of Bucking-ham Palace that we had used to call home. "I'm old enough to go too—it's only fair."

"Then you must ask them," I said, knowing how persuasive Margaret would be. "But perhaps it would be a good idea to say hullo and how are you first? Remember, you have hardly seen your parents since Christmas."

CHAPTER SIX

Surely they don't expect two young women to return to nursery life? I stood in the doorway of the palace day nursery, unchanged in five years. The rows of toy cupboards, the fire guard in front of the nursery fire, and two rocking horses by the window were all waiting to be useful again.

"No, no, this will never do. Ring for fresh linen, Ruby. I want all these beds stripped and changed again. And those are not the towels we use." Alah sniffed. "We don't use striped towels," she said in disgust. She directed efforts to unpack trunks of clothes and rang for maids to change the sheets on the narrow white beds the princesses had slept in when they were little girls.

"Would you look at the dust!" Alah ran a finger along a windowsill and inspected its tip. "It will take an age to get this lot straightened up. Oh well, that's the war, isn't it? Nothing will ever be the same again."

I could hear her all the way up the stairs to my suite of rooms next to the schoolroom. A relentless tirade of "What happened to . . . ?"

How many families would stare at one another over the coming months, probably even years, and say, "What happened to us? Nothing will ever be the same."

And across the world, after the war was fully over and peace had finally been declared in Asia, when would the grief, as families mourned their dead, their lost homes, their way of life, ever cease?

I was drained: exhausted by the monumental catastrophe that one man had caused. A man, it would appear, who had no compassion, or positive vision, for humankind. Who had led the world into hate, fear, and chaotic disaster. I took off my hat in a room that seemed to have become a holding place for an assortment of chairs and threw it on my bed. Our drive through the city had leached the last of my elation that the war was over. London: the crowds, the noise of the city, all had reduced me to a tired woman who yearned for the simplicity and peace of my mother's cottage and the quiet woods that fringed the River Forth.

Tomorrow I would be ready to celebrate. Tomorrow I would take the girls into the palace gardens and savor the sooty air of London and say, "Home again!" And tomorrow I would tackle Alah, Bobo, and Ruby to resolve the first of their never-ending needs.

I stretched myself full length on my bed and stared up at the ceiling. There was a diagonal crack that hadn't been there before, and I tried to remember how many times the palace had taken a hit in the past five years. Was it nine? I remembered the queen telling me that a bomb had fallen in the quadrangle when she and the king had been at dinner, blowing glass out of windows and destroying the chapel. But the vast and ugly old palace was still standing, surrounded by delirious crowds.

My heart had sunk as we had walked long, empty corridors to the nursery and schoolroom wing. How oppressive palace life could be, with its hushed, heavy library silence. *It's not home; it never will be*, I thought as I kicked off my shoes. *It is a tired, shabby old dump. Built to impress, not to charm or invite you to relax, curl up in a chair, and reread a favorite book.* What would my life have been like if I had not stayed on to become the girls' full-time governess, if I had gone back to Edinburgh at the end of that wonderful summer in 1931? I would have taught in a school, most probably in Glasgow. Taught the deprived children of dockworkers who barely had enough to eat, let alone buy their children the fine library of books that my girls had access to. I would have met someone, a fellow teacher most likely, and married him. I might even have married George Buthlay. I turned my head to the wall, impatient with myself. *But you didn't, did you?* I told myself. *You chose this, and this is where you are right now. No need to make life bitter with regrets.*

Another burst of cheering. Perhaps the king and queen had already gone out on the balcony to wave to the people. I made myself get up from the bed to close the window. My bedroom, sitting room, and schoolroom looked out on the gardens, but I could still hear the singing and cheering from the Mall on the other side of the palace.

"Is it the same, Crawfie?" I turned to find Lilibet standing in my doorway. "My room looks so much smaller. And why are there so many chairs in your sitting room?" Her consideration for my homecoming made me pull myself together.

Was this shabby, unattractive room with its collection of mismatched chairs lined up down the middle really mine? Unlike the nursery, it was terribly dusty. I started to laugh. "Do you know, I have absolutely no idea? Perhaps they forgot you had a governess."

She smiled and came across the room, and with our arms around each other's shoulders we looked out on the still green lawns and the overgrown flower beds of what we used to call the back garden. "But what are you doing here, Lilibet? I thought you and Margaret were going out on the balcony with the king and queen to wave to everyone."

I knew she had come to find me, to make sure that I didn't feel abandoned now that she and her sister were reunited with her parents. She appeared to have little enthusiasm for the balcony. She raised her eyebrows at the prospect of waving to crowds the same way her father was probably doing now. Margaret, I knew, would be standing next to her mother, full of delighted enthusiasm and dressed in her best dress. "We have an hour before we go out with Mummy and Papa. We are waiting for Mr. Churchill. Papa wants him with us."

"And Margaret?"

"She is loving every minute of it. They have put an orange box for her on the balcony, so she can be seen when we do our best Queen Mary waves. Grandmama is with them too: dressed in a tall toque hat and swathed in all her jewels and her furs." She giggled. I could see Margaret Rose being gracious, carefully patterning herself after Dowager Queen Mary, and so could Lilibet. We sat down on my dusty sofa and tried to smother our laughter.

"Land of Hope and Glory" echoed up to us from the Mall, and our giggles threatened to become hysterical. Elizabeth dried her eyes. "I think the drive into the city, with its gaps and ruins, the overwhelming numbers of people waving flags and singing, is a bit overpowering, after Windsor. It's unbelievably loud out on the balcony. But I came to ask you if you would come to the balcony room with me. You will be able to see us go out and wave to the crowds. Papa wanted to be sure we invited you. Please come; there's champagne. And we have permission to go out tonight—to join the celebrations." Even Lilibet couldn't keep the excitement out of her voice. "Three officers from the Guards will take us. Margaret is in ecstasy."

"You're not going to wear your uniform, are you?" If they were to go out, surely there would be dancing, and how could anyone dance in that narrow and skimpy ATS skirt? I realized that I was far from myself, badgering her this way.

But Lilibet looked as if she could take anything in her stride. She smiled. "Of course I'm going to wear it. It took me months to persuade Papa to let me join the ATS. I think I look rather dashing, don't you?" She turned to the looking glass and organized her cap at a jaunty angle. "Everyone will be in uniform, so I must wear mine. Are you going to celebrate?"

"Yes, with a book and an early night!"

"You could come out with us. Why don't you?"

The thought of disappearing into a crowd of loud, half-drunk, and maudlin celebrators didn't appeal in the slightest. I knew exactly how I would spend my evening. A nice hot bath; Windsor Castle's bathrooms were few and decidedly spartan, with water that dribbled sadly into vast tubs marked with a black line to show you what was meant by five inches. I would ring for a supper tray in my room and savor the blissful luxury of curling up in a comfortable bed to read until I fell asleep.

"If you don't celebrate, what will you do?"

"Like I said, I'm reading an awfully good book."

"Well, at least come with me now to the balcony room, before Mr. Churchill gets there first and drinks all the champagne."

I was easily persuaded; it would be vintage champagne if I knew anything about life at Buck House.

If ever there was a man in a less celebratory mood when I joined the family in the balcony room, surely it was the king. He had been his usual courteous and thoughtful self as he had greeted my half curtsy. "C-C-Crawfie," he had exclaimed as I was given a glass of champagne. "Welcome home. Palace looks a bit battered, eh?"

"Nothing a bit of paint won't fix, sir," I said. Ever the doughty

Scots governess, as I thought how much more battered our king looked than his palace. He was even thinner than he had been at Christmas, and it had the effect of making him look smaller. I was glad that I had put on low-heeled shoes with my dinner dress. The last thing I needed to do was tower over this shadow of a man who had diminished in size a little more every year since his coronation.

There was a commotion of congratulations in the corridor outside the balcony room, and before he could be announced, Churchill came through the door, his arms outstretched as if he would take the tiny king in an embrace. Close to him, I was surprised at how short Mr. Churchill was and how effortlessly his bulk dominated the room. I glanced at the king to see how he was taking his prime minister's stage entrance, but he was all smiles. "Come in, Winston," he said, as if anyone could stop the man.

The prime minister bowed low, and straightening up, he took a glass of champagne and raised it in the air. "Long live the cause of freedom, and to your good health, Your Majesty!" he said, and I noticed there were tears in his eyes. I turned my head away, because to drink to the king's health seemed almost to be courting disaster. As if they had heard Churchill, the crowds outside in the Mall took up the cry: "We want the king! We want the king," a burst of cheering almost animallike in its ferocity, as if the people of Britain were baying for their monarch's flesh and blood.

The king finished his glass of champagne as if it was water.

"Another glass, Winston, before we brave the mob?"

They drank to each other, and then the king touched his prime minister on the arm, and the man who had led us throughout the most dangerous years of our war followed his monarch out onto the balcony.

The cheers grew, and when we thought they couldn't be louder, they increased in frenzied volume. The queen turned to her daughters; she smiled. "I think it is safe for us to join them now without being completely deafened." I watched them through the door, and as the queen took her place next to her husband and lifted her gloved hand to stir the air, I could have sworn that the noise reached a level unachieved by the collective human voice ever before.

"Was it fun, Margaret?" My youngest princess was yawning her head off over her schoolbooks.

"Oh, it really was. D'you know, Crawfie, everyone was kissing *everyone*? Complete strangers, even!"

"Really?"

"Yes, really and truly. I got kissed hundreds of times. It was wonderful!"

"Something perhaps best not shared with Alah or Her Majesty."

Lilibet had collected the morning post and was reading several closely written pages. I glanced down at the return address on the envelope. It had come from the Admiralty. Was her secret love in the navy?

I caught sharp-eyed Margaret peering sideways at the envelope too. "Navy—Papa's favorite," she mouthed at me across the table.

The image of the king's exhausted face as he had braved the balcony with Churchill flashed into my mind again. Surely now that the war was over the king could relax and resume the privacy of family life: the "we four" that he cared so deeply for. The "we four" of the little family he had so enjoyed before his brother's abdication.

CHAPTER SEVEN

June 1945
Buckingham Palace, London

It's cruelly unfair, Crawfie. I hate being alone, I really do." Margaret, back rigid, jaw jutting in mutiny, slammed her fountain pen down on the desk. "Papa keeps dragging Lilibet off to do this and read that. He even let her have lunch with him and Mr. Churchill." She was vibrating with hurt feelings as she hurled her homework into the basket for me to mark.

"It is important that Lilibet spend as much time with His Majesty as she can," I explained to tossing curls and folded arms. "The king is teaching her the ropes because he remembers how difficult it was for him to come to the throne untrained. In a few more years, you will be involved too. As the queen often reminds me: the Windsors are a working family, and there will be plenty for you to do when you are old enough. Now, I think it would be a good idea if—"

"Crawfie, don't you ever get tired of coming up with good ideas?" I recognized the edge in her voice that signaled a storm.

My voice was level as I looked her directly in the eye. "It is my job to have them, Margaret, but if you know what you would like to do this evening, then let's hear it!"

I saw the flash and could almost smell the gunpowder.

The door opened and one of the queen's pages came into the room. Margaret, with a triumphant smile, slammed her volume of *The Tudor Dynasty* shut. A pity because I had always thought that the way Henry Tudor first seized the throne after his Lancastrian victory at the Battle of Bosworth and maintained order in his new realm through sheer force of personality, not to mention intimidation, would appeal to Margaret Rose. "Yes?" she said before the page could utter a word. "You may interrupt." Her voice dripped with gracious condescension, and I turned my head away to conceal my smile.

"Excuse me, Your Royal Highness. Her Majesty would like to see Miss Crawford in her drawing room as soon as possible."

"For heaven's sake, Crawfie, everyone gets to spend time with Mummy and Papa except me." I could have ledged a penny on her bottom lip.

I looked at my watch. "I am quite sure I won't be long, and when I come back, perhaps we could practice the songs you are going to sing tomorrow night for the family?"

She was instantly all smiles. "Off you pop, Crawfie, and tell Mummy not to make a meal out of it. She only needs an update on how we are settling in."

I dashed into my room to comb my hair and wash my hands before making my way south to descend two floors and walk three corridors to the king and queen's private apartments. As I paced along, I wondered which sort of meeting I was in for. *Will it be the cozy and slightly conspiratorial "just us girls" that we enjoyed before the war, or does she have a formal agenda?* I would know the moment I walked into her drawing room. The queen's opening introduction, however bland it might appear to be, always informed what sort of little chat we were to have.

The footman opened the door. "Miss Crawford, Your Majesty," he announced, and I walked into the room. Queen Elizabeth, wearing a pastel blue chiffon, with matching high heels and evening bag, sat in the center of a rose pink and fawn silk damask sofa, surrounded by her dogs. She put the book she was reading on a side table, crowded with framed photographs, as I made my half curtsy.

"Good evening, Crawfie. Yes, please do sit. Sherry?" She was drinking her customary gin and Dubonnet. I was given a diminutive flute of Amontillado, and we were left alone.

"So lovely to have you back in the palace again. It's almost like old times! Now, how are you and the girls settling in?" The queen, like Lilibet, had an electrifying smile. Over the years, Elizabeth's smile had become an on-off affair: a quick flash of teeth for those who worked for her, a broader welcoming dazzle for those who mattered. Her smile for me today was cozy, confiding. It reached her bright, deep-set blue eyes.

"Margaret was a little distracted at first, but she is doing well in her studies. She enjoys being challenged, and my only concern is that my curriculum is not vigorous enough for her. I was wondering if Sir Henry Marten might have the time . . . ?" My idea of Eton's provost, who had taught Lilibet constitutional history, coming to teach Margaret was waved away.

"Oh, do you really think so, Crawfie?" The queen wrinkled her nose. "Poor Sir Henry must be getting up there in years, and does Margaret really need to know about the constitution? I would have thought that you provide enough history for anyone."

Margaret's intelligent, curious face flashed to mind. The devilish streak that needed an outlet. I pushed on. "Margaret is an above-average pupil, ma'am. She would be a perfect candidate for university." She was already shaking her head before I had finished. I made one more desperate attempt. "I think Margaret would be happier, more fulfilled, if she was truly engaged in academic . . ."

The queen smiled her kindest smile as she waved away modern thinking. "No, no, no, Crawfie, we could never agree to that sort of thing. University? Goodness knows where it might all end." She took a sip of her drink. "Poor Margaret, just imagine it. She would be a fish out of water."

No, she would be a fish in water—a happier, more challenged one.

"The University of Edinburgh was a dream come true for me. It really brought me out of myself," I persisted.

"And how is Lilibet settling in, do you think?"

I continued with my report, determined to visit Margaret's future another time. "Lilibet has made the transition from Windsor with her usual composure." I took a half sip of sherry, which drained the flute.

"Yes." She tilted her head to one side and looked at me thoughtfully for a moment, as if at a loss to recall the words she had decided upon before my arrival. "Hm, Lilibet. Well, quite." So, she had an agenda, and it was Lilibet.

"She seems to be very contented," I said helpfully, since their daughters' absolute happiness was important to both royal parents.

The affable silence between us stretched from a pleasant pause to a yawning chasm into which the unfortunate might inadvertently slip. I looked down at my hands in my lap, but I could feel the queen was watching me. Those shrewd, intensely blue eyes didn't miss a thing. How had she and the king managed to live in the palace throughout those terrifying years of the Blitz, one might ask. But one look into that resolute, steely gaze was an indication of how strong the queen's nerves were. I took in a breath and looked up.

She was still regarding me as if I was a particularly interesting specimen in a lab, her eyebrows slightly raised as she waited for more information on her eldest daughter. I noticed that her lips were thinner and more compressed than they had been before the war. I had never been much good at the she-who-speaks-first-loses game. I am far too obliging. "Lilibet has really come into her own this year, ma'am," I said, hoping to reassure her. "So grown-up!" I translated as the smile ached on my face.

A little shrug, as she deliberated over this truism and replied with one of her own. "Nineteen is no age, really, but it is a far cry from fifteen."

I acknowledged this accurate observation with a deeply solemn face.

"I know she had her own sitting room at Windsor, but it is time she had her own suite at the palace so she can entertain her friends. We have started to look about for a couple of ladies-in-waiting, and of course staff. If we had not been at sixes and sevens due to the war, she would have been given her own household on her eighteenth birthday." The queen nodded, acknowledging that this transition would take Lilibet away from my care, our daily life together. "I know," she commiserated. "It's awful when they grow up . . . and you . . . and you have to stand by and just let them go." Her voice was husky as she acknowledged our loss.

I felt my throat tighten. *You knew this day would come, so don't get all silly and misty-eyed!* I hoped that they had a plan for Lilibet's future days, weeks, and months, other than representing her mother at the lesser occasions where young royalty cut their teeth, the finishing school where they were groomed for a life of dedicated public service. It was their fate, their lot. *But not my bright, astute, and thoughtful Lilibet!* Surely Their Majesties would come up with something that would stimulate her and help bring her out of herself, and not reduce her to a dutiful ribbon cutter.

I should have known better. Lilibet had been forced into the royal mold the moment her uncle had abdicated. Now she would be prized out of it and put to work. "Mr. Hartnell will be over this week so we can plan her official wardrobe." A fleeting and irreverent image of Lilibet dressed in the misty mauves, powder blues, and pale pinks of the dated, fussy dresses and coats favored by her mother sprang into my mind. I looked down again at my hands folded tidily in my lap so she couldn't see my face.

"She wants Bobo to be her dresser, and we have agreed. It is important she has someone she knows well as she begins public life." It was the perfect choice; Bobo worshiped Lilibet and would sacrifice her entire life to the dedicated selfless service the queen required of the upper servants for her family.

"Lilibet is more than ready to start her public life, ma'am, and to prepare herself for her future," I said, and then I took a risk. "I hope there will be many days with the king as her mentor. We lost so many useful years to the war." For a moment I let myself wonder what would happen if the king became seriously ill—the war years had exhausted, almost depleted, him. If he died, the burden on such a young queen would be incalculable. "I'm sure she would be delighted to be put to work."

"*Her Royal Highness* is delighted, and we must remember to call her that now." I colored at the queen's correction. *Is she annoyed with me?* I wondered. I had never been required to use the princesses' titles when talking with the family; the king had wanted our relationship to be informal, and surely his wife had wholeheartedly agreed?

Elizabeth tilted her head to one side, her expression confiding, and I breathed a little more easily. "When we go to Balmoral, I will invite a group of young men to join us: Johnny Dalkeith and Henry Herbert . . ." She waved her hand at the sons of friends, cousins, and minor royalty. The electric smile came and went—on-off. "Are you aware of any of the young Guards officers at Windsor she particularly liked? I am surprised she hasn't lost her heart to one of them already."

"I have not seen her show a particular interest in any young man, Your Majesty," I admitted, because this was true. I had no idea with whom Lilibet was corresponding so industriously.

"Really? Not one?" The bright, cozy smile vanished. The lines from her nose to the corners of her mouth down to her chin deepened. "I find that most puzz-el-ing, because according to the princess, she is in love." She gave me a second to let this sink in. "Oh, Crawfie!" A tinkling laugh. "And *you* had no idea?"

I had fallen into her trap to drown in syrup. Every word I uttered would sink me deeper. "Her Royal Highness has certainly been rather distracted recently . . . She waits for the post and . . . and is delighted when there is a letter . . ." I stammered and ground to a halt. My hands felt cold, my forehead hot and damp. I saw David Bowes-Lyon, whiskey glass in hand, raising his cigarette to his lips as he had pursued me for gossip last Christmas.

"A letter from whom?" She waited for my answer. "Come now, Crawfie, are you not aware whom she is corresponding with?"

Am I supposed to know these details? I asked myself. *I'm a governess and not an informant—a spy.* Before I could answer, what had become an interrogation continued. "Do you think that Her Royal Highness is roman-ti-cally involved with someone?"

I gathered my wits. "She . . . Her Royal Highness has all the signs of a young woman who is thinking romantic thoughts." I shuddered at my ghastly description. *Why can't I just say that Lilibet appears to be in love with someone, but I haven't a clue who?* This wasn't the Dark Ages. Surely even a royal princess was entitled to enjoy her first love without her family thumbing through the when, the where, and most important of all, the who. I looked for reassurance from someone I had always thought of as a friend, a woman who had always favored informality, little get-togethers, and girlish confidences. She had disappeared, and in her place was my employer. The queen's vigilant expression sharpened. "So, you haven't seen her with *anyone* . . . at all?"

I shook my head. "No, ma'am, I have not seen her with *anyone* in the *romantic* sense," I said with emphasis, because it was the truth, and evidently Lilibet's attentive Uncle David had not discovered her secret.

"So, she was not involved with anyone at Windsor," she said, more to herself than to me. This seemed to satisfy her, and she was all sociability again. "Oh dear," she said, almost apologetically. "It's going to have to be one of those half-finished conversations—the bane of my life these days!" Her quick smile. "So sorry to bother you with all of this, Crawfie. The answer obviously lies with Lilibet."

A quick glance at the tiny diamond watch on her wrist. "Where does the time go? I'm so sorry, Crawfie, we must sit down one evening and have a real chat, but now . . . such a rush." She rang the bell and the doors opened for my escape.

Chapter Eight

July 1, 1945
Buckingham Palace, London

Hullo, Crawfie." A sad pair stood in my doorway: Lilibet, and behind her Susan with her head down and her long ears sideways.

"Come in, come in. I'm finished with my marking." I looked up at the clock. "Time for a glass of sherry. Will you join me?"

She closed the door. "Yes, thank you. Why is life so terribly difficult and disagreeable sometimes?"

I patted the space on the sofa next to me. "Come and sit down here with me, and let's see if I can help." I had been waiting for her visit since my little chat with the queen.

"It's about last Christmas, when everyone came to Windsor." She plumped herself down next to me, and Susan leapt into her lap. "Someone was there who I knew years ago when we went to the Royal Naval College—before the war. Do you remember? Papa, Mummy, Margaret, and me, we sailed into Dartmouth on the yacht?

You were there with us—we were shown around the college by that tall boy."

Dartmouth. I remembered the tall boy, quite clearly. He had spent a muscular half hour demonstrating how easy it was for him to leap over a tennis net. I had forgotten his name, though. "When we left in the yacht, he rowed after us, was that the one?" I asked.

"Most of them did." She was right; there had been at least eleven Dartmouth college skiffs escorting us out of the harbor. "But one of them rowed right out to sea with us. Papa had to call out to him to go back." I could still see the strong back and broad shoulders as the rower had fought to keep pace with a yacht under full sail. At the time I had felt sorry for him; there was something so desperate about his strenuous effort, as if he was calling out to us: "Don't leave me behind!"

I smiled. "Yes, I remember him clearly." Later on, as the figure in the skiff had dwindled to a mere speck, I had felt embarrassment for his evident desire to impress. Surely all that bounding about the tennis court had been enough of a demonstration of his physical abilities. If a girl had been so conspicuous, it would have been called showing off.

"That was Philip," she said with pride, as if adolescent exhibitionism was an act to be treasured.

Philip! Of course, I had seen him recently, at Windsor. He had been sitting in the front row of seats in the Waterloo Room to watch our pantomime, *Aladdin*. He had appeared to be completely enchanted despite the dreadful puns and the frightful double entendre. Everything fell into place with a neat little click: *So, Philip is the reason she spends more time in front of her looking glass and gazing out the window.*

"You are talking about Philip of . . . of . . . ?"

"Prince Philip of Greece." She might as well have said "The god

Adonis." Her voice was reverent and her eyes shone with admiration.

"Did you tell Her Majesty?" The smile when she had said Philip's name disappeared. "I started to tell her about him the other day . . . and then I lost my nerve. But I did today. We had tea together. I think I put the wind up her a bit."

This was the time for me to say absolutely nothing. To question her about what she had told the queen would put me right in the middle of the two women. I sat there with what I hoped was a neutral expression, and not one of monstrous panic, and waited.

"I asked Mummy when she had fallen in love with Papa. When had he told her he loved her? How had they met? I just wanted to know . . ." Lilibet's expression was unruffled, but her hands were clasped tightly in her lap. "Mummy said she was much older than me when they married. And then she asked me if there was anyone I cared for . . ." Lilibet looked down at the top of Susan's head, so I couldn't see her face. "Before I even had a chance to answer, she rushed in with advice. She told me nineteen was much too young to be serious about things like marriage, that at nineteen we hardly know our minds." She concentrated on stroking Susan's ears flat against her neck and watching them spring upright again. I waited patiently, knowing exactly what was to come. "The upshot was that she told me that she certainly didn't care for anyone until she met Papa. She said she waited for the right man to come along, and when he did, she knew it right away!" She cuddled Susan close, hunched over her protectively. Her brows were down: Lilibet looked almost mutinous.

"I think your mother is being naturally cautious, and rightfully so. She doesn't want you to rush into things. The war took a toll on enjoying the lighter side of life, of going to dances, and . . . and enjoying the company of young men. She wants you to have fun!"

"I did meet young men—all the time. I have known most of them all my life. I was talking about something more serious!"

"And you are quite sure about your feelings for Prince Philip?" I asked. Wondering if perhaps now that she was back in the fold, the "we four" her father so lovingly called his family, this Philip might disappear into the landscape.

Her look was derisive. "Of course I am! The same way I've always felt, right from the moment I met him at Dartmouth. I love him; it's as simple as that. I feel *right* when I am with him. He is straight-forward, he is honest, and we *connect*, if you know what I mean." She looked away. "I think of him all the time. He is so different from all the other men I know, so *himself.* I know it's love. I'm sure it is." She spoke with conviction, not the kind when you are trying to convince yourself; I could tell that she was far past that phase of infatuation. Lilibet was so completely sure of herself that everyone else could go fish.

I loved her absolute certainty. Her declaration for Philip had me on the verge of tears; I opened my eyes wide and inhaled. "If only all of us could be so sure that the man we are attracted to is the right one for us," I said, trying not to sound too entranced by her convic-tion. "So, why is life so difficult and disagreeable?"

There was one of those silences of which the queen is so fond, but Lilibet was thinking hard, not waiting for me to go first. "When Papa joined us, I told them it was Philip I loved; they were almost disap-proving." She glared down at Susan's round head. "They didn't say a word, either of them. But they gave each other one of those looks. It was awful. I want them to be happy for me, and they are not."

It seemed to me that the Windsor family put far too much impor-tance on a state of constant happiness. In my experience, happiness was not the bread and butter of everyday life; after all, how could you revel in the highs if there were no lows, or at least some ordinary everyday disappointments? But I was a stoic Scots girl, grateful when the sun came out a couple of times in July and it didn't rain on your picnic. "Give them time to adjust to the idea; be patient."

She nodded, and after a few minutes of grooming Susan with her fingertips: "Crawfie, have you . . ." Her solemn gaze became apprehensive. "I mean have you ever, you know, been . . ."

"In love?" I finished for her. "Yes, I thought I was."

"If you were in love, really in love, wouldn't you know, definitely?" She turned her head back to the window to avoid looking at me directly. "What about Dickie Henley, did you care for him?"

Dickie Henley? It took me a moment to remember who he was. Dickie Henley was a Guards officer at the castle when we first moved to Windsor. All I could remember was his big, red, shiny face as he laughed uproariously at our jokes.

"Captain Henley?"

"He was awfully keen on you; at least Margaret and I thought he was. All right, then, what about Malcom Sutteredge?" I frowned as I tried to recollect. Lilibet laughed. "He was awfully keen on you too. So, no one, then, Crawfie, no one you particularly care for?"

"Yes, there was someone I cared for, perhaps I still do, but the war came, and now he is off somewhere in India. So, all romance in my life is on hold."

"You are still in love with him?"

I shrugged. "I certainly care about him . . ." I let my feelings for George Buthlay tail off; good manners would prevent her from asking more about the elusive George. "Now, about Prince Philip and how you feel about him. I understand that you don't want to upset your parents, especially since there was no real family life during the war. But it is important for you to be able to tell them how you *feel* about something that matters to you—don't you think?"

She gazed unseeing at the far wall over my shoulder, deep in thought and I realized that talking about one's feelings was not something the upper classes went in for much.

"Where is he now . . . Philip?"

"He's still in service to the Royal Navy—in the Pacific. But I wanted to tell Mummy and Papa about him now. So that . . . so that they can get used to the idea."

"That's a good plan. I can see you have thought this through carefully."

"I think Papa quite likes Philip—I mean, after all, Philip is part of his family. I'm just not terribly sure about Mummy." I thought this was an astute observation. What I could remember of Philip of Greece when we visited Dartmouth, apart from his overt masculinity, was his confidence and his thoroughly outgoing personality. *I can't imagine the queen appreciating another magnetic individual, especially a very young man—she is the one who waves the magic wand and tells the jokes.*

"Hasn't he visited Windsor more than once?" Most European royalty were related; they connected back to that prolific breeder, Queen Victoria. "Surely, your parents know him quite well?"

Lilibet waved her hand at me as if I was being particularly dense. "His uncle is Louis Mountbatten—but the family calls him Dickie." I frowned. "Crawfie, of course you know who Mountbatten is. Well, perhaps you don't; he was away all through the war."

"Yes, I remember." I nodded in my enthusiasm at recognizing the name. "He is His Majesty's cousin. He's an admiral—an important one. Surely there isn't a problem, then?"

Another sigh. "But Uncle Dickie is not one of Mummy's favorites, which is why I think she has taken against Philip." She tipped Susan off her lap and stood in thought for a moment, her head bent as she gazed down at her shoes, reminding me of her father. I understood where the queen was coming from. *Of course she wants to slow down any runaway feelings of romance—they are dangerous.* The future Queen of England must marry someone eminently suitable, someone who would fit in perfectly. A man with a strong sense of tradition, with the utmost respect for the monarchy. No one knew how much that mattered better than Lilibet's mother. She had rescued the Crown from the public self-indulgence and flagrant unsuitability of her brother-in-law.

"The queen has worked hard for her country; both of your parents have. It is their duty to be cautious. Lilibet, I know you understand how important your future marriage is, when you will be queen one day." A brisk nod; she was barely listening. "Why do you think she doesn't approve?"

"I have absolutely no idea! He is far more royal than I am, and these things matter very much to Mummy. His mother is Princess Alice." Seeing my puzzled expression, she burst out laughing. "Wake up, Crawfie—you are the historian here! Princess Alice was born at Windsor Castle, her great—I have no idea how many greats—grandmother was Queen Victoria."

And his father was who? I wanted to ask, but she was off again.

"I can't imagine why Mummy has taken such a dislike to him."

"Did she say she disliked him?"

"No, not in so many words. But when I told them who I wanted to marry, she nearly choked on her scone and sat there gazing at me as if I was the biggest disappointment in the world. When I left, I was barely through the door before she exploded about Philip being far too old for me, which is ridiculous. He's only twenty-four; he's five years older than me—the same age difference as there is between Mummy and Papa." She shook her head, lips compressed, and her eyes reddened. *She knows that to take on her mother will be a fearsome task.* I couldn't bear to see her defeated before she tried.

"Her Majesty will adjust, Lilibet; she really will. And the king, what did he say?"

Lilibet scooped up Susan and planted kisses on her furry brow. "I don't know what's got into Papa these days. He said absolutely nothing at all—he just left it all to Mummy."

I watched her soothing Susan and realized how naive she was underneath all that calm composure and schooled reticence. I wanted to say, "Don't you know that there is nothing wrong with your father except poor health and exhaustion? He works hard at a job he never wanted in the first place. It is a heavy burden for him to be king." But why would I tell her what she already knew? She had seen her father walk into his study to spend long hours there, she had watched him chain-smoke his way through the day, and now that she was back in the palace, she must have seen that he drank too much scotch in the evening to relax.

She needed to brace up. If she was ever to become her own person, she had to learn to speak out—to trust that her parents loved her enough to listen to her.

"The king is a caring father, Lilibet. He wants you to be happy. I am quite sure he will come around if Philip means so much to you. When you go up to Balmoral this summer, he will be much more open to listening to how you feel and to considering marriage to Prince Philip. But I think it is important to be patient about this. After all, nothing can be accomplished now; even if both the king and queen are agreeable to your wanting to marry, no one knows how long this war in the Pacific will go on for. The Americans aren't going to back down until they have broken the Japanese for Pearl Harbor."

A brisk shake of her head. "It is not about my being too young. If I had announced that I was in love with Porchey Porchester, Mummy would have called up Norman Hartnell and told him to start work on my trousseau immediately."

I clapped my hands briskly together to break the gloom that threatened to eclipse this glorious summer evening. "I honestly don't see a problem here, Lilibet," I said to keep morale from collapsing. But in my mind, I could see the queen's cool gaze, the one she adopted when she was working out the best plan for everyone, and one that did not put her at a disadvantage, as Lilibet happily announced that she was in love. "Remember that you have been feeling this way about Philip for quite some time, and this is news to your parents. Be patient with them and all will be well!"

"I'm not being selfish, am I, Crawfie?"

"Why would you think so, when I have never known you to be?"

When Lilibet left, I found myself mulling over the queen's words to her daughter. *She didn't care for anyone until she met the Duke of York?* I had tried not to show surprise, or any reaction at all. Lady Elgin had recounted an entirely different story of how the queen had come to marry the king on my last visit home in January.

"You must be so proud of your girls," she said, after she had reassured me that her son, Andrew, my first pupil, was on the mend from a war wound and would be home at the end of the week.

"I can't believe how fast they have grown up, especially Lilibet," I said, my pleasure in both my girls clearly evident.

"She'll be married before you know it. I remember when her mother was being courted by the king. Poor Bertie, he was potty about her, absolutely potty. But everyone was in love with Elizabeth Bowes-Lyon in those days." She rolled her eyes at the careless gaiety of the roaring twenties. "She was such a lively young thing." She leaned forward, her eyes alight with memories of summer flirtations. "But in those days, poor Bertie didn't stand a chance: her particular passion was for James Stuart and Bertie's older brother."

My jaw must have dropped. In fact, I know it did, because Lady Elgin giggled. "Are you telling me, Marion Crawford, that after all these years of working for the family, you didn't know that Elizabeth Bowes-Lyon had a desperate crush on David when he was the Prince of Wales? Long before she met Bertie—of course."

I shook my head. "I have to be so careful; the court is full of gossip and rumor. I've always found it best to stay away from it."

But my natural curiosity got the better of me. "She must have been so young."

Lady Elgin nodded. "She was indeed, and such great company! She was completely bowled over by David—well, we all were. He was so incredibly handsome. Nothing came of it, of course. The Prince of Wales was an odd duck even then. No time for straightforward, fun-loving girls like Elizabeth Bowes-Lyon. He liked his women older, preferably married, and *very* sophisticated. He nearly drove his poor father mad with his affairs. Yes, there was something a bit off about David, there was always . . . that sense—" She stopped herself. "Well, water under the bridge now, poor chap. I wonder if he ever regrets giving up all that"—she waved her hand in the air to conjure palaces, state occasions, and the aching monotony of being king—"for a woman like *her*." The image of Wallis Simpson on that afternoon long ago when I had met her in the hall of Royal Lodge popped into my head: the cold, hard stare, her overt sexuality toward the king. The Duchess of York's trilling laugh and frozen stare.

"Awful woman—I'll never understand what he saw in her, other than sex. And not very nice sex at that, or so I've heard." I was spared her outspoken thoughts by the arrival of a maid with a tray. "Ah, here's tea." She organized the cups and saucers, searched for the milk jug, and without prompting resumed where she had left off. "Poor David was always rather weak when it came to women. How do you take your tea? It's been so long I've forgotten!"

We sipped in silence for a few seconds before she was off again. "Bertie must have proposed to Elizabeth at least three times, that I knew of." She shook her head at the king's plight. "Poor man—he was so lovesick and so desperate for her." She put down her tea and leaned forward. "He would propose, she would say no, then he would spend weeks writing her apologies and begging for them to be just friends. In the meantime, James Stuart went off to America to make his fortune, and Elizabeth just threw in the towel and said yes to Bertie! The king and queen were so grateful when she accepted him." She nodded at her next wise words. "I think they knew, you see, that David would never cut it as king, and they saw Elizabeth as a perfect wife for Bertie if things went awry, as they did. They knew that she would be the one who would hold it all together."

"Which she has done, and done well," I said firmly: all I dared allow myself to say, as my head spun at the thought of the young Elizabeth Bowes-Lyon flirting with the playboy Prince of Wales.

"Ah yes, underneath all that winsome charm, she is a very practical woman. Who was it who said that she is like a marshmallow made on a welding machine?"

It had been Cecil Beaton, but I said nothing.

Now, as I sat in my little sitting room holding my empty sherry glass, I felt nothing but sympathy for the lively young woman who had become our queen. Poor Elizabeth. I remembered the year after the abdication, when the royal family faced its biggest crises since changing their name from Saxe-Coburg-Gotha, during the First World War, to Windsor because everything German was actively hated. *No wonder she would prefer Lilibet marry one of the straightforward nice boys of her girlhood. A solid, rather dim English aristocrat who would do his duty as the heir presumptive's consort.*

CHAPTER NINE

July 6, 1945
Buckingham Palace, London

G ood afternoon, Miss Crawford. We were hoping you
would come and see us today; there are so many things to
discuss before we go up to Balmoral." I took my place in
the only unoccupied armchair in Alah's sitting room. "We know
that you will be going home to your mother for the summer, but
will you be accompanying us on the train?"

How many years had we played out this scene? Alah asking me
if I would be traveling on the royal train. My answer was the same
it was every year since 1931. "Yes, Mrs. Knight, I will be on the train
as far as Stirling."

The old nanny nodded, confirming that once again, I was cadg-
ing a free ride in the luxury of the royal train instead of slumming
it on the London and North Eastern Railway line.

An impatient cluck from Miss Margaret "Bobo" MacDonald.
"You see, Miss Crawford." Bobo's straight back and gracious smile
had become more regal now that she was no longer Lilibet's nurse-

maid, but her dresser. "There is very little room in the nursery coach, as I am sure you will remember from last time."

"And it's even more crowded now, with Lilibet's dog," Ruby added.

The MacDonald sisters—one tall, one short, both solid, flat-featured women with heavy limbs, thick ankles, and tightly permed hair—had been imported by the queen eighteen years earlier from a tiny hamlet somewhere in Angus. Trained to Victorian standards of servitude by Alah, they both took over the role of nursery tyrants during the war years. To her infinite satisfaction, Bobo was regarded with acute fear by members of the royal household. Her gorgon stare was fixed on my face. "There are only five couchettes in the nursery coach," she told me, as if I had never been on the royal train before.

"Yes, I am quite aware of that, Miss MacDonald. I will travel, as I always do, in the third coach."

With an effort at her old vigor, Alah tried to master the situation. "Yes, that might work."

I was not going to acknowledge the silliness of Alah's need to stress arrangements that were the same every year: there was something in her demeanor that troubled me. It was the malice in Bobo's manner toward the older woman that made me uneasy for her.

"You might have to sit up all night; there might not be enough room for you—even in the third coach." Bobo's smile revealed huge yellow teeth. Both the MacDonald sisters could snap a steel cable in two with those gnashers.

I made as if to get up from my chair. "Good, that's settled, then. Now, is there anything else I can help you with?"

"We are concerned about the princess, Miss Crawford. Bobo had to take in her pink evening dress, the poor mite," Alah complained, her heavy face doleful. "It's simply hanging off her, ever since we moved back into the palace."

Ruby rushed to agree. "She's lost pounds."

"She'll wear herself out with grief," Bobo put in.

It took me a moment to realize that they were referring to Lilibet. "Oh, I think that's putting it a bit too strongly. Why, for heaven's sake, is she grieving? The war is over; the family are all back together again. Anyway, I rather like her new svelte appearance." I caught Ruby's skeptical look. "Her new *adult* figure," I reminded them.

"A bit too sharp-boned for my taste. But she knows her own mind, does my little lady—she'll find a way to marry that young man." Bobo looked down her nose at us.

I am sure my jaw dropped before I could recover myself. *How does this crew of old harpies know about Philip?* I racked my brain to think who could have told them and came up with the one person who not only knew but might have confided in her old nanny.

Alah glared at Bobo, a hard, fierce stare, and suddenly I didn't feel that she was quite so helpless at the hands of the nursery bully. "Bobo, what are you saying? Lilibet is far too young to know her own mind. If she was older and we hadn't been cooped up in the castle for years, she would know that that young man is a disaster." So, it was Alah who had been informed by the queen.

"And that's putting it kindly, Alah. It is evident that he's a leech." Bobo quickly sided with her old boss.

Ruby lapsed into her native dialect. "He's a penniless naebody: nae naem, nae haem, an' nae coontry." And kindly translated for Alah: "He has no surname, and he's homeless—from nowhere!"

"That's quite enough, Ruby. We do not gossip in the nursery." Bobo's thin lips almost disappeared with disapproval, and her sandy eyebrows drew together in a tight frown.

Nursery gossip be blowed, *I* needed clarification. "But Philip's father is Prince Andrew of Greece. And Philip's mother, Princess

Alice, was born at Windsor Castle, the great-granddaughter of Queen Victoria. Isn't that name, home, and country enough?"

The nannies tittered, united by my ignorance and their desire to set me straight. "Clearly Miss Crawford is ready to believe anything she is told, eh, Bobo?" said Alah.

Bobo's smile was patronizing. "Philip's father, Prince Andrew, was kicked out of Greece, so he's prince of nowhere. I am surprised you didn't know this."

"But he is Prince Philip *of Greece*, isn't he?"

Her smile became pitying. "A courtesy title only. His family fled from Greece during the revolution when Philip was a baby. They had to run away to France, without a stitch between them, and with that poor baby stowed away in a bread basket! Was it a bread basket or an orange box?"

"An orange box," Ruby said with triumph.

"Anyway, it was such a grueling experience for her that Princess Alice went insane and had to be locked up." Bobo lowered her voice. "Prince Andrew left his five children and mad wife to be looked after by his rich relations, while he ran around"—she whispered the words—"with other women!"

Alah's voice was more forceful, her eyes indignant as she crossed her arms in judgment. "Shameful behavior. No wonder Princess Alice lost her mind."

Bobo lifted her voice to ring over Alah's. "So, Ruby is right. Philip has neither family nor country, and especially no money. I can't imagine how he would make a good husband for the future Queen of England." She glared at the three of us, daring us to disagree.

Their voices lifted in competitive discord.

Ruby repeated, "Nae naem, nae haem . . ." like a demented parrot.

Alah interrupted her with a loud, "Preposterous! A penniless nobody . . ."

"Pushing himself forward . . . !" Bobo the loudest of all.

"I think we should lower our voices," I advised. "Perhaps Lilibet doesn't know about any of this."

"Of course she does." Bobo's vociferous impatience gave way to an aggressive hiss. "But she doesn't *think* it matters. This is why Her Majesty is so terribly worried. Even though she only wants Lilibet's happiness, as does His Majesty."

"So, now you know the truth of the matter, Miss Crawford." Alah sat back in her chair, her chin tucked down in disapproval. "Now, come on, you two, we have a lot to do to get us ready for our summer up at Balmoral. Will you excuse us, please, Miss Crawford? So much to do, and His Majesty has still not decided on which day we are leaving next week—because of this travesty of a general election. As if I don't have my hands full enough as it is with Margaret Rose."

"Margaret?" I looked for enlightenment. "But she's so happy to be home again."

"She's going through a phase," said Alah with painstaking loyalty. "Just a bit shaken up with all the changes."

"What changes?" A long-suffering sigh from the royal nanny, and Bobo sniggered into her handkerchief. "When we come back from Scotland"—Alah enunciated slowly, as if I had lost my hearing—"Lilibet will have her own suite of rooms, with Bobo to look after her and two ladies-in-waiting. She will of course be participating in official state occasions. You have *heard* this, haven't you, Miss Crawford? Her Majesty *must* have told you."

"And this has upset Margaret," put in Bobo, who was not impressed with the adolescent Margaret's bullying if she didn't get her way. "And she's acting up . . . as usual." A malicious glance as she scored another point against a woman who had been her senior in the nursery.

"Acting up?" I said with genuine disbelief. "How extraordinary," I continued, as if my experience of Margaret was nothing but tranquil. "Yes, I had heard of the changes for Lilibet. Ah well, it's all part of life, isn't it—change?"

Their eyes widened at my outrageous remark, glancing at one another as if I had lost my mind. I escaped to my own rooms to pack and ponder Lilibet and Philip's plight—and what sort of mood the king would be in with a landslide victory for the new Labour prime minister, who had ousted his old friend Winston Churchill.

I was interrupted in my packing by the arrival of Percival Blount, a small man with narrow shoulders and ears that stuck out from his well-barbered head and glowed pink if the sun was behind him. Mr. Blount was deeply devoted to schedules, to timetables, and to his boss, the king's private secretary, Sir Alan Lascelles. "Good afternoon, Miss Crawford. My apologies for interrupting you so late in the day."

He made a funny little bow and stood stiffly in the doorway of my sitting room. "Please do come in, Mr. Blount." I closed the door on the evident upheaval in my bedroom. "May I offer you a glass of sherry?"

"I wish I had the time, Miss Crawford. I am here to run over the travel arrangements for the trip to Balmoral." He passed his hand in a light downward movement from his nose to his chin, smoothing his mustache. His manner never deviated between a blend of courtly primness to me and a reverent deference when referring to the family. I composed my face to listen to the detailed minutiae that I knew would follow.

"Everything has been thrown up in the air because of this wretched election."

"And who would have thought"—I could not help myself; had

the devil got into me today?—"that Mr. Attlee would be our next prime minister! The results were announced in this morning's newspaper!"

A cough, a grimace, as he frowned at his clipboard. "I have no opinion on the matter, of course, but Mr. Churchill has served us selflessly throughout the war. I feel"—his eyebrows waggled in consternation—"that we have let him down. Such ingratitude after his great sacrifice to the people."

"But a Labour prime minister—and by a landslide too!" I bit my lip. I did not want it to flash around the palace that Their Royal Highnesses' governess was a socialist! I was not quite sure what Mr. Attlee would bring to our depleted and economically exhausted country and its weary and battered citizens, but I believed it was time for a change. We needed some new blood in government.

Some pompous throat clearing from Mr. Blount made me tone it down; my upcoming summer holiday with my mother was having a breezy effect on me. "Now that the king has formally asked Mr. Attlee to form a government in his name, we are free to go to Balmoral." He rustled through the papers on his board. It was time to talk train schedules.

"I understand from Her Royal Highness Princess Elizabeth that you will be traveling with us, as usual, to Stirling?" I nodded. "May I ask you to supervise the princess's dog, Susan? She must be kept in another coach when Her Majesty's dogs board." I managed my surprise. "Her Majesty has decided that all the dogs will travel with the family this time." A brief shake of his head at the challenge this presented. "Which complicates everything because there are eight of them, and Her Majesty won't hear of them traveling in the guard's van. Unfortunately, Susan bit Honey yesterday evening and got into a scrap with Dookie, so we must separate them." I understood instantly! The nannies had refused to supervise Susan and decided to make her my responsibility. "I would be delighted to," I said. It was entirely typical of the Windsor family that travel arrangements started with the dogs.

"Apart from that, everything is the same as last year. Now, any questions?"

"None at all, Mr. Blount. Thank you so much for everything."

He placed a small, neat tick against my name on his list. "Yes, well, it has been quite a business, hasn't it?" Despite himself, he couldn't leave the election alone—the shock of a Labour government was reverberating throughout the palace. The corridors were alive with the news: the name Clement Attlee had been whispered, muttered, and exclaimed at since the first newspapers had been opened. "If a coalition government was good enough for us during the war, surely we could have continued with one, at least until the end of the year; such inconvenient timing."

I nodded and got up from my chair. "If you will excuse me, Mr. Blount, Her Majesty only has one dresser this evening, and I promised to run an errand for her."

He was already bustling to the door. "Thank you, Miss Crawford. On that train by seven, if you please—and whatever you do, do not forget Susan."

I walked the half mile between my rooms and the queen's private apartments with a copy of A. J. Cronin's popular novel *The Green Years*. I couldn't for a moment imagine that she would read it, but it was necessary for her to have a copy lying around at Balmoral in case any of her guests were curious enough to venture beyond the first two pages.

"Just a moment, Miss Crawford. His Majesty is with Her Majesty right now." The footman standing outside the queen's private apartments held out his hand, palm toward me.

"Where is their ruddy gratitude?" The king's voice, shaking with rage, came through the closed door. "I could hardly look Winston in the face when he came to give me his resignation. It was sheer bloody hell!" The footman and I stared away from each other to opposite ends of the corridor. This sounded like the beginning of one of the king's gnashes.

A murmured response from the queen.

"Yes, of course I agree! I think Attlee did a reasonably good job during the war in a subordinate role. But he has no real presence, no real personality. Not like Winston. And he has some crackpot ideas . . . he is far too leftist. This isn't ruddy Russia!"

Another murmur, this time louder: the queen's voice rose in a question.

"Yes, yes, of course I did." His voice lowered from a shout. "Attlee was right there on Winston's tail! I hardly had time to think before he was ushered in, clutching that hideous hat in his hand."

A short, sharp question from the queen.

"Yes, I heard you the first time: I asked Attlee to form a government in my name, and he said something irrelevant, and I waited for him to get the hint and bugger off."

The queen started to say something but was drowned out by her husband's fury. "Dear God Almighty! I *am* thinking about Winston. We have let the man down!"

It was fully fledged gnash and time for me to go. "Please give this book to Her Majesty for me. Thank you."

I tramped the long corridors and staircases back to finish my packing. *Who could possibly imagine that an outmoded and ailing old imperialist like Winston Churchill would be the man to lead his people after the hell Britain had been through in the last five years?* I leaned back against the closed door of my bedroom before I returned to my packing. Life in peacetime was going to be very different at the palace. By the end of this year, Lilibet might very well be a married woman, and I would be making plans for the rest of my life at home in Scotland.

. . .

At a quarter to seven the following evening, I arrived at King's Cross station carrying my small overnight bag with an overexcited Susan swarming ahead of me on her leash. "Good evening, Mr. Blount."

A polite nod and he turned back to supervising the organized chaos of boarding the household and their luggage. "Her Majesty's dogs are already in the saloon coach," he said over his shoulder. "So you are free to get settled in the third."

Susan surged ahead, her eyes bulging and her tongue hanging out in anticipation of another encounter with the formidable Dookie. We trotted past the saloon coach, shaking with canine activity inside, as Dookie and Honey jumped up on chairs to shriek at us.

"Disappointed?" I said to Susan as we climbed up into the empty third carriage next door. She sniffed the air and then threw herself down on the floor, and I pulled a book out of my handbag.

Gradually, the scrum of nannies, dressers, and valets on the platform organized itself in a boarding party as they were settled in their allotted coaches, and I looked out the window to watch Their Majesties and the princesses walking down the platform to the train, followed by the king's equerry and his private secretary. The queen was dressed in mauve: tweed dress, coat, hat, gloves, handbag, and shoes. *How does she manage in those crippling heels?* I wondered. *She looks as if she is walking on springy turf.*

The queen turned to the king, and her bright smile flashed in response to his gloomy shrug. *Oh dear, the election is still weighing on him.*

The saloon coach door banged shut, and I could hear the Windsors organizing themselves: the queen's fluting questions, Lilibet's bell-like answers, and Margaret bossing the footman. Susan sat up, her attention focused on the connecting door, and catapulted forward as Lilibet pushed it open.

"Hullo, Crawfie. Thanks for bringing Susan. What a naughty girl you are!" she cried as the dog jumped up into her arms, her little tailless rump agitating with delight. "Mummy says that Susan and Dookie have to be friends, so I'll take her in with me." I got up to hold the door open. Behind her, the king, his hands rammed deep into his coat pockets, argued with his private secretary, Sir Alan Lascelles, or Tommy, as he was affectionately called by Their Majesties and no one else.

"Jesus Christ all-bloody-mighty, Tommy!" the king exploded at the silent Lascelles. "Just tell the silly bugger I have no ruddy intention of inviting him up to Balmoral. It's my damned holiday, and I want to spend it with my bloody family." Everyone froze and looked down at their feet. To catch the king's eye at this point would be fatal.

"Sir, if I may." His quiet drawl gave no hint that Tommy was intimidated by the royal temper. In his time he had seen flying ashtrays, books, magazines, and sometimes a whiskey and soda, first from the abdicated king and now from his present boss. Tommy made no attempt to pacify; neither did he, like the rest of us, avoid eye contact. "We always have the prime minister to stay at Balmoral for his weekend in the summer, sir. We can, perhaps, organize it for later on, at the end of August, before we return to London."

The king raised his hands in the air and shook them. "No, and no and no, damn it! Dreadful little man—probably eats his peas with his knife." Lascelles straightened his tie and waited, hoping as we all did that the worst was over.

Margaret piped up in her best Mrs. Mundy: "There's nuffink wrong with eating yer peas thataway, sir. How else can you get 'em in your mouf wivout droppin' 'em in yer lap?" And her father threw back his head and roared with laughter, delighted to be rescued by his cheeky daughter.

"All right, all right, Tommy. You can tell the silly sod that he had better come at the end of August; by that time I'll be ready to accept that the country has treated Winston abominably—absolutely ruddy abominably. After all the man has done for us." He stomped off to his favorite spot in the corner of the saloon, lit a cigarette, and puffed away furiously as his family went about the business of settling in.

The train rolled forward and pulled out of the station, and I returned to my couchette at the back of the third coach and tried to find my place in the book I was reading. If the king was this upset by the election of a prime minister whose only fault was that he came from the middle class, I dreaded to think how he felt about his eldest daughter, his pride, marrying a man with nae name, nae home, and nae country.

CHAPTER TEN

July 8, 1945
The Royal Train—London to Stirling, Scotland

The train clattered north at the leisurely pace required by the queen for a long journey, and I used the time to do nothing at all. With my book open on my lap, I leaned my forehead against the cold glass of the window to watch the country unfold. Now clear of the dreary, war-scarred London suburbs, the world was fresh and green. The summer sun had started its leisurely descent to the horizon, glazing the backs of brown cows to a vivid clay red as they grazed in emerald-gold pastures and drank from opal ponds.

The intricate piecework of fields and pastures bound by hedgerows, dark woodlands, and wide, serene rivers rolled past my window. A village nestled among beech trees was a snapshot of black-and-white half-timbered houses. We slowed, but did not stop, at the Midlands county town of Northampton. I leaned forward to catch a glimpse of a quiet street on the edge of the town: the thin spire of a church steeple pierced the thickly leaved trees on the slope of a hill; a strong-shouldered shire horse pulled an empty dray effortlessly up its incline, the driver leaning back, reins slack in his hands. England was at peace again!

As the light began to fade to dusk, more sheep appeared in pastures than cows—we were in the north country. The rhythm of the train lulled me away from the outside world, and I looked down at my lap. Slotted between the pages of my book was a letter from my mother that had been handed to me by the palace postman as I was leaving.

I slit the envelope open and pulled out two closely written pages, both sides covered in my mother's economically small but clear handwriting.

My dear Marion,

All is ready for your arrival. Betty and I have been baking (she has made more oatcakes than we could possibly eat) and we have marked off each day on the calendar that brings you closer to us.

Our VE Day in Limekiln was a quiet one compared to yours, but it was good to see families reunited again. We were let off lightly in the village this time around: the MacFiggis eldest, Fergus, was killed in the Battle of Britain, and of course the Archers lost both their boys in '44, and the Dewar family are still hoping that there will be news of Amos.

We put out flags and bunting down the high street and set up trestle tables. Everyone brought along something to eat, and the Bruce Arms set up a keg! I have to say the Limekiln Pipers put on a good show! How I wish you could have been with us to share in the fun.

One face in the crowd was such a welcome sight. Do you remember George Buthlay? I should say Major (!!!) George

*Buthlay lately returned from India of all places! He sat down
with me and the Rev. and Mrs. Blair at our church supper last
Sunday. He certainly remembers you and asked after you!*

I told him all your news . . .

My pulse thudded a warning in my ears, and I looked up from
the page and closed my eyes.

What had my compulsively outspoken mother told George
Buthlay? That I would be delighted to see him? That I talked about
him nonstop, avid for any news of him? My cheeks flushed and I
felt uncomfortably warm. I unbuttoned the top button of my
blouse. *For heaven's sake, would you get ahold of yourself, Marion? She
only gave him your news!*

The last time I had seen George Buthlay—now *Major* Buthlay,
emphasized by my mother's exultant exclamation points—was in
the late summer of 1939.

What was it about this tall, silent Scot that had fixed him so
firmly at the back of my consciousness over the years? As soon as I
read his name, I could picture him quite clearly the last time we had
seen each other, five years ago. I counted on my fingers—could he
really be forty-seven now? Would he be bald and stooped, his health
broken by three years of the war in India? I opened my overnight
bag and pulled a worn leather photograph folder from the inner
pocket of its lid. George's serious, unsmiling face gazed out at me;
even five years ago I hadn't thought this photograph a good like-
ness. George didn't need to smile to share a joke.

I saw him in my mind as if it were the first time. I was in Edinburgh at school when I was introduced to a tallish, wiry man with
dark, serious eyes. He was talking with two of my professors—men
of his own age, both of them old friends. The most striking thing
about George was his silence—his expressive silence. Where others
chattered easily, on and on and on, George shared his observations

in subtler ways. A look was all that was needed to enjoy a private exchange about the chattering group around us. Our silent communion, so intimate that I had often felt we were alone among the buzzing, noisy crowd of my friends, was what attracted me most to him. His eyes expressed pleasure, concern, and derision with eloquence, until his gaze turned inward and he retreated from the world. Then his silences were complete.

My mother of course knew all about him—she had been close friends with George's widowed mother before she died. When I first became attracted to George, I knew she would have more information about this rather enigmatic man.

"Why has he never married?" I asked her—already fascinated by this deeply private man and flattered by his attention whenever we met at local events and get-togethers.

"He might have had someone he was sweet on before the last war, but I can't remember. He was studious, a quiet boy was George, and barely eighteen when he got his call-up papers. They were filling the ranks with conscripted boys from all over the country in 1916: new recruits pitched straight into the Battle of the Somme on their first day in France." She nodded. "Yes, *that* battle." I said nothing, but I waited to see if she would go on. My two brothers, Ian and John, had both died at the Somme. I wondered if this was why my mother took such an interest in George; he was about three years younger than our Ian and the same age as John.

"Anyway"—her voice was brisk—"no need to dwell on the bloodiest days of that war. So, George was one of the lucky ones, if you can call surviving the carnage of the Somme lucky." She frowned down at the peas we were shelling, immersed in troubling memories of the past.

While I was playing with my friends in flower-filled meadows, George Buthlay and young men like my brothers were struggling for their lives, and those of their men, in the trenches of Belgium and France. I finished shelling peas and fixed my eyes on my mother's face, willing her to continue. She looked up. "Ah yes, George Buthlay. When the war finally came to an end, George came home—one of many heroes. He was mentioned in dispatches for conspicuous gallantry, even awarded a DSO. And like most of them who had survived uninjured to come home again, he had changed—there was a piece missing."

She sighed and shook her head. "Those were terrible times. No one can imagine the horror those surviving men had suffered." She didn't mention my father's pain-racked last months. His lungs, ruined by mustard gas, failed him completely that winter. I had heard his voice calling for help in his nightmares, and at times we had both been strangers to him. My mother's face was prematurely lined with the burden and grief the war years had brought to most women of her age. When my father died, we left Dunfermline to live with my spinster aunts in Aberdeen. They looked after me when my mother went back to teaching.

"George hadn't been wounded in battle. But he was a faded version of the young man who had gone to do his duty. His mother said she could count on one hand how often he spoke to her. He never opened his mouth: a nod was all you got if you saw him on the street. His nerves were shot, of course—like so many of our brave lads. And then he disappeared up north. Mrs. Buthlay said he couldn't take the crowds of people on the street, at the market, or anywhere really." She shrugged off Dunfermline's quiet community as if they were an out-of-control football crowd on their way home from the pub on a Saturday night.

"It was what we used to call shell shock. It was so common, we didn't really talk about it." She acknowledged my raised eyebrows. "George got himself a job on a sheep farm—up in the Hebrides. He wanted to be alone—completely alone."

"So, he only came back to Dunfermline recently?"

"He came home when his mother was diagnosed with a heart condition. Mr. Carstairs, who was the bank manager at Drummonds back then, gave him a job at the bank. He was still the silent type, of course, but he had somehow managed to find himself again." She swept the empty pea pods off the kitchen table into a galvanized bucket for the pig. "You're awfully curious about George Buthlay." She cocked her head on one side, her eyes alert with curiosity.

"I'm not really *that* curious."

"Oh yes, you are!"

Sometimes it was hard to be my mother's only surviving child—her only daughter. I could have told her that George Buthlay was not the marrying kind, but she chose to hear what she wanted to. "I find him a bit confusing," I said, and hesitated. To tell her too much would mean a thorough interrogation. "I think he likes me because he always seeks me out in a group or a party. He doesn't flirt or anything, but I get the impression he likes my company . . . But there has been no . . . no progression."

She nodded. "He's from a different generation from you, Marion. The way some of your girlfriends carry on is downright embarrassing. George simply respects you."

I nodded agreement. Sometimes it was the best thing to do when my strong-minded mother expresses an opinion. But I knew there was more to it than that. Something was holding George back from coming forward, and I didn't know if I had what it took to break through that self-protecting wall of reserve.

My friendship with George became sporadic when I was offered my job with the Yorks and went south—for what was only supposed to be the summer but turned out to be for years.

It was cold sitting next to the black glass of the window. I reached up, pulled down the blind, and moved out of the way to let the steward make up my couchette for the night. George and I had seen each other often in Dunfermline whenever I came home to be with my mother for my summer holiday, for Christmas and the New Year. The last time was in 1939, just two months into what we optimistically called the Phony War, at the wedding of an old school friend.

I spotted George at the Kincaid Hotel standing with his head bowed respectfully as he listened to Archie McLaren, whose agitated hands were waving in the air. Archie's face was beet red, and I suspected it was either the whiskey, or more likely they were discussing Mr. Chamberlain's undeniable avoidance in confronting Hitler's brutal occupation in Czechoslovakia to "protect" the ethnic Germans living there from their supposed suffering.

I had never seen George in Highland dress before. And I had to say there was nothing more off-putting than a man with short, bulging calves or thin, white, hairy legs in a kilt. I slid a downward glance at George's long, well-shaped calves sticking out from under the blues, red, and greens of Anderson tartan and, encouraged, let my eyes wander up to his black cropped jacket. It fit smoothly across broad shoulders and sat snugly into his waist. I turned away in a flutter of embarrassed anticipation as he looked up, caught my eye, and excused himself from Archie's vehement and scarlet face.

"Hullo there, Marion. You are looking well."

"Archie seemed pretty upset."

His eyes glinted with merriment. "I sincerely hope I don't have to hear any more from Archie McLaren on the base interest rate tonight." He brushed wedding cake crumbs off his chin and cocked his head toward the scrape of a fiddle as it was tuned. "I think they are opening with a strathspey . . ." His tone became so somber you would have thought that I had overdrawn my account at his bank. "Would you like . . . care to dance?" He made a funny little half bow in invitation, and his serious face softened in pleasure when I said yes. He took my hand and tucked it in his arm, and his quick sideways glance of approval made me glad that I had worn the organdy dress my mother had wheedled me into wearing.

Light on his feet, his kilt swaying, he was an unostentatious dancer, unlike some boisterous Scotsmen who bounced about, clapping their sweaty hands and shouting out encouragement to one another. I felt as if I weighed ounces as he took me through the elegant measures of the dance. And the next one, and the one after that too, until it was so hot and airless in the low-ceilinged room that the pipers, red in the face, called for a break. Sweating brows surrounded us, and there was a strong whiff of mothballs and damp wool in the air.

"Something to drink?" George asked, but the line for the bar was long. I fanned my cheeks with my hand. "I don't think there's a scrap of air left in this room," I suggested.

George nodded to the terrace door standing open to the night. We hesitated on the threshold, greeted by the sound of overexcited laughter and squeals of pretended modesty from the darkness of the shrubbery.

"Let's sit over there." George led me to an open window with a deep seat at the far end of the room, away from queues for food and drink, and before the band, refreshed with a pint, picked up their instruments again.

Quite suddenly I felt nervous: my throat was tight, my knees quivered, and it wasn't from the exertion of dancing. Surely he would ask me to go walking with him after church tomorrow: the Dunfermline version of an evening at the cinema watching the latest American film, which I enjoyed with the occasional boyfriend in Edinburgh.

"Marion, there is something I want to tell you." George sat down next to me.

Tell me? My heart started to beat like a bird caught in a net. I swallowed and looked at the empty dance floor so I wouldn't have to see his face.

"I joined up yesterday." I turned what I hoped was a face free of any expectations back to him. "Of course, I'm too old for combat—but they want me as an instructor for officer training at Catterick, until they decide what to do with me." He raised his eyebrows, and his dark eyes shone, not with pride but amusement. "Who would have thought that a forty-two-year-old bank manager might be useful in war? Someone even mentioned India!"

"India?" My mind stuttered on white men with ginger whiskers wearing pith helmets and barking orders on the hot stamped-clay earth of a maidan surrounded by natives dressed in white saris and dhotis. "Which part of India? Will there by fighting there?" I asked as I waited for him to take my hand and promise me that he would be safe from rabid dogs, disease, and failing drains.

He cleared his throat. "Maybe—India belongs to us, so it's possible."

The horror at the thought of real war must have shown itself on my face. "It's the *Officer Training Corps*, Marion. I doubt we'll see any action. But it is important to me to do my bit." His eyes, fastened on mine, were earnest, asking me to understand.

I nodded and let the silence fall between us, forcing him to explain.

"I should get my papers any day now . . . so it will be goodbye for a while, but Catterick is in Yorkshire, so not that far away."

If I was so at ease with this man, so comfortable being myself around him, then why couldn't I ask him to spend time with me before he left for training? But I couldn't: the right words didn't seem to come easily, and I thanked God that the awkward, clumsy ones stuck in my throat unuttered. All I could do was blithely nod encouragement, a stiff smile on my lips as I held back selfish tears. How my throat had throbbed with pain, longing, and despair.

George's face was rigid with tension. He licked his lips, and then, as if plucking up courage, he asked, "Marion, I was wondering . . . do you think you'll have time to write to me?"

Write to you? Here I am, sitting here in front of you now! *What on earth is wrong with now?* I felt tears of embarrassment and pain sting my eyelids. The effort of keeping them in was agony. He did not take my hand or move closer. He just sat there his white starched collar, still crisp at his throat for all the dancing he had done.

So, we were going to part as good friends. I was to be his pen pal, not his fiancée, or even his wife, waiting for him to come home at the end of the war. The delight of dancing with him vanished, the flounces of my dress were stuck to the backs of my legs, and I wished I was anywhere than in this hot room, now empty of couples, who were all locked in each other's arms outside under the cover of the dark.

"Of course I'll write, George," I managed to force out, even though my throat felt rigid, as if it were made of cardboard. "When did you say you were going?"

"Probably by the end of the week." His eyes held a despairing light as they gazed steadfastly into mine, or so it seemed to me. Perhaps I had been wrong in believing that I understood George's silent method of communicating—perhaps I read what I wanted to see in his expressive eyes when he was thinking of something quite mundane, like the base rate of interest at the Bank of England.

The train slowed to pass through another lonely village station. I pulled the last page of my mother's letter from my handbag and read it through carefully, trying to make out if George was single or married to a nurse from a British Army hospital in Bombay or Calcutta.

George returned a month ago from India! A bit on the thin side, but he looks fit and well. He's been taken back by Drummonds Bank and made senior manager. We talked of old friends and when the war would end with Japan, but he was only waiting to ask one question: "How is Marion?" When I told him that you would be up in Dunfermline within the week, he didn't hide his smiles!

I pushed the blind to one side and looked out into the dark, shadowless world of night. The blurred lights of a village, off in the distance, streamed past the windows. In wartime I had made this journey through an implacably black, endless night. Now once again there was light in our world.

CHAPTER ELEVEN

Summer 1945
Limekiln Cottage, Dunfermline, Scotland

The clear air smelled of pine sap and pollen from the wildflowers that crowded the ditch along the lane to our house.
I rounded the corner and there she was, waiting for me, at
her garden gate.

"Only staying for the night, Marion?" my mother said when she
saw my little bag. I smiled, put my arms around her tiny frame, and
gave her a long hug. *Is she thinner than she was in January?* I inhaled
her clean scrubbed skin: the faint aroma of beeswax and carbolic. The
palace, with its rigorous schedules, formality, and never-ending list of
must-dos, evaporated into the gritty air of London, to be replaced by
weeks of weeding the rich earth of the vegetable garden, searching the
henhouse for eggs, and long, leisurely walks by the river's edge.

"My bag will be sent up from the station this afternoon."

"And you walked all the way from Dunfermline?"

"Yes, all the way. I wanted to stretch my legs, and the air here is
glorious after London!"

"Aye, well, come on in and take your rest. I know how hard they work you."

We walked into her immaculate house: a jug of wildflowers on the kitchen table and the sweet astringent aroma of well-polished wood. Home again!

"You look so well, Ma." There was a plate of shortbread, another of oatmeal biscuits. "Mm, you made my favorites."

"Well, I don't have much to do now that I am retired. Though I do still take on the odd pupil for piano lessons, just to keep my hand in. Betty came over and helped with the heavy work. I am quite sure she will be back again tomorrow morning, to hear all your news." She shook her head at her neighbor and old friend's garrulous nature. "Took me longer to get your room ready, what with all her gossip, but ne'er mind, Betty means well."

I took off my smart city hat and hung it on the peg by the door; it would be the last time I wore it until I caught the train back to London.

Ma put the kettle on the hob. "Your young man is coming over to lunch after church tomorrow."

"I hope he doesn't know that you call him that. Because he isn't my young man, however much you want him to be."

"No need to get into a flap. Of course he wants to be your young man, Marion, who *wouldn't*? He never married, you know."

Unlike my mother, I didn't see this as a particularly hopeful sign. "He's forty-seven, hardly a young bachelor."

"Well, he's my young bachelor, then, since I am twenty years his senior."

If the war hadn't come along, would George have asked, or would I still be waiting for him to invite me out for tea? *Haven't I learned by now to accept that he's not a marrying man, as much as I am destined to continue life as a spinster?*

"I'm glad that George has returned safe and well from India, but

I am not interested in him in that way, Ma." She started to shake her head. "No, really, I'm not."

She looked up at the ceiling and laughed, as if I was being particularly dense. "Just the fact that he leapt at my invitation to lunch is surely an indication that he is very fond of you, Marion. He's been made *senior* manager at Drummonds; did I tell you?"

"Yes, you did, in your last letter." She gave me one of her nods, her I'm-serious-don't-mess-me-about one. "Doing very well is George. And he particularly impressed on me how much he was looking forward to seeing you."

I took her by her shoulders and looked down into her lined, laughing face. "I really came home to see you," I said. She reached up and cupped her palm around my cheek. "My dear, sweet girl, it is possible to love more than just one person at the same time. Now, drink your tea, and let's go for a nice walk before we make dinner."

George and I did the washing-up together after Sunday lunch. He with mop and suds, and me drying and putting dishes away. He was a methodical washer-up and even in his rolled-up shirtsleeves, with one of my mother's cheerful red paisley pinafores wrapped around him, he looked dignified, like a bank manager doing the washing-up.

"I was wondering if you were free next Sunday. We could take a picnic to Blackness Castle: the views of the Firth are supposed to be magnificent from the old ramparts." George handed me a plate to dry. An invitation to a walk: I was so astonished by his question that I dried it over and over, too stunned to reply.

"That would be nice." I tried for nonchalance and failed.

"Good. Next Sunday it is." A silence fell that I did not rush to fill: I couldn't think of a thing to say.

George applied himself to washing the pattern off my mother's best china. "So, what is it like, working for the King and Queen of England?"

He didn't look up but gave the plate he was washing all his attention. He carefully rinsed it and handed it to me to dry.

I opened a drawer to put away knives and forks. *Why this question now?* I was quite sure that Ma had warned him that it was dinned into us by palace courtiers that we should never discuss the family.

I leaned up against the wooden draining board to answer this new, talkative George. "Well, it took a lot of getting used to, after the abdication," I said. "And the war, coming as quickly as it did, didn't help things." Those days were a world away now, but I could still remember how sad we had been to say goodbye to Royal Lodge. "We moved to Buckingham Palace: it is a great barn of a place, miles of corridors, hundreds of rooms, and an army of staff to keep it. The move was very hard on the princesses—well, everyone, really. The children hated the palace, the queen hated Wallis Simpson, and the king seemed to . . ." I was going to say, "dwindle before our eyes," but I kept it impersonal. ". . . work far too hard." I wondered how best to describe the loyal, wholly decent man, driven by duty, who was our monarch, and decided that I had said enough.

George nodded. "But what is it like for *you*, working for them?"

"Oh, it's all right. I am very fond of the princesses; they are sweet-natured, good-hearted girls. Lilibet is very conscientious about things like obligation and doing her best, and Margaret . . ." I laughed—I simply couldn't help myself. "Well . . . Margaret is full of life and remarkably bright. I often worry that she outstripped my abilities as a teacher long ago. If she was from an ordinary background, she would probably go on the stage, or better yet to university." He had stopped washing dishes and was listening carefully. "I like to think I have brought some sort of ordinariness into their lives, some sense of how it is to be one of us."

I looked up; surely he was bored to tears listening to all this chatter about a very conventional family. But he nodded me on. "The war was a blessing in its own bleak way. We lived at Windsor, and I had full rein, so I tried to introduce everyday things into their existence among the bowing and scraping that all palace officials and servants effect. It is so bad for young children—well, for anyone, really. Lilibet is gracious and thoughtful to those who serve, but Margaret can be . . . well, she can be queenly enough for both." I stopped, aware that I was prattling. His invitation to go to Blackness Castle had thrown me completely, and I was babbling on, trying to cover how flustered I was by his invitation.

He smiled his solemn smile. "You care for them very much, don't you?"

"Yes, I do—as if they are my own children."

"Surely Elizabeth doesn't need a governess any longer. How old is she now, nineteen, twenty?"

I couldn't look at him because his simple inquiry was so unexpected that the tips of my ears began to burn. *Is he wondering how much longer I will be needed as governess to the princesses?* I had been down this road before; interpreting the thoughts of others was a dangerous business.

I cleared my throat and concentrated on drying a saucepan lid. "Lilibet is too old for a governess, but Margaret needs a strong influence in her life. She runs circles around the nannies, and now we are back in the palace . . ."

I didn't say that I had thought about leaving and returning to Scotland because I had packed that idea away for another day. Lilibet needed someone to stand with her in her crusade to marry Philip. But the pulse beat in my ears at his question, and I hoped that he would ask more of them.

CHAPTER TWELVE

Summer 1945
Dunfermline, Scotland

W e could hear George's arrival long before he pulled up outside our kitchen door.

"Marion, Marion! George is here," my mother called up the stairs. "Did you hear me? It's George!"

I walked out of the kitchen door. Could this possibly be Major Buthlay, senior manager of Drummonds Bank, standing astride this machine?

"The bike belongs to my cousin," he explained as he saw my gaping surprise. "Er . . . both the bike *and* the jacket—he was a fighter pilot during the war."

"A pilot?" I laughed. "You never told me you had one of those in your family."

"Mac was always a tearaway as a boy. His war was nothing like mine: he was in the Battle of Britain when he was only twenty. Told me that they drank brandy for breakfast before they flew off to fight the Hun. He's in civil aviation now, so I expect he finds life pretty dull these days." He held out a leather helmet and a pair of goggles for me. "Better put these on; it can be blowy even on the back."

"But your first war was pretty hair-raising too, wasn't it? You were certainly in the thick of it." I made a business of tucking my hair up into the helmet to give him time to answer. If our friendship was to go forward, the only way I could think of accomplishing it would be if he trusted himself to unfold a bit more.

There was a long pause as he looked down at the dust of the lane. He put his hands in his pockets.

The sweat broke out on my palms. *I've gone too far: I have reminded him of a place that holds such dread he had to isolate himself in the Outer Hebrides for ten years.* I clenched my hands until my fingernails bit into my palms.

He lifted his head, his eyebrows slightly raised, mouth down at the corners. I couldn't tell if he was angry . . . or if he would simply ignore my question.

Well done, Marion, you've only messed up what promised to be a perfect day. I racked my brains for something to say that would steer us away from the pain of death and loss. He leaned up against the side of the bike. "Yes," he said. "You're right, the first war was hair-raising." He paused as he pulled off his gloves and laid them on top of the bike's handlebars. "Though not quite in the way that Mac means when he tells us tales of derring-do." He shrugged and half squinted at me in the sunlight. "Actually, it was hell . . . hell for every one of us caught up in that nightmare. And I'm sure it was hell for most of us in this one too."

I fixed my eyes on his face. He would either talk to me or turn away to start up the bike.

He turned his head to look up into the shade of the tree and then back to me, and to my relief, I saw the corners of his mouth lift. "I was very young, that first time. And I could certainly have done with a bit more than brandy for breakfast on a cold morning in the

Somme, before we went over the top with only half our strength. I can tell you that!"

He must have seen the anxiety in my face. "It's all right, Marion. That time doesn't frighten me anymore. It's gone—exorcised. But when Chamberlain made that speech announcing that we were at war with Germany again, after all the hemming and hawing of appeasement, I knew I had to put my civilian life on hold until it was all over. We ended it badly the first time." He rotated his right hand. "Reparations . . . making Germany pay for what they had done . . . well, everything." He picked up his gloves and slapped them against the engine cover. "We even called the first war 'The War to End All Wars.' How ironic was that, eh? I don't know how many nights I woke up when I came home to Scotland, scared to death and drenched with sweat—reliving . . ." He shrugged away the burdens of a generation. "It had to be done; I had to do it." He started to put on his gloves. "Despite the whole wicked waste that first time around, it all had to be done again."

My eyes swam with tears, and I looked down at my feet to blink them away, when all I wanted was to step into him and put my mouth against his.

"I hope that is enough of an explanation for you, Marion . . . why I just signed up and went off . . . without saying anything more than . . . or committing to—" He cleared his throat, and his quiet eyes sought mine. "You see, I had to be sure that I could last it out a second time. I didn't want you waiting for . . . a broken-down crock to come home. Not when you had such a wonderful job . . . and a fine, independent life in London."

He started the bike and then extended his hand to help me onto the pillion.

I got onto the pillion seat behind him, stunned with what he had told me as he revved the motor, and we accelerated down the dusty lane.

A broken-down old crock? I could have laughed out loud with joy. The man in front of me, so close I could wrap my arms and legs around him, was more vital and alive than the one I had danced with six years ago. *Has his second war given George the confidence to release himself from the past?* Perhaps I would never know what he had lived through in all his years of war, but here he was back again, apparently neither mentally scarred into silence nor aggressively angry at his lot. He would never tell me the details of his war when he was a boy, and I didn't want to know them. It just mattered that he was here and that he wanted to be with me.

I gave myself up to the day as we coursed along the glowing green-gold tunnel—now bright sun, now dark shade—of the lane that led to the bridge.

"This is wonderful!" I said to George's back as he turned onto the narrow road that dipped down to the edge of the Forth. I tightened my grip on his jacket as the bike accelerated, and the hedges blurred to a smudge of soft green. "This is what it must be like to fly!"

I was almost used to the speed and the mixed sensation of exhilaration and fear when we leaned to the left to take the turn and climb the short slope to the lip of the Kincardine Bridge.

We have to cross that on this? One slip and we'd be through those railings. We would drop like a stone into the deep, swift-moving water far below us. My prudent governess's heart thumped in my chest. I held on to George's waist as we hurtled forward.

The familiar sweet salt smell of the Forth reassured me that all was well, and I opened my eyes to be amazed that we were still on the bridge—the water still on its way far below us. I tilted my head back to laugh up at the blue void of the sky as the summer air whipped sharp and clean across my face, and the wide river transformed into a band of gleaming, dancing light.

The bike leaned into the curve of the road, and George lifted his left arm and pointed. Ahead of us, sitting on a far-off promontory, was the ship-like shape of Blackness Castle, a black cutout against the sky.

The bike slowed as we coursed along the narrow flint lane with the river on our left. The road became an uneven dirt track, and the bike's engine made soothing put-puttering sounds as George steered us around its deep ruts.

Almost too soon we were bumping over the short turf toward the base of the castle's granite ramparts. George switched off the engine, and silence crashed in on our ears. I laughed at the tremor in my legs as he helped me off the back of the bike.

"Looks like we have the place to ourselves," he said as he took off his helmet and goggles. "You all right? That bridge can be a bit overwhelming on a bike. Not too fast?"

I wasn't quite sure that I could walk straight with muscles that still trembled from the vibrations of the bike's motor. "How fast were we going?"

"About sixty back there on the road."

A strong brackish-laden breeze came up the Forth from the sea, and my tongue tasted salt on my lips. I pulled off the helmet, pushed my hair back off my forehead, and looked at the world through new eyes: it was brighter, greener, and smelled sweeter. The sound of gulls wheeling over the water was strong and insistent. For some inexplicable reason, my eyes filled with tears of complete happiness. For the first time in years, I felt such a strong sense of freedom, of release from duty, from the drab grayness of the war and the constraints of palace life, that I wanted to laugh and then cry from absolute joy.

George unstrapped a green canvas rucksack from under the bike's pillion. "Shall we eat first or explore?"

"Let's eat first," I said with such eagerness that he laughed.

"Picnic spots are important. Where do you want to sit?"

I looked around and saw the ideal place. "There," I said. "We can look right up the river to the bridge. And if we sit with our backs to the wall, we will be protected from the wind." *And from anyone who wants to explore the castle.*

He shook out a square of mackintosh for us to sit on. "I brought a bottle of wine; all I know is that it is white." The bottle was wrapped in wet newspapers to keep it cool, and with a flourish, he unwrapped a greasy parcel. "Cold chicken. Mrs. Bannock roasted it last night, and the smell was more than I could stand." He handed me a drumstick. It was as if I had never eaten chicken before; despite the tantalizing ways the royal chefs could devise to tempt the palate, nothing came close to that first bite of cold chicken.

Bathed in sunshine and cooled by salty breezes, we finished it off between us, and then we topped up our wineglasses. George leaned his back against the sun-warmed stone of the castle's ramparts. "Now it's time to work for your lunch. Will you tell me about the castle?"

"Strangely enough I don't know anything about it, except that it belongs to the crown, and we are sitting on the king's land. So, you can thank my boss for the view and this smooth turf lawn."

"Your Majesty!" George raised his tumbler with a flourish of thanks as a small herd of black-faced sheep came around the corner of the castle wall. They stopped and, in the foolish way of sheep, stared at us. Their leader bleated a warning before dropping her head to graze.

"Hebridean sheep." George toasted them with another wave of his wine. "Tough and enduring—just like us Scots." Was it the ride out to this lonely spot on this glorious day, or was it drinking wine and eating cold chicken in the soft summer air? George's hair ruffled by the breeze, his eyes shining in his sun-reddened face, he looked as carefree as he must have looked when he was a boy. It was nearly too much to take in, in one day.

We lazed on the ramparts to finish our wine and watched stately clouds coast in from the dark horizon of the North Sea. Sunlight and shadows dappled the grass around us, and within minutes the first drops fell. When the wind shivered the surface of the water, we were already sheltering in the old guard room that looked out onto the stone pier below.

"It'll soon pass." George wrapped the mackintosh around my cold arms, and my heart started to bump as his arms tightened around me. We stood for a moment and watched the rain jumping up off the water below us. "Marion." The way he said my name made the tiny muscles around my mouth tremble. I turned my head to lift my face for his kiss, and my heart bounded up into my throat. His mouth, soft against mine, was warm and the winey taste of him so sweet that I fell against him.

The kiss, longed and hoped for, made me feel languid and ardent in the same moment. I was so swept away with delight I couldn't bear for it to end. As we clung together, all I could hear was the rain drumming on the river and every pulse in my body skipping for pleasure. Who would have thought that this quiet, reserved man was capable of such passion—or that I was?

The kiss ended, and we stood close in each other's arms, our lips still touching, unwilling to release. George smoothed my hair back and pulled away to look down into my face. "Such a rich, deep auburn," he said, and he put his nose into my hair and inhaled. "You could only be taken for a Scotswoman, with your wide slate gray eyes and your lovely hair: beautiful Marion." He took my hand in his and raised it to his lips to kiss. "I know you take your work very seriously and that you really care for your girls, but surely there will be a time when Lilibet is married off and you are free?" He let go of my hand and pulled me to him; his chin rested on the top of my head. His warm breath made me shiver and step closer. "You see, I have cared for you . . . loved you . . . for so long, another year or so won't make any difference. Would you . . . would you consider?" He hesitated for a moment to laugh his silent laugh, at himself. "I mean, Marion, will you marry me?"

He loved me—he had always loved me! I was not condemned to keep living my lonely life on the fringes of someone else's fuller one. I would share mine with George: kind, gentle, and passionately caring George.

"Yes, yes, I will." In my happiness I saw Lilibet dreaming on the window seat of my room. He bent his head and kissed me again, and I hoped it would rain for the rest of the afternoon.

I skipped up the path to the kitchen door like a silly young thing and stopped in the scullery to comb my hair through with my fingers in the tiny mirror over the sink. *Why, I look almost normal—no one could possibly guess how I've spent the afternoon!* My cheeks were perhaps a bit pink, but only from riding on the back of a motorbike. Were my eyes too bright, too wide? Easily come by from an afternoon of fresh air and a windswept river. I smiled at my everyday self in the mirror and called out, "Hullo, Ma. I'm back!" as if I was still plain Marion Crawford.

She was in the kitchen making bread. There was a smile on her face as she dusted flour over the dough. She looked up at me and her smile broadened.

"George . . ." My voice broke in elation. "Has asked me to marry him . . . and I . . . I said yes!"

"I knew it the moment I saw you both." My mother put a floury hand on my shoulder and kissed my cheek. "It took the poor man long enough; all these years?" She dusted off her hands and took mine in hers. Her eyes swam with tears of happiness and something else. It was relief. My mother had guessed at my isolated loneliness in the palace, and she had prayed for George Buthlay to declare himself.

"We'll have to wait another year." The practical governess emerged.

"Another year?" Her incredulity filled the kitchen, and her hand latched itself onto my arm, a familiar emphatic grasp. "Whativver fur? Surely, those two great gurls have enough fawk tae look after them? Nay, Marion, you go back to London and tell Her Majesty that you are to be wed." She drew in a long breath, her eyes fixed on my face as she shook my arm. "No more waiting, Marion: start your life with George!"

She must have seen the consternation her outburst had caused me. She lifted her floury hands and took my face tenderly between them. Her voice softened. "Listen to me, my darling girl, it's time to say goodbye to the Windsors." Her gray eyes peered up into mine. "And be firm the way you put it to the queen." She took a tea towel to dust off my cheeks then folded her arms. "If you ask me, which I know you won't 'cause you didn't when you took this job, your Queen Elizabeth enjoys wielding her bit of power—she's not afraid to put a bit of stick about, is that one. So you need to be firm."

Her dislike for the queen jabbed through her practical words of counsel. "*George* understands, Ma. He is quite prepared to wait."

She shook her head and turned back to kneading dough. "No man"—she dusted more flour over the dough and herself—"is prepared to wait for long, Marion. Ye're thirty-six years old. Do yerself a favor and give them a month's notice as soon as you get back." She picked up the dough, slapped it back on the board, and gave it a good thumping. "Their Majesties can look about and find some nice young woman to look after things."

Despite the warmth of the kitchen, my hands felt cold and stiff. I reached for the kettle to make tea.

"George said he would wait," I said.

"Aye, and the next time you see him, when they give you a bit of time off, the first thing you'll hear is that he's been a-walking out with that Miss Stewart at the grammar school—she's got her eye on him has that one."

All girlish thoughts of weddings and, dare I say it, babies were blown away like smoke in a sharp breeze. My mother might have been narrow in her view, but she understood human nature. I had felt happiness for a day, and now I began to worry that it might be taken from me.

Ma was sitting at the kitchen table with her breakfast cup of tea and the *Aberdeen Press and Journal* when I came down the next morning.

"Japan surrendered," was all she said and continued reading.

"Then it really is the end." My mind immediately went to Prince Philip of Greece. *With Japan's surrender, he will come home now. Lilibet must be beside herself with excitement.* "What else does it say?"

"Not much." She took a sip of tea and read: " 'Newly elected Labour Prime Minister, Clement Attlee, broke the news of victory in a midnight radio address. Relaying Japan's acceptance of defeat, Mr. Attlee thanked Britain's allies and her people, saying, "Here at home you have earned rest from the unceasing efforts you have all borne without complaint through so many dark years." ' Someone needs to tell that wee man that we are still living in the dark years. It would be nice to have some sugar for our tea and a bit of coal for the winter. Doesn't he know firewood is getting scarce here in the north?"

"Anything else?"

" 'Declaring a three-day national holiday, the prime minister concluded, "For the moment let all who can, relax and enjoy themselves in the knowledge of work well done." ' Just you tell me what *that* man has done all these years—sitting on his backside talking, that's what. Lord, how these men like to jabber into a microphone!"

I poured tea and scraped margarine onto my toast. "A three-day national holiday, now, that's something. Let's make up a picnic and invite George to come with us to Culross woods—it's only a thirty-minute bus ride!" The sun streamed in through the windows. "What a perfect day to finally end the war!"

Ma was up out of her chair. "I'll check the hens; we can take egg-and-cress sandwiches, and there are some oatmeal biscuits, and look"—in triumph—"Mrs. Ross swapped eggs for cheddar. I'll make cheese-and-pickle sandwiches too."

I picked up the newspaper. "I wonder what made the Japanese surrender so quickly." I read through the brief account again. "We thought the war in the Pacific would go on for months." I scanned columns for more information.

"Don't worry about all that now, Marion. I have no idea where Japan is, and neither does anyone else in this part of the world." My mother bustled back in with a basket of eggs and an apronful of apples. "Run upstairs and put on something pretty while I make the sandwiches!"

CHAPTER THIRTEEN

September 1945
Dunfermline—Buckingham Palace, London

It was raining. Dark spots spattered George's gray mackintosh. Behind him a train pulled out of Platform 2 bound for the Hebrides. I hung out of the window of my second-class compartment, my hand so firmly held in both of his that my engagement ring cut into my fingers. I remembered our last walk together. "I almost forgot, Marion, that I should give you a ring, and so—" He took a battered square case out of his pocket and flipped it open with his thumb. "This was my mother's ring, and before that my father's mother's ring." It lay in his palm: a rich gold band with a bright sapphire in its center. "It is a modest ring," he said as the little jewel winked at me in the sunlight. "But I know my mother would have been proud to know you—delighted that you would be my wife." He had slipped the ring onto my finger and, turning my hand, kissed the palm.

"Well, this is a bit of a change from the way I arrived," I said to break the tension of our parting. I wanted to lean out and kiss away the tense lines around his mouth, but I caught the eye of a disapproving matron holding the hand of a solid, dull child and behaved with the required Scots propriety. George nodded; there were deep creases at the corners of his eyes, a sure sign that he was hiding behind his bank manager's face. I stretched out my other hand to stroke the creases away and tried to swallow down the tight, awful feeling of dread. *I am going away from everything and everyone I love the most.* London and the palace were not my home; they belonged to a world apart from cottages and homemade oat bread, from motorbike rides and picnics, and from kisses in country lanes that made each walk shorter in length than the last.

"Don't go, then, Marion." My mother's firm voice rose above my panic and the clash and clatter of steam engines pulling into the station from the south. *But I must, it is my job, and Lilibet needs me.*

"Will someone pick you up at King's Cross? Your suitcase is very heavy." I was grateful for George's prosaic inquiry, his calm voice, his warm hand tightly holding mine.

"A porter will help me with the luggage, and I'll catch a taxi to the palace." He nodded, unused to women fending for themselves in large city stations. The life I led was already pushing me away from George—from home.

"I'll write as soon as I get back, and we can plan your visit to London this winter." The thought of him coming to London took the edge off my fear about leaving.

He held my hand tighter. "Let's plan for before Christmas, rather than after?" A pause, and I waited for what I knew would come next. "Will you tell the queen of our engagement?"

"Yes, of course I will." Just how would I phrase the news of my engagement to her? I heard my mother's urgent voice telling me to be firm.

He sensed my withdrawal: our goodbye. The door opened, and he stepped up into the compartment and took me in his arms. He kissed me gently on the mouth. "Don't worry, Marion, just think about the time when we can be together." He kissed me again. The shrill whistle of the stationmaster and his cry of "All abo-aard!" made me jump, and George got down onto the platform and slammed the door closed.

As the train pulled out of the station, he took off his hat and waved it, and covering the side of his face with it, so no one could see, he blew kisses.

"Crawfie!" Margaret swanned through the schoolroom door, pulling Susan on a leash behind her. "You are back—finally! We have *missed* you so much." Susan dug her back paws into the carpet, her head down. "Susan was behaving like a little animal—she bit Dookie again—so Mummy says it's leash time.

"Thank you for your birthday card, by the way. It would have been so much better if we could have celebrated here, instead of hateful old Balmoral." She tossed Susan's leash on the floor and sat down in a chair: her head thrown back and her eyes closed, with the world-weary air of a woman who had been tried beyond her endurance. "You would never believe how *boring* Balmoral can be." She raised her head to look at me. "You are *so* lucky not to have to go: all that endless heather; all those detestable craggy views. It just goes on and on." Her glance flicked around my room. "That's a pretty hat; where on earth did you get it?"

"Edin—"

"Of course, Lilibet spent every day with Papa, stalking deer! Such a pointless waste of time." She raised her arms in a languorous stretch. "Crawfie, it's *wonderful* to be back in London." A delicate yawn of boredom. "I just came to say hullo. Now, I can't stop for long. I must have my hair washed, because Mummy's invited Johnny Dalkeith and Sunny Blandford for dinner. Do you think, if I twist her arm, she'll let me go out dancing at the 400 with them?"

"I shouldn't bank . . ."

Margaret rolled her eyes at the irritating habits of parents, and I had to bite the insides of my cheeks to stop myself from laughing. Was this gorgeous sophisticate the Margaret Rose of the tantrum years? She had left for Scotland an untidy girl and had come back a woman of the world—or at least an elegant parody of one.

"My goodness, Margaret, how you have come along. You have grown, surely?"

"Not in inches, though, unfortunately." She held out a slender foot clad in a high-heeled peep-toe shoe.

"Aha!" I said.

"Yes, no stuffy old Norman Hartnell for me—the dress and the shoes came from Paris, but don't tell Mummy or Papa. I saved all my coupons for them. Alah thought I was buying underwear; that's why I'm here, because she was so furious with me when this dress arrived!" The gleam of delight in her eyes was alluringly softened by long, sooty lashes. *Is she wearing mascara?* I peered into her face. She was certainly wearing lipstick. She laughed as I stepped back to take in the whole effect of her new wardrobe and obligingly undraped herself from the chair. The hemline of her silk voile dress floated a hair above her knees, revealing the curve of pretty legs sheathed in sheer nylon; the wide belt emphasized a tiny waist and the rounded curve of her hips. "Can't stay, Crawfie . . ." She undulated across the room in a perfect imitation of Betty Grable in *The Dolly Sisters*, high-stepping over Susan and looking at me over her shoulder.

As she reached the door, it opened again for Lilibet's entrance. Her lightly tanned face and glossy hair shouted, "I've spent every single day in northern country air."

"Crawfie, welcome home; we have missed you so much." Her sincerity was absolute.

I gazed at the two sisters standing in front of me, Margaret in her elegant postwar French finery and Lilibet in a skirt with an uneven hem and a faded blue blouse. My girls! Both utterly different and at the same time so very alike. I held out my arms, and when they leant their pretty heads on my shoulders, all my homesickness and regret at leaving George began to slowly ebb from pain to acceptance. *I am needed here: this is the job.*

"How bonny you look: the Scottish air has done you both the power of good. And Their Majesties?"

"You will find out at teatime." Margaret was off toward the door. "Simply must dash." And she was gone, leaving a whiff of an expensive scent in the air and the sense that an entire world was waiting for her: a world of debonair men in superbly cut suits who drove long, shiny, low-slung cars to take her to dimly lit clubs where dance bands played until dawn.

Lilibet watched her sister leave and then glanced at me. "She shut herself away in a small sitting room for hours at Balmoral, reading stacks of fashion magazines, listening to her record player, and existing on tiny little meals served to her on a tray. She even practiced smoking—I thought Alah was going to have a heart attack. She ate oranges to disguise the smoke on her breath. You have to talk to her, Crawfie." Lilibet frowned. "She was absolutely impossible. And it's all because I have Bobo as my dresser and my own apartment in the palace." She took up her habitual perch on the window seat, with a grateful Susan on her lap. "Terrible about Japan, isn't it? I can't see how they will ever recover."

While the Japanese people of Hiroshima and Nagasaki had been dying under a blow so formidable, so profoundly total in its destruction, I had been strolling through pine woods, full of egg-and-cress sandwiches, hand in hand with George.

"Thousands upon thousands died—just like that. And Britain had to agree to it, the bombing, because of the Quebec Agreement. Papa was devastated."

I nodded. That morning, when I had read every horrifying news report on the consequence of ignoring a new world power and seen the photograph of the gigantic mushroom cloud sixty thousand feet high, I had heard that split second of fear and terror as mothers, children, babies, and frail elderly people were thrown upward to die in a collision of fire, smoke, and the remnants of their world. I had combed newspapers for accounts and had worried over reports that had justified the use of this terrifying new bomb. I wondered how we could live with an act so amoral, so cruel.

"I am struggling, Lilibet—desperately trying to come to terms with what America believed it was right to do."

Felt it was right to do? I know my face showed my horror as she lifted her eyes to gaze serenely at me, as if we were discussing the weather.

She faltered. "But the American government did warn them, though, didn't they? They asked for an unconditional surrender, and the Japanese emperor didn't even respond. I suppose the Americans felt it was the only solution."

I realized with a bolt of chilling clarity that this sort of conversation with Lilibet was a huge mistake. She had been trained not to express her political views, and here she was displaying the sort of detachment that appalled me. And I didn't want to be appalled by Lilibet, not when I was giving up so much for her.

"It is an awful thing, this new A-bomb," she observed pacifically.

"An awful thing?" I simply couldn't help myself. "It is a . . . a moral disaster . . . a world disaster! Whoever thought of, and then made . . . a thing that could do so much wicked damage is a demon. A godforsaken demon! Don't you remember how devastated you were, Lilibet, when we drove in from Windsor on the morning after the war in Europe ended? Don't you remember how shocked you were at the chaos, the upheaval, and the terrible waste caused by the Blitz and the V-2 bombs? Not to mention what we did to cities like Dresden?"

"Dresden?" Her eyes were wide with astonishment at my anger. I knew that the last thing I should do was even touch on the horrors of Dresden.

"What happened to us all in Europe was outrageous: a horror against humanity, but nothing to what those poor souls in Hiroshima and Nagasaki experienced in the last moment of their lives. What happened to their world was . . . unconscionable." I stumbled to the window and threw it open. I leaned out, hands on the stone sill, to cool my hot face and breathe the mercifully uncontaminated clear air lifting in cool drafts from a garden so exquisite in its late-summer glory that it made my heart ache for the wreckage of Japan.

I looked over my shoulder at Lilibet; her face was flushed with bewilderment. I was quite sure that she had never seen her solid, dependable governess quite so beside herself before. I had broken one of the queen's rules. I was not playing the Windsor game: if you find something upsetting or distressing, the best thing to do is ignore it. Better that than to overreact.

And if you can't ignore it, I fumed, *push your head down underneath the silk cushions on the sofa, stay there, and count to ten, until the ugliness passes. And when you emerge, do so with composure, dignity, and a gracious smile.*

"Perhaps we shouldn't talk about it," Lilibet suggested.

"Most certainly we should not!" I responded with more asperity than she could have possibly wished for.

A pause from Her Royal Highness before she said, "I heard from Philip the other day. Unfortunately, he will not be coming home for a few months." Her tone was flat and unemotional. "Now that we have liberated Singapore, he has to stay and help bring home all our prisoners of war."

I struggled to subdue my trembling voice when I answered. "Prisoners of war in Singapore?" How many more hideous facts about the war in Asia were still to come? I cleared the emotion out of my throat. "Are there many?"

She darted a quick glance at me and licked her lips, wearing a slightly worried frown as she tried to decide how much of this catastrophe she should reveal. I tried to imagine cool mountain brooks and lambs in springtime to steady my voice. "It's all right, Lilibet, you can tell me. I won't explode."

"Well, that's a relief." But her gaze was still uneasy. "Yes, Crawfie, there are many prisoners: thousands, in fact. Philip says mostly British, New Zealand, and Australian POWs. The Japanese made their prisoners of war build a railroad all the way up through Malaya, Burma, and into Thailand so they could invade India. Countless died building it: Asians mostly, and . . . Europeans. He says Singapore is in chaos, with trainloads of POWs coming down from the peninsula, and there are not enough hospitals for them. It will be some time before we see Philip again."

I nodded, trying to keep an impassive shop front, but I could hear my breath still ragged with outrage: one man and a handful of psychopaths, greedy for power, had started this horrifying mess six years ago.

I bit down on words I would regret. I would not say that even if the Japanese military had annihilated half the world and enslaved thousands, we were surely sinking to their grotesque level of inhumanity by using the atom bomb.

"Crawfie?"

"Yes, Lilibet?"

"I agree with you, you know."

I borrowed an expression from George: eyebrows raised; corners of the mouth turned down.

"I mean I *really* agree with you. It *is* barbaric what happened . . ." I noticed she did not mention who the barbarians were. "But you know how it is, don't you?"

I took out a handkerchief, blew my nose, and stowed it away back in my pocket. "Yes, of course I do. And there's no need to explain anything, Lilibet. I must be on edge to be so . . . so emotional." My outburst had probably been considered ill-bred, my lack of restraint vulgar. I knew who had brought up this kind, well-meaning, and compassionate young woman to be so terribly repressed. *It is your fault*, I said to Alah and the queen, standing shoulder to shoulder in my mind, *not Lilibet's.*

"Won't you tell me how Their Majesties are, after their break in Balmoral? Are they reconciled to Philip?" I struggled with my still burning anger. Struggled to inquire with polite interest, and not like some out-of-control hoyden who could only embarrass and cause more pain.

She straightened her back, and her mother's tone was so clear in her voice I had to stop myself from laughing. "No rill chenge on thet front, Crawfee. We have reached a stellmate: Mummy, Papa, and I." She smiled at my palpable relief. "But I worked on Papa when we were alone together, and he says that when Philip comes home I may invite him to the palace so that he and Mummy can get to know him better." Her gaze was earnest. "And we are good at waiting, aren't we? The war taught us how to do that very well." She was appealing to me to not be angry with her for things she had no control over, and I rushed to reassure her.

"The time will simply fly by now that you are taking on more official engagements, Lilibet. There's nothing like being busy to get through the day."

She smiled her princess smile, and lifting her chin, she said with the immense pride of a young woman who had led an overprotected life with emphasis only on doing the expected, "I'm going to Belfast early next spring to launch HMS *Eagle*, Crawfie. It is an absolutely massive aircraft carrier. Mummy was going to go, but Papa and Tommy Lascelles said that I should, that it was time for me to do something more than just visit hospitals." *She's been launched*, I thought. *The dress rehearsals are over; from now on it will just be Margaret and me.*

She got up from our window seat. "I'm here"—her smile glowed in her healthy face—"with an official invitation. To invite you to tea with Papa, Mummy, Margaret, and me." I was touched by her desire to include me; it was as if she was reassuring me that even though she would be off christening aircraft carriers and inspecting hospitals and factories, she still had time for me.

"Thank you, Lilibet. It will be very nice to say hullo to the family." *And*, I thought, *to see how your papa is doing.* It was important for me to gauge the mood of the entire royal family, the "we four" of the Windsors, before I broached the subject of my engagement to the queen.

CHAPTER FOURTEEN

October 1945
Buckingham Palace, London

I had no idea you had such a sweet tooth, Crawfie." The queen's appraising stare when I joined the family for tea had unnerved me into taking a large slice of chocolate biscuit cake. The king, as if accurately assessing his wife's mood, lit a cigarette, looked at his watch, and said, "Have to be off in a minute; Townsend's waiting for me."

"You should have asked him to join us, Papa." For all her newfound chic, Margaret pouted like a six-year-old denied a treat.

"We can't bore Peter with schoolroom chitchat." The queen turned to her youngest daughter in a dazzle of shining teeth.

"We'll ask him next time, Margaret." The king blew a stream of smoke down his long nose: an aging dragon whose inner cauldron had long since ceased to boil. He stared down at his plate at a diminutive crustless sandwich with one tiny corner missing before he looked up, and I averted my eyes. He had drunk half a cup of tea, forced down a quarter of an inch of sandwich, and smoked four or five cigarettes in quick succession as we women nibbled and sipped our way through a spread that could have fed a large family for a week. I thought of my mother existing on eggs from her hens and vegetables from her garden—it would be a struggle for her this winter when they stopped laying and she had eaten her last winter cabbage.

"My greatest concern is that although Margaret's French appears to be fluent, her grammar is faulty. So, let's have more French, Crawfie, please, and less history. Margaret only seems to be able to converse in the present tense—I can't imagine why!"

Why is she doing this now, in front of the family? I sat in my chair, a chastised child, as the queen pecked holes in my curriculum for the autumn. Her voice was reasonable in tone, but her eyes were gray frost as she tore a slice of bread and butter into pieces and tossed them to her pack of snapping corgis. *No wonder,* I fumed in hot-faced silence, *her dogs are so fat; that's pure blasted butter she is throwing at them.*

I could feel resentment and anger burning up inside me and swallowed down the defensive replies that threatened to burst out of me. After all, it was she who had done away with Mademoiselle, insisting that I was more than capable of teaching the girls French—and now this? I squashed down my offended feelings, refusing to acknowledge my hurt. *You are doing this woman a favor,* I reminded myself. *Putting your life with George on hold to ensure a smooth transition as the girls take up their royal duties, and helping them back into the swim of things at Buckingham Palace.*

"Mon français parlé est parfait, et au moins mon accent est meilleur que le vôtre, Maman." Margaret tripped perfect French off her tongue, her hands folded in her lap, her mouth a moue of disapproval.

"Mais non, ma petite. Ce n'est pas vrai! Pas du tout, eh, Crawfee?" the queen cooed as she invited me with an icy glare to join them. If I weren't so disconcerted by her determination to correct me in front of her family, I would have shrugged off her cold stare and launched in. The queen returned to her French conversation sounding like a plump and frazzled English tourist with a phrase book in her hand, with her daughter a fierce little Parisienne with her eloquent, rapid French.

The queen threw a challenging look at me. "Et vous, Crawfee," she challenged in her schoolgirl French. "Qu'est que vous pensez?"

Do not ask me what I think when I am this upset, was my unspoken reply. How I managed to say in such a cool voice, "Je pense que le vocabulaire française de Margaret s'est considérablement developpe," I have no idea. But it was a response that went unheard, as the queen and her youngest daughter fought a battle of French verbs in shrill voices.

A polite voice that betrayed only the slightest tension asked, "C-C-C-Crawfie, you are from Scotland. Does your family enjoy stalking?"

Hysterical laughter boiled up in my throat, and I gulped it down. *Stalking? What is wrong with them all today? Where did he think the Crawford family would stalk deer? Down Limekiln's short High Street to the butcher to join the queue for the last wild rabbit?*

"No, Your Majesty, not in the last two hundred years."

He nodded at me through a haze of smoke. "Relaxing way to spend a day," he said. "You should come up to Balmoral with us—you like walking in the open air, d-do-don't you?"

"I do, sir, very much," I said, taking the opportunity of a quiet aside with him to consider the state of his health. He looked a lot better than he had eight weeks ago. There was more color in his face, the tick that had made his left eyelid jump uncontrollably had almost disappeared, but he was still too thin, too hollow-eyed. He nodded, stubbed out his cigarette, and lit another almost immediately. Inhaling smoke deep into his lungs, he turned to join in the

French conversation as he exhaled. But he wasn't quick enough to keep up with Margaret. The fingers of his left hand beat a light tattoo on the arm of his chair, and I noticed that his long, thin legs were crossed tightly at the ankle. Such tension! He dropped out of the French argument and returned to his inner preoccupation as if it demanded his complete attention. *No wonder his favorite occupation is shooting*, I decided. *He can bang away with his guns for hours, effectively blocking out all conversation and obliterating his anxieties with each fallen creature.*

Elizabeth waited until there was a lull in the Gallic conversation, which had all the tone of a first-class spat. "Crawfie, will you come with us to Windsor this weekend? I promise you won't have to stay in the Victoria Tower." She lifted her voice: "Will she, Mummy?" I smiled at the memory of wartime Windsor and my long nightly walk from the dining room to my bedroom in the tower. I shivered my shoulders in exaggeration and Lilibet laughed.

Finally, the queen drew breath. "What did you say, Lilibet? Non, Marguerite, c'est assez."

"We must make sure that Crawfie is not landed in the Victoria Tower this weekend, at Windsor."

"Now, darling, you know perfectly well that Crawfie can't come *this* time. I promised Porchey, Sunny, and Johnny a Windsor weekend. And Hugh Euston is bringing Pamela Mountbatten, Ann Fortune, and Mary Cavendish." A broad smile of pleasure. "And I have invited Noël to keep us all entertained. The castle will be packed, so I will have to be duenna, *not* Crawfie . . . Crawfie can have a bit of time awff." Her voice maintained its playful tone, but the look she shot me was unkind. It was worse than Susan when she nipped Dookie or made a nuisance of herself.

What have I done? Stunned by her offhand dismissal of my help as a chaperone, I caught my breath and exhaled carefully, so that it didn't sound like a sigh.

The queen had rounded up the eldest sons of the richest and oldest aristocratic families: pleasant chinless wonders without an ounce of drive or originality, but assuredly every single one reliable, appropriately grateful, and completely in the queen's thrall. But what was clear now was that she viewed me as belonging to the other side: a Philip supporter.

I glanced across at Lilibet's face. It was a polite blank, but I saw her hands clasp each other so tightly in her lap that her knuckles turned white. The irrepressible Margaret jumped in. "Sounds like you've invited your entire cricket eleven to Windsor. Poor Lil, you're going to have to dance with all of Mummy's suitable suitors for you. Or perhaps she's inviting them for Noël!" A shocked silence. Lilibet's puzzled expression crinkled her brow, the queen's eyebrows lowered in a full frown, and I wondered how an overprotected sixteen-year-old girl could possibly know about Noël Coward's fondness for men. The king, whose head had whipped round like a ventriloquist's dummy, with his wide mouth open in surprise, threw back his head and roared with laughter.

The queen finished her scone in two delicate little bites, as if Margaret had not spoken. "Crawfie, we are agreed that Margaret"—a fond shake of her head toward her naughty youngest daughter— "will join you in the schoolroom from ten until three on weekdays, unless she has a more pressing engagement, for some serious study of French grammar. Good, that's settled, then. Thank you, Crawfie, we mustn't impose on your free time."

If she had jerked her head toward the door, she couldn't have made it plainer, and I rose hastily to my feet.

"Yes, ma'am, and thank you, sir."

Lilibet got to her feet too, and the queen put down her teacup. "Oh, Lilibet, a moment, darling, before you rush awff. Lady Astor told me that Marina telephoned. She wanted to invite you to Coppins this weekend. Will you telephone and tell her that we are going down to Windsor?" She glanced at her wristwatch. "Better do it now, while she is having tea."

I glanced back over my shoulder as I scuttled through the door. Elizabeth had already picked up the receiver, but the look she gave me as I stepped over the threshold was anxiously sympathetic.

I didn't want anyone to see me gallop to the haven of my rooms, so I made myself walk slowly to the foot of my staircase and strolled down the corridor. I opened the door, stepped inside, and stood with my back against it, as if at any moment the queen might throw it open and accuse me of aiding her daughter in pursuing an unsuitable relationship. My thoughts were so stricken that all I could do was stare blankly at the wall.

Breathe! I instructed myself. I sat down on the sofa. *Breathe!* I felt like a parlormaid who had carelessly chipped a cup. My face flooded with embarrassment and shame. *Why is she so angry with me?* For fourteen years there had always been the feeling of "just us girls" in my schoolroom chats with the queen. She had always been welcoming, lighthearted, always willing to see the funny side of life. We had enjoyed each other's company. I had been part of her family—hadn't I? Now, all of a sudden, she had become my employer, a disappointed one: cold and admonishing.

Was I guilty of coming between a mother and her daughter? Had I tried to usurp the queen in Lilibet's affections? It had always been my conscious intention to not try to replace their mother, but I couldn't help but feel motherly toward them. And when the war came, we were marooned at Windsor. We lived with an ever-present undercurrent of fear: the bombs, the bleak, implacable blackness of night. And with that a continual nervous concern about the king and queen's safety at Buckingham Palace. Those years had made us closer, especially my relationship with Lilibet as she had grown into womanhood. She had come to me with all her questions and concerns: the first time she got the curse; the facts of life, and the hysterics we had shared at Alah's severe hints about storks, cabbage patches, and gifts from God; the mystifying attraction of some Guards officers and the guilty giggling about those we thought repellent.

I backtracked through conversations I had had with Lilibet about Philip, looking for clues as to whether I was culpable of conniving with daughter against mother for popularity. Surely, all I had done was listen to Lilibet, encouraged her to be open with her parents? I examined my conscience as rigorously as any penitent. *No—* I dashed tears away with the back of my hand—*no, I have not encouraged Lilibet to do anything but be honest and forthcoming to her mother. And neither*—more tears rolled—*have I tried to take the queen's place.* Perhaps Lilibet had told her mother that she had confided in me, and this was the reason for this secretive woman's animosity? I shook my head. Lilibet was guarded with her feelings and rarely one to speak out. I searched for my handkerchief and blew my nose. Margaret, then? Chatty, bright Margaret, who would say anything to be the center of attention? But Margaret had no idea that Lilibet had confided in me about Philip. The queen, I realized with a slow and painful exhalation that bordered on a sob, the queen somehow knew that I was her daughter's confidante, and she didn't like it.

"How on earth do I tell her of my engagement and that I will be leaving?" I remembered the conversation we had had in 1940 when I had suggested to the queen that I should join up to do real war work and showed her my half-completed application form to the Women's Royal Naval Service. "Oh, Crawfie, no! Surely not? I mean the WRNS is a wonderful organization, of course it is. But your war work is here at Windsor . . . looking after the girls. Without you, *we* wouldn't have a moment's peace to do our important work for the country." Her tone had been light, reassuring, and I had been flattered by how important I was to the family.

"What will she say if I tell her I am leaving to get married?" I asked the pale green and cream walls of my sitting room. The queen had made it quite clear, several times during tea, as she nibbled at a petit four, that twenty-one was the perfect age for a young woman to think of marriage. "Two more years!" I wailed. "I can't do it, I really can't!" The room's silence closed in, echoing only disdainful disappointment at my disloyalty to a family that depended on me.

I turned my head and wiped my eyes on the antimacassar on the back of the sofa. *Will George be content to wait two whole years?* I most certainly would not. How I wished I had listened to my sensible mother and had written to the queen, offering a month's notice from the safety of Scotland. I isolated the one thing that had become so important to me from the tangle of my shocked and hurt feelings. However grueling my remaining time at the palace might be, I couldn't bring myself to leave Lilibet in the lurch—not after having heard her brave declaration for Philip.

I got up from the sofa and walked across the room to my modest drinks cabinet and poured myself a whiskey. Its peaty warmth was comforting; it was so smooth I didn't even cough. "Better not make a habit of this, Marion," I said to my empty glass. *Or of talking to yourself!*

CHAPTER FIFTEEN

December 31, 1945
Limekiln Cottage, Dunfermline, Scotland

I don't think we need any of Marion's lovely Glen Avon now that George has brought us such a generous pile of firewood to keep us warm." Ma smiled at her hero as George added a last log to the fire and dusted his hands.

He put three glasses down on the table. "Uisge-beatha—the water of life—and a roaring fire! What more do you need to celebrate Hogmanay—except of course each other?" He smiled and the corners of his eyes crinkled at some inner joke or secret. "I have a little bit of good news to share with you. I was offered a job at Drummonds Bank in Aberdeen the day before yesterday."

"As what?" I asked.

"Bank manager, of course, but not at first. I'll be learning the ropes for a month, and then when Mr. Whitelaw retires, I will step into his shoes."

"But what about Drummonds Bank in Dunfermline?" The shock of the unexpected made me sound ridiculous.

"I'm afraid I can't manage both banks, Marion. I am offered nearly twice the salary in Aberdeen—think of the money we can save for my retirement!" He took both my hands in his. "I didn't dare tell you about the interview—I was sure they would give the job to a younger man."

I didn't look at my mother because I knew what expression would be on her face. "There is a daily bus service between Aberdeen and here." I felt the need to reassure her.

"It takes three hours because of that long stop in Perth," my mother put in, "and the faster train journey is an expensive one to make every weekend." My mother launched into a pet theme. "And they never run on time, not since the war. They should get on with this nationalization business—then perhaps we'll have cheaper fares and trains that run on time. That's why we voted Labour—so that the government could do something for the country."

George put his arm around my waist and pulled me to his side. "The trip to Dunfermline at weekends will be nothing at all"—he waved his arm in the direction of the window—"in my new car: I bought Mr. McAlister's Baby Austin."

It was a fait accompli. I felt as if the rug had been pulled out from under my feet.

"That little car of McAlister's? However long will the trip from Aberdeen take in that titchy thing?" My mother's scandalized face would have been amusing at any other time.

"Two hours. When Marion is home from London, I'll leave at five o'clock on Friday and be with you both for supper and leave again on Sunday after tea. Come and see it!"

He walked me to the parlor window, and we contemplated the shadow of a very small car standing in the lane. "Think of the lovely drives we can make together on Saturdays—even when it's raining." George's voice close to my ear made me shiver in anticipation, and

I wrapped my hand in his. "I'll even pop over to Dunfermline when you are in London and take your mother for lunch and a day of shopping in Edinburgh!"

Ma appeared and frowned at the car. "Petrol is expensive these days—and then they always announce some shortage or other," she said. "And Aberdeen is a very expensive city to live in. And where will you sleep when you are here? We have only two bedrooms." She glanced at us both out of the corner of her eyes, a quick, sly look, and George burst out laughing. "On the sofa, Mrs. Crawford, where else?" He pulled me closer to him. "When Marion retires . . . this summer, I will have enough money saved to retire too! And then we'll buy that old cottage down the lane, fix it up, and be your neighbors." He turned me away from the kitchen, and my mother pretended to tut about the cost of petrol, when I could see she was delighted at the thought of us living next door.

"What do you think, Marion, shall I say yes to Drummonds in Aberdeen? . . . It will only be until the end of August. We can be married in September."

"You haven't accepted already?"

His brows shot up, his eyes wide. "No, of course not. I wanted to ask you what you thought first. But I must give them an answer on Monday."

A horrified squawk from behind us. "Chew it over later—just a minute to go to midnight."

George topped up our glasses with the deep amber spirit, and we sang "Bliadhna Mhath Ùr," a happy New Year, as the silvery chimes of the carriage clock rang out the twelfth hour.

"Time to let in 1946." Before we could stop her, my mother threw open the kitchen door, and a blast of air, straight from the arctic, filled the room. "That's enough, Ma," I cried, as tears of cold welled in my eyes and oxygen-fueled flames leapt in the grate.

"Here's to you both, and here's to George's new job!" Ma raised her glass to us, and with the first sip of whiskey warming our throats, we sang:

A guid New Year to ane an' a'
An' mony may ye see!

George took me in his arms and slowly waltzed me out of the kitchen and around the ground floor of the cottage. At the bottom of the stairs, we got ourselves caught up with the coats hanging on their pegs, and he gave me a long, malty kiss. "A happy New Year, my beautiful Marion. I think 1946 is going to be our year."

We were standing at the foot of the stairs that led to my bedroom, and the thought of my quiet room with its welcoming bed was nearly my undoing. If my mother had not been scurrying around our kitchen tidying things away, I would have taken him by the hand and led him up those stairs. The whiskey made me laugh at such wicked thoughts. Presbyterians didn't melt with longing, their legs were strong and steady to keep them upright in God's service, and Scots governesses, even in our modern century, did not imagine what it would be like to be in bed with their fiancés, however thoroughly they were kissed. But I was betrothed to this man; we would be married; surely that took the shame out of our desire?

I laid my head against George's chest. I could feel his heartbeat quicken as my lips touched the skin above his tie. He lowered his mouth to the top of my head; I could feel his warm breath in the parting of my hair. In that moment, I made my resolution for the year: there would be no more dithering and procrastinating about how or when I would tell the queen that I would be retiring this July when they left for Balmoral. I lifted my head. "I think you should say yes to the Aberdeen job, George. I will arrange with the palace to leave in the summer."

. . .

"Someone here to see you, Marion." My mother's voice came up the stairs as I pulled a heavy sweater on over my blouse. The window-panes were covered with my frosted breath from the night's heavy freeze. I scraped away the rime with a fingernail and peered out into a glittering winter world. Icicles hung along the undersides of the bare boughs of the mulberry tree outside my window, and the wait-ing pond was a disk of pewter ice. I glanced at the alarm clock next to my bed. *George is here awfully early for ice-skating.* I brushed my hair and put on my shoes.

"How he got that ridiculous motor up our tiny little lane, I'll never know." Ma greeted me at the bottom step. "No, Marion, it isn't George." Lowering her voice to an audible whisper, she said, "It's someone from the king!" Her eyes gleamed with excitement. After all these years of hearing about kings, queens, and courtiers, one of them had turned up on our doorstep. I walked past her into the kitchen.

A uniformed chauffeur stood with his back to the fireplace, his eyes watering with cold.

"Mr. Hughes!"

"Good morning to you, Miss Crawford. Sorry to arrive unan-nounced, but something has happened, and you are needed at San-dringham."

The king! I composed myself to hear the worst. Ma pulled up on the pump handle at the sink and put her half-filled kettle down. Drops of water plinked on the kettle lid. The king was dead. The silence in the kitchen was like a shout. If the king is dead, Lilibet will be queen. *No*—I shook my head at my thoughts—*not yet! She's too young!*

"What has happened?" I heard myself ask.

Mr. Hughes glanced at my mother as she wiped her hands on a tea towel.

"Mrs. Knight died in her sleep the night before last."

"Alah?"

He nodded. It wasn't possible. She hadn't been that old, surely? *Poor lonely old woman*, I thought, as relief flooded through me that Lilibet was spared the monarchy.

"And Their Royal Highnesses, the princesses, are very distressed; the Princess Margaret is inconsolable."

"What sad news," my mother said. "But surely, Mr. Hughes, you can't be saying that Marion should leave with you?"

He looked so baffled that I stepped in.

"Alah was like a mother to the princesses and to the queen. She brought them up, looked after them, cared for them as if they were her own children." I could only imagine how grief-stricken the princesses must be. Their indomitable nanny, the life force of their childhood, had gone from them so suddenly.

Mr. Hughes turned from my fierce little mother with relief. "How long would it take you to pack, Miss Crawford? Her Majesty asks that you come to Sandringham as soon as possible. Both the Misses MacDonald are in shock. And Her Royal Highness Princess Margaret has been asking for you. You . . . you are needed."

Ma folded her arms under her bosom.

"You're not going anywhere with my daughter until she has a good breakfast inside her. What about you, Mr. Hughes, have you eaten this morning?"

She put down three earthenware porridge bowls on the table and just as quickly followed them with cups, saucers, the milk jug, and a pot of tea. "Hope you can take your tea without sugar—there's been none here for months. Cut some bread, Marion. How long did it take you to drive here from the south, Mr. Hughes?" She glanced out of the window at the preposterously huge car that filled the lane in the same spot that George's Baby Austin had parked just hours ago.

"It's a day's drive, ma'am. I spent the night in Dunfermline. And thank you, ma'am, a good breakfast is always welcome."

"No need to ma'am me; I'm plain Mrs. Crawford. There's no bacon to be had, and the hens stopped laying in October. But there is oatmeal porridge, and we Scots eat it with cream and a little salt. So, sit yourself down, Mr. Hughes."

CHAPTER SIXTEEN

January 1946
Sandringham House, Norfolk, England

I leaned forward to peer out of the window into the dark Norfolk night as Mr. Hughes steered the car through the gates of Sandringham. As we rounded the corner and the lights of the house came into view, I saw his shoulders droop from the tension of his long drive on icy roads. I caught his eyes in the rearview mirror: red-rimmed in a face lined with fatigue. We had stopped only twice and that was for petrol. I looked at my watch: we had been on the road for nearly twelve hours. With a sigh of relief, Mr. Hughes pulled up at the side door to the servants' hall.

"Well, here we are at last, Miss Crawford." He opened the door and helped me out of the car. My legs were cramped and stiff, my feet so cold I couldn't tell if I was standing on them. I walked forward. *So, this is how a sailor feels after weeks of being at sea.* I turned to the man who held my arm in his supporting hands. "Thank you so much, Mr. Hughes, you must be exhausted."

"Nice cuppa tea with a splash of whiskey in it, and I'll do, Miss Crawford. Here's Mr. Ainslie to welcome you."

The door opened, and the king's butler came down the steps. He took my other arm, nodding to Mr. Hughes that I was in safe hands.

"My dear Miss Crawford, I would say welcome to Sandringham, but what a sad occasion. The family are deeply distressed, as are we all." In all the years that I had known him, I had not met a single baron, viscount, or marquis who possessed the considerate courtesy or gentle manners that Mr. Ainslie had. I felt as if I had been welcomed by a favorite uncle. He looked over his shoulder to the man who had driven nearly eight hundred miles in snow, black ice, fog, and sleet. "Mrs. Mundy has kept dinner for you, Mr. Hughes, whenever you are ready." The chauffeur wished me a good night's rest and got back into the Daimler to drive round to the stable block.

"You must be very tired, Miss Crawford; such a long, cold journey for you. Come along inside and let's get you warm. I expect it's much colder up in Scotland." A shaft of Norfolk wind blew through the leafless trees, and I shook like an old woman with the ague. Mr. Ainslie ushered me into a chill, poorly lit servants' hallway and up the back stairs to the second floor of the house. He pushed open a green baize door and we walked off cracked linoleum into a wide, thickly carpeted and brightly lit corridor. The scent of forced hyacinth filled the air: the queen was in residence.

"I have put you in the East room; we have no guests at Sandringham at present, only family. I hope you will be quite comfortable here." He opened the door into a sumptuously furnished sitting room. A bright fire on the hearth, deep, comfortable chairs, heavy velvet curtains drawn against the frigid East Anglian night.

I stood, dazed and a little disoriented, as a footman carried in my suitcase; a maid followed close behind him to unpack it. They disappeared into my bedroom. I took off my hat and started to fumble at the buttons of my coat. Mr. Ainslie helped me off with it and handed it to the footman. My head swam; all I really wanted to do was to stretch out on the bed and sleep. Mr. Ainslie took me by the arm and steered me into a chair by the fire. "I will tell Her Majesty that you have arrived. She asks that you come down this evening, if you are not too tired?"

I stared up at him, my face blank. I had been received at Sandringham with the sort of deference only extended to the royal family. I must pull myself together. "Thank you, Mr. Ainslie; yes, of course, I will go to Her Majesty immediately."

I am not here for her, I reminded myself. *I am here for the girls.*

"As soon as you are ready, Miss Crawford, just ring, and I will take you to the family."

The footman set a silver tray down on the table: ham sandwiches, a pot of coffee, a covered soup tureen. It was clearly going to be a long night. I drank two cups of coffee liberally laced with fine white sugar. It was hot, sweet, and strong. I went into my bedroom to wash my face and hands. A white face, topped by untidy hair, looked back at me in the looking glass. I found my comb, put on some lipstick, and rubbed some onto my cheeks. I rang for Ainslie and followed him the length of the house and down the great staircase to the drawing room.

The king was nowhere to be seen, but the queen, Margaret, and Lilibet were sitting in front of an immense fire in the salon; its light danced on beige silk damask walls, dark wood paneling, and huge armchairs and sofas upholstered in floral chintz: the Edwardian taste of the king's grandfather lingered everywhere in the house.

"Crawfie." The queen lifted a heavy head. She looked exhausted, from her slumped shoulders to the hand that listlessly held her customary gin and Dubonnet. Stunned by Alah's abrupt death, they looked like survivors of a shipwreck washed up on a lonely beach—orphans of the storm.

Any rancor I had felt toward Her Majesty evaporated at the sight of her round, forlorn face as she said my name again. "Crawfie, thank you so very much for making time for us," she said, as if I had popped over from next door.

"My condolences, Your Majesty. Such a terrible shock."

I turned to the two girls. Lilibet reached out a hand to me. "Crawfie, such an awfully long way . . . in this terrible weather." Her eyes swam with tears; she drew in a breath and, in complete control of herself: "Thank you so much for coming." She came over to me and, taking my hand, led me to the sofa. I gave hers a squeeze as we sat down together. If we had been alone, she would have laid her head on my shoulder as she used to when she was ten and Margaret was plaguing her.

"Your Royal Highness," I said to Margaret, and she was up out of her chair by the fire and beside me on the sofa. With the two girls on either side I looked across the room at the queen.

Queen Elizabeth was always poised to take command of every situation, with the robotic serenity of a woman who has weathered countless royal tempests, but tonight she was deeply unsettled. There were dark circles under her eyes, and a network of lines around her mouth and chin puckered as she tried to smile reassurance that all would be well. Her wavering gaze hovered on the faces of her stricken children. She lifted her glass to her mouth and took a sizable sip of her drink. She was shaken to the core by her nanny's death; the stability and security the old lady had provided all three women had gone. *Alah's brand of loyalty cannot easily be bought in postwar England.*

Her Majesty's gaze flicked over to me, rested briefly on my face with a smile of new recognition, and then passed on to the hot, clammy-handed, and snuffling Margaret. Her smile faltered, confirming everything that I had thought during the long, cold hours of my journey to Norfolk. *She needs my help, and she particularly needs it with Margaret.* Bobo and Ruby were stubbornly loyal to the queen, but Bobo worshiped Lilibet and had no time for Margaret except to criticize, and Ruby was easily bullied. I held the only other position of trust in Her Majesty's life. I was her daughters' teacher and companion of many years: providing unquestioning care, dedicated guidance. Why, even up until last May, I was thought to be utterly reliable, the queen's ally.

The queen's weakening smile became a valiant one. She took in a breath, and I saw her shoulders lift. "It does my heart good, Crawfie, to see you here with us again. The girls have been most awfully distressed; we all have. Poor Alah, we had no idea her health was so bad. She was such a stalwart soul, always ready to soldier on. Kind, dear Alah." She lifted her glass. Her sad gaze was fixed on my face—there was no challenge, no cool assessment of my flaws, reflected there. Just the hope that I would rally to the cause.

I nodded and said, "Yes, Your Majesty," and watched her shoulders come down a notch or two.

"She was all alone . . ." Margaret's breathy voice broke. "She died alone. She had lunch with Bobo and Ruby . . . then went to her room to do some mending. That was at half past two in the afternoon." A deep, gusty sob. "No one knew she had died until her maid took her tea . . ." I put out my hand to hold Margaret's hot one. *I will not let this happen to me. I will not soldier on, long past my useful life, to die alone in some little-used corner of one of their houses like poor Alah.*

"Margaret, dear, she wasn't alone. She was with us, surrounded by those who loved her." The queen closed her eyes briefly and then treated me to a gentle smile of gratitude. "I said to His Majesty, we must ask Crawfie to come, and thank heaven you did. You can only imagine what a state poor Bobo and Ruby are in. Alah was like a mother to them too—to all of us." Her voice wavered, just a little. Margaret forgot she was far from being a woman of the world and trembled beside me as a fresh torrent of tears broke.

I could feel Lilibet next to me, struggling to keep control. *Poor little thing,* I thought. *Why on earth shouldn't she give way to her grief?* I turned her to me and stroked the damp tendrils of hair back from her forehead. She gulped back her tears and pressed my hand.

I reached into my handbag and distributed the clean handkerchiefs that nannies and governesses always carry. Margaret mopped her face. "The doctor said she wasn't in any pain, she just went"—a shuddering sob—"in her . . . s-s-sleep." Margaret desperately needed to talk about her nanny's death. However much Alah worshiped Lilibet—diligent in her training, watchful of the respect accorded to the heir presumptive—she had adored fat, pretty baby Margaret Rose. So much in fact that she kept her corralled in her pram, playpen, or high chair when she was long able to walk.

I smoothed the palm of Margaret's hand. "It must have been such a shock for you, Margaret. I can only imagine how sad you must feel."

Margaret lifted a tear-streaked face to me, desperate to confide. "I was so unkind to her the other day. But I didn't know; I just didn't know."

"Of course you didn't, Margaret." I put my arm across her bowed, shaking shoulders. "Alah probably didn't know how ill she was either. She was happy and purposeful looking after her girls. She loved you both very much." I turned to Lilibet to include her. "She always told me that you were her own little girls. She was so proud of you both."

"We'll miss her terribly," Lilibet said; her eyes brimmed and she blinked hard.

"Yes, we . . . will," choked out Margaret.

"Of course you will; of course you will." Margaret trumpeted into the handkerchief again. Her hair stood up in the front in damp tufts.

"Why didn't we know that she was so ill?" she asked her mother— her challenge rang out across the room. "We should have known, Mummy. Doctors or something . . . then we could have looked after her—properly."

"There, there, Margaret." The queen put her empty glass down on the table and looked around the room. *She could probably do with another drink. God knows I could do with one.*

I held the girls' hands in mine.

"Just remember Alah with a glad heart," I said, remembering the stern rules and comportment she imposed on them: rewarding the three-year-old Lilibet with a sugar biscuit when she managed to control her bladder for an entire morning.

"Remember her often, with gratitude." Two-year-old Margaret might only play with one toy at a time, returning it to the cupboard before choosing another. In my mind I saw the patient face of a woman who unswervingly accepted the rigid class divisions of her generation: her strong jawline, her frown of admonition, how cross she became when she was worried or unsure. Kind enough in her own stoic way, but a woman with little to no imagination. Rigid loyalty, consistent rule.

And the result? Lilibet was far too self-controlled and often controlling. Margaret's frustrations as a toddler led her to throw tantrums of such monumental fury that the two nursemaids, Bobo and Ruby, caved instantly when Alah was not there, teaching Margaret a vital lesson in how to bully.

Clara Knight—Alah, such an absolute name. A mispronunciation of Clara made decades ago by the queen when she was a child. Allah means "the God" in Arabic. The two-year-old Elizabeth Bowes-Lyon had named her nanny after the Almighty. No wonder the entire palace staff walked in fear of Mrs. Clara Knight. No wonder she had insisted on creating her own protocol among nursery servants, where she was treated with the same deference as the queen.

Margaret blew her nose again, and her breath came more evenly. Lilibet let go of my hot hand.

Was it my empty stomach or Margaret's that growled? "Margaret, have you eaten anything at all today?" I asked. She shook her head; silent tears still seeped from the corners of her swollen eyes. "Do you think you could manage a wee bite?" She shrugged and snuffled into the handkerchief. "Let's ask Mr. Ainslie to arrange for some soup to be sent up to the schoolroom."

"No need to go the schoolroom, Crawfie." The queen was on her feet. "I will arrange something for you in the dining room." She smoothed the front of her skirt. "I must go and see that the king has everything he needs."

She hesitated in front of her youngest daughter and, bending down, lifted Margaret's chin to dry her cheeks with a tiny scrap of lawn and lace. "No more crying now, my darlings; best foot forward." A motherly peck on two blotchy cheeks. I remembered how much Alah had dinned into the royal princesses that displays of any sort of emotion at all were vulgar. *This is why self-disciplined Lilibet has managed to gulp down her tears more completely; her training at Alah's hands was far stricter than that of Margaret's.*

The queen turned in the doorway. "Crawfie, will you talk with Ruby and Bobo?"

"Yes, ma'am," I said. "I will pop in and see them first thing tomorrow."

"Good," said the queen, as if everything was now settled. "They have been asking if you would come." I realized in that moment that Alah's death heralded a new era for the Windsor family. Bobo was already Lilibet's dresser, and now Ruby would continue as Margaret's maid. The Windsor nursery would be disbanded until Lilibet married and had children of her own.

CHAPTER SEVENTEEN

February 1946
Buckingham Palace, London

I bent over my desk, crossing through lists I had made all week, so furiously engaged I didn't hear Lilibet come into my room. "What's happening, Crawfie? You look so desperate. Has Margaret . . ." I looked up into her face.

"No, Margaret is delightful these days . . ."

"But something is bothering you."

"Bothering" was putting it mildly. I fretfully crossed out another item on my list. I had left it too late to organize George's visit to London properly, and now I was in a right tizzy. "A family friend, Major Buthlay, is coming down for the weekend, and I have left it too late to get tickets for *The Winslow Boy*. I had no idea the play was so popular, and I can't even get tickets for anything else. And on top of that, I have no idea where to go to dinner or where the poor man will stay." I had no need to add that palace inmates were like schoolchildren when they were let out in the great wide world.

"A visitor from Scotland!" I glanced up, expecting to see curiosity; all I saw was concern. "You must be looking forward to show-ing him London." And as the rest sank in: "I wish I could help you, but I don't know anything about that sort of thing either." She sat down and considered. "We must talk to Papa's equerry, Peter Townsend. He is so helpful, and very approachable. Mummy says he can make anything happen." She knew that I would rather die a thousand deaths than bother the senior palace staff; they could be so very . . . chilling was probably the kindest way to put it. "Let me ask him if he can help, and if he can, he'll let you know."

The last thing I wanted was the rumor mill whispering that Miss Crawford was entertaining a male friend. "I don't want to be any trouble."

"How could you be any trouble?" She got up and came over to my desk, where I was frowning at my crossed-through lists of hotels all in the wrong neighborhoods or else, to my dismay, terribly ex-pensive. "Peter can help with everything, Crawfie. Don't worry about where Major Buthlay can stay. Peter has a genius for organiza-tion. Mummy and Papa call him the wizard!" She put her hand on my shoulder and glanced down into my panic-stricken face. "Oh, I see. Yes, I understand. I think we can trust Peter; he is very discreet and would completely respect your privacy. What have you planned so far?"

I cleared my throat and picked up my plan for George's arrival on Thursday. It looked like a schedule for a school outing.

"Most of it is really simple: we both enjoy wandering around museums and galleries. Do you remember our visits to the Victoria and Albert and the National Gallery before the war, Lilibet?"

She nodded. "Yes, but my most favorite outing was when you took us to Woolworths to shop for our Christmas presents, and we went there on the top of a double-decker bus. Do you remember that? And you gave us both our tuppences so we could pay the bus conductor ourselves. Margaret and I played passengers and bus conductors for weeks. But let's concentrate on you, for once. The play you want to see, what's it about?"

"It takes place in the early 1900s, about a young boy, a student at the Naval Academy in Osborne, who is sent home in disgrace for stealing a five-shilling postal order. His father believes he is completely innocent, and his sister, who is a suffragette, has a friend who is a really good lawyer. The family all work to prove his innocence." I looked up to see that I had lost her. "I know it sounds really dull, but the reviews are wonderful."

"That sounds exactly like the sort of thing that Philip would like," Lilibet mused. "Do I have your permission to have a word with Peter Townsend about getting tickets for the play, and maybe recommending a restaurant for supper? He might even know of a reasonably priced hotel close to us. He is awfully good at making things happen. We all adore him."

"This play is very good indeed." The curtain closed for the entr'acte of *The Winslow Boy*.

I was thrilled to have provided a treat—for both of us. I had glanced at George occasionally through the first act, and it had made me quite unreasonably happy to see him so completely engrossed. "And the seats, Marion, the seats are absolutely first-class." I was smiling with delight as he took my arm to steer me through the throng to the bar.

"When I read the reviews, I thought it would be the sort of thing you would enjoy—it's about all the things you believe in."

"Which are?"

"Honor, for one thing . . . loyalty."

"My generation were brought up to believe that honor is sacred. Why don't you wait here, and I will get us something to drink?" And he joined the queue at the bar.

"So, what are you thinking about? Honor still?" George was back with our champagne.

"I think the thing I find the most touching about the play is just how far the family are prepared to go to prove the boy's innocence."

He gave me a glass of champagne, and I lifted mine to salute him.

"Let's drink to honor and loyalty," he said. "You know, don't you, Marion, that I understand your reasons for sticking with your job? For seeing things through." *Even if I haven't told the queen that I am leaving in July?* I felt a stab of panic. Was I being honorable to George by being loyal to Lilibet and Margaret? *I will tell the queen as soon as George goes back to Scotland.*

"To honor and loyalty!" I raised my glass and sipped that first delectable, teasing taste of champagne. I felt elegant and sophisticated in my dark blue velvet evening dress, surrounded by the stylishly dressed crowd eagerly discussing one of the most critically acclaimed plays of the season.

George touched his glass lightly to mine. "And to us, Marion, and thank you for a wonderful evening." He looked around the bar. "I think I could get used to living this high on the hog!"

"So could I. But it is Peter Townsend, the king's equerry, we have to thank. He arranged everything for us. How is the hotel?"

"It is really very nice indeed, comfortable without being grand: a quiet room with its own bathroom." He drew closer to me. "After we have had dinner, if you are not too tired, perhaps I could take you dancing?"

The bell rang for us to return to the auditorium. "Oh, I won't be too tired. But I am not sure where . . ."

George laughed. "I don't know whether to be jealous of Townsend's flattering attention to detail on your behalf. But there was a note from him in my hotel room with suggestions for two or three clubs in Knightsbridge where we could go to dance. I can't imagine a better end to a perfect evening."

I didn't explain to him that equerries spent their lives pleasing those they worked for, and I prayed once again that Peter Townsend, gifted magician that he was, was also the master of discretion.

The taxi set us down in a quiet corner of what I guessed was Leicester Square, and the driver pointed out the discreet entrance to the 400 Club. *They'll never let us in*, I worried as an impeccable doorman who stood well over six foot, with shoulders like a navvy, folded his arms at our approach.

George lowered his voice. "We are here for Operation Spitfire."

"You are very welcome, sir." And the doors were opened for us immediately.

George eased the starched collar away from his neck. "That was a bit like open sesame, and I was waiting for him to turf us out on our ear." Our entry into one of London's most exclusive clubs made me feel that I had become a sparkling socialite, as we were ushered to a table by the dance floor.

"I wonder why Operation Spitfire." George helped me off with my wrap before I was seated.

"The only thing I know about Wing Commander Townsend is that he has a drawerful of decorations for valor and courage as a fighter pilot in the war. I wouldn't be at all surprised if the doorman of this very select establishment is aware of that." I laughed. "He might even be ex-RAF."

Intimately lit tables were grouped around us, and on the edge of the dance floor, an eighteen-piece orchestra was playing. "Have we been somehow transported to an American film? That band is awfully good. I had no idea there were places like this in London!" George sat forward in his chair as he looked around at the fashionable crowd.

"I recognize all the tunes because Margaret spends most of her time singing and dancing, and since she lives in the rooms just below mine, I often have to ask her to turn down the volume on her gramophone." I hummed along to a favorite with the girls from the show *Oklahoma*: "People Will Say We're in Love."

A waiter appeared with a bottle of Pol Roger and an ice bucket. George raised his eyebrows at me across the table. "Throughout all the years I have known you, my darling, the one thing I have been consistent in asking you is will you dance with me?"

He took me out onto the dance floor and drew me to him. "Far too crowded for Scottish reels." His breath in my ear made my arms shiver and I stepped in closer. He gave me an experimental whirl. "Oops, I think we need another glass of champagne."

The taxi pulled up outside the entrance to the Rembrandt Hotel, and the porter came down the steps to open the car door. I turned to George. "I don't think I could bear it if there are sly, knowing glances from the hotel staff."

He held the door closed. "I can tell the driver to take us back to the palace, and we can meet here tomorrow morning for breakfast. I don't want you to be embarrassed or feel awkward. You know that, don't you?"

The porter turned away from the car; perhaps he thought we were having a tiff: an overtired middle-aged couple out on the town, bickering about the cost of dinner.

The giddy effects of champagne and dancing dissolved, leaving me nervous and unsure. "I feel as if I am doing something wrong."

"Of course, Marion, of course I understand. I just can't imagine anything more right for us." His hand closed on mine, the touch light; there was no pressure. "If you want to wait, then that is what we will do."

But wait for how long? Another year? Two? Empty years pushing me further into middle age? Someone told me that if we are still virgins at forty, we simply shrivel up. My mouth was dry from the champagne. We had toasted to honor and loyalty. Why hadn't we toasted to love? I closed my eyes and listened instead to the refrain of the sentimental song we had swayed in time to at the 400 Club: "It had to be you . . . It had to be you . . ." George's arms holding me close, his warm breath in my hair.

What do I want to do? "I want to be with you, George," I said.

He raised my hand to his lips and kissed its palm before he opened the door of the cab and held out his arm to me.

"Good evening, Major Buthlay, Mrs. Buthlay, I hope your evening was enjoyable." I was neither dressed like, nor young enough, to be the sort of girl men took back to their hotels after a night of dancing and champagne. I lifted my chin as I slipped my arm through George's. The porter opened the door for us, and we sailed into the hotel lobby as if we had been married for years.

"Good evening, sir, good evening, madam." The lift operator closed the doors. "What floor?"

I glanced up at George's face as he put the key in the lock of his door. "I thought for one moment your Presbyterian upbringing would win out down there," he said.

"It nearly did. Where we come from, it's no holding hands until you are engaged."

His face was studiously solemn as he pushed open the door, and before I had a chance to worry that the entire royal household would know by breakfast time tomorrow morning that the princesses' governess was carrying on in South Ken with a man who she said was her fiancé, George took me in his arms.

Chapter Eighteen

March 1946
Windsor Castle, Windsor Great Park, Berkshire, England

D o you have time to go for a walk, Crawfie?" Lilibet's clear,
bell-like voice in my quiet room took me by surprise. My
head came up so swiftly from the book I was reading that
she laughed and took my beret and scarf off the hook by the door,
holding them out to me. "It's quite brisk outside—so wrap up."

I didn't have time to exclaim with shock as a north wind hit me
like a sledgehammer and my eyes filled with freezing tears, because
the minute we were outside, she caught me by the arm and turned
me to her. "He's coming home, for good!" Her hand was clasped
tightly around my wrist and she shook it in time to her next words.
"He's . . . coming . . . home!" she shouted as if the bitter wind that
swept up the hill might scatter her words and Philip's homecoming
would no longer be real.

I gently detached her grip, my teeth chattering with cold.
"When?" Was she completely impervious to this penetrating cold?

"Any day now. He could be docking at Southampton within the

week. And as soon as he is done with all the red tape and navy bumpf he is going to drive up to London—to be with me!" Another gust made me wish we could have had this chat indoors. The cold dry air and her long-hoped-for news whipped color into her cheeks, and her eyes blazed such a deep and ecstatic blue that somehow the cold didn't matter to her any longer. "My dear, how wonderful."

To my utter surprise, the staid Lilibet lifted her arms above her head and did a high-stepping jig of triumph, clapping her hands together and uttering sharp cries of Celtic delight. She took me by the hands and whirled me in a circle as the wind blew our hair about, and I lost my beret to another blast from the north. There was nothing like a state of anticipation for stirring the emotions, and the poor girl had been on edge for weeks.

"Is Philip just going to arrive at the palace and have dinner?" I asked.

Lilibet was laughing as, still holding one of my hands, she pulled me through the Henry Gate. Obviously, she had a good deal to tell me, if we were off for a walk in Windsor Great Park. I steered us down the west side of the walk, out of the wind.

"I have made a plan," she said. A quick glance out of the corner of her eye to catch my approval. "No slapdash approaches, because first impressions matter." I liked her practical determination. "First of all, I have to talk to Papa. Actually, I've been talking to him quite a bit about Philip, and I think he is coming around."

And the queen, is she coming around too? "So, the king is on board?" I asked the easier question.

"Not *quite* on board, but he is getting used to the idea of Philip. I bring him up quite often and in a very casual way, so Papa can get used to hearing me say his name. Nothing too shattering, no declarations of love or sentiment of any kind, because it would embarrass him and make him nervous," she said with complete understanding of what made the king tick. "I tell him about Philip's navy duties in the Far East—it fascinates him, even if some of the details are rather depressing."

She stopped, and we watched a herd of deer amble across the Long Walk. "Look, they have their babies with them."

"Yes, so they have." We watched the dappled flanks of the fawns fade into the trees. "Have you told the king that Philip will be home this week?"

"No, not quite just yet. I wanted to talk to you first."

A prickle of unease made its way up my spine, and I huddled down into the protection of my tweed coat, pulling the rabbit-fur collar up around my ears. The last thing I wanted to do was to conspire with Lilibet against her parents. The queen had been particularly affable to me since Alah's death, and I was trying to pluck up the courage to tell her of my seven-month-old engagement.

Lilibet's next words banished any complacency I had about sharing my own happy news. "You see, Crawfie, it doesn't really matter what Papa thinks about Philip, whether he likes him or not, because it is Mummy who matters. And she is pretending she has never heard Philip's name at all. She is still inviting all her favorite young men for me to Windsor weekends. She favors Hugh Euston right now. It's quite exhausting." She closed her eyes, and I laughed at the picture that sprung into my mind: Hugh Euston's earnestly serious face as he asked her to dance.

"You have no interest in any of them, not even Lord Porchester?"

She shook her head. "Porchey? No, of course not, not in that way," she said in her brisk, no-nonsense voice. "And don't be silly and ask me about Patrick Plunket either . . . he is more like a brother to me than anything. They are all of them good friends, but they all know they will only be friends without me having to tell them, which is a relief.

"So, what do you think the best plan would be, Crawfie? Go to Mummy and ask her to include Philip in a Windsor weekend? Or would it be better to tell her that I would like him to come to dinner at the palace, with just the family?"

I wondered how Philip would cope with one of the queen's especially penetrating looks as she relentlessly pried information out of him to be used against him later. How old was he anyway? Five years Lilibet's senior made him twenty-four. What man in his mid-twenties would be a match for Her Majesty, with her soft, cozy charm, her flashing smile, and her will of iron?

Lilibet's eyes were crinkled at the corners with anxiety, her hands twined into each other, the skin drawn tight across her knuckles. I didn't hesitate. "Not dinner: too formal and too long. Keep it short the first time. And luncheon won't work because His Majesty is always so . . ."

"Grumpy at lunch?" Lilibet laughed.

"I was going to say that he is often too busy to come to lunch, *and* you need Margaret there to lighten things up if they get bogged down." Loyal and loving Margaret could be trusted with her role as court jester, but only just so far.

"Tea, then. If we have tea together, Papa will be more relaxed, and Margaret will be there in case we need a diversion."

Yes, that would work. I narrowed my eyes as I schemed. *Teatime is the queen's affable hour.* Alarm fluttered through me: I had been pulled into conspiracy again. "Tea will be perfect. A relaxed gathering where you can get up and wander around. That way Philip won't get trapped by too many probing questions."

"Should I alert Margaret?" Lilibet asked.

I could quite clearly see Margaret, eyes snapping with delight as she strutted around the Victoria drawing room in her new high heels. "I would just play it by ear with Margaret. If Her Majesty agrees to your inviting Philip to tea, I am quite sure Margaret will be at your back, so to speak. But I wouldn't tell her just yet—you know, sometimes she anticipates a bit too wholeheartedly." More strategic advice; what was I thinking? *In for a penny, in for the whole blasted shooting match. Come on, Marion, there's no need to get in a fluster.* I pushed windblown hair out of my eyes and said rather recklessly, "If the queen agrees to tea, tell Margaret after lunch on that day. We are polishing up our French verbs in the afternoons; that will take the steam out of her a bit." I was already embroiled, so what did it matter if I gave unasked-for advice? "When will you know that Philip's ship has docked at Southampton?"

"He will write as soon as he arrives."

"Good. Wait until you get his letter, and ask the queen to invite him to tea when she is with the king, since you have already prepared the ground there."

"Oh yes, of course I was going to do *that*!"

I laughed as she brushed my contribution aside. "What on earth do you need me for?"

"Because it is very important that you come to tea too. I want you to meet Philip. You know how I feel about him, more than anyone else."

"Thank you, that's very thoughtful of you, Lilibet. I can't wait to meet him." But this left me with a quandary of my own. Should I tell the queen of my engagement before tea with Philip or after it? *You'd better get it over with before you lose your nerve entirely.*

I was ushered into the queen's presence at half past seven in the evening, the day after we returned to the palace from Windsor. My mouth was a desert, my palms damp with humidity. And if that wasn't enough, I had started a cold, thanks to my walk with Lilibet, so I was as deaf as a brick in one ear. I took the chair closest to the queen on her right side.

The queen shot me a suspicious look. "Not coming down with anything, Crawfie? You look a bit peaked."

"No, ma'am, just a little chill. Nothing infectious."

"Good. Inhale a drop of eucalyptus oil in a bowl of hot water under a towel. Then you won't be so stuffed up. But first of all, Crawfie, I really want to congratulate you. I am so pleased with Margaret. She seems to be coming out of her awkward phase at last. It's incredible how quickly they mature these days. I can't believe she will be seventeen when we go up to Balmoral this summer." I allowed myself a long sigh of relief that Margaret's French was no longer a vexing issue. "Now, what is it you would like to chat about? I only have a few minutes because my brother David is arriving at any moment." She had not offered me sherry, which was an indication that she was eager to get on with the rest of her evening.

David Bowes-Lyon? Oh, dear God, please not him! "How nice, Your Majesty. How long is he staying?"

"A week, maybe two." I took a long, steadying breath and pressed my hand against the base of my rib cage. Philip would be in London by the end of the week, and the worst thing imaginable that could happen would be upon us this evening.

I pictured Uncle David's triumphant face as he was introduced to Philip over an inviting, highly caloric spread of sandwiches and cake. Each delightful morsel of Philip's flaws and his lack of suitability would be handed to her brother, on a tea plate, by his sister. And everything Bowes-Lyon had suspected at Windsor last Christmas would be passed on to his gossip-grinding cronies, suitably embellished and enacted in a series of comic vignettes.

A solution to this almighty hiccup would have to wait. After my weekend with George, I simply would not let my fears of Uncle David, his waspish tongue, and the damage he could do with it stand in the way of informing the queen of my marrying.

Stop being such a little coward and get it out, Marion.

"How delightful, ma'am. It has been a while since your brother was here," I said, and she wrinkled her nose in much-looked-forward-to pleasure.

"As you know, Crawfie, my brother is such good company, such immense fun: charades, putting on little plays, games of dumb crambo. The times simply flies. Now, how can I help you?"

"Some good news of my own, ma'am," I said with a commendably steady voice. "I am engaged to be married." There was a brief pause, and I bit the inside of my lip to stop from rushing into explanations.

The queen put her head on one side; her smile widened as her eyes bored into mine. "How very delight-ful. And who is the lucky man? He must be a Scot!"

"He is, ma'am, from Dunfermline. His name is George Buthlay, Major Buthlay."

"And what does Major Buthlay do for a living?"

"He is a bank manager at Drummonds Bank, ma'am."

"In Edinburgh?"

"No, ma'am, in Aberdeen."

"Ah, so a small bank, then, how nice. Well . . . congratulations, Crawfie. What splendid news." But it wasn't splendid. I could tell by the glacial expression and a smile that had snapped off as soon as her words of congratulation had managed to slide between her teeth. I steeled myself for the worst part of my happy news.

"George and I are planning to marry when the family go up to Balmoral this summer." She treated me to a long silence, but I screwed up my courage to wait her out.

She said something, but between the pulse booming in my cold-deafened ear and sheer panic, I wasn't quite sure I had heard her right. I shook my head.

"I said, Crawfie, that Major Buthlay will have no objection to you returning to your post at the beginning of September?"

Return at the beginning of September?

I tried to swallow, but my throat muscles didn't seem to be working. "I actually don't think I—"

"You do see, don't you, Crawfie, that leaving us now would be *most* inconvenient. Margaret . . ." She paused. "Still such a child, not yet seventeen. Now that poor, dear Alah has gone, she needs a firm, steadying hand. And you, Crawfie, have such a stable effect on her."

I stared at her, aghast. "Margaret is very mature for her age," I reminded her. "And immensely intelligent. I thought perhaps some tutors might be engaged. I often feel that she has long outstripped my abilities."

She waved tutors and a more challenging curriculum aside. "We are talking about Margaret—not Lilibet! Margaret is a very head-strong girl. She needs structure to her day, a framework, not a hap-hazard schedule from an array of tutors! You simply cannot abandon us now, Crawfie. It would be unthinkable."

I had plucked up my courage to talk to her about my eventual departure, and, damn it all, I would see it through. I would set a date with her now and hold her to it.

"Yes, I understand your concern, ma'am. I am quite willing to wait—"

"Yes, that will suit us perfectly. Make your plans for when Mar-garet turns eighteen—the summer after next. When she takes up her royal duties."

"The August after next? Perhaps . . . I am not quite sure . . . Maybe . . ." My words tumbled out of me as if someone else had said them. I heard them dully in my congested head and realized too late what I had done. *Do not agree to another year!* The nails of my right hand dug into the palm of my left.

The ice that was building in the room thawed a fraction. The queen looked down at her lap for what seemed like a long and dusty age. She sighed and, lifting her head, gazed sadly across at me, as if I was the most disappointing creature she had ever had to deal with.

"You are free to come and go as you please, Crawfie. No one

would dream of asking you to stay longer than you wish to." A small hurt smile. "But"—she dropped her voice to a murmur of gentle rebuke—"we would be so grateful if you would at least give us until August of *next* year. Unless, of course, something untoward happens."

I was witless, completely lost for thought or words. *It's not quite so bad. A year from this August I will be married to George.*

"I am so glad you understand the situation, Crawfie."

And with that she was done with me, and I was free to race for the cover of my sitting room. "Something untoward happens?" I said to my sitting room as I closed the door. Would some shadowy character waylay poor George one night and bash him over the head? I threw myself down on my sofa, breathless with laughter. I had done it. I had told her that my time as royal governess had an expiration date.

My laughter faltered and ended on a hysterical squeak. Lilibet and Philip's engagement would face a serious setback if David Bowes-Lyon sat down to tea with a man whose father was branded as a careless boulevardier and whose mother had lost her mind when he had deserted her and their children to hopeless poverty. I hoped that Philip didn't just look like a Viking; I prayed with all my might and main that he had the courage and brass of the entire blasted Danish horde.

Chapter Nineteen

March 10, 1946
Buckingham Palace, London

Prince Philip of Greece, suntanned from weeks in the tropics, strolled into my sitting room with all the athletic élan of a Hollywood film star, and I understood for the first time what the *Woman's Own* magazine meant when they referred to "chiseled features."

No wonder Lilibet is walking on air. I fixed a severe expression on my face, determined to pay attention to the more important aspects of his character and not be submerged by charisma.

Lilibet performed introductions. "Philip, this is my dear Crawfie," she said, and conscious of the need for a little more formality, she added, "Miss Crawford is my governess. Crawfie, this is Prince Philip of Greece."

The Norse god in front of me extended his hand as I was trying to decide whether protocol required a half bob. The hand was warm and dry as it briefly clasped mine—a nice firm handshake said a lot about a man.

"Hullo, Crawfie, how are you?" A pair of intelligent, clear gray eyes gazed steadily into mine. "Friend or foe?" they seemed to ask.

"I am very well, sir, thank you."

"Crawfie is coming to tea with us, Philip."

"Good show, we need to mass our supporters." I was used to the stiffness of foreign royalty when they were talking to those who serve, so I was struck by how at ease he was with me.

He continued to gaze at me. "Actually, I remember Crawfie quite clearly." His serious expression softened. "Didn't you come with Lilibet and her family to Dartmouth—years ago?"

Had she reminded him that was where he had first met me? I didn't think so. His demeanor might appear to be relaxed, but his observant eyes were alert. Prince Philip of Greece was here to make a good impression.

"Yes, I remember it too. You rowed all the way down the river Dart when we left in the yacht. You almost put out to sea!"

"One way to escape the press-gangers." He glanced at Lilibet's beaming face to see if he had made her laugh.

"It must be wonderful to be home again," I said to keep the conversation going, as clearly Lilibet was just going to stand there and smile.

"It most certainly is." He glanced at Lilibet again. "But I forget how cold and orderly England is after the Far East." He turned to Lilibet. "Do we have to wash our hands and comb our hair? It *is* getting on for half past four." He laughed. "Ahem, sorry, navy punctuality."

She laughed. "We are having tea with Papa and Mummy, not the nannies."

"Same thing," he teased. "I'm afraid I arrived a bit early," he explained to me. I noticed that although his uniform was impeccably well brushed and pressed, it was far from new, and he had clipped the edges of his frayed cuffs. This shabby, postwar lack of vanity was endearing, as were the well-polished shoes that needed to be reheeled. Philip's easy confidence made little things like an impoverished wardrobe seem of no consequence at all—at least to me. I wondered what stiff-upper-lip and highly starched Tommy Lascelles would have to say about a down-at-heel prince with shiny lapels.

"I had better run and change." Lilibet, reluctant to leave him even for the negligible amount of time she lavished on her appearance, walked to the door. "I won't be more than a few minutes." And she left me there with this young matinee idol who strolled around my sitting room and inspected a gallery of photographs of the princesses.

"Margaret, now, there's a character." He shook his head in smiling admiration at a photograph of her standing on her head in the middle of a Girl Guide sing-a-long. "Someone had better find an interesting job for Margot, or watch out!" He sat down in a chair facing mine by the fire.

"Oh, I think she is settling down admirably well, considering all the upheaval." It was too early to share family anecdotes and secrets.

He gave me what I later came to call his gimlet look: a quick appraisal followed by a short, thoughtful silence. "Yes, of course." A brusque nod as he registered my evident loyalty to the Windsor family's personality girl. "Someone told me that living in the tropics thins the blood. I had forgotten how cold it can be here in March." I wondered if he meant the palace or just England in general.

"You are talking to the wrong person, sir. I'm from the frozen north."

"Ever been to Lossiemouth?"

"Nowhere colder on earth than Lossiemouth, sir." *A teensy-weensy bit competitive, are we?* I kept my smile on the inside.

"You're right, their weather comes straight down from the Arctic. I used to dream of swimming in those frozen waters when I was sweltering in my bunk on board ship in Singapore—ninety-nine degrees and so humid it stifles your breath. D'you mind if I smoke?" He got up from his chair to offer me one. When I declined, he lit his with a battered navy-issue lighter and stood before the fire, careful not to block it. He exhaled a plume of smoke that caught in a draft from the window and eddied around his head. He laughed. "Good thing I like camping out!" And I realized that he already considered Buckingham Palace his home.

I realized he was watching me closely through half-closed eyes. "Lilibet says"—his voice was well pitched, with only a trace of the arrogant drawl of Britain's upper classes—"that she trusts you more than anyone else in the palace."

More than her own family? I wanted to ask.

It was flattering to hear such praise, perhaps a little forthright considering he had been introduced to me not five minutes earlier. I smiled at the obvious compliment. Philip apparently was winning me over. "We have been together through some difficult times," I said. "The princesses and I were at Windsor throughout the war. It was inevitable that we would become very close. Both Their Royal Highnesses—"

"Speak of the devil." He smiled as the door was flung open, and the irrepressible Margaret was with us. "How did *you* know I was here?"

"I offer bribes to a network of pages and footmen." She was laughing. "We have an additional treat this afternoon: Uncle David is coming to tea." She glanced at me out of the corner of her eye to see if I recognized this as a major drawback to Philip's interview, as she called it.

"What?" Philip looked so stunned, I wondered what he had heard. "I thought he was in Paris, with you know who!"

Another outspoken remark! I realized that Philip had a reckless side to him. Margaret shot me a derisive look and laughed. "No, *not*

Uncle David the Duke of Windsor. The other Uncle David: Mummy's younger brother, David Bowes-Lyon. Blimey"—her Mrs. Mundy voice meant that she was in top form—"now, that *would* be sumfink, mate." She saw my frown and ignored it. "If *he* turned up, poor old David Windsor might just get a jam sandwich, as long as he didn't bring Queen Cutie with him."

Philip was already laughing as he lit another cigarette. *He is nervous*, I thought, *and utterly grateful that Margaret is here. He is hoping her playfulness will lighten this meeting.* I prayed that Margaret didn't send things over the top.

"Queen Cutie?" he asked.

Before Margaret could reply I explained, "Noël Coward's pet name for Mrs. Simpson. I mean the Duchess of Windsor. And, Margaret, don't you dare mention Uncle David Windsor this afternoon."

Lilibet swished through the door, her bay-brown hair gleaming in waves to her shoulders. A rich blue twin set deepened the shade of her eyes to dark sapphires and emphasized her complexion, as delicate as the unfurling bud of a rose. I glanced at Philip, who had almost come to attention as she came into the room, and saw the admiration in his eyes. He pulled up a chair so that it was close to his and waited for her to sit.

I tried not to watch them too closely as they laughed together. Philip had turned in his chair so that his entire attention was directed solely to Lilibet, who leaned back in hers, one leg crossed over the other, her high-heel-shod foot swinging, as he recounted a wartime near miss on HMS *Whelp* in the Strait of Malacca.

"And then there was heavy fire, all around us. We were surrounded! And a midshipman piped up, 'We're for it!'" Philip affected the falsetto of the young and scared as he lifted both his hands up in an appeal to a higher authority, and Lilibet's robust, delighted laugh joined his. "And I heard myself mutter, 'Not on your bloody life, mate!'"

I looked over to Margaret, and she gave me her cat smile, and I allowed myself a nod of approval.

This was it! This was surely the real thing, their unaffected and complete delight in each other. How unselfconsciously at ease they were! A misty moment of my own: *Stop it, you silly sentimentalist!*

Remembering that they were not alone, Lilibet turned to Margaret and me. "The weather is supposed to be lovely this weekend!" We both nodded enthusiastically. "Philip, are you perhaps free Friday to Monday? Because we are going down to Windsor—all the daffodils will be out!" She smiled as if this was a prize worth winning.

"Windsor? Love the place." Lilibet blushed at his enthusiasm. "I'm on furlough for two weeks, so, yes, I'm free. What do I bring?"

She laughed. "Come as you are, and if you have riding boots, bring those too, but we have a tack room full of them."

Her understanding of his limited wardrobe was touching. *There is nothing like being twenty and in love*, I thought with some wistfulness. I wondered how George and I would have fared if we had been younger and bolder, before the world had taught us to be cautious and sensible.

Margaret, unable to contain herself, would not be left out. "No, we are not going to talk about horses, Lilibet. Do you like to sing, Philip?" she asked him. "I hope you do. We are all in love with the songs from *Oklahoma*."

He threw back his head and laughed. "You had better hope I don't—tone-deaf!"

"Dance at all?" She was at her most challenging.

"Oh yes, I'm a fabulous dancer, aren't I, Lilibet?"

"Leave him alone, Margaret. You can be in charge of all the

entertainment at Windsor, and we will do whatever you want." And to Philip: "That means she will sing all the tunes from the show for us over and over. Once she lifts the lid of a piano, she's at it for hours!"

"And you and I can dance to them all. So, that takes care of the entertainment. What about riding?" He brought the subject back to one Lilibet most enjoyed.

"There's a perfect mount for you at Windsor: he is well over sixteen hands, so a good size. He has a nice temperament and enough spark to make him interesting," she said, her face grave and considering as she thought of the best choice for him in Windsor's large stable.

"That wasn't the horse I rode last time, was it? My God, it was a nightmare." He looked at the three of us and shook his head. "Mouth like iron with a will to match, and he certainly had it in for me." He lit a cigarette and sat back in his chair. He stretched his long legs out in front of him, crossed at the ankle. "What completely unnerves me about horses is how smart they are: they know the minute you get up on them exactly how well or poorly you ride. They take two or three minutes, pretending to be docile, while they work out all your faults. After that it's curtains for the novice rider."

"Philip, when were you last on a horse?" Lilibet asked.

"Well, let's see, I am a sailor . . . so not much riding during the war. I believe the last time was Christmas 1944, and it was at Windsor, on this particular horse. Whatever direction you were riding in, it insisted on an alternative route. We galloped knee-deep through slippery mud, forded ponds, dashed under low branches." He looked around at the three of us giggling away and smiled. "My legs were jelly by the time that bastard was done with me. When we finally got back to the stables, hours later, everyone had gone in for tea. As I slid off him, he turned his head and nonchalantly bit me in the backside. I think his name was Beelzebub."

"You're exaggerating quite terribly," Lilibet said as she blinked away tears. "Philip is really very passable on a horse, for a 'novice,' as he calls himself. Though I do believe the bit about being nipped on the backside. I know which horse that is, and you are not riding him next weekend."

As I watched Philip's good-natured teasing of Margaret and courteous ease with Lilibet, I realized that he was far worldlier than either of them. I was quite sure that he was used to being surrounded by incandescent females.

Another thought occurred, causing a flutter of apprehension. Lilibet, constant, loyal, and a little bit on the unimaginative side, was the vulnerable one of the pair. She was not a personality like Margaret, who loved to fascinate and demanded attention as her right. If Lilibet were to marry this gorgeous breath of fresh air, would her solid dependability be enough to hold him?

But Philip wasn't interested in bowling over rabbits. He did not overtly flirt with Margaret, or even Lilibet. If anything, he was rather brotherly, and both princesses were captivated. After the plain bread and butter of young men like Porchey Porchester, Billy Wallace, and even the outgoing Hugh Euston, who deferred, bent their necks, and laughed at everything the princesses said, Philip was a breezy combination of high-seas buccaneer and knight errant. I looked at my watch.

"Oh, good heavens above. We will be late for tea!"

"Unforgivable of you, Crawfie." Philip opened the door for us. "You know how important it is we don't keep the grown-ups waiting."

CHAPTER TWENTY

March 10, 1946
Buckingham Palace, London

Grateful to be a mere onlooker during tea, I quietly enjoyed a plate of superb ham sandwiches as I watched them all sort one another out. Philip, as I had expected, was the center of everyone's attention.

The queen, a permanent smile fixed on her face, was at her most winning. "Philip, how lovely to see you again!" She went about putting him at ease, with only an occasional sideways glance at her silent brother David, who never took his eyes off delicious Philip for a second.

The king's welcoming "Good of you to pop by and say hullo, my boy," although agreeably pleasant, did not pull him out of his preoccupation as he puffed smoke all over the tea cakes.

The queen, naturally, led the conversation. "Now, do tell us all about Singapore, Philip. Duff and Diana Cooper say that the climate is unbearable."

"Yes, ma'am. Humid and very hot. But there is so much color: the whole of the Far East is a riot of color; it's a wonderful distraction from the flies and . . . regrettably, the stink at the docks." A shriek of laughter from Margaret at Philip's outspoken description. *Ease it down a notch*, I silently advised him, as Uncle David tittered and gave his sister a discreet nudge with his elbow.

The king accepted his wife's offer of a sandwich and a cup of tea but touched neither. His large, thoughtful eyes had fixed on Philip's face at his outspoken remark about the Singapore docks as he lit another cigarette. He laughed at Philip's jokes, which were many, and every so often, his eyes would slide over to his pride. Lilibet was shining. She sipped her tea and nibbled half a scone, her attention on Philip as he effortlessly kept up with the queen's interrogation.

"I really enjoyed the food, though," he said in answer to another question from Her Majesty, "even if I wasn't quite sure half the time what it was I was eating."

"I have heard that they eat eggs that have been buried in the earth for a hundred days," said Margaret. "To preserve them," she added. "That's what Lady Cooper told me. She said they are a delicacy."

The queen laughed her tinkly laugh as if Margaret had said something witty, and David Bowes-Lyon emerged from his watchful silence to be condescending. "I think she was teasing you, Margaret. Everyone knows that Diana Cooper will say anything to be sensational."

I saw Philip's gimlet gaze direct itself briefly to Bowes-Lyon. In that second, I realized he wasn't taken in by the queen's apparent interest in him, or that of her younger brother. *He's no fool*, I thought. *Of course he has heard of David Bowes-Lyon's venomous reputation and his cruelty to those he considers defenseless because they are not quite socially up to the mark.* I watched Uncle David give his sister a sly glance, and my greatest fears were confirmed: *He is taking notes. He is storing away Philip's weaknesses and flaws for when he and the queen are alone together.* I saw the feline smile on Her Majesty's face, the gracious dip of her head as Philip of Greece answered yet another of her innocent questions.

It is not Philip's background that she objects to, I realized as I finished my fifth ham sandwich. *It is his self-assurance—his confidence. She wants Lilibet to marry the compliant Porchey Porchester, who will be grateful to Her Majesty for his place as royal stud in the line of succession and submit gracefully to the Dowager Queen Elizabeth as she continues her position of power through her daughter when she becomes queen.*

The hairs on the nape of my neck stirred, and I shivered, not because I had been seated farthest away from the fire, in a direct draft from an ill-fitting window, but because David Bowes-Lyon was once again on the hunt for scraps of information that could be useful. I clenched my hands into tight fists. This miserable little viper was assessing the love of Lilibet's life as potential fodder for some of his more outré all-male gatherings, where he would entertain with brilliantly cruel snippets and sink Prince Philip of Greece and all of Lilibet's hopes.

My eyes swiveled back to Uncle David's victim as he dutifully strove to answer more questions from the queen. "What are your future plans, Philip? Will you stay in the navy?" A loaded question uttered in an innocent silver voice.

"Oh yes, ma'am. I think it offers the best career for me." A good answer: it was a royal duty for princes to serve in the senior service, and it didn't make him look as if his one purpose in life was the pursuit of England's heir to the throne.

"And where do you stay when you are in London?" Her smile was winsome, her head tilted in fascinated curiosity.

"With my uncle, Dickie Mountbatten." Oh dear, this wasn't such a good answer, but what else could he possibly say? Mountbatten was, after all, his uncle, who had sponsored him in the navy and probably paid his school fees at Gordonstoun.

"Ah, dear Dickie, how is he? And Edwina? I really must congratulate him; what a terrific job he did in recapturing Singapore." The queen waved a half-eaten eclair at one of England's war heroes.

"In spite of some spectacular blunders earlier on!" put in Uncle David.

"Mountbatten has just been made a Knight of the Garter and created Viscount Mountbatten of Burma as a victory title for war service, David," the king warned him.

Uncle David raised supercilious eyebrows. Dickie might be the king's cousin and onetime confidant when the king was new to his job and worried about everything, but David knew he was far from a favorite with the queen. I saw her glance at her brother with a brief shake of her head, and he responded with a small moue of contempt for the vulgarly ambitious Mountbatten. I could almost hear his querulous complaints to his sister when they were settled with their cocktails before dinner. "Mountbatten—wouldn't you know he was behind Philip's interest in Lilibet? Always so relentlessly ambitious—and so frightfully pushing! Do admit that his shoving in like this is too sickening for words!" he would say in that high-pitched flat little voice that seemed to come from the back of his throat. And his sister would sigh as she picked up her gin and Dubonnet. "I wouldn't go quite so far as *that*, David." A small smile. "But I wouldn't dream of trying to convince you otherwise . . ." Thus giving permission for David to sink Philip with rumors and innuendo.

A peal of laughter from the queen brought me back to the present, as she glanced at her husband, who was gloomily staring at a half-eaten sandwich on his plate. "Dear Dickie and Edwina, please say hullo to them for me . . . for us." She beamed at Philip. "Edwina: so talented, so beautiful."

"Oh yes, indeed." The king stubbed out a cigarette and opened his case to take out another. "We simply must have them over for dinner sometime. Or better still"—he turned to his wife—"let's have them up to dear old Sandringham for some shooting. Dickie's a superb shot."

"I will do what I can to fit them in." The queen put down her cup and saucer. "Poor old Sandringham will be packed to the rafters when we go up in October."

The king knew better than to insist. He forced his wandering attention back to their guest. "Interesting to see what Dickie will do now that there is peace. Did you see much of your uncle when you were over there, Philip?"

"Not really, sir. Lieutenants don't rub shoulders with admirals much. But I am staying with him while I am in London, so we will have plenty of time to catch up."

"Somebody had better think of something for him to do." Bowes-Lyon was sitting on the edge of his chair, leaning forward. "An idle Mountbatten means work for everyone." A bright little laugh. If you closed your eyes, you would have thought it was the queen speaking.

The king frowned. "I have no doubt at all that he will be given something important to do, David, because Dickie's gifts are many."

"They certainly are, sir," David responded quickly. "Our Labour prime minister is very grateful for the support of the great man, especially one who publicly endorses Bevan's nationalizing our railways, and this wonderful national health plan for the people I keep hearing about." I saw Lilibet's eyes widen in concern and Philip's half smile, as if he had learned something else about the deeply conservative David Bowes-Lyon.

A brief pause in the flow of chatter, and Margaret jumped in. "Mummy says you are coming down to Windsor this weekend?" And with a glance at her sister: "Let's exercise *all* the horses; they were all looking awfully fat when we were there a fortnight ago. The weather is supposed to be lovely."

"Do you shoot at all?" the king asked Philip, grateful for the neutrality of slaughtering wildlife.

"I've never had the time or the opportunity, sir."

"Done any stalking?"

"Not as much as I would like."

"Well, we'll have to change all of that. You had better come up to Balmoral when we go in August."

"I would enjoy that—thank you, sir," was Philip's immediate response.

Lilibet turned a look of gratitude and love on her father of such bright intensity that I stopped fretting about Uncle David for the time being.

Chapter Twenty-One

March 15, 1946
Buckingham Palace, London

I think we're gaining ground. Windsor went really well." Lilibet had come to visit, and we sat down together on the window seat of my sitting room at the palace.

"Which part?" I hadn't seen her since Philip's invitation to tea and the family's return from Windsor.

"*All* of it, Crawfie. The weather was superb, and we rode every day. Papa came out with us twice! Philip made him laugh so much that he had to stop, get off his horse, and have a drink of water, because he couldn't stop coughing."

She gazed out the window for a second or two. "And Philip is going to spend four weeks with us at Balmoral in August. He's going to come stalking with us—Papa and me, that is. And he is coming down to Sandringham for the grouse. So, you see, everything is going frightfully well in that department."

"And the other department?" I wanted to ask, but she was ahead of me.

"Mummy was very nice to him too."

She always is. I remembered the encouraging peal of laughter as the queen pried information from him. *And after a session or two with her younger brother, all sorts of rumors will start to fly.* His older sister made the bullets for David to fire.

"Philip is quite a good horseman, actually. I mean, he doesn't ride often, but he is naturally athletic, so everything comes easily to him." Lilibet's voice brought me back into the room.

"Everything *is* going well."

"Yes, it really is. Now, come on, Crawfie, what do you think of him? You can be quite candid."

I couldn't remember the last time I was really candid with the family since they had become the Windsors. "I like him. He appears to be open and direct, which I find refreshing. He is certainly good company." I paused before the important part: "I am very pleased that the king has invited Philip to spend more time with your family so you can get to know him better too." I said the last bit with conviction. *Of course, Philip has taken your breath away and undoubtedly you are in love.* What I felt she really needed to discover was whether she actually liked him, and if that liking could be sustained over a four-week-long country-house shooting party, and then hopefully for the rest of their lives together.

A question popped into my head from the David Bowes-Lyon tea. "What did your uncle David mean about Lord Mountbatten's support of the present government?"

She closed down, as she always did when politics came into the conversation. She considered for a moment. "I suppose what he was driving at was that Philip, like his uncle Dickie, is very modern in his thinking."

That was what I had gathered at tea. I remembered her father's reaction to Clement Attlee's Labour Party winning the election. Clearly Dickie Mountbatten, and perhaps his nephew Philip, batted for the wrong side. The taint of socialism, of a government voted in by the people for the good of the common man and not leadership by the ruling class, was calculated to panic even the most stalwart of families who had governed for centuries.

"Good, I'm glad you like him, Crawfie," she said. "Because Papa has also given me permission to invite Philip to dinner here in my apartment, whenever I want to. With you as our duenna and Margaret as chaperone, of course! Now I must rush." She was so pleased at the way things were progressing that she swooped down on me and planted a kiss on my cheek. "You have been such a good friend to me, Crawfie, really you have. I can't thank you enough."

A relentless April rain had driven down all day, and by ten o'clock I was tucked up in bed with a book and a hot-water bottle under my cold feet. But my thoughts kept straying from the plot of my Agatha Christie, and in the end, I gave concentrated thought on how things were going for love. Not just on the main stage of the palace, for Lilibet and Philip, but off in the wings, for George and me.

I plumped up my pillows and lay with my hands folded on my stomach, and with the blankets and eiderdown pulled up to my chin, I schemed.

His Majesty's invitation for Philip to join the family at Balmoral was a significant step forward. I saw the three of them walking the rolling heaths with Lilibet adoringly between the two men. The king impressed by Philip's athletic skill and patience, and his future son-in-law as a respectful and attentive student. The lonely beauty of Balmoral would provide a perfect backdrop for a proposal, with a benign father smiling on the two young people as they picnicked in the heather!

I beamed up at the ceiling, enchanted with my fantasy, and took it one step further: Philip, dressed in his slightly dilapidated dress navy uniform—it was a pity he could lay no claim to a tartan; he would look marvelous in a kilt—gallantly dancing with the queen in an enthusiastically executed eightsome reel. There would be no David Bowes-Lyon to mess things up for him, and with his vitality and determination to have a good time, Philip would win over Queen Elizabeth in short order, and when they all came back to London, Philip and Lilibet's future would be in the bag. *They could be married as early as this September, or October at the latest!*

Which meant that when Margaret turned eighteen next August, I would be free to marry George, having fulfilled my duty to Lilibet and to the queen.

My water bottle had lost its comforting heat as the spring rain pounded against windows that rattled in the cold north wind and wailed down the vast chimneys. Its dreary, insistent voice showed me all the miserable cons to my lofty pros. The king did not want his daughter to marry—anyone—and his wife didn't want her to marry a man she had not chosen for her. And I wouldn't be there, at Balmoral, to counsel Lilibet over any little setbacks that occurred, because I would be taking my summer vacation in Dunfermline.

I thrashed onto my left side. My feet were clammy and cold, my forehead dry and hot. I pushed the hair out of my eyes. All my dark fears that David Bowes-Lyon would make trouble for Philip flapped around my bed like crows. Thoroughly demoralized, I flipped my pillow to its cooler side and tried to distract myself with Christie's bestselling *Sparkling Cyanide*.

I was red-eyed and tired the next morning, so it didn't take much to push my already overtaxed imagination over the edge. Still lost in thought, I dropped off my household expenses for the nursery at Percival Blount's office and turned into the main corridor of the official wing of the palace. Courtiers' offices lined its sides, with two lanes of traffic traversing the center: one coming east from the state-rooms, the servants' quarters, and the private residences, and the other returning west. As I plodded along, Tommy Lascelles, the king's private secretary, and his assistant private secretary, Michael Adeane, striding side by side, swung out from Adeane's office. I was almost on top of them.

"*Where* did you say he went to school, Michael?" Lascelles asked his subordinate.

"Gordonstoun, sir." Michael Adeane shot his cuffs and smiled.

Gordonstoun? They are talking about Philip's eccentric public school. I picked up the pace to close the distance between us.

Lascelles's affronted face turn to Adeane. "Where on earth is it, anyway?"

"It's a boys' boarding school in northern Scotland, sir, with an emphasis on building *natural* leaders. Never heard of it before—had to look it up!"

A short laugh from Lascelles, who at the best of times was the driest of sticks. "So, not Eton, then, not one of us."

Michael Adeane coughed and smiled a tight, reluctant smile. "No, sir, I think it might explain his somewhat bumptious manner."

"It's not his manner I am worried about, Michael; it is his background. He is not the sort we need at the palace. He has leftist leanings, and I dread to think what the public would have to say about his sisters' Nazi affiliations. I am hoping it is just a fleeting thing, this attraction that Her Royal Highness has for this—"

"Bounder, sir?"

"That's putting it mildly, Michael, and *something* must be done. Now, about His Majesty's schedule for next Tuesday . . ."

Nazis? There had never been any mention of Nazis before! How on earth had Philip's sisters—I didn't even know how many he had—manage to get themselves tangled up with Nazis? I dodged down a narrow corridor that led to the back stairs to the floor below and, once in the safety of my sitting room, sat down to ponder this new catastrophe.

Breathe! I instructed myself. *For God's sake, woman, breathe!* I replayed Lascelles and Adeane's condemning conversation over again. Tommy Lascelles's view carried weight in the palace, and his opinion counted, not just with Their Majesties but with the government. The king had come to rely heavily on Tommy. He trusted him, and not just about appearing in the wrong uniform at public events. *If Lascelles and Adeane are going to turn their noses up at Philip*, I thought as I stared bleakly at my sitting room carpet, *Lilibet's plan to marry him might take more than just a few cozy weeks in Balmoral.*

I realized that I hadn't had much sleep the night before, and I was anxious and on edge about my own future. No sooner had we taken a step forward toward Lilibet's happiness than something cropped up that threatened my life with George. I simply had to get a grip.

CHAPTER TWENTY-TWO

May 1946
Buckingham Palace, London

Lilibet stood in the center of her palace apartments, her arms folded across her bosom and her head on one side.

"No, no, that's much too formal." She rejected the Louis Philippe Sèvres with a dismissive wave of her hand. Two footmen started to stack the rejected plates onto trays.

"Do you even know what you want?" Margaret was losing patience. "What about the old blue-and-white Willow pattern from the kitchen?"

"Something simpler, something plainer. I can't remember what it's called."

"You can downplay things too much, you know." Margaret's tone held a warning. She tilted her head back and stared down her nose at Lilibet. The last thing we needed was a falling-out between the sisters.

"The Royal Worcester is white with just a plain gold band at the rim. Would that do?" I asked.

"What does it matter, Lilibet?" Margaret thumped plates around on the table, and I winced. "You never notice what you are eating, never mind the wretched china, and I am sure Philip doesn't notice either."

Lilibet turned to a footman hovering with an ornate arrangement of roses. "No, please take them away. I feel like I'm in Mummy's bedroom." She turned and walked slowly into her drawing room, as if seeing it for the first time. "Crawfie, what on earth is wrong with this room? The last time Philip came to lunch, he took one look and asked me when I would be completely settled in. Does it look so uninviting?" Margaret pressed her lips together; she wasn't going to advise her sister in this mood. They had already had several arguments about what Lilibet should wear. "Perhaps we might move that sofa over there?"

Two rather hot-faced footmen lifted a heavy sofa and moved it a couple of feet toward the wall.

"Oh dear, I think that's worse." Lilibet caught her bottom lip with her teeth.

"Just get rid of the thing altogether; there are too many of them. You only need one sofa here, and then two chairs, here and here. The smaller ones can go back against the wall or form a little group here." Margaret waved away the sofa, and it was removed from the room.

"There, that's better, not so cluttered." Lilibet turned and surveyed the dining area that opened off her drawing room, an area of her apartments that she never used. "What time is it?"

"Five o'clock. Come on, Lil." Margaret took her by the arm and led her to the door. "Let's walk the dogs. Fresh air and lots of it is what we both need. What did you order for dinner, by the way?"

"Lamb chops and mint sauce . . . what? Why are you laughing?"

"Followed by apple tart?"

Lilibet looked at the two of us with our hands over our mouths.

"He *likes* lamb and apple tart. What's wrong with it? It's simple and filling." I prayed she had some other more romantic ideas for after dinner.

"Lamb chops? Lovely!" Prince Philip of Greece picked up his knife and fork with the gusto of a man used to eating his rations in a crowded wardroom. Margaret, as fastidious about food as she was about her wardrobe, picked her way through dinner and for once did not take over the conversation.

"How long were you in the ATS, Lilibet?" Philip asked.

"Only about six or seven months; it was all they would let me do."

"What *did* you do?"

"We were mechanics, you know; we repaired motor engines. I loved it. It was hard work, but I learned a lot about truck engines. And it was good fun. One of our instructors was a bit overwhelmed when he found out that I was in his class. He was so thrown about being 'in the presence of a real-life HRH,' as he put it, that he dropped everything he picked up. It was like a Charlie Chaplin film," she said, her eyes two azure crescents of delight. "His jaw was set, his eyes were glazed, and his face a deep, fiery red. The only thing he said for five minutes was 'S'trewth,' under his breath. The ground around the truck's engine was littered with bits of metal and tubing that he had fumbled and dropped, and then he lifted this huge oil can . . ." She bowed her head with laughter and then looked up at us. "And the entire group stepped back!"

It is astonishing what love can do for the introvert, I thought to myself as we rose from the table.

We took our coffee in Lilibet's drawing room, but Philip wasn't interested in too much sitting. He drained his coffee, put down his empty cup, and walked to the door. "Come on," he said over his shoulder. "Don't just sit there. I want to know what all the rooms on this floor are used for." We followed him out of the drawing room, through the double doors, and into the corridor. Two footmen stood to attention. "You can leave us now. We'll call you if we need anything," Margaret said as we gathered in the wide corridor that ran east to west along the north side of the palace.

"I can't get over the size of this place." Philip, hands on hips, looked up and down the corridor. "Are these rooms ever used?"

"Sometimes, but normally they are just shut up," said Lilibet. "When we were children, we got lost in the palace all the time."

"This corridor is double the length of a bowling alley," Philip said. "You could put skittles down that end, and bowl from here. If you order a set, I'll show you how to play."

He walked along the corridor, opening doors to rooms furnished with heavy and ornate furniture—most of them covered with dust sheets. "It's like a museum, and this one looks like the set of some provincial pantomime."

"Not a very interesting one, and most of the things in it are falling apart. But we can't throw them away apparently, because they belong to the Crown," said Margaret. "Lilibet, Crawfie, and I used to play hide-and-seek and sardines on this side of the palace when we had friends over for tea."

"What a splendid idea. Sardines it is." Philip took a penny out of his pocket and spun it in the air. "Heads or tails?" He caught the coin and slapped it down on the back of his hand, keeping it covered as Margaret shouted, "Tails!"

"Right, Margaret, you win. So off you go. We'll count to fifty and come and find you."

"Stay in this wing, please!" Lilibet shouted after Margaret as she picked up the skirt of her evening dress and belted down the corridor.

We covered our eyes and listened to Margaret's receding footsteps. A door opened and shut with a bang.

"Fifty . . ." Lilibet finished counting. "She went up the corridor and turned left." And she started to run east.

He doesn't know about all the mid-stairs or the little hidden rooms for footmen and pages, I thought as I opened a door on the left of the corridor to the servants' staircase, passageways, and pantries that formed a behind-the-scenes network in the center of the palace.

Ten minutes later, I squeezed into a broom cupboard and wedged in beside Margaret and Lilibet. "I haven't hidden in here for years." Margaret sneezed. "I've been squashed up in the dark surrounded by cans of Brasso and floor polish for hours. What took you all so long?" She hugged her knees and giggled as we heard Philip's feet pounding past the concealed door.

"He'll never find us. Come on, we have to give ourselves up. It's not fair . . ." Lilibet whispered, but we didn't need to break cover, because the door flew open and we all shrieked.

"You gave yourselves away." Philip's long shadow fell on us. "I could hear you giggling together a mile away."

We came out from the cupboard. "And you all smell like cleaning women." Philip carefully smoothed away a dusty cobweb from Lilibet's glossy curls. "Good, so now I've got the lie of the land, I'll hide next."

"Oh no, you won't," Lilibet said. "You were last to find us, so you lost, and it's my turn. Let's see if you've really got the layout of this old mausoleum." And she was off up the corridor.

"Who would have thought that Philip would enjoy playing nursery games?" Margaret said the next morning as we toiled away over French grammar.

They aren't always nursery games. I smiled as I remembered Lady Elgin telling me that guests at Edwardian house parties always enjoyed playing hide-and-seek and sardines. It gave everyone a chance to arrange who would visit whose bedroom later on. "Since we are duenna and chaperone," I told her, "we have to be alert to finding those two in a tactful but timely way—otherwise we will be derelict in our duty!"

She nodded, her face solemn. "I know *all* of Lilibet's hiding spots. I just make sure I forget them when Philip comes to dinner." I laughed at her obvious scheming.

"Why are you laughing?"

"Because if you look as if you are too hot on their trail, I am very clever at diverting you."

"She never wants to play hide-and-seek with Porchey Porchester or even gorgeous Hugh," Margaret pointed out. "She's completely besotted with Philip."

"And he with her?" I asked quickly, because sometimes I worried that after a while, the potshots about his family and Gordonstoun would take their toll, and Philip would fade from Lilibet's life.

But Margaret knew otherwise. "Any man who has to eat lamb chops, or ghastly Dover sole, every time he visits has to be besotted, Crawfie."

Lilibet appeared in my doorway. "Invite me in for sherry, Crawfie?" I poured two glasses as she filled me in on Susan's latest battle with Dookie.

"Things are looking distinctly off on the Philip front," she said. "No sooner does one issue resolve itself, another pops up. But this one is serious because it comes from Tommy Lascelles; it is the larger of his many concerns about Philip." She paused to gather her thoughts. "I know it is his job to keep us from inadvertently doing anything to tarnish the monarchy . . ."

"Well, he cut his teeth as an assistant private secretary when your uncle abdicated, so he knows a thing or two about tarnishing."

Lilibet considered her glass of sherry and examined the pattern on the edge of the Turkish carpet. I bit my lip to stop myself from prompting. Finally, she lifted her eyes and gazed at me as she decided what she should reveal, and I struggled with patience.

"Mummy . . ." My heart sank. "Mummy told me that Tommy told Papa that he has quite a few concerns about Philip's sisters. They were married to prominent Germans: Nazi sympathizers. One of them had dinner regularly with Hitler." The slightest tightening of her lips conveyed what? Her distaste? Her disbelief? "This is not common knowledge, by the way, Crawfie, but Tommy believes that if the Great British public knew, they would be offended and upset at my marrying a man whose sisters were all married to Nazis."

"But every German was expected to be a member of the party, Lilibet. It wasn't a choice—the German government was fascist. Hitler was a dictator. There was no free choice, not even for 'true Germans,' the ones who loathed Hitler and were horrified by everything he set out to do!"

She pressed her lips together and shook her head. "Yes, I understand your point, Crawfie, but the British react very strongly to fascism—we put Sir Oswald Mosley in prison because he was leader of Britain's fascist party."

"There is a huge difference between having sisters who married Germans, and an Englishman starting a fascist party in England and palling around with Hitler. I am quite sure our workingmen and women can tell the difference." I did not say that before the war there were many aristocrats in Britain who were rather partial to Hitler's brand of politics: jealous of the success of Jewish-run businesses, full of admiration for the new Germany with its restored culture, trains that ran on time, and immaculate city streets brimming with willing workers. I braced myself with another glass of sherry. "Tommy Lascelles is only being punctilious because it is his job. But I understood that all Philip's brothers-in-law were military men and not connected in any way with the SS or Gestapo."

She was staring thoughtfully at the wall behind me as she continued. "Margarita, Theodora, Cecilie, and Sophie. Cecilie died with her husband and their two children in a plane crash. I think she might have been pregnant at the time. Philip was still at Gordonstoun; he went to Berlin for her funeral. It was packed with high-ranking Nazis." I nodded. "And then there is Sophie, Philip's youngest sister. She married Prince Christoph von Hessen, who was one of the directors for the Third Reich's Ministry of Aviation."

I waved Prince Christoph away. "That does not make him guilty of war crimes. He was working for his government during the war—everyone did that in every country. That does not make him a criminal."

She took a long breath. "Sophie and Christoph named their eldest son Karl Adolf, after Hitler. Tommy says they ate dinner with Hitler regularly."

"Oh."

"And then there is Margarita. She married Gottfried, Prince of Hohenlohe-Langenburg, a commander in the German army. He was very pro-Hitler in 1939. Luckily toward the end of the war, he came to his senses and joined a plot organized by fellow aristocrats to assassinate Hitler and was dismissed from the army. It all sounds terrible, especially when we are inundated with the Nuremberg war crimes trials." She dropped her head, too humiliated by what she had learned to continue. "The trials are turning up all the terrible things that happened . . ."

"And his eldest sister? Theodora?"

She shrugged her right shoulder. "I haven't heard anything much about her, other than her husband, Berthold, flew for Germany's Wehrmacht until he was injured."

"But that was because he was a German. He was doing his patriotic duty, for heaven's sake."

I could see that she was taking this badly.

"Well, it seems Prince Gottfried tried to do the right thing, Lilibet. Don't look so desperate. Look, Philip fought for Britain. He was on our side. If you were a German living in Germany from 1933 to 1937 it was easy to be fooled by Hitler during those years—they had no idea what his true nature was, or what his plans were. He appeared to do so much for the German people after the Allies reduced Germany to poverty and shame in the reprisals following World War I. But don't you see? The war and what happened are finished now. Over and done with. Nazism and the Third Reich vanquished and the world at peace. I don't think—"

Lilibet held up her hand to interrupt, her eyes bleak. "*Second* thing that Tommy Lascelles and Clement Attlee object to is that Philip's father, Prince Andrew, fled Greece and lived in the South of France, *Vichy* France, governed by Pétain during the war." She finished her sherry, tied a few knots in a rather grubby handkerchief. "He made no attempt to reunite with his wife and children when the war ended but went to live in Paris. Luckily for them, they were looked after by his mother's family." I noticed she did not use the words "philanderer," "mistress," or "mental asylum," but they were relevant to the story I had heard. Either she had not been told the full facts, or she was omitting the ugly parts of Prince Andrew's behavior, even to herself.

She sat up straight in her chair to tell me the worst. "And as it turns out, Philip isn't actually a British citizen, so he can't continue to serve in our navy as an officer." She looked at me as if everyone at the palace was mad except her. "I mean, that does sound unfair, doesn't it? He fights for us all through the war, and now it's 'Thank you and goodbye. Off you go; you are not one of us after all.'"

The boneheaded stupidity of it, I fumed to myself. *Why are the English obsessed with their public schools and their stupid navy?* "And the *king* believes these are important issues?" Had she heard these words from His Majesty, or was the queen putting her own interpretation on things?

She nodded. "I think he has to, because Tommy Lascelles and the government think they are." She stared down at her hands, now folded quietly in her lap, and then up at me. Her frank gaze fixed itself on my face, appealing for confirmation that she had it right. "You see? It is not as simple and straightforward as we had first thought." In a few short months Lilibet had accomplished a monumental leap of understanding that had brought her out of her nursery paddling pool into the salty ocean in which the rest of us mere mortals struggled to keep our heads above water.

But she has inherited her mother's steel and her never-say-die determination, I thought as I watched Lilibet's chin come up and her face take on the sort of resolve I had seen in the queen when she had made up her mind what was to happen. "But we mustn't give up even if things are not looking quite so hopeful, must we, Crawfie?"

It seemed nonsensical to me that a great-great-grandson of Queen Victoria didn't measure up. "Lilibet, I don't see that any of these issues really touch on who Philip *is*. They are situations that surrounded his family during turbulent times." I cleared my throat, searching for the right words. "What about his uncle, Lord Mountbatten—the man who recaptured Singapore? I heard that he is going to be our next viceroy in India. So, he obviously carries some weight. I am sure Lord Mountbatten is in support of Philip continuing here in England and will sponsor him to become a British citizen. It's done all the time, isn't it?" I watched her resolute expression dissolve into one close to despair.

"Yes, I wondered when you were going to ask that. It seems that Uncle Dickie is a bit of a two-edged sword: on the one hand, Clement Attlee and his cabinet approve of him because of his liberal views, but as a new prime minister, Attlee worries about supporting anything that might be controversial. It wouldn't take much for everyone to decide they don't like Attlee's policies and run back to Mr. Churchill. And even though Uncle Dickie is one of Papa's oldest friends, he finds him a bit too pushing these days."

Or rather your mother does. I remembered that Winston Churchill, whom the king revered, was not too keen on Mountbatten and referred to him as "the man who wants to give away India." Because part of the new viceroy's mission to India was to ease the way for their independence.

"Why does the king think he is pushing?"

"Mountbatten is considered to be overly ambitious." She opened her hands palms upward, as if asking for divine intervention. "He is too enthusiastic," she explained. "It's his style that sometimes upsets people. Anyway, it is not Papa's way to be obvious and thrusting." She dropped her head and shook it at Mountbatten's determination to shine. "It annoys Papa. I think he feels that Uncle Dickie is somehow encouraging Philip to . . ." She couldn't bring herself to finish.

To push Philip to marry you? Did it really matter that much to Uncle Dickie that his nephew marry the future Queen of England?

It was important not to let her dwell on Mountbatten's possible engineering behind the scenes. "In England conspicuous ambition is frowned on. The approved style is to murmur nothings and look modestly down one's nose as accolades are heaped on us. We are expected to greet acknowledged success with a polite murmur of thanks and a deprecating cough." Lilibet laughed and the tension that had been building in the room eased up a fraction.

"When it is seen that none of Philip's in-laws are war criminals and he has become a British citizen, I am sure you will be able to iron all these wrinkles out with His Majesty when you go north to Balmoral. It's just a question of standing firm and not giving up."

"I just wish that Lascelles and Adeane and all the rest of them would stop nipping at Philip's heels."

"They will as soon as your father gives his consent to your marriage."

"Well, it's all down to Balmoral, then, isn't it, Crawfie?" She got to her feet. "Heavens, look at the time."

"Will your uncle David be joining you at Balmoral?" I asked, and she looked surprised. So, she hadn't worked it out about him yet.

"Yes, of course he will, but he has no say in the Philip thing at all."

I wouldn't be so sure of that, I thought.

CHAPTER TWENTY-THREE

Summer 1946
Limekiln Cottage, Dunfermline, Scotland

Day after day of sun had graced our usually gray-skied summer, and I couldn't have been more miserable if I tried. George, now firmly established at Drummonds in Aberdeen, announced his arrival for the weekend with a postcard: *Leaving Friday at five. Should be with you by seven thirty! George.* The postcard had plopped through the letterbox on my first Friday morning in Dunfermline, followed by George's arrival that evening.

The following week the postcard arrived promptly on Friday morning. *Marion, Pressure of work—unable to get away—perhaps next week. George.* The forward-slanting handwriting, interspersed with dashes, was an indication of his haste to return to Drummonds' banking demands. I was disappointed, but mostly for George working away in his stuffy bank during one of Scotland's most lovely summers. When he canceled his next visit, I was concerned he was overworking; the following week, I was resentful. Now I was close to despair.

"I think we should pick the last of the green tomatoes and make chutney." My mother's voice interrupted my brooding. I straightened from weeding a row of sturdy plants laden with fruit that would never ripen, even in this glorious summer.

"George said we should have grown our tomatoes under glass." She wrestled a large vegetable marrow into the wheelbarrow. "We can make marrow jam . . . I wonder if Mrs. Ross has any ginger."

"I had no idea he was an expert gardener as well as a banker."

"Marion, there is no need to be sour. This new job means a lot more responsibility for George." I struggled for patience as I turned the earth around rows of broad beans. "Drummonds in Aberdeen is five times the size of the little branch he ran here." She shaded her eyes so she could see my face. "He is working for a *larger* pension for both of you. It's quite simple, dear girl; he's just too busy to get away."

I knew otherwise. George had been very clear about his view of how things were between us when he had come for his first, and only, visit at the beginning of summer.

"I'm not getting any younger, Marion." He did not sit down on the picnic blanket with me but hovered on the edge holding a large thermos of tea. "I had really hoped you would have some idea of when you would be leaving them by now."

His expression was so closed off I couldn't tell whether he was angry or hurt. I scrambled to my feet, scattering cheese-and-pickle sandwiches. "You see, it has been a year since you said yes, and now you say that you only informed the queen this spring about our engagement." He wasn't exactly angry, but he looked down at the thermos in his hand as if it was holding back on him. "And when she pressed you, you agreed to continue until this time next year. I don't understand. Are you . . . ?" He turned his head away.

I didn't know what to say. I put my arms around his waist, but he started to pull away. I stepped in and put my head on his shoulder, locking my arms behind his back. "Surely they could find another teacher for Margaret. Why does it have to be you?"

Because they don't think that way. I was trapped between my love for George, my duty to the queen, and Lilibet and her rocky road to love.

"George." I tried to keep the fear out of my voice. "It's really not like most jobs. I can't just up and leave them like that. I have a duty to the Crown—something that is expected of me. Most of the household staff work for the family for life, or else they find it so demanding that they only last two or three weeks. After all these years I can't leave them stranded." *I can't leave Lilibet to struggle on alone.*

He detached himself from my embrace. "Stranded? Marion, I feel stranded!" He lifted his arms out to the sides as if he was alone on a rock in the middle of an empty ocean. "And what about your duty to yourself . . . and to me? Is it because you don't want to give up a life of glamour for the humdrum of being married to a retired provincial bank manager?"

To my relief, the pain had gone from his voice—somewhat. "Of course not, George! But this has been my job for most of my adult life. I have to leave it in a way that I feel is right!"

He reached down and put the thermos on the ground. I noticed that his face was thinner, and the sunlight showed up the gray in his hair.

"Even with the car, it is at least a two-hour drive from Aberdeen to Dunfermline, and the cost of petrol has gone sky-high. I had hoped that we would be married by now and setting up a home together." To my relief his voice took on a slightly accusatory note. Anything was better than seeing the puzzled hurt on his face.

I did not say that his decision to take the Aberdeen job had complicated our lives, because it had. "I hoped so too, George." Were our dreams fracturing under the pressure of a long-distance relationship?

"My promotion means a larger pension when I retire, but if we were married now, we could be together in Aberdeen until then. I know it would mean a small flat, and not a house of our own in Dunfermline, but it would be so much better than nothing at all."

I bit back recriminations about his new job. "But, George, we never talked about living in Aberdeen. We talked about living in Dunfermline to be near my mother when we both retire. The plan was to retire together so we could live down the lane from her. I can't live with you in Aberdeen and leave her here alone!" Although she had lost none of her spark, my mother was looking older and skinnier with each visit. And even if she didn't say so, I knew she was lonely. "I can't bear the thought of being so far away from her."

"You are certainly far away from her now. And you haven't given notice so we can be married in December. You are staying on for another six, or seven . . . or however many months she requires!"

He ran his hand through his hair, making it stick up in the front, and his lips thinned in a tight and uncompromising line. *Is it my fault that he feels the years are slipping away? I should never have caved to the queen, never agreed to wait until Margaret turned eighteen!* But I wasn't the one who had taken a job in Aberdeen—I was doing everything I could to leave a career of fourteen years as carefully as possible.

"Your mother isn't the problem, Marion. She can always come and live with us in Aberdeen. But until you leave the Windsors—" He broke off to frown . . . a full frown: eyebrows lowered; his chin sunk down onto his chest. "Well, until you leave the Windsor family, there is no us."

I swallowed down frustration. "Yes, I understand about leaving the Windsors, but we never discussed my living in Aberdeen . . . ever!" I folded my arms across my chest.

"Well, like you, I have no choice, it seems. The bank wants me to stay on until April, and they will make it worth my while financially. And you haven't left the Windsors, have you?"

I saw a way out of this impasse. "But that's just it . . ." I cried, as if we had both been given a gift. "You have to stay on longer at the bank, and I have to stay on at the palace." I spread my hands out to show how easy our new plan would be. "Then when you are released from Drummonds, it will only be three months before I am with you. We can buy the cottage, arrange for the work to be done on it, and it will be ready for us to move into by next August!"

A long silence as he peered into my face, his eyes narrow with suspicion. "Are you quite sure about that? Are you quite sure you will be free next summer?"

"Yes!" My voice sounded firm and sure, but I felt anxiety stir. *What about Lilibet? You haven't explained to him about Lilibet!*

He laughed as he watched my face. "You are not sure, are you? Of course there will be another year required of you. Maybe if we are lucky, they will let you leave in two years." He walked away from me and stood looking out toward the river. When he turned back to me, his face was stern. "What I would like to know is this. When you told the queen that you were engaged and would be marrying this year, what did she say?"

"She asked me to wait until Margaret was eighteen."

"What an unreasonable expectation. And it's hardly as if it's a full-time teaching job, is it? She just wants to keep you there to suit her convenience because Margaret is a handful she doesn't want to have to manage."

He was quite right, of course. Having spoiled their youngest daughter all her life, both of her parents were at a loss as to how to deal with Margaret's headstrong and willful ways. If Alah was still alive . . .

Go on, get it all out, tell him what worries you most. Tell him about

Lilibet. "It's not just until Margaret is eighteen. I can't leave Lilibet until she is engaged to marry Philip." I watched his jaw clench. "It . . . it has not been easy for her, George. It seems that neither the king nor the queen wants her to marry just yet. And when she does, I think they would prefer someone more conventional for her than Philip . . . and she is very much in love with him."

"And I am very much in love with you, Marion, and neither of us are getting any younger." He put his hands in his trouser pockets, looked down at the picnic blanket and the scattered sandwiches.

A flutter of panic started in the middle of my chest. "She is only twenty, with no one in her corner but me," I pleaded. Surely he would understand? "If Philip were from an old aristocratic family, educated at Eton, and belonged to all the right clubs, he would be a shoo-in. But he's not."

He snorted: he could give a damn about Philip's suitability. "God knows I am a conservative man, Marion, but quite frankly, these people still behave as if we were all in the 1800s. All this expected deference and allegiance is outmoded; their type of monarchy is a remnant of the past. Do you know how people see them?" His frown returned, his brows so far down I couldn't see his eyes. "As a useless bunch of parasites and, worse, a drain on taxpayers' money. Dear God, anyone would think they actually did something useful for the country." He glared at the view for a moment before turning a scowling face back to me. "And anyway, isn't Philip a prince? What more do they want for their daughter? Europe has run out of kings, unfortunately." He heard himself, and thank goodness he stopped glowering. He ran both his hands through his hair and shook his head. "I'm sorry, I didn't mean to be unreasonable. Come on, don't look so stricken," he said with a little more grace. "We'll find a way. Let's do what your mother does when things look bleak. I'll pour us a cup of tea. Though whiskey would be more welcome."

We sat down on the blanket and poured tea into Bakelite cups. A strained and awkward silence gathered between us. *We are not out of the woods yet*, I thought.

"Does it really matter who she marries?" He poured more tea into my cup.

"She will be the Queen of England one day. Of course it matters who she marries. Her life will be one long round of duty and hard work: endless functions, endless public appearances, with very little time for her own family. It is important that she has the man she loves by her side."

He grunted and shrugged his shoulders. I could see that he didn't understand, couldn't possibly understand, the myriad of duties expected of a constitutional monarch, and he seemed rather cynical about the notion of having one's true love by one's side in the daily battle of life.

"She's far too young to know her own mind—an overprotected child. What does she know of this Philip?" Impatience for a family he considered useless returned. "From what you've said, she hardly knows him. And all European royalty chase women, are serially unfaithful, and keep mistresses. Imagine coping with that over the banquet table."

"Oh really?" I said, without bothering to consider that his accusation might have grounds. "And what do you know about European royalty, eh?"

We had reached a stalemate. There was no more to be said. I packed up the remains of our picnic, and we drove back in silence to my mother's cottage. Ma, after accurately assessing our mood, lost no time in wading in with her tuppence worth.

"I think you are being a wee bit stubborn for your own good, Marion," she whispered at me as we made supper together in the kitchen.

"No, Ma, when George asked me to marry him, he knew exactly what my situation was—"

"Would you look at the man, Marion? He puts in hours at the bank all week, gets up at dawn to drive to see you here, drives again all Sunday afternoon to be back for Monday morning. He's nearly fifty; he should be able to put his feet up in his own house on a Sunday afternoon, with his wife making a nice supper for him, not waiting months, years, for her to give up her job to marry him." She put three kippers under the grill. "You could earn more money teaching at Dunfermline grammar school. When was the last time they even gave you a raise? I can't believe how stingy they are . . ."

"Ma, please don't do this. Please don't erode everything I have done."

"I am doing nothing of the kind. I am merely pointing out that by kowtowing to that woman's unreasonable expectations, you are jeopardizing your future."

I turned away from her and threw my tea towel on the kitchen chair, cornered and defensive. "I am disappointed that you can't see my side, Ma. For years you were proud I had a career and that I held a position of responsibility too. Neither you nor George seem to consider that the princesses are like my own children. I will not end my relationship with the family in a way that will make me regret it for years."

I glanced through the door. George was in the living room with a newspaper over his face and his feet up on a leather pouf. "He is having a snooze now, for heaven's sake, and there are *two* women in the kitchen making his supper."

"There is no need to get sharp with me, Marion. Give in your notice, or you might lose George."

Chapter Twenty-Four

Summer 1946
Aberdeen, Scotland

George was too busy to come to us the next weekend, and the following Monday, unable to bear not seeing him, I wrote to him and told him that I was coming up to see him in Aberdeen. There was a fine drizzle falling when he met me at the station.

"Welcome to Aberdeen, Marion." He took me into a nearby café for a cup of coffee. I wasn't used to seeing George in his banker's dark gray pinstripe, and his starched wing-tip collar with a bowler hat on his head. It made him seem distant and formal: armored in his business attire.

We sipped our ersatz coffee.

"Last train to Dunfermline is at six o'clock this evening," I said.

"That gives us the whole day together. What would you like to do?" He smiled at me, but there was a touch of formality in his voice, as if he was escorting a friend of his mother's for the day.

I reached across the table and took his hand in mine, a gesture that was immediately noticed by the prim little woman in gray sitting at the table next to us.

"I love you very much, George. You know that, don't you?"

"Yes, Marion, I do. Now, what shall we do with our day? I know." He patted my hand and let go of it. "The art museum?"

We made the rounds of the Aberdeen Art Gallery in the morning. We ate lunch in a little restaurant next to the museum: pale, tasteless ground-mutton rissoles that I could hardly bring myself to eat; the mashed potato was lumpy, the overcooked cabbage watery. Just as we were finishing our gooseberries and custard, the sun came out. "How about a stroll in the botanical gardens?" George had eaten both his lunch and most of mine.

The leaves were turning rich russet and gold as we strolled in the Cruickshank gardens. There was a sweet-sharp smell of decaying leaves and a mist coming up off the river to gather under the trees. "My landlady, Mrs. Patterson, has invited us to have tea before you leave." George didn't look too enthralled with the idea. "She is a good person, but perhaps not very . . ." He shrugged. "She has had a hard time of it . . . I could tell her there wasn't time."

But I wanted to see where he lived. "Oh no, let's say yes. I can imagine you in your home surroundings when I read your letters."

He laughed. "I am quite sure she would never let you see my 'home surroundings.' Unfortunately she would consider it most improper."

"Oh dear, she must be one of Aberdeen's correct landladies."

"Mrs. Patterson has made frugality into a virtue: she is a one-bar-of-the-electric-fire-only sort of woman, but lodgings are hard to find in postwar Aberdeen," George warned me as we walked up scrubbed white steps to the dark brown front door of the grayest and most austere-looking house in the terrace. Not one late-summer flower hung on in her smoothly raked gravel front garden; no cat slept in the last of the sun on her front-room windowsill.

Mrs. Patterson of Aberdeen was exactly how I had imagined her: thin, worn, with iron-gray hair scraped back off a face that was as cold and unwelcoming as her house. She cast an appraising glance over me from head to toe and, judging that I was safe to admit, stepped back to allow us to enter. A strong, institutional smell of Harpic toilet cleaner wafted toward us down the stairs, reminding me that all three of Mrs. Patterson's paying guests were men. We followed her down the narrow corridor to her second-best parlor, where tea was already laid on a round table. Everything in the room was brown. It was like sitting in a sepia photograph.

"So, you work for the royal family," Mrs. Patterson stated in a disbelieving voice, and then sat back and regarded me with compressed lips, as if someone from the south might steal her tarnished apostle spoons. She poured tea and handed me a half-filled cup.

"I suppose you take sugar in your tea, Miss Crawford?" She dipped a tiny teaspoon into the sugar, and I rushed to reassure her that I did not. There were net curtains at the windows, shrouded by a festoon of brown velveteen drapery, so it was difficult to see how much milk to put into my cup. I sipped the weak tea: it tasted sour, and small curds drifted to the surface.

She handed us each an oatmeal biscuit as thin and dry as hardtack.

"Well, I am sure you would like to visit awhile before you leave for the station," she said in an offended tone.

"Thank you for the tea, Mrs. Patterson." She left us, her mouth drawn in tight with disapproval because George was sitting next to me on her hard and unwelcoming dun-colored sofa. She also left the door open so we would not be encouraged to misbehave. *No wonder George is miserable,* I thought. *No wonder he feels as if life is passing him by.*

. . .

My suitcase lay open in my room, and I was packing in a distracted and disorganized way. I folded a sweater, dropped it onto the floor, and used language the king would be ashamed of. George had been working hard at his bank and had not managed to get away for the last two weekends.

"I should have gone up to Aberdeen today, to see George, and caught the train to London from there," I told Ma when she came into my bedroom with a pile of laundered underwear.

"It's not too late, Marion. You could catch the ten thirty; you would be there in an hour! I can finish your packing for you. But you would have to come back; there is no train from Aberdeen to London until tomorrow morning." Was it her intention to drive me into leaving the palace by reminding me that there should be no improper access to my fiancé? I didn't put it past my determined little mother.

Anguish swept through me. Tears pricked behind my eyes, but I blinked them away. If I cried I wouldn't stop. *Am I being stubborn about not leaving the Windsors?* I gulped down the agony of indecision. *I don't know what to do!* It was hard to rely on my judgment for years and then throw it to one side. There was comfort in knowing what I must do, having practiced it all my life, and complete fear in jettisoning what had become a habit. *Is this all my working life has been?* I asked myself. *A habit? Perhaps it is too late for me,* I thought as I rolled stockings, snagging my nail and laddering a perfectly good pair. I stood looking out of my bedroom window, biting my thumb. *Perhaps I have already become a narrow, closed-off spinster, with no room in my life for anything but my job.*

The lump in my throat grew until my breath was coming in short gasps. I had lost him! I had lost George. I had disappointed him so often that he couldn't bear to care anymore. It was easier to shut himself away in his bank and worry about other people's money. I turned to my suitcase, my eyes blinded by tears of despair. I wouldn't go; I wouldn't get on that train and leave Scotland.

"What on earth is all that commotion? I thought you ordered the taxi for Monday morning." Ma bustled back into my room, went to the tiny window, and poked her head through. She laughed and waved. Turning back to me she said, "Go wash your face and comb your hair, my darling girl. You have a visitor."

I put my head out the window. It was George, his tired face alight with pleasure as he honked his car's horn. "Marion, I worked overtime on Friday. So here I am."

I ran down the steep stairs at breakneck speed and into his arms. "Did you think I wouldn't come?" he said as he caught me to him. His hand stroked the back of my head. "We will make it work, my love. Somehow it will all come right for us."

CHAPTER TWENTY-FIVE

September 1946
Buckingham Palace, London

Hullo, Crawfie. It's good to be back." Lilibet greeted me in a voice so flat, so expressionless, that my head came up from my book like a hound scenting danger. I was up out of my chair in a moment. She gave me a quick peck on the cheek before sitting down on the window seat. The clocked ticked the seconds away as silence built, until I couldn't bear it.

"How was it?" I asked. "Philip's visit to Balmoral?"

She lifted her head. "It was very pleasant." There was a frog in her throat. "I have a bit of a cold, which is surprising because the weather was spectacular." She smiled—at least her mouth performed the job—a joyless excuse for one. It was hard to read her expression with the sun coming in through the window behind her, but she radiated misery.

I swallowed down unease. "Philip enjoyed his first experience of deer stalking?" My encouraging inquiry rang across the room, and she cleared her throat again. "Oh yes, it was perfect weather for it.

We only got one good shot in, but I know Papa loved showing Philip the ropes—like you, Crawfie, Papa is a natural teacher." Her voice fell away, and she returned to removing dog hairs one by one from a skirt covered in them.

"Well, that sounds like good news. His Majesty rarely bothers to spend time with those who bore or annoy!"

Lilibet folded her hands in her lap. I could have screamed with impatience as I waited for her to make up her mind what, or what not, to reveal. "I'm rather afraid to tell you this, and I really shouldn't. I think Mama and Uncle David have it in for Philip."

David Bowes-Lyon! I clamped my jaws tightly together to stop myself from blurting. So, Uncle David had braved the discomforts of a summer at Balmoral to be at his sister's side. I saw him standing in the drawing room, surrounded by old pals, with the newest American cocktail in his hand: the polished clubman telling stories about how much the tweedy set and their heather-covered moors and craggy outcrops of rock bored him to death.

Perhaps she sensed my anger, because she lifted her wrist and looked at her watch. "I don't know, Crawfie. Perhaps I have been rash in wanting to marry Philip. Anyway, I've got to run. We have to go to Windsor this weekend—Mummy wanted to make sure you knew you were coming too."

"Things were all right in the beginning," Lilibet finally admitted the following morning as I packed my overnight bag for Windsor.

"Between who?" I asked.

"Oh, between Papa, Philip, and me. We set out after breakfast with a picnic lunch to stalk. And"—her laugh was warm with affection—"Philip was particularly good at it. He had an expert ghillie, and Papa helped him understand the subtler points of stalking, but he's a natural sportsman."

For the life of me I couldn't understand why anyone wanted to spend the day trudging the tundra in the pursuit of an animal that was inevitably doomed to die. What were shotguns for but to kill prey at long distance and get the whole thing over with quickly?

"So where was the difficulty?"

"There really wasn't one. Except perhaps that Philip sometimes says things that are . . . you know . . . a bit . . . off course."

Off course? What did that mean? Vulgar, unmannerly, too outright? I shook my head. "He always strikes me as being willing to fit in—to get along with everyone."

She folded my handkerchiefs into rigid little squares and put them in my bag. "When everyone else arrived, it was as if he was trying too hard. And . . . sometimes he is a bit boisterous, and . . . well, you know, rather forceful."

A horrible thought struck me. "When did your uncle David arrive?"

"About four days after us. He had a cold, so he couldn't join the rest of us on the moor. He stayed inside and kept Mummy and Tommy Lascelles company."

I almost snorted in disgust. David Bowes-Lyon wouldn't join anyone, except by the fire in a drawing room for the sort of gossip that demolishes reputations.

"Unfortunately, Philip pulled Uncle David's leg about his cold: told him to gargle with warm seawater and advised him to get out on the moors and walk it off rather than shut himself up in a stuffy drawing room."

Well, good for him! I was glad that he hadn't put up with any of Uncle David's sniping in corners.

"It didn't go down too well with Mummy . . ."

"Who else was there when Philip was with you?"

She counted their names off on her fingers: a few of the king's

ponderous old shooting cronies and their wives, and the effete
bachelor friends of the queen. No wonder Margaret was at a scream-
ing point when she came back from Balmoral or Sandringham.

I watched her struggle with being too critical of the man she
loved. "Oh, I think I am making too much of it." She shrugged her
shoulders and laughed.

"So, tell me." I was as direct as I dared to be, and I saw her eyes
widen at my candor. "Apart from Philip not getting along with
Uncle David?"

She laughed. "He thinks him a witless pea brain. I am afraid
that Philip rather put their backs up," Lilibet admitted.

"Whose back up? How?" I asked.

"We-ll, Tommy Lascelles for one. I know he doesn't like Philip. And
he tries to trip him up, rather, which Philip deals with very patiently.
But then Tommy keeps on picking and in the end Philip bristles."

"Tommy is a bit of a fossil."

She brightened. "Yes, he is, rather, isn't he?"

"Yes, it's his job. What was he picking about?"

"Just little finicky things . . . He had a go at Gordonstoun being
too experimental and eccentric, and when Philip sneered at Eton—
which he should not have—Tommy went off and told Papa, and
Papa told Mummy, who told me that Philip is often . . . 'tactless'
was the word Tommy used."

And there we had it.

I could hear the spiteful whispers: "Philip is not the one for Lilibet. Philip is an outsider. Not to be trusted. He has sisters who
married Nazis. And he is tactless."

"Papa was a bit cold with Philip after that." She turned away, but
I saw her eyes stare away tears.

I folded a shawl, put it in the suitcase, and closed the lid. And
we walked into my sitting room as the maid brought in my morning
coffee.

"And after that?" I asked when we were alone.

"Papa says that I am too young to get married. But his tone to Philip was snubby."

And your mother? I silently prompted as I handed her a cup of coffee.

"And Mummy says the same.

"Philip did his best, but . . ." She lowered her head and gazed down at the cup balanced on her lap. "Everything is so tiresome, Crawfie. Even Bobo told me this morning that she thinks that Philip is beneath me."

I clenched and unclenched my hands. I would have difficulty not strangling that wretched Bobo MacDonald the next time I saw her. But I said nothing about Lilibet's loyal dresser. "How much influence do you think Tommy Lascelles really has with the king?" I asked her. Lilibet shook her head slowly from side to side and shrugged her shoulders. If I was a fatalist, I would believe, as they say in the American films, that it was "curtains" for Philip.

"You know something?" I said, trying to be the only one not to put the kibosh on love. "I think this will all work itself out. All these hiccups and reactions are just the result of your introducing the idea of change."

She opened her eyes wide and drew in a deep breath. "It is all such a mess. Philip can't even become a British citizen with all the civil unrest in Greece at the moment. And he can't stay in the navy if he's not a citizen."

It was time to boost, not commiserate. "First of all, if your father gives his permission for Philip to marry you, I promise you his citizenship will not be a problem. And your mother will come around; she is just being cautious because she worked hard to reestablish the monarchy after all that business with the abdication." I didn't know if she was listening or not. She had fixed her gaze at the bottom of her coffee cup as if she was about to tell fortunes. Sad ones. "Lilibet,

I think we shall just have to sit tight and wait them all out. All that happened at Balmoral was that your mother and father got to know Philip a little better—people take a while to adjust to change. Don't back down now."

She lifted her gaze from her cup. "I don't intend to, Crawfie. I will simply tell them that the only husband I want is Philip."

"What does Philip have to say about it all?" I couldn't help but ask.

Finally, she smiled, her sweet, generous smile. "Philip thinks we have to be patient." A quick glance at me out of the corner of her eye. "But he did ask Papa for his permission to propose to me." She laughed outright at my expression.

"Lilibet, why didn't you tell me this at the beginning?"

She put her finger to her lips. "Because I wanted your advice on the unfortunate bits first."

"And His Majesty said *yes*?"

"His Majesty said *not yet*. That I was only twenty and he would like Philip to hold off until next year, which Philip agreed to." She stood up and smoothed the front of her skirt. "And that is why we four are off on an official trip to South Africa. We are leaving in February next year. We will be gone for three months."

"Three *months*?"

"Yes, it was Mummy's idea that Margaret and I should go with them. It's a test, of course. To see if I will forget all about Philip."

"Something has to be done, Crawfie, and quickly too." Margaret's hand on my arm brought me to a sharp halt as we labored up the hill from the Victoria walk later that afternoon, followed by a crowd of panting dogs.

"En français, Margaret. Nous devons pratiquer nos verbes," I said, but I was too distracted to care.

"No, Crawfie, it's too important for French. The Lilibet and

Philip business is serious, much too serious to be fumbling around for the future tense of 'to be.' I know Lilibet is all dewy-eyed about Philip and believes quite wrongly that all is going well, but things are unraveling, and she hasn't any idea how fast."

"What seems to be the problem?" I asked, mindful that Margaret was a blurter.

There were no thoughtful pauses from Margaret. She took in a deep breath. "First of all, Mummy is very much against Lilibet marrying Philip. She will go to any lengths to prevent it. Do you know what I mean? No, of course you don't, so I'll tell you.

"While Lilibet, Philip, and Papa were off stalking, Mummy spent a lot of time with Tommy Lascelles. Tommy doesn't approve of Philip to begin with. But after a session or two with Mummy and Uncle David, he holed himself up in his office and spent his time busily writing letters and getting answers to them. It has to do with Philip's family and his suitability as a future consort to Britain's queen."

I had to turn my head away; her urgent voice and deeply serious expression would have been amusing at any other time. Margaret was playing her role of intelligence gatherer to the hilt. "Tommy thinks that Philip has a bit of a reputation . . . as a lady's man."

I shook my head. "What? No, it's not possible. In fact, it's ridiculous."

"Yes, it is a fact, because I heard Uncle David telling Mummy that Philip is too sophisticated and far too European for words. And everyone knows what that means."

This was just the sort of thing that David Bowes-Lyon would come up with. If Philip was handsome, virile, and good company, of course he had to be a lecher.

"I overheard everything. Everything! According to Uncle David, Philip has always had lots of girlfriends. Even when he was writing to Lilibet during the war, he was always with some woman or other.

But for years, he has been very close with that glamorous Hélène Cordet." She looked at me in a kindly, pitying sort of way. "Now, I know you don't know who she is, Crawfie, but I do. She is a singer—a really good one, actually. And she is absolutely gorgeous. Much more gorgeous than Lilibet—she has what they call sex appeal. And please don't tell me that you don't know what *that* means." I started to ask her how she knew what sex appeal meant, but she waved an impatient hand. "Philip is godfather to her children." She lowered her voice, but its clear tone rang ahead of us up the hill. It was as much as I could do not to put my hand over her mouth. "Uncle David says there is a rumor that he might even be their father."

I pushed the hair back out of my eyes and stared at her in horror. *If only half of this is true, it makes Philip look tawdry, shopworn, and certainly not the man I have taken him for.*

"Crawfie, you are gaping."

"There are always rumors—Philip is a good-looking and an attractive young man."

Her laugh was derisive, and it was patronizing too. I frowned at her until she apologized.

"And then there is Papa. He is not very keen on the idea of Lilibet and Philip *at all*. Not one bit."

I was not a poker player. I knew my face expressed the fear that threatened to submerge me, to send me running to my room to try to work out how we could overcome this hurdle.

"Does he believe that Philip is—?"

"A womanizer? I don't know what he has heard. But Papa is furious with Uncle Dickie because he is not only sponsoring Philip's naturalization to become a British citizen and giving Philip his name, but he is telling *everyone* that Philip and Lilibet are secretly engaged to be married."

"But they are not, are they? So, it is just another rumor."

She reached out her hand and joggled me by the elbow. "Oh,

Crawfie, please wake up! Uncle Dickie has put Papa's back up, and he is digging in. On top of all this womanizing business, Philip is looking more and more like an unsavory gold digger by the minute." She put her hands on her hips and glared at me as if I was being obtuse on purpose.

I remembered my role as governess. "Please don't put your hands on your hips, Margaret."

She folded them across her bosom. Her Windsor blue eyes flashed outrage and fury. "Don't you see? Papa doesn't want Lilibet to marry *anyone* at all right now; he just wants it to be 'we four' again. And it doesn't help with everyone biting at Philip's ankles and running him down, behind his back, to Papa!"

I was still too taken aback by the "womanizing" accusation to offer any suggestion that would be of use.

"Lilibet has *no* idea!" Margaret threw her hands up at her sister's naivete. "No idea at all what is going on. It makes me so angry with all of them." Her brows came down and she took a step closer. "So, what are *we* going to do?"

We had reached the top of the hill, and the corgis threw themselves down in a panting heap. I fanned my face with my hand. "Well, there is nothing whatsoever we can do, is there?"

"What?" she exploded. "We can't just let them ruin Lilibet's one chance of happiness." Her cheeks were scarlet, and her hands were back on her hips. "We can't just stand by and let this happen. Lilibet wouldn't let *my* happiness be destroyed by a bunch of old gossipers and starchy out-of-date courtiers . . . she just wouldn't!" Tears welled up in her fierce eyes and her lower lip jutted.

I put my arm around her shoulders. "Margaret, life isn't that simple, I'm afraid. Especially for the heir to the throne."

She shook my arm off. "*Don't* start talking to me about duty. How can Lilibet possibly do the job of being queen if she's married to some dull chap that Mummy chose for her? Answer me that one.

Philip is perfect for her; he will stick up for her and give her confidence." She didn't wait for an answer. "She has no one at all, except you and me." She broke away and started to stump off toward the castle gate, and I puffed after her.

"I know how upsetting it is, but we have to have some faith in Lilibet."

"She is such a Goody—"

"Yes, I know she often comes across as dutiful and obedient."

"I was going to say that she is a wretched Goody Two-shoes. It makes me so bloody furious. Sorry again, Crawfie."

"And *I* was going to say that we must not forget that she has learned patience and self-discipline: two attributes that have made her strong and steadfast. All she has to do is not back down and wait them out. All this fuss and bother, all of these rumors about Nazis in the family, philandering fathers, and mentally ill mothers, and now Philip's affairs with other women, are all simply fuss. I am quite sure that Lilibet will prevail. And it is our job, Margaret, to stand by her. Encourage her and help her stand firm, and that means doing just that and absolutely *nothing* more. I hope I am being clear."

"You don't think we should at least say something to Papa?"

The gleam of battle had not gone from her eyes. I thought of all the passionately well-meaning damage she could do, and I tried not to clutch at her in my panic.

"Margaret," I said slowly, forcing calm. "If you really want to know what I think, the very best thing we can do is to let Lilibet deal with this in her own way. She knows we care; she knows we love her. I promise you she will come through." I had almost convinced myself.

"Yes, Crawfie, all right." She wiped her eyes with her handkerchief and on we went together toward the castle gate. "Mentally ill mothers? I didn't know that about Philip's mother. Do you mean to say she actually went bonkers?" I hadn't the energy to reply.

CHAPTER TWENTY-SIX

December 1946 to January 1947
Limekiln Cottage, Dunfermline, Scotland

Two days before Christmas I went north to the stinging winds and the sullen skies of Dunfermline.

My mother had lost weight, and when she wasn't moving, her hands went to the small of her back. "Just a touch of lumbago; it's the chill off the river," she said as she pulled me into the kitchen and wrapped her arms around me. "You look bonny, Marion. Look, this came in the post for you." She handed me a Christmas card. It was from George.

I wish you the Merriest of Christmases, his neat handwriting informed me. *And if all goes well I will be with you both to celebrate Hogmanay. All my love to you both.*

But all did not go well. At the last minute a severe storm locked us in its freezing grip. The roads were sheets of black ice and gale-force winds howled from the north. On the morning before New Year's Eve, as we were making our porridge, the blizzard was so thick we couldn't see out the windows.

"Good Lord above. If this keeps up we'll be snowed in," my mother said with the complacency of a woman who planned for every season with a well-stocked vegetable cellar and enough lamp oil to last a decade.

For the first time since the war, Ma and I celebrated Hogmanay alone. I was determined to make it a good one for her because it troubled me that she was showing signs of slowing down—of aging.

"There is plenty of wood, so I have built up the fire. Come into the parlor and leave those dishes. I'll take care of them." I tried to coax her to sit, to do nothing but enjoy an evening in front of leaping flames.

"Come and do them with me, Marion. I can't have dirty crocks sitting in the sink for the New Year." We had cleaned and polished all day to welcome in 1947. "No Scot worth her salt welcomes a New Year into a dirty house. It must be all those servants who have made you so lazy."

It took me a minute to wash and dry dishes for her to put away. Then I poured two generous glasses of Glen Avon and led her to the fire.

"To you, my darling, girl. To you and George." We drank, and she leaned forward and held up her hand, palm facing me. "I'm not offering any advice to you, Marion. None at all. But I have a feeling in my bones that all will come right for you both this year." She raised her glass. "Do shlàinte agus do àm ri teachd." To your health and to your future. We drank.

"Ah yes, that's the right good stuff, all right." My mother put down her empty glass, and I poured her another splash or two. "I love the warmth as it goes down. A nice bright fire, a good dinner, and a glass or two would put anyone right." This tiny scrap of a woman was hard hit by her belt of whiskey as she gently slurred her blessing. "Uisge-beatha: the water of life." She raised her glass and sipped slowly as she gazed into the fire. "Now, tell me about this trip you are all taking to Africa."

"It's quite a business, these official tours," I explained. "Which is why I must leave tomorrow, to help get them ready. Lilibet will be celebrating her twenty-first birthday in Africa! It will be a tremendous amount of work for the family too. They will visit hundreds of towns to say hullo to the people of South Africa."

"What a fuss," Ma said and took another sip—her eyes were drowsy. "And in this terrible weather too."

"They'll escape our winter, at least," I said. "It will be summer where they are going. They will be traveling all over South Africa in the White Train: the coaches have been built especially for this trip and are the last word in luxury."

A grunt of derisive scorn. "What a carry-on: I hope we are not paying for this shindig."

"Funnily enough the king said the same thing when the trip was in its planning stages. I have no idea who is paying—probably the South Africans."

The king, like my mother, had shrunk in height and weight the last time I had seen him standing in the middle of the queen's drawing room, looking on as the women in his family exclaimed over fabrics that Norman Hartnell had produced for their summer wardrobe for the trip. Surrounded by the bright display of gauzy silks and cottons, he wore a strained expression of polite interest as Mr. Hartnell chirruped with enthusiasm and models paraded dresses, coats, and evening gowns. He had withdrawn into a corner of the room, eyes tired, face drawn and pale, and his responses to his wife's delight were monosyllabic.

"The king doesn't enjoy public life," I explained to my mother. "He dislikes meeting new people. I think he is dreading this trip."

Ma shrugged her shoulders in incomprehension. "Why go all

that way for a country that's not ours—why not stay here and meet his own people?"

"Because it is important to solidify South Africa's standing in our new Commonwealth. Their prime minister, Jan Smuts, is worried he will lose the next election. Smuts is outspoken in his dislike of segregation, and it has made him unpopular with the Afrikaners, and his opposition leader, Malan, is pro-apartheid."

"Apartheid?"

"Keeping mixed race and black people separate from white people. I can't imagine living in a country where they are prevented from being with the rest of us, can you?"

She looked into the fire, her gaze soft as she remembered another time, when she was young. "The first time I saw a black man in Scotland was in 1918. Your father had just come home from the war, and I was in Glasgow to meet his ship. We had heard of them of course, in Dunfermline, but I had never met a black man, or woman, or even seen one." She nodded at her memory. "They came from the Gold Coast in Africa and the West Indies to help us fight the war. They were welcome everywhere and treated like the heroes they were—with respect. I can't imagine what these South Africans are thinking to force them to live apart from white people. They must be a very unpleasant bunch."

She raised her glass, and the leaping flames caught the deep amber in the whiskey. "It's about time they gave back those countries they stole and end all this imperialism and taking what is not theirs—as if England were put on this earth to rule!" She sipped from her glass and wrinkled her nose in disapproval. "It is not good for a country to have so much power over those who have nothing; it gives it a sense of superiority it doesn't deserve. Repression, Marion, is a terrible thing—it blocks out hope for generations. Anyone would think God was an Englishman the way they talk south of the border." If I poured her another dram, she would be on about Scotland's secession from England and the cruelty of the Sassenach. "That Mountbatten, now, he's got the right idea about quitting India."

"Winston Churchill refers to him as 'the man who wants to give away India.'"

My mother laughed. "Oh aye? That must be one in the eye for the establishment," she said. "So, Philip's uncle wants to help India to independence. I think I approve of this boy. Well, good for the Mountbattens; perhaps they'll bring some sense into that lot for once."

I steered her away from the Windsors. "Anyway, there will be a lot to do in the next month to get the family ready for their trip. I'll be very busy."

"It will be an experience for you, Marion. To see another part of the world!"

Part of me yearned to travel and see the world, but I would not pass up three months with my mother and George, if I could. "Well, we'll see. Lilibet is definite that she wants me to go."

"Then I expect that is what will happen." She was warm, and rosy-cheeked from the fire and Glen Avon, and her eyelids drooped.

I smiled and took her hand in mind. "Yes, I expect that is what will happen." But she didn't hear me; her eyelids had closed, and she had drifted off to sleep.

CHAPTER TWENTY-SEVEN

February 1947
Buckingham Palace, London

"I wish you were coming after all, Crawfie. It just doesn't seem fair: all this on-and-off-again business. I am furious with Mummy for changing her mind at the last minute." Margaret, her lovely face flushed with excitement, pranced into my sitting room. "I wanted to show you my favorite coat and dress—I absolutely love this shade of pink. What do you think?" She strolled up and down my sitting room, turning with her coat held open with all the flare of a mannequin. She pirouetted, and the cyclamen silk dress underneath her shell pink coat shouted her joy at being Margaret: young, pretty, with rich parents who were going to take her on a cruise with trunks of outfits as elegant and as charming as this one.

She stopped mid-spin to return to her outrage that I had been told yesterday afternoon I would not be going to South Africa. "I asked Mummy again, this morning, if she would change her mind, but she said that there simply wasn't room on the train."

I wondered when I would wear the cotton dresses and tropical-weight linen coats I had bought at the last minute, when I had been told five days ago that I should expect to board the royal ship at Southampton. I shuddered at the thought of short sleeves. The sleet-battered windows made the room dark and cold. I plugged in the electric fire. Just one bar, we had been cautioned by the palace in these times of austerity.

I rubbed my hands together and put a heavy Shetland cardigan on over my jumper. "Is it snowing again? I am so glad we are leaving this awful weather." Margaret gave an exaggerated shiver of shoulders clad in soft bouclé wool. The wind moaned up the corridor from a hundred drafty windows. I squared my shoulders so that our goodbyes were not tainted with the gloom of the bitter weather and my being told to stay behind at the last minute.

"Take lots of photographs"—I took her warm hands in mine—"and if you have time, I would love a letter or two. But there is something else, Margaret. Please listen." She had broken away to return to the looking glass.

She stopped, her eyes wide at my tone. "What is it? . . . I don't look like Mummy in this hat, do I?"

"No, not at all. It's about your sister."

She smiled at me. "Yes, I know, Crawfie, don't worry. Bobo and Mummy are against Philip, so I have to be there for her. Did you know that Mummy said Philip might not come down to Southampton to wave us off when we set sail? Talk about shortsighted—anyone would think this was Tudor England."

I wanted to gather her in my arms and kiss her. But Margaret was practicing; she was a sophisticated woman of the world stepping out onto a stage that would applaud her. The last thing she wanted was her old governess hanging on her arm and telling her to be kind to her big sister.

· · ·

"Crawfie, how very sweet of you to spare me the time when we are all up in the air with last-minute packing." I was ushered into the queen's drawing room that evening so she could reassure me how sad she was I could not go with them. "Yes, please, do sit, dear Crawfie." It was the familiar routine: the bright welcome, the little chair, and a glass of sherry.

A sorrow-filled sigh, a slight shake of her head, and the queen stretched out a hand to ruffle Dookie's ears. "I am so sorry that you are not, after all, able to come with us to South Africa; what a terrible disappointment it must be. We had no idea that the White Train was almost as cramped as our train here!" She put her head on one side; a frown corrugated her forehead for a moment and was gone. "Lilibet and Margaret were so looking forward to your joining us."

I was not concerned for Lilibet: marooned on first a ship and then a train with Bobo's determined dislike of Philip, and her mother's regretful concerns about his unfortunate family. Neither was I anxious for the king and the grueling months that a state tour promised for a man who disliked travel of any kind outside his own country. And I felt only relief that I would not spend the next three months with the forceful personality sitting in front of me anticipating the adoring crowds who would cheer her, and the opportunity to dance the night away at gala balls. The queen's state visit to South Africa would be her moment in the spotlight: her London Blitz all over again, but with better food and no danger of falling bombs.

I nodded along; her voice a distant, eager buzz. My only thought was for George. The blessed relief I had felt when I was told, "So awfully sorry, Crawfie, you're not coming," had been washed away by his letter.

I slipped my hand into my skirt pocket, and my fingers closed around the envelope that I had opened just this afternoon. My fingernail caught on the rough edge of the torn paper, and I swallowed down an irresistible urge to get to my feet and say that I was urgently needed elsewhere. *When will the bright, empty chatter ever stop?* I needed the sanctuary of my rooms so I could lay my aching head down and cry away my pain.

"And then there is Margaret . . . she has been so wayward recently . . ."

My hand gripped the letter that I had read over and over again until the paper was limp in my hand.

"What is it that makes young women so antagonistic—to their mothers, I mean? She can't do enough for His Majesty."

One glance through the letter, and I had pulled down my suitcase from the top of the wardrobe and started hurling winter socks and sweaters into it as fast as I could.

My dear Marion,

"And then there is the unsuitability of her choice of clothes— that awfully bright cyclamen pink. She positively bullied poor Mr. Hartnell . . ."

Your mother came to Aberdeen last week to visit her sisters. Fortunately, I had time to give her tea before she caught the half past six train back to Dunfermline. She told me how excited you were that you were going on the royal tour to South Africa, and we both thought how lucky you were to escape this bitter winter!

I realized when she left how much your life with the royal family means to you. And how wrong it was for me to have pressed you to leave a job that I know means everything to you. It was selfish and thoughtless of me, and I feel like a self-centered fool for not understanding before.

> *I am releasing you from our engagement—I know it will
> be best for both of us. I hope we can remain good friends when
> we meet. But for now, I wish you bon voyage and a wonderful
> adventure in Africa.*
>
> *Yours,*
> *George*

It seemed that George no longer wanted to be mine. The shock
of his words froze all thought; all I could hear was the hammering
of my heart, the pain in my chest so intense I thought I was going
to die. *But I'm not going to South Africa. I have been given an eleventh-
hour reprieve.* The words on the page had connected with my brain,
and I booked a seat on the express train leaving for Scotland.

I had three months, while the family were away, to concentrate
on just one thing. If I had not already lost George—I nearly burst
into wails of agonized tears—I must do everything I could to bring
him back to me.

The queen's voice, from the center of her sofa, demanded my
attention. "Did you say you were leaving for Scotland tomorrow
morning, Crawfie? Is that wise? I hear the weather in the north is
even worse than here!"

I got to my feet and made a half curtsy, even though she had not
given me permission to leave. "Yes, I must go to Scotland," I said,
my words so heavy with emphasis that she blinked. "Bon voyage,
Your Majesty. I know the tour will be a great success." And I left her
already instructing her two dressers and three pages in a close hud-
dle of detail.

I could not, dare not, imagine what my life would bring me over
the coming months. I merely thanked God that I was free to try to
rescue my future.

· · ·

The train ground to a stop for the third time in as many hours. I peered out the dirty windows of my drafty second-class carriage. *What now?* I opened the window and stuck my head out to look up the line. My breath hung in the frozen air, and my ears and nose burned with the cold.

"Close that window, miss." The conductor came through the carriage. "Snow blocking the line ahead; we'll be here until they can get it clear." A large woman with a cheerful red hat and a bright blue woolen scarf made a tutting sound. "Come on, ducks," he said. "Come and help me dig away the snow." There was laughter all round. The Great British public were showing how doughty they could be.

I couldn't bring myself to ask how long it would take to clear the snow from the tracks. British Railways had a wonderful way of being jocular when their schedules went haywire, as if they were planned events for our entertainment. I unscrewed my thermos and drank the last cup of tea, brewed at seven o'clock this morning and presented to me by Mr. Ainslie. "Blizzards in the north, Miss Crawford. It will be slow going, I'm afraid. The cook has made some sandwiches for you and some of her fruit cake." He handed me a beautifully prepared little hamper. "There is a coal shortage up there too—thanks to this terrible weather. Perhaps you should consider waiting a few days? I mean, after all, the journey will be . . ." He lifted his hand to heaven: only the Lord knew what he had in store for us.

But I couldn't wait another moment. I had to get to Aberdeen; I had to get to George. I lifted the Bakelite cup to my lips and took a sip. The tea was cold and tasted sour.

CHAPTER TWENTY-EIGHT

February 1947
Limekiln Cottage, Dunfermline, Scotland

"Marion!" My mother's face was puckered with concern as she pulled open her door. "What's happened? Is everything all right? I thought you were on your way to Africa. Oh, for heaven's sake, what possessed you to make the journey in this weather? You're perished." She put her arms around me before drawing me into the kitchen. I was rigid with cold; my hands and feet ached, my nose a peak of ice in the middle of my face. I was so exhausted I hadn't the energy to speak.

"How on earth did you get here from the station?"

She took me by the shoulders and guided me to the heat of the Aga. "Hot tea," she directed herself. "Or would you prefer soup?"

"Yes, soup, please." My stomach was an empty pit, clamoring for food. I was close to breaking down with remorse and fear that everything I held most dear had been put to one side for the Windsor family, who were now setting off for three months in the sun.

"The lane's been blocked for two days. No one can get down nor up. How did you get through?"

"Mr. Mackenzie and his tractor . . . they dug out the lane yesterday evening. Mr. Franklin gave me a lift in his truck. There is a box of groceries on the step outside—more snow coming in tonight. Mr. Franklin said to expect at least another foot. They'll dig out the drifts in the lane so they can get more supplies to us."

My mother chafed my hands in hers. "Parsnip soup . . . with oatcakes. And tomorrow we'll have chicken stew . . ."

I nodded, too tired to care.

Her accent broadened as she sensed the despair I felt. "Somethin' has happened; your face is as white as milk." The skin at the corners of her eyes creased in concern. "Ne'er mind, soup first."

"It's George." I was too drained, too distressed, to cry, but it was hard to get the words through the tight band around my throat whenever I thought of him. "George has released me from our engagement. It's off, Ma."

"What on earth are you saying?"

"I think he has had enough of my job and the Windsors." I tried to laugh, but I couldn't.

She smacked her hand to her forehead, her eyes wide. "It's ma ain fawt. Marion, I told him you were going away to Africa for three months, because you said you were!"

Her face was so distressed that I caught her by the hand. "No, it is not your fault. It is mine. I should have given notice when George asked me to marry him. I was selfish, terribly selfish and stupid."

"You did what you thought was right." She bent down and gathered me to her. I closed my eyes and rested my aching head on her narrow shoulder, surrendering my burdens and returning to childhood as she rocked me in her thin arms. After a while she released me and sat down on the settle next to my chair. "Now, what are you going to do?"

That she thought I should *do* something was reassuring. "As soon as the snow clears, I am going to Aberdeen. I am going to see George and tell him that I will leave my job immediately and marry him. Do you fancy a winter wedding, Ma?"

She laughed and chucked my chin. "That's my girl. You go up and stay with your aunts Madge and Mary. Go and see George and talk him round."

My plan was a simple one. I would go to Aberdeen on a Friday morning and stay with my aunts. I imagined their joyful welcome as they pulled me into their house and scolded me for arriving before a weekend.

"You know we do the flowers at St. Peter's Church every other Saturday, silly girl." Aunt Madge was bigger and sterner than her little sister, and it was she who insisted they still make the two-hour bus journey, twice a month, to the parish they had grown up in to do the flowers for Sunday service.

"Don't say that, Madge. She is welcome whenever. You can do the flowers; I'll stay here." Aunt Mary would be beside herself with happiness.

They would argue, but both would agree that on Saturday afternoon they would set off for the church to do the flowers for Sunday with the vicar's wife. And stop the night for Matins the following morning. They would skip lunch at the vicarage and be home for lunch and tea with me.

"If we leave after Sunday service it will give us plenty of time to catch up . . . I am surprised you didn't go to Africa with the queen. Your ma was right proud of you going all that way!" I heard my aunt Mary say.

When they were gone, God help me, I would go over to George's house, not ten minutes' walk from Cameron Avenue, and bring him back to the privacy of their scrupulously tidy living room. I could see the fire burning in the grate lighting the well-polished shabby whatnots and little tables and their fat old orange tomcat sleeping on the windowsill. George and I would have a chance to talk things through—alone, without interruption, without tea cakes on doilies and the elaborate teatime ritual of spinsters. If all went well, we had the night alone together, and we would have time to make our plans. When my aunts came home again on Sunday, it would be to a happier, more betrothed woman than the one they had left on Saturday afternoon.

My overnight bag was packed in readiness for my train journey to Aberdeen the next morning, but my bedroom was as dark as night at eight o'clock when I awoke. I turned over to grope for my alarm clock; the top sheet crackled with a thin layer of frost, and a long icicle, formed by my breath, scraped against my cheek. I swung my legs out of bed and shivered as my feet, scuffing for my slippers, touched the icy floor. I pulled the curtains back. It had snowed again in the night, enough to bank up on the roof below my bedroom window. I put on half my winter wardrobe and went downstairs. Ma had made porridge and tea.

"I let you sleep; you were all in last night." Her lined face was less tired than it was two days ago when I had arrived. She was glad I had come home.

I took a short walk to the end of the path to the lane. The dip in the road was full of snow. I looked up into a dark sky. I would not be catching a train anywhere. "I don't think they can get the tractor down the lane," I reported to my mother. "I'll have to put off going to Aberdeen." Neither could I possibly leave my mother snowed in. "We have to bring in more wood from the shed. And I have to do something about the chickens," I said as I started to eat my porridge. "Would you put on the wireless, Ma? We can catch the nine o'clock news."

A static crackle and a high-pitched intermittent whistle as Ma twiddled the knob of the wireless I had bought her for her birthday last year. "I can never get it quite tuned in," she said fretfully as she tortured more atmospherics and shrieks from the dark brown box. "I think the snow is blocking the airwaves somehow."

The wireless whined; then clear as a bell came a human voice. "For the Fife area . . ." A hail of static. "The worst blizzard for twenty-five years in Dunfermline, Ballater, Kirkcaldy . . . three feet of snow with ten-foot drifts. Many of the county's main roads are blocked." The weatherman's voice was drowned in a crackle of interference.

"Ninety Fife villages . . . cut off. A major road in Dundee city center is covered in a sheet of ice . . . All bridges in the county are impassable." An unearthly screech of distorted sound. I couldn't stand it any longer. I got up from the table with a cup of tea in my hand and knelt by the radiogram.

"You have to move the dial slowly . . . and watch the needle as it moves to one-five-zero to the Home Service," I explained as a voice came through the wireless, loud and clear. "Aberdeen broke its record for snowfall . . . with more snow on the way. In Edinburgh for the fifth day in a row, the disruption of transport, including coal trains, has led to power cuts and the restrictions on use of domestic electricity for five hours each day, under threat of fines or imprisonment."

"Good Lord above, as if we didn't know *that*. The shortages are worse now than they were in the war. Switch it off, Marion, please. I can't listen to the same weather report morning after morning. It makes me itch."

On the fourth day of what was to become the worst winter on record, we had carried in firewood and stacked it in the hall. The pump handle froze, and we melted snow for water in a big pan on the Aga.

"Never had any use for electricity anyway; if we could get a line down this road, it would collapse in all this snow." My mother went about the daily task of filling her oil lamps. "I don't think the chickens will make it in this cold." She filled the last lamp, trimmed its wick, and sat down in a chair by the Aga.

"Will you stay here and tend the fire, Ma? Boil enough water so we can have a nice bath. I will go and do something about the chickens." I put on my thickest coat, barely able to button it over three sweaters, pulled my beret down to my eyebrows, and wrapped a scarf around my face below my eyes to my neck.

The front door of the cottage faced south: the air was almost balmy when I opened it. I allowed myself a minute to admire the beauty of the pristine filigree world that surrounded us before making my way toward the henhouse. When I came around the corner wall of the cottage, the north wind slammed into me with such violent fury it sliced through layers of wool like needles of ice and whirled my beret off my head. I crouched in the lee of the mulberry tree's thick trunk to get my bearings, and then, half-blinded by flying snow, I fought my way to the chicken coop and wrestled open the door. It blew back out of my hands and slammed against the wall.

Inside the air was cold, but the coop had been built by John Mackenzie and, like our cottage, was strong and stout—made for harsh winters. "Everyone bearing up?" I put my hand into the nearest nesting box. Surely they couldn't have survived? The warmth of soft feathers. No music was sweeter to my ears than the irritable clucking as I disturbed her sleep.

I tobogganed bales of straw from the barn down to the coop and used them to pad the henhouse walls for insulation. I fed the chickens their corn and helped them back into their boxes, reassured by the drowsy sounds of contentment. I filled the water troughs again and prayed they would not freeze too quickly.

"Thank God you have always led a simple, practical life, Ma," I said as I stood in front of the Aga, trying to warm my freezing bum.

She looked up from chopping onions, her eyes watering. "There should be enough root vegetables, cabbages, pears, and apples in the cellar, and we can always kill a chicken or two." She put down her knife and went into action. "Your face is blue with cold; come on, sit here and get warm. No, not too close to the fire, you'll get hot ache." With one hand she put the kettle on the hob, and with the other, she wiped melting snow off my face with a tea towel. "Good Lord, your eyelashes are frozen. Just how long can this terrible weather last? Here, drink this." She wrapped my hands around a mug of tea.

"When we've had our supper, let's light the oil lamp, and I'll read to you."

She brightened up immediately. "What'll it be? Dickens? Austen? What about an adventure story? It's been a long time since we read Robert Louis Stevenson—he's pretty good."

I pulled down a couple of books from the bookshelves. "*Kidnapped* or *Treasure Island*?"

I stared into my bowl of porridge and put the spoon down on the table. I would never have thought I would hate the taste, the smell, and the texture of oatmeal as much as I did now. Across the table my mother sipped her tea, pausing to cough and then take another cautious sip.

"I'll get out there and organize a chicken for more soup." Her voice was a whisper, a faint echo of her usually robust and cheerful tone.

"I can do it. You can't possibly go outside. The wind will cut you in two."

"Have you ever killed a chicken?"

"I've seen you do it often enough."

She started to laugh, but it turned into a cough, hard and tight. Her shoulders heaved and her face turned red.

"There's nothing to it, Ma. I will 'organize' the chicken if you'll peel the vegetables."

I sat by the window and wrote to George. Letter after letter, in the last of the afternoon light.

Dear George, I begged. *Please, forgive me! Ma misunderstood me about South Africa.* I crossed out that line; it was not her fault. *I am coming to Aberdeen as soon as it thaws.* I wrote on: paragraphs of anguish and regret; then, snatching up the paper, I ripped it in two and tossed it on the fire.

Dear George,

I am so terribly sorry. I have tried, badly, to manage my job and our new life together . . .

I scored a heavy line through my words and tossed the page onto the fire.

Dear George,

I am snowed in at the cottage with Ma. She is sick and I am frightened. We are cut off from the world. The drifts are so deep, and no one has come to us from the village. Please come.

The band around my throat tightened as I scrunched the page into a ball and tossed it into the fire, reached for my coat, and went out into the storm to carry in more firewood and feed the chickens.

When I came back into the kitchen, I found my mother bent double, hacking and gasping for air, her face a deep, congested purple. I put a heavy pan onto the hob to reheat the chicken soup I had made from the old hen I had killed this morning. Was it really today that I had done that? It seemed like a year ago.

I could still feel the hen's scrawny neck under my fingers as I had laid it on the chopping block and tried to justify my brutality with the pragmatic excuse that she had long since stopped laying anyway and that this sacrifice was for my mother. I shuddered, remembering the bright splash of blood on the snow. I wiped my hand down the side of my skirt, but the soft, downy neck feathers were imprinted on my fingertips.

CHAPTER TWENTY-NINE

March 1947
Limekiln Cottage, Dunfermline, Scotland

The short, dark days, howling wind, the bank of snow that obliterated daylight, and my morning trip along a tunnel of ice to the henhouse took their toll on my morale and my mother's health.

Then one morning as I waited for the kettle to boil, I tuned in to the BBC Home Service. "Ma, they have just announced that there is a thaw in the south, and because it warmed up so quickly, there are now floods—everywhere. We should expect our freeze to ease up soon." I sat down on the edge of my mother's makeshift bed in the kitchen next to the fire and washed her face and hands in warm water. "Ready for some breakfast? You look better today. You didn't cough quite so much last night."

"Has the Forth flooded?"

I shook my head. "I don't know, but if it does, we are too high up for floodwater to reach us. Don't worry."

Her face was the color of parchment, and there were dark shadows under her eyes. They looked huge in her thin face, but worse than that, they had lost their spark. That indefinable quality that was the essence of my mother's energy, her drive and her determination—the qualities that had kept this little woman going through the years of my childhood, two world wars, and an economic depression—were now faded as they gazed blankly into my face.

I propped her upright against a wall of pillows and pulled her shawl up close around her neck and shoulders. Then I carefully put a cup of tea into her hands, wrapping them around the cup before I let go. She took a sip. "Great heavens above, there is sugar in this tea. Did Johnny Mackenzie get his tractor through?" Her voice was as dry and scratchy as the branches of the mulberry tree that had scraped against the kitchen window in the wind, a creature desperate to come in out of the cold.

"Yesterday afternoon. You were sleeping. He brought bacon, bread and butter, and a pot of Mrs. Mackenzie's marmalade, Ma. I'm going to make you breakfast—it will be a feast." He had also promised me that he would bring the doctor for my mother.

"Bacon—whatever next? And what is that you have in your hand?"

I held out an envelope with what I hoped was a steady hand. "A letter for you. John Mackenzie brought it—he says it came this morning."

She squinted up at it. "That's George's writing, you had better open it."

I took a breath to steady the tremor in my fingers and tore open the envelope. The letter was postmarked the fifteenth of February—the day after I had arrived here nearly three weeks ago. The day before the worst blizzard in history hit Great Britain and most of Northern Europe.

I pulled out a single sheet.

Dear Mrs. Crawford,

I was hoping to drive out to you on Sunday, but the roads are either blocked with snow or covered in ice—with more on the way—so I might have to postpone my visit for a week. I imagine your plight is worse than ours here in Aberdeen, since you are so isolated—even from Dunfermline.

My greatest concern is that with Marion away, you will not be able to get to the shops for supplies before the next storm, so I have telephoned Mr. Anderson to put a box together of basic things like bread and milk, and he says as soon as the roads to your house are clear, he will deliver them.

I hope you have enough firewood to see you through the storm, and hopefully I will be able to get down to you next week.

I don't want to labor the point but having a telephone installed in your cottage might be a good idea!

Yours,
George

The news, so welcome that it restored more energy to her tired body than a cup of tea, roused my mother to harrumph at the idea of the telephone in her house. "First thing that happens in a good, strong storm: the lines come down . . . Why anyone would want . . ." She was about to start in on "the" electricity, but it turned into a coughing fit.

"He thinks you are in Africa," she said, and took another mouthful.

I turned away, overcome by a dozen conflicting thoughts. I couldn't let her see my unease. She had been so sick in the last week that I believed I might lose her. What she needed most was the hope that George had not deserted me. That when she went, I would not be alone. My mother understood how hard it was to live on your own. "Drink your tea, Ma. I'm going to make us a disgustingly hearty English breakfast—no porridge oats for us today."

The next morning, I was trundling a wheelbarrow of fresh straw from the old barn to the chicken coop when Dr. Marley arrived.

"There's flooding along the banks of the Forth," he said by way of greeting. "Good thing you are up this high. How on earth you and your mother survived that freeze I'll never know."

I wanted to say that she survived only by the slenderest of threads and because she was one of the toughest women I knew, but he was in no mood for chitchat. I led him into the house to where she was sitting by the Aga, bundled up in her old Shetland wool cardigan and a thick plaid shawl around her shoulders.

"I knew you would outlast that wicked weather, Mrs. Crawford," he said as he took out his stethoscope to listen to her heart. "Now, a little cough." He nodded as he listened. "Heart as strong as a horse, but your lungs sound a bit too thick for my liking." He sat down next to her and took her pulse and put a thermometer under her tongue.

"Just a bit of a cold," Ma said.

"Don't talk, please. Aye, it might very well have started as a cold; then it went to your lungs; now you have the pneumonia with a fever." He rummaged in his bag and fumbled with a large bottle of pills and a cardboard container with fingers still clumsy with cold. He turned to me. "I can't do this without going to the window, Marion. Count out twenty-eight of these pills into this container." He turned back to my mother. "I am leaving penicillin with you, Mrs. Crawford. You are to take two tablets a day for the next fourteen days: one in the morning with your breakfast, the other with your supper. Finish all of them, even if you are feeling better. You should be full of beans in a few days' time, but you are to continue to rest. And for heaven's sake would you please eat something? You are as thin as a switch—not a good idea, at your age, to begin dieting." His feeble attempt at a joke made my mother smile. "I'm going into the grocer at Dunfermline with a list from your daughter, and they will deliver everything to you this afternoon. I want you to eat lots of nourishing chicken soup, until your stomach can cope with meat." He only looked a little offended as we both laughed off chicken soup. "If I ever eat chicken again," my mother said as she held her handkerchief to her eyes, "it will not be too soon."

"Will you keep each other company?" I asked my mother's friend Betty, our nearest neighbor, who had come to visit. "I have to go and clean out the coop. It stinks to high heaven."

Betty nodded. "Better you than me." She sat back in her chair and stretched her feet to the fire. "I could smell it as I came through the wood. What a pong!"

I raked out the coop, piling slimy-wet straw, thick with manure, into the wooden wheelbarrow. On the far horizon, huge ink blue clouds loomed, and I worked faster. If more snow was on the way, I couldn't possibly think of leaving Ma, even with Betty to look after her, for the three days of my planned visit to Aberdeen to see George. I raked wet straw in a fury, anxious to be out of the wind. My eyes watered not only from its northern bite but from the acrid stink of old chicken bedding. I braced myself on the slushy ground and stood upright for a moment to ease my back. The world looked desolate: the meadow grass yellow-brown and sodden with pond water; the looming slate gray skies and the howling wind promised only more winter, more snow, and a return to isolation.

The old argument started again in my head: *Stop making excuses. You have to go to Aberdeen.*

I will, as soon as I can leave Ma.

She will be fine with Betty staying here: you have to go now. You have to go and see him before it's too late, before not seeing him becomes normal.

I resumed raking: lifting and dumping the filthy straw into the back of the barrow. I saw George standing in the doorway of his landlady's house, his expression as cold and unforgiving as the weather. I closed my eyes and shook my head as I heard my meek, stuttered words of apology. It was an image that came into my head every day. On good days George reached out and pulled me into his arms, stroking my hair as he held me tightly. On bleak ones I turned away from his silent frown to trudge back down the pathway to the street, alone.

My God, Marion, anyone would think you were Margaret with all this drama. Go tomorrow morning, catch the ten o'clock train—Betty will stay with Ma!

Resolve made me stronger, and I picked up the thick wooden handles of the laden wheelbarrow with renewed vigor and hefted it forward. My wet wool gloves slipped on the handles, worn smooth with use. I tightened my grasp to steer my load through the gate of the chicken run. The heavy barrow tilted, and I struggled to keep it upright, ramming my leg against the post of the gate.

I hauled in a breath, set my teeth, and shoved my load up the slope to the compost heap outside the barn. The soles of my boots slid in the slick mud. "Come on, will you?" I could have sworn the barrow leaned its weight against me in response. *I should never have loaded it so high.* I braced against the heavy barrow and its reeking pile of straw, throwing my weight forward. For a precarious moment, I felt my feet slip in the mud and then hold. I growled under my breath and pushed again with all my might.

We must have looked like something out of a Charlie Chaplin

film, the wheelbarrow and me. My legs began to slide away, and however frantically my feet tried to keep up in the wet mud, they lost the battle. The joints of my wrists burned as the barrow twisted out of my desperate grasp, and I came down with an almighty thump on my back. For a moment the barrow teetered as if it was trying to decide whether to flip to the right or roll back on top of me. It made up its mind with a cumbersome cartwheel to come crashing down on its side an inch from my head. As a final contemptuous coup de grâce, it rained its stinking load down on me.

"God damn it all!" I shrieked—profanity learned from my employer. "God damn it all to . . . to . . . to buggery!" I lay on my back in freezing slush covered in a blanket of chicken filth.

The weeks of the blizzard, the bleak cold, the long hours of slog just to stay warm, clean, and fed; the exhausting worry of Ma's illness; and the heartache and fear of losing George rushed in on me in a tidal wave of furious anger and outrage. I lifted my head clear of the acrid stench of muck and half-decomposed straw and rolled onto my stomach, tears of rage choked in my throat as I tried to wipe the filth out of my eyes. When I could draw breath, I lifted my head for another round of profanity. "I swear to . . . God!"

"Marion? Is that you?" I turned my blinded eyes toward a voice I had yearned to hear in all the dark days of the storm. It was George. Tears welled and tried to break through the mask of mud.

"Marion, what on earth are you doing here?" Two hands clasped me under my arms and lifted me to my feet. I was so covered in sludge I couldn't see him through the mat of mud-filled hair that hung in a curtain across my eyes.

"Be still, you're covered in . . . in chicken shit." It *was* George's voice. It was George! "Let's get you up to the house." We began to move forward as I was half-dragged, half-carried up the slope toward the kitchen door.

My mother's voice. "Dear heavens above, Marion! What happened? George? What on earth is going on?"

"I'll tell you what happened. Poor bairn went down in the muck, didn't you, Marion?" Betty's strong arm joined George's around my waist.

"I found her outside. Good Lord above, Marion, are you all right?" Careful hands felt my arms and pushed back the layers of wool. "No bones broken, but that's a nasty bruise on your arm." I was put into Ma's chair. My bedraggled hair was pushed back out of my eyes. A warm, wet towel made a track through some of the filth on my face; cornstalks were pulled out of my hair.

"How did it happen?" Betty was trying to untie the laces of my slimy boots. "Oof, but that's a strong smell. Put newspaper down there on the floor, George, that's the way."

I started to shake my head, tears coursing tracks down my grimy face. "The wheelbarrow . . . too heavy . . . I slipped . . ."

"She's exhausted," said Ma. "It has been a long and terrible go of it. Poor girl. It's all right, Marion; George is here now. You just rest while we get you cleaned up and out of these sopping clothes."

I couldn't bear to look at him.

His hands were on the front of my coat as he unbuttoned and pulled it from my shoulders. "I'll take care of her, Mrs. Crawford. You look all in too. Sit down, please—next to the fire. Betty, would you make something hot for her to drink? Cocoa, or tea with sugar, if you have it."

He took off my wet coat, brought more hot water, and washed the dirt from my face and neck.

"Stand up, Marion, lean on George." Betty wrapped me in a warm blanket and somehow peeled off my skirt and stockings from underneath it. All the while Ma told George the tale of how long we had been cut off.

"Even I had a job to get through to them 'til two days ago." Betty put a cup in my hands. "We were all fine out here, until Mackenzie's tractor broke down a fortnight back. Take a wee sippa this, Marion, it's ma ain hot beef broth."

I drank as Ma's voice picked up the tale. "More like a month it felt like, Betty. I lost track of time. The pump froze—we had to melt snow. Marion had to keep bringing in logs . . . from the woodshed . . . a tree came down in the gale, fell like the crack of doom, just missed the cottage . . . we had to rescue the chickens . . . thank the Lord the winter stores lasted. The days were so short, the night seemed to go on forever. We ran out of candles, barely a pint left of lamp oil."

"Marion, let me help you up the stairs so you can put on clean clothes." Strong arms lifted me again.

"I can take her, George, I can take her." Betty was at my side.

"No, I'll manage. It was only a tumble." I was desperate to clean myself in the privacy of our bitterly cold bathroom.

"You look so pale . . . my love." I still couldn't look at him.

"I'll be fine . . . after a bath."

"Marion"—my mother used her commanding voice—"sit down by the fire and let Betty clean up your hair. George, you have to carry up hot water for her bath. Heat it on the Aga."

George filled up our bath kettles and put them on the hob. Then he sat down on the floor next to me. "What are you doing *here*? I thought you had gone to South Africa!"

"She arrived the day before the storm," Ma said for me. "Thank God she didn't go to Africa. I would not have made it through alone."

The next day George and I left my mother in Betty's capable hands with a pantry stocked with food and drove back to Aberdeen. I had instructions from Ma to reassure her sisters all was well and a list of provisions to buy that could not be had in Dunfermline's sorely depleted shops.

When my aunts left to make their traditional visit to do the flowers in their church, George and I climbed the narrow attic stairs to the top of the house and the room that had become mine in 1918 at the end of the war when my father had died.

"My mother and I came to Aberdeen from Gatehead when I was a little girl; I was about nine at the time. My brothers were killed in the war. My father made it through, but he died, months later, from the aftereffects of mustard gas.

"We lived with my aunts until I was fourteen. My mother taught in the local primary school. It's just up the road from here—the one on the corner. My aunts Madge and Mary looked after me. I walked to school, came home to warm shortbread and a glass of milk, and two determined middle-aged women to help me with my home-work. Then Ma got a job teaching in Dunfermline and we moved to Limekiln."

George hesitated in the doorway of my old room, and I watched him take in the rows of schoolbooks lined up against the wall on their shelves, the little blue painted desk and its chair, and the un-adorned cross hanging over the narrow bed with its white coverlet. His eyes widened at the room's scrupulously clean emptiness; it was a shrine to schoolgirl chastity.

"It feels awkward being in here. I feel as if I am trespassing."

"This has always been my room. Please don't feel strange. I'm inviting you!"

We stretched out on my narrow single bed and took an entire afternoon to rediscover each other.

"I think I have been very shortsighted about my life with the Windsors," I said as he drew the coverlet up over our legs and backs, to our chins. "I never meant to be. I just couldn't see a way. I didn't know how to leave them: Lilibet and Margaret."

He stroked my hair and kissed my face. "Beautiful Marion." His fingers lifted my chin for more kisses. "There is no fault—just the habits and duties of adult lives, of the time we found ourselves in. I was quite convinced that when I came home from India and saw you again, you would have found someone else. You can't imagine my joy when your mother told me you were still single. And when you said yes to marrying me, I wanted everything, immediately. I tried to be understanding about a job you obviously enjoy: a place where you are truly needed with two little girls you love. Most of the time I managed it, but I felt such resentment.

"When your mother told me that you had gone to South Africa, I thought you had made a choice to travel rather than come back to Scotland. I wondered if we had made a commitment to each other too late. That you didn't care quite enough to leave the Windsors, and that I was still trying to recapture my youth, to recover it some-how, by marrying you. I can't imagine how you must have felt when you got my prissy letter." He put his hand over his eyes briefly and shook his head.

I tried to smooth away the lines of regret around his mouth with my finger. "We none of us ever have a complete choice; we are never completely free. Fate interrupts our plans—our lives. But I want to be with you, before anything else. You do believe that, don't you? When the family come back next week, I'll leave. I truly will."

He took my hand in his and kissed its palm. "No, don't go back on your word to her, to the queen. God only knows what that poor girl will have to endure before they will let her marry the man she loves. But when you come north in July, let's be married then. You can finish your commitment to them, but there is no need for us to wait; we can be married this summer. Then whenever you come home, it will be to me in our own house in Aberdeen. What do you think? Would that work?"

All is not lost! "I think we should start looking for a place together here in Aberdeen before I leave to go back to London." His arms tightened around me as he planted firm kisses on the crown of my head.

"Do you think your mother would agree to moving here?" He turned on his back, nearly falling off the narrow span of my bed. "I hate to think of her living alone in that cottage; she looks so frail."

"I have no idea if she will agree—I doubt it," I said. "She is an obstinate one is my mother, but"—I kissed his warm mouth and inhaled his sweet breath—"I think we should ask her."

He moved into the middle of my bed, and we were pressed together by an unyielding wall. Our breath quickened and I closed my eyes.

CHAPTER THIRTY

Margaret swept past me at the turn in the great stairs, the wide skirts of her fashionable dress brushing against my legs. "Philip has just driven through the gates." She glanced back at me over her shoulder, trying out her insouciant, careless, woman-of-the-world look. It was evident she had been practicing on someone who appreciated it. "We have only been back a day." She pulled me to the window that looked down on the family entrance to the palace. "Just look at that darling little car. It's an MG—Peter says they go like the wind!"

Peter? Peter who?

I put a restraining hand on her arm, but she shook it off as she continued down the last flight to the hall. "Where are you off to, Margaret?"

Lilibet in a midnight blue dress with a tall collar that stood around her neck appeared at the top of the stairs. She frowned down at her sister. "Thank you for making Philip feel welcome," she said as she pulled on long gloves, "but I think I can manage on my own."

If she was beside herself with the anticipation of seeing Philip again, Lilibet appeared as serene as a summer day in June. Her shining eyes reflected the blue-violet lights of her silk dress, its tightly fitting waist emphasizing its narrowness and the fullness of her bosom. Her mouth was a sensuous, red-lipsticked curve of a smile as she smoothed her gloves and waited at the top of the stairs, her eyes on the door below.

The trip has changed her, I thought. *She has become a self-possessed woman with no doubts at all about her destiny.* Her speech to the world on her twenty-first birthday had been evidence of that.

"You look perfect," I said as I looked up at her and remembered the words that had meant so much to me as my mother, George, and I had listened to her birthday speech broadcast to the world. The twenty-first of April—the day Lilibet had turned twenty-one and the day George had signed a short lease on a tiny little two-room flat in Aberdeen.

I declare before you all that my whole life, whether it be long or short, shall be devoted to your service and the service of our great imperial family to which we all belong.

I had been so moved that I had had to duck my head and clear my throat. Lilibet's bell-like voice transmitted from Cape Town in South Africa was as clear as if she was with us in my mother's cottage in Dunfermline. "Now, that's what I call a commitment." My mother turned to George and me sitting on the sofa, our arms around each other, as she recharged our glasses for a toast. She raised her glass of champagne. "To a long and healthy life to the princess"—she extended her glass to us—"and a happy and speedy marriage to you both."

Margaret brought me back from my mother's cottage to the ornate Victorian panels of the palace staircase. "I can't wait to go to the 400 Club." Her voice was wistful. Her eyes flashed up the stairs in an appeal to her sister. "I'm sure if you asked, they would let me . . ."

Lilibet gave her gloves a final tug and settled her fur stole around her shoulders. "Crawfie, would you do me a favor and take my sister off to your rooms and offer her a glass of something? Lemonade, perhaps, although I am quite sure she will twist your arm for Glen Avon."

We laughed at Margaret's tut of exasperation, the whirl of her full skirt as she turned to walk back up the stairs. I almost expected her to cry out, "It's just not fair!"

"Of course you will come to the 400, but not tonight!" Lilibet's mouth widened to a full smile as Philip came into the hall, his hat held under his left arm, his right smoothing his hair into place.

He looked up in the bright light at us, grouped together on the stair. "Hullo there. Welcome home . . . all three of you," he said, but his eyes were on Lilibet as she continued on down the stairs in a heavy rustle of silk and floated across the hall to him.

He took her hand in his and bowed his head. Then, straightening up, he kissed her on each cheek. "The European way," I heard him say.

There was none of her customary reticence as Lilibet came through my sitting room door the next day.

"Everything is going to be perfect, Crawfie." Her radiant smile flashed her happiness. "Philip asked me to marry him last night!" She perched herself on the arm of my chair. "While we were away, his mother told him to take her tiara to Antrobus and have him break it up for an engagement ring. Isn't that the most wonderful thing you have ever heard? Her tiara—her last piece of good jewelry. The kindness . . . generosity." I looked down at the diamonds on her left hand.

"Oh, Lilibet, it's quite beautiful. I am so happy for you." In that moment I decided my own announcement should wait; nothing must be taken from her on this day.

"But no one knows, only Mummy and Papa."

My eyebrows shot up into my hairline and she laughed.

"No, Crawfie, not exactly ecstatic—especially Mummy, but she had to honor the agreement we made before we left for South Africa. They knew that the only way they could get me onto that ship was to promise that if I felt the same way about Philip when we came back that I might marry him. The first thing I said to them when we docked in Southampton was 'I want your blessing to marry Philip.' They had to agree." She pressed her lips together and gave me a gruff nod, the way her father did, and I laughed.

"Then apart from your parents, let me be the first to congratulate you."

"Thank you, Crawfie." She took my outstretched hand. "You have been so kind to me, so understanding. Now I wonder why we were ever worried that it might not happen!"

I remembered the nights I had lain awake, worried that if my fate was allied to hers, it would be years before I would be free to marry George.

A shaft of sunlight made the ring sparkle on her hand. "Princess Alice picked up the ring from Antrobus Jewelers, just to keep the press off the trail, because we have promised Papa there are to be no announcements—for another month or two."

Aha, then they are still holding out. How cautious they were, how unprepared to let this lovely girl marry her threadbare prince. Did the queen imagine that Porchey Porchester or Hugh Euston would find what it took to sweep Lilibet off her feet at the last moment? I laughed at the idea.

"Where did you go last night, you and Philip?"

"We danced." She got up and twirled across my room. "Danced until three at the 400."

"Did you go alone?" I was curious how these things were managed if the press were eagerly trailing Lilibet and Philip for news.

"Oh no, we can't do that; it would be in all the papers. We made up a party." She reeled off the names of the old set, the ones who had come to Windsor for her mother's cricket-eleven weekends.

How difficult it must have been to be so well-known, so beloved by the people, that the press must pursue their princess and now her fiancé wherever they went. Camera bulbs flashing, questions shouted from the crowd: "When are you going to marry him? Where's Philip?"

"Have you set a date?" I asked.

"No, not yet. We are giving the parents a week to settle to the idea. But I want to be married soon . . . no long engagements." Her mouth was set in an uncompromising line. I supposed when you had publicly promised to dedicate your whole life to the service of your people, little things like wedding dates were yours alone to decide.

I got up from my chair and put my hands on her shoulders. "Well done," I said as she tightened her arms around my waist—a hug, then a quick release; she had never been one for long embraces, not like her little sister. "Well done, Lilibet. You managed it all quite beautifully: grace and dignity, backed up by steely determination, will get you everywhere." We laughed. "I am so proud of you and so happy for both of you."

She stood back from me, her tranquil gaze fixed on my face. "He is wonderful, Crawfie. I am so awfully lucky. There is no one quite like him, you see, certainly not for me."

"All bloody hell to pay, Crawfie." Margaret came through my door for her French history lesson, cigarette holder in her right hand, poised like a dart.

Why is she smoking? What on earth is she thinking?

I waved a disapproving hand at the cigarette and her language. "Good heavens, Margaret, I thought for a moment that I had been transported to a dive in Soho! There is no smoking in here; that is the rule and it hasn't changed." She stopped mid-stride; a mutinous glance, her right shoulder raised in defiance.

"Do your parents know about the smoking?" I pointed to an ashtray on a side table. She shrugged off her parents' fuddy-duddy opinion and walked, ever so slowly, toward the table, took the half-smoked cigarette out of its holder, and tossed it into the ashtray. "It isn't quite out," I said. She ground it out with emphasis before she looked up, her mouth sulky.

"You said something had happened," I said, trying to keep my voice neutral. I crossed my fingers and prayed that the queen had not discovered some new social horror committed by Philip's family or, even worse, that David Bowes-Lyon knew the name of some sophisticated nightclub chanteuse that Philip had met in Singapore during the war.

Margaret's eyes shone with glee—mischievous glee. "Papa has been shouting at Tommy Lascelles and Michael Adeane for the past twenty minutes. He even shouted at Mummy. Tommy is running around like a chicken with its head struck off. And poor old waste-of-space Clement Attlee is on his way over to the palace. And all because a member of the press—which newspaper I do not know, so don't ask—saw Philip's dear old mum walk into Antrobus's jewelers. How did he know she was Philip's mum? Because nuns rarely visit Bond Street jewelers, and while they wait for the package they have come to pick up, they certainly don't light up a fag." Margaret's vulgar use of the term for a cigarette was unpleasant, but not as unpleasant as her news. "Yes, Crawfie, the cat's out, all right, and Papa is hopping mad." She looked up at me, laughter creasing the corners of her eyes. "It's hard to believe, isn't it, that what started as a wonderfully generous act, made possible by the loving sacrifice of Princess Alice of Battenberg's only piece of remaining jewelry, should end in such a catastrophe."

I bit my lip. *Why is she looking so pleased?* Surely this loving little sister was not crowing because, once again, there was a hitch to Lilibet's happiness? *Play it down*, I advised myself. "It is hardly a catastrophe, Margaret, just a hiccup. Of course the king is angry because he expressly asked that no announcement be made—yet. But it is the sort of thing that happens, and he will come around."

"Well, he's absolutely livid, so don't count on it."

Poor man, I thought, unsurprised at the king's anger. Mr. Ainslie had told me that the king's tailors had arrived the day after the Windsors' return to the palace to alter suits that hung off the king's thin shoulders. Even his favorite equerry, Peter Townsend, was not immune to the king's irascible tongue. "I think a lot of your father's concern is because this winter has left the country tottering, Margaret. If Britain was in bad financial shape after the war, we are in dire straits now. Thousands upon thousands of livestock froze to death in the fields this winter. And the resulting floods caused massive damage. It probably means another massive loan from America, and a royal wedding after a long, stressful trip is probably not the best of news for your father."

She shook her head. "Yes, I know all about that." Her shrug at Britain's economic plight betrayed her superficial maturity. "That'll all sort itself out. What Papa is struggling to come to terms with is the fact that Lilibet is going to get married," she said with finality. Her mouth twisted up at the corners—I couldn't call it a smile. "Ring's too big anyway. It has to go back to the jeweler." But there was none of the snap and spark in Margaret's eyes when she was making trouble for the pure hell of it. Her shoulders slumped as she stood by the window looking down into the garden.

"What's troubling you, Margaret?" I put my hand on her shoulder and turned her to me. Her face had lost all its gleeful malice. It was long, and sad with misery. I pulled her down next to me on the window seat.

She shook her head and pressed her lips together. "Nothing."

"It is about Lilibet getting married, isn't it? For the longest time we had to champion her cause, be in her corner, and now all of a sudden it's happening. It's really hard to get used to the idea after all this time, isn't it?"

She nodded, and a tear made its way out of the corner of her tightly shut eyes and flashed down her cheek. I handed over my handkerchief. More tears; a deeply steamy sigh. "What will happen?" she said, her voice thick with distress. "What will happen when she goes away to be with him?"

So, this explained the I-could-care-less attitude, the cigarette, and the cruel remarks about catastrophes. Margaret's big sister, her companion and her protector, had someone else in her life, and Margaret saw herself forsaken and isolated in a palace full of courtiers, advisers, and her doting parents, who had spoiled her and now couldn't cope with her tantrums.

I smoothed her hair back from her damp forehead, and she leaned into me.

"She is always the first," she muttered through her tears. "The first to leave the nursery, the first to fall in love, the first to marry."

I heard the six-year-old Margaret Rose pounding after her sister down the corridors of Royal Lodge: *Wait for me, Lilibet; wait for me!*

What would there be for this princess, who would only be next in line—until Lilibet and Philip had a son? What was the function for those who had no real role to play in the monarchy? Margaret would chair charities and open hospitals—neither of which required the sort of flair and imagination she possessed.

She needs to be mentally challenged or there will be hell to pay. I could see Margaret at Cambridge joining the Footlights Dramatic

Club. Surrounded by a group of energetic extroverts: people of her own age. Away from the empty pomposity of royal life, she would flourish. Without direction and a purpose, she would become the palace tyrant.

"Lilibet won't be going anywhere," I said, knowing that this was not quite true. "There is nowhere for them to live. They will have their own apartments in the palace while Clarence House is refurbished from top to bottom for them. It will take months and months to put that old house to rights; it's almost derelict."

After a moment she pulled back and blew her nose. "I'm not a complete baby," she said furiously.

"No, you are not," I said. "But you and your sister have both been close to each other all your lives, and it is understandable that you will miss her." I saw two little girls playing in the rose garden at Windsor Castle during the war years: training dogs to jump over benches, riding their fat ponies across Windsor park. Sitting by the nursery fire in their nighties as I read to them and then, when the air-raid siren sounded, running downstairs to the bomb shelter in the castle cellar, clutching their favorite dolls. *Don't be scared, Margaret—it is just another cowardly German with a bad aim. Jerry couldn't hit a fly!* Lilibet's voice echoed down through the years.

"I don't care—I don't need her," Margaret said, the tears still streaming.

"You will be busy with your own royal duties. Your own life: dancing the night away at the 400 with all your friends."

Margaret turned an exasperated face to me. "Crawfie." She jogged my arm as if I wasn't paying attention. "I don't want to do any of those silly things; they are not essential. What I want is my own life!" She trumpeted into my hanky. "I want someone there for me too, my own person. Someone who belongs only to me."

But who? I stroked tendrils of damp hair out of her eyes. *The leftovers from the queen's cricket eleven? None of them can possibly ap-*

peal to her. She is too intelligent, for one thing . . . and much too demanding. "You will meet someone wonderful; I know you will—when you least expect to!"

She balled up my handkerchief in her fist. "And if I ever meet someone in this godforsaken dump, it will be no one they want for me, just you wait and see. Mummy hasn't a clue about anything except being queen!"

Was there someone now? I studied her face, trying to see if there were secrets concealed behind this outburst of despair. Margaret's explosions usually revealed what she felt—her expressive face gave everything away—but she was the master of cover-up too, when it mattered. Determined not to be waylaid by the queen and accused of slacking in my duty to my charge, should Margaret suddenly decide to tell us that she was engaged to marry the butler's son, I considered all possibilities. *Every male in the palace, apart from the servants, is over forty! Her tears are simply those of an adolescent girl whose big sister is about to start her life with the man she loves.*

CHAPTER THIRTY-ONE

July 1947
Buckingham Palace, London

I dithered in the doorway of my wardrobe, taking down dresses and then putting them back on the rack. Everything I had chosen to wear for my wedding day looked all wrong. I gazed down at a row of shoes and then up at a line of hats on the top shelf. *Which dress, the silver-blue or the gold?* Margaret came swishing into the room, and I jumped, feeling guilty. The Windsors' governess was planning something close to an elopement.

"Crawfie, I can't believe you are going off to Scotland, not with all this wedding kerfuffle going on." She plumped herself down on my bed and tried on the hats that lay there.

"I like this one, this pretty rolled straw; it's a lovely shape, perfect for you." I turned with my newest hat in my hand, the one I had intended to wear with a silver-blue shantung silk suit.

Margaret shook her head at it. "Horrid, quite horrid. It looks like a helmet."

"But this style is all the rage now. I thought it looked rather elegant."

She shook her head dismissively. "Yes, perhaps on a crabby old spinster . . . it's too severe."

She put on the rolled straw. "What's the occasion?"

My cheeks flamed. I had no intention of telling any of the Windsors that George and I were to be married in five days' time. But I would not lie to Margaret.

"It's for a wedding," I said.

She laid a forefinger against her cheek, her head on one side, and batted her eyelashes as she admired herself in the mirror. "This is the hat for you: airy, summery, and so pretty with your oval face." She got up and transferred the hat to my head. "I would have said almost bridal." She reached into the wardrobe and pulled out a full-skirted dress in royal blue. "Where did you get this? It's dreamy: look, it almost floats. Is it a posh wedding?" I shook my head. "Then this is perfect; all you have to do is take the ivory rose off the hat. And tie a blue silk scarf around the crown. See?"

Her woebegone face of the last week was replaced by the enthusiasm of dressing up. Margaret whisked around my room laying out the dress and shoes on my bed. "May I?" Without waiting for my agreement she picked up some nail scissors and cut a navy blue silk scarf in two. I turned to the looking glass. The hat was pretty; its crown was rounded, the brim dipped softly aslant my face. I have a small head and sometimes hats make it look even smaller. The fine ivory straw filtered light to my face, making me look years younger.

Margaret took off my hat and waved the scissors at it in inquiry. "These dreadful droopy roses have to go." She neatly snipped them off and tied the scarf around the base of the crown in a soft bow at the side. "See? Much better now."

I watched her serious face as she reached up to put my hat back on my head.

"It's quite lovely, Margaret!"

"Yes, I know. Now, hold the dress up against you and kick off those black shoes and put on these." Gray high heels on my feet, indigo blue silk dress, and a pretty hat on my head—I looked bridal, an elegant summer bride.

"You have the perfect figure, Crawfie—you can wear anything. I wish I was as tall and slender as you." Margaret peered into the looking glass with me. "You might want a little padding in the bosom, though. You know, just to give you *something* there." She picked up the remnants of the silk scarf and the scissors. "Come on—you never know who you might meet at a wedding!"

I backed away, laughing. "I love what you have done to the hat. It looks absolutely perfect." I turned back to the pier glass and then glanced over my shoulder to share my pleasure in the outfit with her. But she had gone over to the window. All interest in her creation had evaporated in one of her startling changes of mood. Her brows were down, and so were the corners of her mouth as she glared at a bird who had the gall to perch on a twig outside my window.

"It's all such rubbish, really," she said. "Mummy is making such a fuss over something only she cares about—cake! Thousands of ration coupons are being squandered on a cake! Do you know it's nearly fourteen feet high? Why don't they do what everyone does these days? A cardboard replica with just real cake on the bottom layer? Isn't that the done thing in these days of grueling austerity?"

I didn't say that if this were her wedding cake, twenty towering feet of sugar, butter, eggs, and flour would not be tall enough. She came back to my dressing table and tossed the rose she had discarded there onto the floor. I hadn't the heart to tell her to pick it up, or not to lounge round-shouldered on the stool in front of my mirror. "When I get married, I will choose my own dress, and it won't be made by Norman Hartnell." She propped her chin on folded hands and stared into the mirror. "It will be made by Christian Dior, with a fabulous full skirt so I can sweep down the aisle in splendor."

I sat down next to her on my dressing table stool and met her eyes in the reflection of the mirror. "Norman Hartnell is the court dressmaker. Of course he will design Lilibet's gown. Her dress must be symbolic of our ancient traditions. We are Great Britain, proud and enduring. Not France, broken and capitulating. Anyway, Dior's New Look squanders yards and yards in the skirt. It would be an insult when people can't buy new clothes!"

She sighed as if I had let her down. "But we can use up thousands of coupons on a stupid cake." She got up from the stool. "When are *you* going up to Scotland?" she demanded.

I jumped to my feet, galvanized back into activity. "Tomorrow morning, first thing."

"And when are you coming back? I'm amazed Mummy is letting you go at a time like this."

But I was too busy deciding what to pack for our honeymoon to answer her. In twenty-four hours I would see George again. In another twenty, I would be standing beside him at the altar of our local church. I put on my wedding hat, and laying my forefinger against my cheek, I tilted my head to one side and fluttered my lashes to peals of laughter from Margaret.

July 1947
Loch Goil, Scotland

The half-timbered lodge at Loch Goil stood on the lip of a deep lake. There was an air of genteel dilapidation in its wide, creaking pinewood boards, the peeling paint of heavy sash windows quivering in their frames in the bright summer breeze that blew down the valley from the hills.

An elderly porter with skinny, bent legs greeted us formally in the lobby, ignoring the trail of rice that fell out of George's pocket when he pulled out his wallet. He insisted on carrying our suitcases and, as soon as we had washed our hands and returned to the dining room, seated us at a little round table graced with a red rose in an alcove away from the whispering silence of the other guests twice our age.

"Roast duck tonight, sir. Mrs. Cullum does it with a simple port-wine sauce. Would you care to see the wine list?"

"This old building may have seen better days, but there's nothing wrong with their cook." George lifted his glass of red burgundy: "To my wife. To our life together."

Our honeymoon! I smiled as I remembered my mother's delighted face as we said goodbye to her and half of Dunfermline at the Kincardine hotel. "No, my darling girl, don't you give it a second thought. Off you go—good Lord above, you only have ten days before you have to go back to London. Betty and I are going to put up our feet and enjoy a nice little glass of Glen Avon."

Two hours later we unlocked the door to our bedroom with a heavy iron key that had been forged in the time of the Gaels. The giant brass bed had been turned down and the much-mended velvet curtains drawn against the dark glass. I sat down on the bed's edge and leapt to my feet again. Every coiled spring rang out its welcome. George put his hand in the middle of the mattress and bounced it up and down. A chorus of deeply solemn, rhythmic creaks.

"It makes complete sense that the bed would be geriatric too." George moved the nightstand into a corner and slowly slid the mattress off the bedframe and onto the floor. His face was scarlet when he stood upright. "I'm so sorry, Marion, but I think the mattress has done for me." Giggling like schoolchildren, we undressed and got into bed.

In the morning, I stood in the cool draft from the window and pulled open the curtains. The lake was smooth and still; its polished surface reflected the black and slate blue hills that ringed it around. I watched the morning mist lift up through the tops of the pines and the stars fade as the sun came up in a pale lemon sky, flushing the mirror surface of the loch to a deep rose.

I turned back into the room. The top of George's head was barely visible on the pillow. I crept back to our mattress on freezing feet and searched in vain among the sheets and blankets for my nightgown. Thoroughly chilled, I slid in beside him.

"Dear God, woman, are your feet made of ice?"

"I think you had better warm me up, George; there is a draft coming through the window frames straight from Greenland."

He pulled me toward him and wrapped his arms around me.

At the more civilized hour of eight o'clock, we were awoken by a gentle knock on our door and a throat being cleared loudly in the corridor.

I lifted my head from the pillow. "I'm praying it is someone with tea and hot buttered toast with marmalade." My stomach growled, desperate for food.

George sat up in bed, groped around for pajamas, and had to make do with his dressing gown. His hair stood up in a coxcomb on his head. "It had better be a bit more exciting than toast," he said as he tied the belt around his waist. "I ordered the works: bacon, eggs, black pudding, and all the rest. We have to keep our strength up for all the hikes I have planned." He was awake and alert as he scuffed across the floor in his old felt carpet slippers. "A nice brisk walk along the loch this morning with a picnic, a long afternoon nap, and then it's to work on dinner." He swung open the door, and our waiter trundled in a trolley so laden I thought its wobbling wheels might spin off and bounce across the room.

George poured tea and brought it to me. "Now, what can I give you? There's bacon, sausage, scrambled eggs, mushrooms, and what looks like a nice rich black pudding. Everything? Ah, Marion, I knew you wouldn't disappoint me!"

CHAPTER THIRTY-TWO

August 1947
Buckingham Palace, London

The train pulled out of Stirling station, leaving my husband standing on the platform waving his hat in farewell. I could not bear to pull in my head as I watched the lonely figure recede in a pall of oily gray smoke.

I settled in a corner of the empty carriage. The next three and a half months of my life would be one long round of lists, errands, plans, counterplans, and finally a wedding. But more than all the preoccupation with the width of the wedding dress's skirt, the height of the cake, and the length of the guest list, my greatest concern was for Margaret.

The twitch of anxiety that had run like a misfiring motor became a full-throttled throb of concern when she came into my room the day after I got back to the palace: defiantly smoking a cigarette, determinedly offhand about the exhaustion of wedding details that took up every waking hour, and as fragile as Venetian glass about her role as chief bridesmaid.

"Far too many of us, really." She blew a thin plume of smoke and put her cigarette out in the ashtray. "Lilibet couldn't have chosen a more scatterbrained bunch of girls. But there you are, Crawfie; there is no end to the mindless fanfare." She counted on her fingers. "Princess Alexandra of Kent, she's the best of the lot, and that's saying something; Lady Caroline Montagu-Douglas-Scott, unreliable as they come and bound to do something really daft at the last minute; Lady Mary Cambridge, I mean blah blah blah never stops talking; the Hon. Pamela Mountbatten, who knows absolutely everything, which makes her nothing but tiresome; the Hon. Margaret Elphinstone"—she lifted her nose with her forefinger—"such a rotten little snob; and Diana Bowes-Lyon." She waved her hand dismissively at her cousin, too weary to mention her flaws. "William and Michael as page boys—so you can imagine the chaos." She held up her hand before I could say something to retrieve goodwill. "And the pièce de résistance is that Philip is insisting that that silly ass, David Mountbatten, is his best man, so we can only hope that they are not too hungover after the stag night to find their way to the abbey."

Underneath the throwaway manner and the makeup, I saw the dark smudges under her eyes and the tense fingers that played with her cigarette holder. I had been away for two weeks, and she had lost weight—too much of it.

"What fun we will have!" I was determined that somehow I would help this reluctant bridesmaid find something to enjoy about her sister's wedding. She had worked hard to champion Lilibet's cause, to see her through to marrying Philip; there must be some way she could enjoy the triumph. "Is the dress decided on?"

She nodded. "Dull as ditchwater, even though he insists his inspiration was taken from Botticelli's *Primavera*." A snort of derision, but her restless eyes held a bleak expression.

"Have you seen it?" I asked, and she nodded.

"Well, not exactly seen the actual dress, no one is allowed to, but

I have seen the drawings. No one"—she pointed her empty cigarette holder as if it was a spear she was about to throw—"not even you, Crawfie, will see it before the day. I only saw the drawing because I insisted. Hold on a moment . . . where are you off to?"

Did I tell her now, or should I wait until I had met with the queen?

"I shouldn't be more than a few minutes . . . I have an appointment with Her Majesty."

She got to her feet, brushing down the front of her dress. "Well, don't let me keep you."

"Wait for me here?"

She laughed. "I don't know what she has to say to you, but it's probably about the cake. She is obsessed with it! The icing, the decorations, the emblematic theme. She is the Norman Hartnell of cakes." A dismissive wave of the hand as she threw herself down on my sofa and picked up a magazine.

The queen, surrounded by fabric samples, barely looked up when I came into her sitting room and made my half curtsy.

"Crawfie, thank goodness you are back. Margaret has been impossible. So disobliging and critical. What on earth are we to do with her?" She picked up two almost identical swatches of baby blue silk and held them up to the light.

"She'll settle down soon enough when it's all over, ma'am." I had decided not to talk about Margaret until I had been congratulated on my marriage.

"This one is better for me, don't you think?" She held the two folds of fabric up against her face, one on each side.

"I like the apricot gold," I said, pointing. "Yes, ma'am, that one, to your left. Rich, sumptuous, and the sheen is beautiful. When you stand next to Her Royal Highness, you will be a perfect foil for her gown."

She held the swathe of apricot up to her face and walked to the mirror, standing this way and that to let the rich glow play on her face. "It is very pretty."

"It's regal," I flattered her.

"Indeed." She let her arms relax to her sides, trailing the silk on the floor, and turned toward me. "Margaret . . ." she insisted.

I nodded. "Yes, I have just come from her. I think she would enjoy being part of the planning, and she has such a wonderful eye. May I find her some part to play, other than being a bridesmaid? Perhaps the flowers for the table, for the reception?" The queen shook her head; flowers were her preserve.

"The bridesmaid's bouquets?"

A little moue as the queen considered. "Now, that is a nice idea, Crawfie. Yes, let her do that—they will have to match the wreaths they are wearing in their hair, and they must be very small bouquets, nothing that would get in the way of their being useful. Now, how can I help you?"

She came back to her sofa and pushed the dogs off a heap of silk rectangles.

"You could congratulate me, ma'am," I said, hoping that my voice didn't sound as quivery as my wavering resolve. "Major Buthlay and I were married in Scotland: a small, private ceremony—just the family."

The smile slid from her mouth as if it had been stripped off her face. A dark shadow of silence threatened to engulf us both. I held my breath and waited. "Have you told the girls yet?"

"No, ma'am, I wanted you to be the first to congratulate me."

She graciously recognized my loyalty with a dignified lift of her chin. "Quite right, Crawfie, quite right. Well! What wonderful news!"

"Of course, I will honor our agreement to remain until August of next year: when Margaret turns eighteen. Both of us"—my voice gained strength from the imaginary George, standing behind my chair, his hand resting lightly on my shoulder—"that is, George and I are quite happy to abide by that agreement. The only difference will be . . ."

"That you will return to your husband when you go to Scotland."

"Yes, Your Majesty."

"Mr. . . . Boothby, is it?"

"Major Buthlay, ma'am."

"Yes, of course. A lovely old Scots name." She became thoughtful. "Perhaps he might wish to come and live with you here in London, so that there is no need for you to return to Scotland at all, except to visit your mother."

I saw the years stretching away as I kept Margaret company until she married and had children. Another Alah, but with a husband, living in a poky flat in Kensington Palace. I watched the queen turn my marriage into a benefit—so much easier to cope with a married-off retainer than a lonely old maid going through the change.

She finished thinking through her plan and smiled. I couldn't bear to hear what she had in store for me.

"There is so much for you to think of right now, ma'am. The wedding is less than three months away. There is all the time in the world to make our plans for Margaret and the future."

She tossed the apricot silk aside and picked up a square of ice blue silk, the color of water in early spring. "Con-grat-u-la-tions, Crawfie. I see you have not wasted time in following up on your engagement to Major Buthlay. If you do indeed honor our arrangement, there will be a generous pension for you when you retire." She hesitated, and her smile flashed. "And we will have to see about a little grace-and-favor for you in Kensington Palace." Once the queen embarked on a plan, there was no stopping her.

A flat with a kitchenette? A one-room bedsit? Kensington Palace was full of little hutches for the no longer useful.

She needs me more than I need her! I waited, curious now to see if she would reveal how generous she would be. "Nottingham Cottage is empty and is such a dear little house, perfect for two." I must have looked surprised, because she sat back among the cushions, her smile complacent as she crossed her ankles. She smoothed a square of silk with a pale, plump hand. "Strangely enough, I said to His Majesty just the other day, what a pity that Nottingham Cottage is empty. It is not good for lovely houses of that age to be left vacant. Did you know it was designed by Christopher Wren?"

GOVERNESS PIPS LILIBET AT THE POST were the headlines that greeted me on my breakfast table a week later at Windsor Castle. And if they greeted me, they were certainly shrieking in unison to Her Majesty, who enjoyed all our national newspapers with her morning cup of tea.

"Congratulations, Mrs. Buthlay!" Two footmen bowed their compliments as I came through the terrace door from my morning walk.

"Good morning, Miss Crawford, I mean *Mrs.* Buthlay!" Bobo's tight-lipped smile froze on her sour face as she scuttled down the corridor.

"Congratulations, my dear Mrs. Buthlay." Mr. Ainslie beamed. "What tremendous news. What do they say in Scotland? 'A long and canty life together'?" He closed the gap between us and said in a low voice, "Miss Burford, Mr. Markham, and myself would like to toast to your happiness this evening. Would you be free at seven o'clock for dinner with us?"

And finally: "Blimey, Crawfie. You are a dark horse. Does Mummy know? I would give anything in the world to have seen her face when she picked up her *Daily Mail.*"

"Stop it, Margaret; not everything in life is a joke." Lilibet got up from my sofa. She was holding a bunch of deep red roses, still dewy from the garden. "Congratulations, Crawfie; we are so very happy for you. We got up early to pick all the red ones!" I buried my face in the sweet fragrance. "Mr. Bonner sent his compliments and said their scent will be stronger as they warm up!"

"Mummy does know, doesn't she, that you are married?" asked Margaret.

"Oh yes, of course. I told her as soon as I came back from Scotland. There really is no harm done, except for the cheeky headlines. I wanted to tell you my good news in my own way."

"I expect she's furious, though." Margaret was enjoying the situation too much. "She hates being taken by surprise."

Lilibet sighed. "Margaret, don't—"

"Don't what? It's true. I wouldn't complain if she was pleasant when things don't go her way. She is still picking apart my suggestions for the bridesmaids' flowers."

Lilibet wasn't listening. She was gazing out of the window, lost in her own thoughts, untouched by the tension in her family.

Friction in the Windsor family was well above simmering point. Tea yesterday afternoon had been a torment for everyone.

"What's wrong with a little color!" Margaret's eyes flashed when the queen had vetoed her flowers for the bridesmaids.

"Darling, they are wearing coronets of white orchids and tiny little roses—to go with their dresses." The queen barely glanced up from checking off one of her lists.

"Oh!" Margaret rolled her eyes. "So much easier if you had told me their flowers were decided on before you asked for my help!"

"Where are they all going to stay?" the king snarled at Tommy Lascelles and Peter Townsend. "I don't want carloads of people rolling through the bloody gates, expecting to stay with us!"

A collective exhalation of relief echoed around the drawing room from the courtiers as the queen answered, "Darling, it won't be a problem at all. Our train will shuttle them back and forth from Southampton to London. Peter, find an appropriate hotel, will you? The Dorchester or the Savoy—somewhere large enough to take our guests. They can all stay there, together. A chance to catch up, to spend time. All your uncles, aunts, cousins, and second cousins, Bertie, all together again. They will love it!" She focused her smile on the king and waved her hand as another hitch was smoothed over and made to sound like fun.

My attention came back to the argument between the sisters in my room. "She was not cross at all—and especially not with you, Margaret." Lilibet rushed to defend her mother and mollify Margaret's hurt. "She is having the time of her life." Lilibet clipped a couple of inches off rose stems as I arranged them in two large vases. "I think she's marvelous: she has a solution for every problem. If she wasn't married to Papa, she would make a perfect managing director of a large business consortium! She is so busy and happy. And the last thing in the world she cares about is a silly headline about Crawfie getting married before me. I should imagine most people think it is charming that the woman who looked after us all these years has only just said yes to her longtime sweetheart."

She beamed at Margaret's scowling face. "I love your idea for the bridesmaids: white chrysanthemums and ivy. Just don't mention it again for a while so she can adjust to the notion. Come on." She linked an arm through Margaret's. "Now I must dash—Mr. Hartnell is coming for a fitting!"

"Is he bringing all three hundred and fifty seamstresses?" Margaret asked.

She giggled. "No, just three this time. The rest are all shut up in some warehouse with the windows whited out and trying to sew with gloves on—poor things."

"Where's Philip?"

"With Uncle Dickie; he wants to show Philip our wedding present." And to my questioning eyebrows: "Broadlands—Dickie, or rather Edwina's, country house. No, not giving it to us, Crawfie; it is where we will be spending our honeymoon."

. . .

"The main idea of all this carry-on, of course, is to distract the Great British public from the deprivations of postwar austerity." Margaret was slumped down in my sofa; her agitated foot caught the leg of the coffee table with a clout. "Sorry."

"How are the bridesmaids' flowers?"

"Do you know something, Crawfie? I'd rather do French verbs than talk about flowers—Mummy has taken that part over, and I have no idea what flowers they are going to use—if any at all. At least the cake has shrunk to four meager tiers and stands a pitiful nine feet: Papa put his foot down. And please, Crawfie, don't ask me about the wedding breakfast menu. I am so tired of talking about food. When it's not about food or flowers, it's unpacking hundreds of awfully ugly presents and saying, 'How original.' With four days to go, I am completely sick of weddings. I'm going for a ride in the park with Peter. It's our last day here before we all toil back to the palace to get ready."

She marched off across my room and was out of the door before I could say a thing, leaving me to mull over her lightning changes of mood, which had now turned into what amounted to sour grapes.

Who was she riding with again? Peter? I was aware that Peter Townsend and Margaret had formed a friendship during the South Africa trip, but surely there was no need for him to play chaperone since their return? I had a soft spot for Peter ever since he arranged George's visit to London with such painstaking care, but it did seem rather odd to me that he should still feature so prominently in Margaret's life.

My head was aching from the endless Windsor family arguments, and the queen's pressure on all of us to make the wedding the event of the year. I would go for a nice long walk; that should surely clear my head of Margaret worries.

CHAPTER THIRTY-THREE

November 1947
Buckingham Palace, London

W hen is Major Buthlay coming to London for the wedding, Crawfie?"

"He arrived this morning."

"Staying nearby?" Lilibet did not look up from a thank-you letter she was writing. Our days, even some of our nights, had been taken up with reading lists, amending lists, and then rereading them all over again, and Lilibet dedicated two hours every day to write thank-yous to wedding-gift givers. "Good, because I want to meet him before everything takes off. Do you think he is free for tea tomorrow? Because I have a surprise for you both. At least I hope it's still a surprise, because Margaret was in on it."

I sent a fervent prayer that George wouldn't be stiff and silent when he met my princesses. He had a way of hiding behind his reserve, and it made him come across as just another dull and dour Scotsman.

George arrived punctually for tea with Lilibet, Margaret, and me. When the doors opened and the footman announced, "Major Buthlay, Your Royal Highness," my face flushed, and I could hear my heart thudding thickly in my head.

And there he was, dressed correctly in his best suit. He paused inside the door and bowed from the neck. He looked so composed, so at ease, as if coming to tea at Buckingham Palace was a part of any working day at the bank. But who could possibly be anything but relaxed when they were welcomed by the sweet, smiling face of Lilibet?

We poured tea, and Susan showed how clever she was at finding ham sandwiches inadvertently dropped behind the sofa cushions.

"They are hunting dogs?" George inquired.

"Herding," Margaret said. "They are used for herding—cattle—in Wales. Hard to believe, isn't it, when you look at how short their legs are. But they are very fast, if you don't let them get too fat, and very bossy."

George took in Susan's round, feathery bottom and her determined digging among the cushions, a look of profound perplexity on his face.

"Her Majesty is hoping you will move to London, Major Buthlay, until Marion retires, of course," Lilibet said after we had poured ourselves more tea and moved the plate of sandwiches to the top of the bureau.

George smiled. "You are asking the wrong Buthlay, Your Royal Highness. It is my wife who decides where we are going to live for the next few months."

"We all hope she decides yes to London. I must say, I think Nottingham Cottage would be perfect for you both. Perhaps Crawfie will show it to you while you are here. How long are you staying?"

"Just for the week." His eyes swiveled over to meet mine. "I . . . I would love to see the cottage."

Lilibet had not forgotten George's love of theater. "Lots of good plays on at the West End," she said, pouring more tea. "Be there in a flash from Nottingham Cottage." She lifted wide, innocent eyes and raised her eyebrows at her sly suggestion. "Just thought I'd mention it!"

I was completely beside myself with happiness. Three of the four people I loved most in the world were sitting together talking museums and theater. "Crawfie always took us to the Victoria and Albert, the National Portrait Gallery, and the Natural History Museum when we were girls—it was always so much fun!" Margaret had forgotten all about her cigarette holder. She sat forward in her chair; the tension of wedding preparations had eased—for now.

"When I was a boy," George remembered, "I must have been five or six at the time, we visited the Natural History Museum in our summer vacation. The three of you are too young to remember, but in those days they had a giant grizzly bear standing in the main hall—stuffed, of course. It was a colossal specimen, standing on its hind legs. I came in through the door, clutching my ticket, and there it was. I took one look and fled. Nothing would induce me to come back into the hall. My mother asked a porter if there was another way in, without going through the main hall. So he took us the back way, through the delivery entrance."

Lilibet laughed, and her whole face was transformed into that wonderful glowing smile. I watched George lean forward, entranced.

Yes, she's beautiful, I silently reminded him, *and sweet—didn't I tell you?*

"We can cap that one," said Margaret. "When we were very little—how old, Crawfie, when Papa pretended to be a tiger?"

"Lilibet was about eight, so you must have been four."

Margaret started to laugh. "One bath time, Papa put on a tiger skin with a huge head; its mouth was open in a roar to show its teeth. It completely covered him from head to foot. Anyway, he came into the bathroom on all fours." Lilibet was laughing so much she started to cough. "We screamed so loudly that Mummy came running in . . . she came running with a . . . with a—"

"A tennis racket!" cried Lilibet.

"Oh God, she was a sight. Alah was only just in time to stop her braining Papa with it."

I stopped laughing for a brief second to remember those days, so long ago. The pleasant, happy family life we had all lived together in Royal Lodge, before the duke's brother had climbed into bed with Mrs. Simpson and the Duchess of York had become Queen Consort of England.

As we got up to say goodbye, Lilibet picked up a list that had been sitting on her desk. "The seating plan for the ceremony in the abbey," she explained. "My life is one long schedule or list these days. Look"— she put her forefinger on two seats marked with our names—"I have put you both in Poets' Corner. Do you see? Yes, that's right in the front. You will be able to see everything from there."

"I had no idea how considerate she was," George said over dinner later that night. "I mean, really thoughtful. That would be your influence."

"No, she is naturally that way." Too many weddings, too close together, had had a sentimentalizing effect on my moods, and my eyes filled with tears. "She has always been that way, right from the day I first met her. She was only six years old, and she was so worried about waking me too early that morning after my long journey from Scotland."

"Her sister is a different kettle of fish altogether—very outgoing and utterly charming too."

"Yes, she is the personality in the family. Margaret is more like her mother, and Lilibet has the same quiet desire to do the right thing as her father." I pulled my handkerchief out of my pocket and blew my nose.

He cleared his throat and, reaching his hand, patted mine across the table. "Now, what's all this about Nottingham Cottage? Have you already seen it? Do you like it?" His mouth went down at the corners. "It's not one of those nicely baited traps, is it? We won't find ourselves living there in twenty years as you run over to the palace because Margaret can't cope with her grandchildren?"

"I have seen it and it is pretty. It's in Kensington Palace grounds, but quiet and private."

His face maintained a look of polite interest. "Has your mother definitely decided against the move to Aberdeen?"

I closed my eyes and nodded that she had. Ma had resisted the idea as soon as I had mentioned it. "I can't say that I would move to Aberdeen, Marion. It's . . ." She had wrinkled her nose in disdain. "So gray, so big, and . . ." She hesitated. "Madge and Mary, however much I love them, they are just not my . . . It's all about the church with them . . . so stifling. And I would miss my garden—the peace and quiet."

"I can't leave you alone, stuck out here, Ma. That winter was a killer."

"How many of those do we get?" She held her hands open palm upward, as if I were suggesting that catastrophic weather would be a normal occurrence in the future. "I have my friends around me, my darling girl. They are important to me. Betty and me, we go way back . . . the Mackenzies, the Rosses. Even Dr. Marley. I'm too old to make the move. When you come to Scotland, I know you will come here to be with me for a few days. And I would love to come to you both for the odd weekend in Aberdeen. Let's just see how it goes."

Inspiration had struck me like a bolt of frigid air—the kind we got in Dunfermline when your mother was getting on in years and lived four hundred miles away. "Supposing Betty was to come and live with you, here? You could share your place; it's big enough."

A long, penetrating look from my mother, the kind that did

more than search your face for telltale signs of daughterly concern. "She would drive me up the wall within a week. All that chitchat. But I see what you mean. I am rather cut off . . . and I don't want you worrying." She sat back in her chair and her thoughts turned inward; I might as well have not been in the room. And then in an attempt to reassure me: "Soon enough you'll be shot of them—the Windsors—and then if I know anything, you'll have had enough of Aberdeen. I have no doubt that you and George will settle in Dunfermline when he retires."

I looked across the restaurant table at my husband, trying to interpret whether the stoic expression on his face meant that he would actually enjoy big-city life. I put down my knife and fork and took a sip of wine. "If we were to abandon the idea of living in Scotland, what on earth would you find to do down here in London?" I hoped this was opportunity enough for him to let me know how he really felt.

"Why, all the things we can't do in Aberdeen, of course! And, sorry to be a banker, but if the rent is free—Nottingham Cottage might work for us. I have a good bit put by, and we could sublease the flat to a professor who teaches at Aberdeen College—he used to be in digs with me at Mrs. Patterson's place—I know he would jump at it. I am due to retire at the beginning of April—that's only four months away. A year of living in London might be fun—we would be so close to everything—the West End theaters, little French bistros, and please don't forget the Oval for cricket!"

London with George! In all the years of living in Buckingham Palace, I had often felt as if it could have been in any large city—I so rarely had a chance to explore it. I was still reluctant to push. "I have seen the cottage. It is delightful, full of light, with a well-proportioned and pretty drawing room, and it's in a secluded part of Kensington Palace grounds. It has a walled-in garden. We can go and have a look at it tomorrow morning. And have a think about it."

CHAPTER THIRTY-FOUR

November 20, 1947
Buckingham Palace, London

The people outside the palace gates had gathered there the day before yesterday and now launched into "For He's a Jolly Good Fellow."

I wish to heaven they would all stop chanting for a moment. Wedding nerves. I laughed at myself. The excitement, with its underlying whisper of tension, had stolen down the palace corridors to my remote rooms, dispelling any possibility of serenity or calm.

My fingers trembled as I picked up my hat: a shallow, wide saucer covered with tiny black feathers, like the breast of a raven. It had cost me a month's salary, but it was a dream of simple, understated elegance with my worsted wool suit in a rich garnet red. *Where is the elastic supposed to go?* I tried to remember the woman in the hat shop's instructions as I pulled the thin black elastic to the back so it would fit under my hair. For the second time I fumbled it, and the elastic snapped me on the ear.

The singing and chanting increased in volume; someone must

have either arrived or left the palace. The din had been picking up in enthusiasm and power since yesterday afternoon: it reminded me of the end of the war—the VE Day celebrations.

A knock on the door, and hairpins spilled from my fingers all over my dressing table. "What is it?" I called out. It couldn't be Margaret; she was on the other side of the palace happily bullying a group of bridesmaids.

"Mrs. Buthlay?" A page came in through the door. "Her Royal Highness asks that you . . ."

"Is everything all right?" I rounded on him holding a hatpin the way Margaret held her cigarette holder.

His face assumed an expression of patience, the patience of a saint about to be martyred. He had been around women dressing for a wedding all morning, and if I skewered him, he would not be taken by surprise.

"Yes, Mrs. Buthlay, ma'am. Everything is in order. But . . ." He hesitated.

"Yes?"

"It's Her Royal Highness's wedding bouquet. A footman put it somewhere to keep it cool, and he can't remember where. Would you—"

"Isn't Bobo there?" Why couldn't the superbly efficient commander of the royal robes track down Lilibet's bouquet?

At the mention of her name, his face flushed, and he looked down. *So, Bobo has already ripped every servant on the second floor a new windpipe.* I stowed away my hairpins in the pocket of my suit coat, picked up my hat, and followed him out of the room.

It took ten minutes of fast walking to get to Lilibet's apartments. As we passed the grand staircase and a line of windows, I glanced out at the crowd surging up to the gates at the top of the Mall. A figure in a morning suit shot across my line of vision outside the window. Was that Jock Colville running like a hunted hare? Jock picked up speed as he crossed the diagonal of the courtyard, his top hat in his hand, his handkerchief in the other. I bent down with narrowed eyes, but he was around the corner and gone from view. *Why is Lilibet's private secretary running a marathon in full morning dress on her wedding morning?*

As we paced on down the last one hundred feet of corridor, I racked my brains as to where a footman would have likely stowed flowers to keep them from wilting. "Not in the between-stairs room?" I asked the queen's footman.

"We already looked, all of us, in every service room there is, Mrs. Craw . . . Buthlay." He shook his head at the idiocy of others not in Her Majesty's retinue.

We rounded the corner from the front of the palace to its east side, and the guilty party slunk into view. The poor man looked as if he was praying for a stay of execution.

As we passed the closed doors of the Chinese Room, I felt the familiar draft eddy around my ankles from under its massive doors. I stopped and beckoned to the footman. "You wanted to keep the orchids cool?" I asked. His ears were fiery red, and now his cheeks suffused with embarrassment. I nodded toward the doors.

"Bloomin' hell." He threw back his head, eyes closed in thanks, before throwing open the heavily carved door. In the shadow of a lacquered tallboy, on a little table by the half-open window, shone a cascade of pearl white orchids and myrtle.

"On we go," I said as he emerged with the flowers.

"Crawfie, have you seen Jock?" The queen was standing behind her seated eldest daughter with a mouthful of hairpins—they seemed to be in high demand this morning. "He left quite some time ago to go to St. James's . . . to pick up Lilibet's pearls." I could tell by the queen's expression that her morning was not going well. Lilibet, on the other hand, looked quite serene, as if she was watching all of us from under the shade of a flowering tree in summer.

"Why are Lilibet's pearls at St. James's?" I asked Margaret.

"Part of the wedding present display. Put there by mistake by some nincompoop." Margaret crossed and recrossed her legs. "He has plenty of time to get there and back, Mummy." She was sitting in her petticoats with a dressing gown thrown around her shoulders, as unperturbed as her sister. "Crawfie, the color of your suit is stunning—more garnet than ruby I would have thought."

"I think it would be a good idea if you put on your dress, Margaret." The queen's eyes flew up to the clock. "We'll be leaving in half an hour."

"Forty-five minutes, actually." Margaret lit a cigarette.

"No, *thirty* minutes, and don't smoke in here, please."

"Lilibet is hardly going to catch light, Mummy."

It was time for the governess to intervene.

"I saw Jock Colville a moment ago as I was walking here. He was running toward the privy-purse entrance to the palace." The door opened and Bobo came into the room. In her hand she had the pearls the king had given to his daughter as a wedding present.

"Poor Mr. Colville," she said without a shred of pity as she arranged the pearls around Lilibet's neck and fastened the clasp. "He had to run *all* the way to St. James's and back; the traffic was so thick they couldn't get the car through." Her hand came protectively to rest on Lilibet's shoulder, and with one of her rare smiles, she continued, her voice smooth with complacency. "Of course, none of the policemen guarding the wedding presents would let him anywhere near the display to look for the pearls, let alone allow him to take them. He had to *telephone* to the palace to Sir Alan and be *verified*. He could barely speak when he got back to the palace, he was so out of breath."

"Poor Jock," said the queen, dismissing Jock's sprint to save the day with a wave of a hairpin. "Now, Crawfie, you are the only one outside of the family, and Bobo, who is going to see *the* dress." A beatific smile. "Are you ready, darling?"

Lilibet got up from her dressing table and stood in the middle of the room. Bobo slid the cotton sleeve protecting the dress over the coat hanger to reveal a shimmer of ivory duchesse satin. "Seed pearls and crystals," Bobo whispered, as the dress shot fire into a room silent with awe. She laid the dress in a pool of rich, glistening light on the floor, and as Lilibet stepped into it: "Mr. Hartnell says it's the most beautiful dress he has ever made." Her voice was hushed with reverence: in her mind she was already standing in Westminster Abbey, hanky in her hand, to watch her little lady walk down the aisle. The queen's senior dresser and Bobo lifted the dress up over Lilibet and helped her to slip her arms into the sleeves before they carefully slid the dress up and over her shoulders.

"The embroidery is exquisite." I stepped closer as they fastened the gown at the back. The queen lifted her hand as if we might in some unguarded moment actually touch the creation that transformed Lilibet into an exquisite, ethereal being: a bride.

"Springtime." The queen's voice was almost an ecclesiastical chant. "Star lilies, roses, orange blossoms, and ears of wheat." She turned her daughter around to close the top button at Lilibet's nape. "Such a classic and simple design, but quite stunning in its detail."

Bobo fastened the train to the back of the dress. "Mr. Hartnell said to keep the train in its bag until we get down to the coach. Is it too heavy? Shall we put it on later?"

Lilibet spoke for the first time since I had come into her bedroom. "It is so light"—she swayed her hips—"so incredibly light. I feel as though I don't have anything on at all."

"Better not say that when you get downstairs!" Margaret guided her back to the dressing table as if she might break, and Bobo slid the veil from its silk sack. It floated in the air: a glittering cloud of crystals as they caught in the glow from the lamps in the room.

"A little this way." The queen took one side of the veil. "Is that center?" They settled the silken cloud on Lilibet's head, and it fell around her shoulders. "Look for the tiny buttonholes, Your Majesty, so that we can secure it to the tiara." Bobo's face was severe with concentration. "Perhaps a little more this way?"

Margaret picked up the Morocco red leather case and, with a flourish, opened the lid for her mother.

With significant ceremony, the queen lifted her fringe tiara in a flash and gleam of a thousand facets of brilliance. "My mother-in-law, your grandmother, gave me this on my wedding day, Lilibet." She held the tiara over her daughter's head. "Yes." She smiled as she lowered the headpiece. "It looks perfect with the veil . . ." Her hands froze, and a look of horror, so awful that I thought for a moment she had been taken ill, held her as if she was made of stone. "Oh . . ."

"Ma'am? Are you all right?" I was at her side. She turned her head to me, her face stricken. Her skin leached of all color underneath her makeup.

"Your Majesty?" I reached out my hand to steer her to a chair before she crumpled on the floor where Lilibet's dress had lain.

"Oh . . ." Her mouth was an open circle of fear. I looked at her hands, held apart, each holding one half of the tiara.

"Bloody hell," said Margaret.

I was across the room to the page standing outside the door. "Where is Mr. Colville? Good. Now, listen carefully: tell him that Her Royal Highness's tiara has snapped in two at the base and that he must telephone to Philip Antrobus and arrange for him to come directly to the palace to mend it. Tell him that we have to leave in twenty minutes for the abbey. I think you had better run."

Lilibet was up from her dressing table, her arms around her mother's shoulders. "It will be all right, Mummy. Oh no, please don't . . . it will only take the jeweler a moment to mend it." The plea to her mother not to cry had me pulling my handkerchief from my pocket. I went over to what I believed was a woman made inconsolable by what she had done. But the queen had recovered some of her equilibrium: her face was no longer slack and lifeless, but tight with fury as she stared at the broken tiara in her hands.

Margaret gathered her robe around her: armor to protect her from her mother's anger. "Mummy, it is not the end of the world. It really isn't—there are so many tiaras lying about the palace; if this one can't be fixed, another will do just as well."

The queen turned from eldest daughter to youngest. "If you hadn't waved the case about like that, it would never have broken . . ." She caught her breath and squared her shoulders, tilting her head to one side in a smile of regret. "I particularly wanted Lilibet to wear *this* one."

Margaret raised her eyebrows; her eyes bored into her mother's for a brief moment before she looked down and saw Lilibet's brief frown of admonition. "Well, if you say so, Mummy. I'm going to get dressed, and then I'll wait for Mr. Antrobus at the top of the stairs." She shrugged as she opened the door, as if her mother had put her hand on her shoulder to detain her. I saw her take in a deep breath before she turned back into the room, looking past her mother to her sister. "You look beautiful, Lilibet; your dress is pure heaven. I'll see you downstairs. We'll all be waiting for you there." She came back across the room and kissed her sister. "Perhaps a little bit more lipstick. Would you like me to . . . ?"

Lilibet smiled. "Thank you, Margaret. I can manage, really I can."

I waited outside the door to Lilibet's rooms until the jeweler arrived and pronounced the tiara mendable.

"A little soldering here, and here, Your Majesty, and it will hold

up perfectly. Maybe five or ten minutes' work; that is all." I watched
him follow Jock Colville along the corridor to a room where he
could work, and leant against the wall to allow myself a moment to
recover, opening my mouth as wide as I could to loosen the tension
in my jaw. Margaret had not been exaggerating; any tiara from the
palace vault would have done as well, and no one the wiser.

What had troubled me most about the little scene I had just
witnessed was how important it had been for Lilibet to reassure her
mother that all would be well. The queen's happiness was more
important than that of her daughter on her wedding day. I wished
I was hundreds of miles away in Scotland, walking down the lane
to my mother's cottage, hand in hand with George.

*George! He is waiting for me at the abbey—how much time do I
have?* My watch was lying on my dressing table back in my room; I
must not be late. I couldn't leave my poor husband stranded in the
abbey.

As if I had shouted my thoughts, a page came down the corridor.
"Mrs. Buthlay, we need to get you to Westminster Abbey now. The
crowds are thick out there."

"Yes, of course." I stood in front of a large gold-framed looking
glass and put on my hat. I was so thrown by the tiara catastrophe
that I realized that I had put it on back to front. I pulled it the right
way around and secured the elastic underneath my hair at the back.
My face was pale. I pinched my cheeks and put on some lipstick.
There now, I told myself. *Everything is going to be perfect, absolutely
perfect. Plenty of time to get to the abbey and George.* But I could still
see the queen's unkind glare as she had turned to Margaret with the
broken tiara in her hands.

"Ah, Crawfie. Now, don't you look lovely?" It was the king on
his way down to the hall. At his shoulder was Peter Townsend,
both of them immaculate in their dress uniforms, the king as First
Lord of the Admiralty and his equerry in RAF blue. "Garnet red,

such a perfect color for you, and I really approve of that hat—simple but very chic. You look absolutely ch-ch-charming." I was so thrown by the beauty of Lilibet in her dress and the queen's reaction to the tiara that I said the first thing that came to mind.

"And so do you, sir."

"All well?" He tilted his head back to Lilibet's closed doors.

"She is beautiful, sir. Absolutely beautiful."

"Good, then shall we go down? I expect you should leave for the abbey now; you can go with Wing Commander Townsend."

I could hear Margaret's voice below us as we reached the top of the stairs. "No, no, no, Pam, you're wearing it too far back on your head." The sound of her clear, confident voice righted me in a moment as we walked down to the great hall, to the bevy of bridesmaids standing around Margaret as she gave her last-minute instructions.

CHAPTER THIRTY-FIVE

June 1948
Nottingham Cottage, Kensington Palace, London

Good afternoon, Crawfie. Do you happen to have the kettle on?"

It was Lilibet standing at the front door of our new home at Nottingham Cottage. Her face a little fuller, her arms more rounded: glossy and sleekly pregnant. "Lilibet, you are the most welcome sight in all the world. You look so bonny!" I shepherded her through the door and into my drawing room.

"Robustly bonny." She put a hand lightly on her belly. "I have gained pounds and pounds."

She stood in the middle of my newly decorated drawing room: pale gray-blue walls and white paneling. She took my hand in hers. "Crawfie, I heard about your mother. I am so very sorry; it must have been awfully hard for you. I expect it still is." Her natural unemphatic sympathy brought tears to eyes that I thought had cried their last weeks ago.

I nodded and tried to say thank you, but the aching void that filled my chest threatened to overcome me. I swallowed and pointed toward the little kitchen. "I'll make us some tea."

She followed me into the kitchen and smiled as I took down my mother's old tin tea caddy. "Yes, a good strong Scots brew. Nothing like a cup of Brodies." She sat down at the kitchen table. "You have done wonders with the place, though, Crawfie. It all looks so homely, so fresh and pretty!" She took in the blue gingham curtains at the kitchen window that I had made myself, the white cabinets, painted by George.

"There are lots of things that your grandmother gave me. The watercolors in the drawing room are a gift from her, and she was so helpful about finding affordable fabric for curtains and covers." I covered a tray with cutwork linen and arranged Lilibet's wedding present of Royal Worcester china to me. Then we carried everything through to the drawing room, Lilibet with the teapot and I with the tray.

She crossed the room and examined the watercolors formally organized on the wall on either side of the fireplace. "Granny's presents are always followed up with lots of advice." She smiled. "Did she send someone over to hang them for you? And then come over herself afterward to make sure it had all been done as she asked?"

I nodded, my shoulders shaking with laughter. "Yes, and then she took stock of our meager furniture and drew up several lists of places to go to furnish the house." Most of it had been completely out of our budget. But the dowager queen had helped solve some of our problems: the curtains and chair covers had been affordable only because the old queen had written to a fabric store on my behalf.

Lilibet sat down and eased off her shoes.

"Swollen feet?" I asked her.

She shook her head. "No, not really; it is just nice to take them off. Honestly, I feel no different at all. He must be a very good baby; he has been no bother so far."

"He?"

"Yes, I am quite sure it is a boy—probably because he is such a lazy thing." She sipped her tea. "When did your mother become ill, Crawfie?"

The quick catch of grief at my throat, hastily swallowed down. "I think she had been ill for quite some time. She never really recovered after that terrible winter, and she certainly didn't tell anyone how serious her illness was. She had a way of dismissing things that irritated her, or which held her up, or simply got in the way." I had still not recovered from the shock I had felt when I had opened Betty's letter two weeks after I had left Dunfermline for London. "It was her friend Betty who wrote to me and told me that I must come home. She had found her, you see, that morning, when she walked over to give her some bread she had baked. Ma had fallen in the night, and . . . had been lying there on the kitchen floor. I was on the next train home." Lilibet's eyes were fixed on my face as she nodded me on. "I was shattered when I saw how thin and frail she had become in just a fortnight. It was pretty much downhill from there." I drew in a breath so I could relate the last with a steady voice. "She was in no pain when she died. The fall and lying on the stone floor had . . . brought on another bout of pneumonia. She had no strength left to fight the cancer she had just been diagnosed with."

I didn't say how unbearably lonely I had felt when I had returned to my mother's empty cottage. Even with the arrival of Aunts Mary and Madge to help me with her things, I had felt desolate, my hands and feet cold, my heart so heavy with loss it was impossible to talk to them. When her house was packed up and Mr. Mackenzie had driven my aunts back to Aberdeen with some of my mother's things, I had offered Betty the chickens.

"All of them, Marion?"

"I can't imagine who else would look after them better than yourself, Betty."

"As a gift?"

"Yes, there is still corn in the barn."

"I'll leave them here and come over and feed them every day. I can check on the cottage, make sure everything is all right."

We had stood together at the top of the rise, and I had remembered pushing up the laden wheelbarrow on the day of the winter thaw. Where George had found me.

The chickens were looking for worms in the vegetable garden. "Mr. Ross says he will come over once a week and take care of the garden. He might even keep the vegetable patch going," I said, reluctant to return to the cottage, to its emptiness.

The rattle of a silver spoon in a saucer brought me back to my drawing room. Lilibet poured us more tea, handing me my cup. Her round blue eyes fastened on my face. I nodded my thanks, reached for my handkerchief, and blew my nose.

"Dr. Marley said that pneumonia is sometimes called the old people's friend. Her ending was peaceful."

"I'm so very sorry," she said as she reached out and patted my hand. "I know how close you both were. How proud she was of you. I am so glad that you have George—he is such an understanding man."

I nodded. "Yes, he is very kind. He got on very well with my ma—she loved him as much as he loved her. Now, enough of all this sadness." I stuffed my handkerchief back into my pocket. "It is wonderful to see you looking so well, Lilibet. When is the baby due?"

She shrugged and shook her head. "When he decides to come, I suppose. The doctors say first week in November. Granny is in heaven; she keeps telephoning with advice and suggestions of what I must eat. Anyway, everything is ready for him: the nursery has been painted yellow. I think it's the same yellow Mummy chose for my arrival—and now she is busy interviewing nannies." *Why aren't you interviewing the candidates?* I wanted to ask her. *It's your baby this nanny will be looking after.*

"Are you . . ." I paused. "Are you nervous about, you know . . . the birth?"

"Oh no, not a bit. After all, it is what we are made for, isn't it?"

I didn't say that it wasn't what I was made for. The doctor had confirmed that George and I would not have children. "Maybe not such a bad thing, after all, Marion," George had said when I had recovered from the news, his gentle face full of encouragement for the happiness of our lives. "What matters to me is that we are both together. I've waited so long to be with you."

Lilibet stretched her legs out in front of her with her hands on the gentle rise of her belly. "It's so quiet here, Crawfie; you would never think you were in the heart of London. It must be the wall around your garden. Are you pleased with this house, now you have everything straight?"

Will it ever be straight? I wondered. The cottage was a charming little place: seasoned red brick with its rose arbor around the door. But I didn't say it was all about romance rather than practicality. George and I had papered our bedroom walls, retiled the kitchen floor, and made papier-mâché filling for some of the larger gaps in the window frames, in an attempt to lessen some of the more penetrating drafts.

"Yes, we have settled in—it is such a pretty little house. And how is the work on Clarence House progressing?"

A long sigh. Lilibet closed her eyes. "When Philip is not at the

Admiralty, he is very busy supervising what has really become a complete rebuild. If this little cottage was rather scruffy when you got it, I am amazed that Clarence House was not actually condemned. It was a mess; actually, half of it still is. Would you like to come over with me one afternoon? You can see all Philip's innovations for yourself. I have never known anyone who loves gadgets and domestic inventions as much as he does!"

Her eyes shone with the pride. "I can't tell you what a relief it is that Philip loves to do things like renovate, improve, and generally take charge." And then, mindful always of others: "Has George settled . . . I mean really settled to life in London?"

"Yes, I think he has. To be honest I was a bit worried about him at first. He has always been such a busy man, but as you can see"—I waved a hand toward the windows into our back garden—"his vegetable patch is extraordinarily productive; he spends a lot of time questioning the palace gardeners on what varieties of potatoes to plant. Mr. Bolton's vegetable-and-fruit garden was the model for this one. Thank goodness my mother taught me to cook—though I am not as good a cook as she was . . . but practice is all I need. When I have the time."

Her steady gaze was neither intrusive nor demanded an answer, but it was keenly focused on my face. Her voice light, almost offhand, she asked, "How is Margaret doing?"

I paused to consider because I am never quite sure. "She is a delight: a pleasure to have in class!" We laughed.

"Yes, that's what you always used to tell Mummy. I hardly ever see Margaret these days; she is such a social butterfly. Mummy says . . ." A long pause. Lilibet lifted her chin and shrugged her shoulders. "Is she really out every night of the week? How can she stay out until all hours and then be ready to study the next morning?"

"My concern has never been Margaret's ability, or her concentration and commitment to her studies. But she is very distracted with her social life." I said no more because to do so would be disloyal. The last thing in the world Margaret needed was to be judged by her essentially obedient sister.

Lilibet picked up her handbag. "Mummy says that you have been a lifeline to Margaret ever since I married Philip. She says she couldn't imagine what life would be like without you there to steady her."

I had difficulty concealing the anxiety that this casual Lilibet remark caused. I knew the queen was an ostrich where her youngest daughter was concerned. She certainly knew that Margaret was out every night with her group of friends but either was too intimidated to correct her nearly adult daughter or simply did not have the inclination to, which was why I was still here. Margaret might have come across as a princess made of steel, but sometimes she looked so wan and apathetic the morning after a night of partying, I worried about her health.

I bit my tongue: my retirement was weeks away; it was time to concentrate on my life with George and not be pulled into what he called "Margaret shenanigans."

"What on earth will you do, Crawfie?" Lilibet asked as I opened the front door to the sight of my husband propping up his bicycle against the gatepost and pulling off his cycling clips. "When you retire?"

I was too busy thinking about the play that we had tickets to see in the West End to concern myself with a serious answer. "What do people do when they retire, I wonder?" I said as my husband came up the garden path. "Perhaps I shall become the next Agatha Christie!"

PART THREE

1949–1977

CHAPTER THIRTY-SIX

April 1949
Nottingham Cottage, Kensington Palace, London

My retirement had almost become complete, except for the occasional call for help from the palace when Margaret threatened to cause havoc or came knocking at the cottage door to wail in exasperation about her mother's demands and contradictions, or her own boredom.

When she had time, Lilibet would bring her beautiful baby boy over for a visit, and I would make tea, and we would play with Charles.

"Do you miss her?" George would ask. "Miss sharing this part of her life?"

"But I do share it, as much as I want to. And anyway, I knew she would be busy. She barely has time to spend with her first baby." And truthfully I didn't. I was too happy to have my own life, my life with George.

·   ·   ·

"Another letter from the Americans." George made two piles: the bills made a taller one than letters from our friends in Dunfermline. "Ah yes, and one from Her Majesty the Queen—I expect Princess Margaret has been up to her usual naughtiness again. Please remember that you have retired!" He handed them both to me.

I waved the one with American stamps on it. "This is from Beatrice Gould. The journalist? Surely you remember? Beatrice and Bruce Gould are editors for the American women's magazine *Ladies' Home Journal*. I had no idea how popular it is, apparently rather like the *Woman's Own* here in England."

His gaze across the breakfast dishes sharpened. "I thought you said no to them."

I picked up my knife and spread marmalade on my toast. *So, he does remember.* I shook my head as I ate. "I didn't respond when the first letter came last month—I threw it in the kitchen boiler. Then I thought I should talk to the queen about it . . . so I talked it over with Lady Airlie a couple of days ago, and on her advice, I wrote to the queen . . ." I brushed away crumbs from my lips and chin. "Lady Airlie told me that the Goulds have been very persistent. They contacted the Foreign Office and pointed out that a series of informative articles about the princesses when they were little girls would go a long way to enhance relations between America and Britain. The American public are fascinated by our royal family."

He nodded and picked up his *Daily Telegraph*.

"It has been done before, you know, when the girls were very young and the queen was the Duchess of York. She and Lady Airlie produced two illustrated books about Lilibet and Margaret Rose. They sold like mad. When I wrote to the queen, I told her that the Goulds had been in touch with me about writing a series of articles about the princesses' education. And here is her reply." I picked up the unmistakable envelope, slit it open with a paper knife, and pulled out two pages of heavy bond writing paper. It had been months since I had felt the embossed crest at the top of the page.

"Aren't you going to open the American one? I am quite sure their letter will be much more interesting."

"It's just going to ask me again for an appointment to talk about my job as governess. Their magazine's slogan is: 'Never underestimate the power of a woman,' which is presumably why this Mrs. Gould thinks that by writing to me every month, she will persuade me to talk to her about the princesses. I wanted to hear from the queen before I respond to her."

I looked up to see what sort of expression his face was wearing. It was neutral, but I saw his lips tighten just a little. I had never been quite sure how George felt about Her Majesty. He outwardly liked and respected Lilibet, and I thought he quite liked Philip's sardonic humor, especially when he came home one afternoon to find Philip tinkering around with our failing boiler. But he kept pretty mum about the queen. I smoothed the pages of Her Majesty's letter, fully aware that George was watching me over the top of his newspaper.

I scanned the first few lines. "Well, she clearly is not happy that the Goulds have contacted me. This is what she says: 'I do feel most definitely that you should not write and sign articles about the children, as people in positions of confidence must be utterly oyster.'"

"'Oyster,' what does that mean?" His eyebrows lifted at one of the queen's favorite expressions.

"It means tight-lipped, like an oyster, of course."

"As we would say in the army: keep your trap shut. Does she say anything else other than a very straightforward no?"

I was already scanning ahead, frowning at the blunt advice offered in the queen's looping schoolgirl handwriting.

"Yes, she does. She says this: 'You would lose all your friends because such a thing has never been done or even contemplated amongst the people who serve us so . . . loyally.'"

George's hand came down, palm flat, to slap the top of the table. "Why would she threaten you like that? 'You would lose all your friends'! How would she know what your friends would do?"

I put the letter down in my lap. "I can't read this to you if you are going to burst out every two minutes because you don't like the way she puts things." I could feel tears of humiliation building behind my eyelids. *No divided loyalties!* I reminded myself. "Shall I continue?"

He closed his eyes tight shut for a brief moment. "I'm sorry, Marion; I'll be a mussel, or whatever it is. Please continue."

I read for a second or two. "The next bit is confusing, so please be patient. I think the Goulds might have contacted someone else through the Foreign Office. I know they are desperate to print this article. Here is what she says: 'Mr. Morrah—'"

"Who is he when he's at home?"

"Dermot Morrah is someone she knows; he is an expert on heraldry and used to help the king with his speeches. I think he writes for the *Times*. He is someone she knows she can trust."

"And she can't trust you? Why can't she trust you? She trusted you with her children all through the war. She trusted you for sixteen years, for God's sake."

But does she? Does she really trust me—after I championed Lilibet to stick to her guns and marry the man she loved? I looked across the breakfast table. George was more than frowning now. He was a thundercloud. If I had wondered before how he felt about the queen, now I was quite sure of his feelings for her.

I folded the letter and put it back in the envelope.

"Was that it? Was that all she said? Be an oyster and don't lose your friends by doing something I don't want you to do?"

"No, I just can't read it to you when you get so cross at every little thing."

"I won't say a word until you ask for my opinion."

"Promise?"

"Promise."

I pulled out the letter. "All right, then. Please just listen, George, and then we can discuss: 'Mr. Morrah, who I saw the other day, seemed to think that you could help him with his articles and get paid from America. This would be quite all right as long as your name did not come into it.'" I cleared my throat, because what she had written next was not only condescending; it was a clear snub.

"'If you want a job, I feel sure that you could do some teaching, which after all is your forte, and I would be so glad to help in any way I can.'"

I couldn't look at him. I felt almost ashamed, as if the only thing I cared about was to make a few extra pounds out of my job as governess to her children.

"May I speak?" I looked up at the face across the table. He put out his hand to take mine and then got up and came around to my chair. He pulled me to my feet and held me in his arms.

"I don't know why she would say that to me," I said. "And she is so confusing. On the one hand she says no, I must not work with the Goulds. And then on the other that it's all right for me to help Mr. Morrah write articles for them about the princesses."

George picked up the letter and read aloud: "'Having been with us in our family life so long, you must be prepared to be attacked by journalists to give away private and confidential things, and I know that your good sense and loyal affection will guide you well. I do feel most strongly that you must resist the allure of American money and persistent editors. Just say No No No to offers of dollars for articles about something as private and as precious as our family.'" He finished reading and then said under his breath something that sounded like "pie-face."

"What do *you* think?" I asked. "I could collaborate with Mr. Morrah so he could write the articles for the *Ladies' Home Journal,* because he doesn't know a thing about the girls, and he would either make them sound like Goody-Goody-Two-shoes, or it would come off as sickly sweet."

"What does it matter? It is clear that the queen does not want you speaking directly to anyone. But a man who has never met them but knows about heraldry can write about her daughters. Isn't that the difference she is pointing out?"

The sting of the queen's condescending advice and veiled threats was receding to be replaced by annoyance. The tips of my ears simmered with hurt indignation.

"That is the only choice she is extending to you, apparently," George said into the top of my head. "Come on, sit down. Let's take it step by step." He threw the queen's letter down among the breakfast crumbs on the table.

We sat down on the sofa side by side. "Tell me what *you* would like to do," he said.

I took his hand. "I'm not really interested in writing articles at all, but I would like our money worries to go away. I know this house is free, but it is expensive to heat, and I thought my pension would be larger." I paused as I remembered the shock I had felt when the Lord Chamberlain sent me my retirement letter granting me a grace-and-favor cottage in Kensington Palace gratis for life, but an annual pension of three hundred pounds per annum had been a blow—it was half a salary that had never been large. Even the letters *CVO*—Commander of the Royal Victorian Order—an honor bestowed on those of us with many years of royal service, had been a wallop to my pride. The queen had clearly hinted at the title of Dame Commander when I agreed to continue on for another few months because Margaret's nerves were so shattered by her sister's marriage. I decided not to mention either of these severe disappointments.

"I know you sit up late at night and worry about how we can

stretch things because London is so expensive. And now with the bills for a new boiler . . . I thought perhaps I could make a little bit of money . . . Perhaps I should go with the queen's suggestion that I help Mr. Morrah."

He said nothing as he stroked the back of my hand with his thumb. His brow puckered. "I feel like a fool for making such poor investments with my pension."

"Everyone is worried about their investments. The lack of jobs, the fuel crisis, and the financial mess we are in after the war. Then that terrible winter created so many more problems, so many more shortages. Everyone is struggling . . . and everything has become so terribly expensive. You mustn't blame yourself . . ."

He turned to me, his eyes searching my face. "I honestly think that we would be better off living in Dunfermline in your ma's old cottage. It would still be cheaper than living in London. It costs us a fortune to have the maid come over and clean . . . and no one told us that it was an obligatory service. I am quite sure Betty would be pleased to make a few bob helping you in the cottage. And I could go back to work for Drummonds. I know they would have me back a few days a week. We have thought it about, but we have been too busy to really consider it."

I had been too busy with the royal family before, and now with my retirement, we were too short of money to really enjoy London. *He misses Scotland*, I realized. "Since Ma died we haven't been north once. I had no idea the train fares were so high. I traveled for years on palace passes—it never cost me a penny. Perhaps you are right. London life is expensive—and we used to dream of going to the theater all through the season!"

I picked up the envelope with the American stamp. The letter's brevity was businesslike but very clear—unlike Her Majesty's lecture on my comportment and her graceless suggestion that I assist Mr. Morrah for pin money.

"I'm going to ask Mrs. Gould how much she would pay me," I heard myself say.

"She's in London?"

"Yes, she is arriving tomorrow and is staying at the Dorchester. She wants to settle things, either with Morrah or me. And she sounds like she is more enthusiastic about me. She says she wants authenticity." I handed over the typed page of Mrs. Gould's letter. "Read it."

When he was finished, he sat back and pulled me against him so that my head rested on his shoulder. "Before you do that, let's do the arithmetic. I don't want you doing something that makes you feel disloyal to the family. Let's consider returning to Scotland. We can rent a little place in Aberdeen and keep Ma's cottage for weekends or selling it. Either way I think the move back would offer a more affordable way of life."

We cleared away breakfast and sat down with the *Aberdeen Press* and read advertisements for house rentals. With the money we would make from the sale of my mother's cottage, our investments, and my pension, we could just about manage the rent in a decent neighborhood and keep ourselves if we were careful. It was a dismal couple of hours. It would be cheaper to live in the cottage in Dunfermline, we decided.

"At least we will not be worried about paying rent," I said. "Would it be too expensive to install electricity in the cottage?"

"I have absolutely no idea. But we can find out. Come on, the one thing we can afford in this city is fish and chips at the Lyons Corner House at Marble Arch. Put on your hat and coat, and let's get some fresh air." As I buttoned up my coat and wound a scarf around my neck, I caught sight of Mrs. Gould's letter on the sideboard and slid it into the pocket of my skirt.

CHAPTER THIRTY-SEVEN

May 10, 1949
Dorchester Hotel, Mayfair, London

Beatrice Gould was the sort of woman who dressed for business. If she hadn't been wearing three-inch heels, I would have towered over her in her perfectly cut charcoal gray suit and white silk blouse. Her hair was cut short in the latest fashion, a cap of blond curls. A broad lipsticked smile and two deep-set watchful eyes greeted me as I walked into her suite at the Dorchester and shook her extended hand. Her long manicured fingers felt like bird claws wrapped around mine.

"Glad you could make it, Mrs. Buthlay. Much better to meet here on neutral ground than at your house."

Mrs. Gould had been persistent in asking for an invitation to Nottingham Cottage: "I want to soak up the atmosphere," she had said on the telephone, "to get the feel of regal ground." I had been deft in dissuading her: George's vegetable patch would not have given her the royal frisson she craved, and the thought of her bumping into someone on the grounds terrified me.

I felt like a traitor as she ushered me into the luxury of her suite. I wanted to blurt that this was a mistake, that I had changed my mind. She closed the door and gestured to a chair by the window. "I can understand your concern with confidentiality, Mrs. Buthlay. We won't be disturbed here. All the time in the world to have a woman-to-woman chat." She smiled; she wasn't quite so formidable when she smiled. Her voice had sounded younger on the telephone, but even with her makeup and the unnatural color of her hair, it was clear to see that she was in her late forties. "How about a cup of coffee?" She didn't wait for an answer but lifted a pot from the tray and poured. The warm air was filled with the fragrance of the real thing. "Cream and sugar?"

She handed me a cup. I inhaled. Nothing postwar about this heavenly scent. I took a long luxurious sip. *Oh God, I'm being seduced by a cup of coffee.* I put down my cup and folded my hands in my lap: ready for business, aware of the assessing gaze that had fastened on me since I had walked into Mrs. Gould's opulent suite of rooms.

"I'll come straight to the point, Mrs. Buthlay. We want *you* to be our writer for these articles: you know everything about the princesses—what was it, sixteen years as their governess?" She waved a thin hand in the air, its nails lacquered a bright red. "You have so much to share with us all. You were part of the family, a part of their lives. Why, if you were any older, you might have been their mother—of course we want you to write these articles! They would be charming, loving—a delightful experience for everyone."

Her confidence that I was their first choice far from reassured me; it swamped me with misgivings. *I shouldn't be doing this; I should be sitting at home waiting for Mr. Morrah to write me a polite letter inviting me to join him as a consultant.* I swallowed and made myself ask the questions I had written down in list form yesterday afternoon. "May I ask . . . I mean, it would be helpful to know what you imagine the princesses' childhood was like."

An understanding nod. "I believe that most people think that the princesses were probably spoiled, waited on hand and foot, young girls with no sense at all of the reality we all have to live with." She lifted her hands in a helpless gesture. "You see, no one in America can imagine what it would be like to be born to rule as part of an ancient monarchy. That's why *you* are vital to this endeavor. Because"—she paused to light a cigarette—"because your story would feel authentic and would put paid to all these fairy-tale images."

I hadn't expected this down-to-earth clarity. I had been waiting for fairy-tale princesses wearing party dresses and eating breakfast off gold plates. But I needed her to be clear where I stood, that if I were to do this, I would not be pandering to a stock perception of two little oddities who were incapable of being children, or who weren't people with emotions who could be hurt by these articles. "Mrs. Gould, may I be clear?"

She waved her cigarette at me to continue.

"First of all, royalty does not live in the real world. They can't; it would be impossible." I thought of Queen Juliana of the Netherlands riding around Amsterdam on her bicycle. "At least not British royalty. And the princesses were very far from spoiled. They were, and still are, kindly, sincere, and considerate people. They were brought up to say their prayers every night, to tidy up after themselves, and to be polite and well-mannered—especially to servants. They played imaginary games for hours—just like other children—hide-and-seek was one of our favorite games. They did not have cupboards full of toys and Victoria sponge cake for tea every day."

As I talked, I saw a brief glimpse of them in my mind's eye: Margaret ate her toast with butter on her chin; Lilibet, careful, one eye on Alah, worried that she might drop crumbs in her lap. "They were brought up by a strict nanny who never overindulged them. This would be the story I would tell." She was nodding intently. I almost expected her to pick up a notepad and pencil.

"And during the war?"

"We certainly had more than our share of air raids at Windsor, of doing without—just like all English children. They didn't see their parents much in those years—hardly at all in fact. There was no glamour, no special privileges." In some way I wanted to prepare her for how unspectacular royal life was. "We lived at Windsor Castle for the duration. I can promise you it was not as luxurious as this." I looked around the claustrophobically heated room, the fashionable furniture, and the thick pile of the carpet that her expensively shod feet rested on. "The castle was practically empty: everything of value had been sent to be stored in Wales, and the building is ancient—underheated and gloomy. Living at either Windsor Castle or Buckingham Palace, even today, is very far from what people imagine." I briefly saw the queen's lavish teatime cakes and sandwiches and crossed my fingers at Her Majesty's sumptuous way of tea. "The Royal House of Windsor are extraordinarily thrifty. I can't imagine describing the children's life otherwise."

She threw one slender, silk-clad leg over the other and leaned forward, her forefinger raised in acknowledgment. "That is exactly what we want, Mrs. Buthlay. Your portrayal of two little girls whose father became king unexpectedly, and how they lived through the war years. What it was like to educate the royal children from *your* perspective," she rushed in to reassure me. "Of course, one of my journalists will help you."

"Thank you, but I don't need help."

"She will simply assist you to write of your job, being governess to the princesses, into story form. Nothing whatsoever will appear that you feel is inaccurate or overblown. It will be your voice the reader will hear, telling the princesses' story. The journalist would be part of your contract with us."

A contract? I hadn't thought of a contract. I wished that George had come with me; he would have been in his element. I would need his help in negotiating anything with this formidable woman.

"My husband, Major Buthlay, will sort that out with you," I said, feeling daring, as I took one step closer to yes. "But one thing must be understood from the start. My name, and that I was royal governess, must not appear anywhere in this series of articles. Otherwise, I will write to Mr. Morrah and offer him my services as consultant to him."

"You won't make any money if you work on this through him." She blew cigarette smoke at the idea and picked up her coffee cup and grimaced as she took a sip.

I realized with colossal embarrassment that I had completely neglected this important element of our discussion. Money was certainly to the forefront of Mrs. Gould's agenda. She was still sitting forward in her chair, her cigarette poised. Her thin, dark, penciled-in eyebrows arched over watchful eyes; her lipsticked mouth gathered in a pout, ready to inhale her next lungful of smoke. Her avid enthusiasm for my writing the story did not match those cold, hard eyes—I saw Mrs. Wallis Simpson, bending over to demand kisses from Lilibet when she was a shy ten-year-old.

"How much are you offering?" I asked, astonished at my temerity. When was the last time I had negotiated a salary? Never.

She leaned back in her chair and tapped ash from her cigarette, her reply swift and sure as she quoted numbers already discussed and decided upon with Mr. Gould.

"Thirty when you sign the contract. Another thirty when you have completed the full series with the help of our journalist. And thirty at the beginning of the release." Her face was without expression; the hand that held the cigarette poised flopped out to the side as she waited.

"Thirty?"

"Thirty *thousand* pounds sterling. Our accountants can organize it so that you won't pay any income tax. What's the tax rate here? Something astonishing if you earn over twenty thousand pounds—ninety percent?" She laughed at the hardship that was Britain's burden since the war.

I was too stricken to respond as I grappled, overwhelmed, with the enormous figures she had thrown at me. Terrified that I had looked like a witless pea brain and she would decide to go with Morrah, I struggled to form at least one intelligent question.

"This is for the *Ladies' Home Journal* in America?" My voice, tentative and unsure to my ears, must have sounded as if I was questioning other sources of income, because she laughed.

"If we sell to other magazines—here in England, for example, or Australia, Canada . . . New Zealand, and South Africa—you will receive an additional five thousand pounds for each magazine. I would suggest that you write a book at the same time as you are helping us with the articles. It could be released just after our series. There are plenty of publishers in the States who would jump at the chance to buy it. I don't think you would regret it, Mrs. Buthlay. Either working with us directly or in following things up with a book of your own."

She allowed me to mull this over. We could continue to live here in London and keep my mother's cottage for summers in Scotland. Or we could leave London and buy a house near Aberdeen, a warm, modern house with views over the Forth—and still keep my mother's cottage. And in the winter we could come down to London and stay in a pleasant hotel and enjoy the theater.

I wanted to be gone from this stiflingly hot room and the hard-faced, brittle creature in front of me. I wanted to find George so we could put on our old shoes and go for a long walk in the cool spring air so I could think this through. I gathered up my gloves and my handbag.

"Thank you, Mrs. Gould. This is very interesting, but I'll have to think about it. I must talk to my husband."

"Don't take too long, Mrs. Buthlay. Mr. Morrah is standing in the wings, sharpening his pencil."

I turned at the door. "You said something about a contract."

She was all business again. "We have one ready for you. Would you like to sign now?"

"No, not quite yet, thank you. At any rate, you must amend it so that neither my name, nor who I am in relation to the family, will appear, *anywhere*. When that is done, we will consider signing . . . not before."

"We wouldn't want it any other way, Mrs. Buthlay. When you have talked to Major Buthlay, just give us a jingle." She laughed. "I would like you to meet my husband, Bruce Gould. Perhaps dinner, the four of us?" Her lips stretched over her teeth in a wide, feral smile.

She opened the door for me, shook my hand, and directed me to the elevator. I turned with one more proviso about my contract and caught the exultant flash of triumph on her face as she closed the door. One half of the heavy double doors with the discreet brass plaque announced that people like the Goulds were so ridiculously well-heeled that they stayed in the Belgravia Suite of the Dorchester when they came to London.

I rang for the elevator and pulled on my gloves. How could I refuse such a sum?

The queen and Mr. Morrah have already decided to publish . . . with or without my help. Beatrice Gould's suggestion that I actually write my own book made my heart bump with anxiety one moment and excitement the next. It had never occurred to me that I could write a book about my years with the Windsors. The doors of the elevator slid open and I stepped inside.

The thought that I might become the published author of a real book made me feel as if I had just bolted down a gin and tonic. *Stop all this nonsense right now.* I could hear my mother's voice. *What is it you really want to do?*

I want to retire, with George, to Scotland, and live a simple, pleasant life that is not made troubling and difficult by trying to work out how to heat our house or find the funds to mend a failing boiler. I would like to roast a chicken in my kitchen and not eke out minced lamb with bread crumbs for rissoles.

I walked through the lobby of the Dorchester and out into the street, eager to rid myself of the heavy scented air. I crossed Park Lane into Hyde Park and slowed my pace. The leaves on the trees cast dappled shadows on paths where birds flew down to peck among flower beds erupting with joyful spring color. But I was still too close to Park Lane and its opulence, its long, sleek, shiny cars, and the fashionable men and women stepping out of them to walk in through the doors of luxurious hotels to drink cocktails as they made plans for the evening.

I kept on going until I found an empty park bench on the edge of the Serpentine. I sank down onto the sun-warmed wooden slats and lifted my face to the late-spring sunshine. *Keep calm*, I told myself as I flexed my fingers, unclenching them from their tight hold on my handbag. With my eyes closed, I listened to the shouts of children playing around me and inhaled the sweet scents of spring flowers and freshly unfurled leaves.

When I opened my eyes, a uniformed nanny wheeling a pram across the grass turned her head to a small four-year-old boy; he had his back turned to her and was digging in a patch of wet grass. Wet mud splattered his legs. She put the brake on the pram and ran back to him, quickly scooping him up from his muddy patch.

He cried out with rage and went flat in her arms like a board—his muddy boots kicking out. She knelt down on the pathway to brush the mud off his legs. I could see her laughing as she scolded. He put his arms around her neck and buried his face in her hair.

They are like our own, I thought as she opened her large handbag and produced a blue ball. Together they ran round the pram, the ball bouncing ahead of them. *And when they grow up, they are still ours.*

CHAPTER THIRTY-EIGHT

January 1950
Nottingham Cottage, Kensington Palace, London

George, look at this. Look what the Goulds have done." Hysteria bubbled up in my throat. I put my hand up to my forehead as I flapped a copy of the *Ladies' Home Journal* magazine at him. There was a photograph on the cover of a pretty brunette in a red cardigan, her wide smile shining in a face vibrant with health and good food. But it wasn't the brunette that had caused me such panic. "*This* is why no one at the palace sent us a Christmas card—and wouldn't come to our mince-pie party!" I flapped the magazine again. I was so shattered when I opened the heavy brown envelope containing the first of the princess articles that I slumped against the front door, my legs too heavy to walk to the kitchen.

George slowly backed out from under the sink. "Two washers and it still leaks." He got to his feet. "This whole place needs a complete renovation."

"George, never mind the leak, look!" He groped around for his spectacles, which were perched on his head. My words were out before he could adjust them on his nose. "It says—in a banner across the cover, 'The Little Princesses. From the time Princess Elizabeth was five, and Princess Margaret a baby, *Marion Crawford* was royal governess.'" I paused, waiting for cries of horror from my husband. For him to snatch the magazine out of my hand so he could roar words of shock that we had been so profoundly fooled by the ruthless Goulds. But George was silent. He had found his spectacles and was polishing them with a tea towel.

"I'll go on, shall I? It says, 'She has written a warm, friendly story of her seventeen years as playmate and companion to the two girls growing up behind the pageantry of royal life at Buckingham Palace. It begins in this issue'! There now, what do you have to say about that?"

George reached out and detached my hand from the magazine. He read it and let the copy fall to his side.

"We have been sent to Coventry; that's what's happened. That is why no one at the palace has been near us for days—except Lady Airlie. She kindly dropped in a moment ago and gave me *this*." My hands were beginning to shake and so was my voice. The humiliation of Lady Airlie's cold, clipped words, when she had always been so particularly kind and warm to me over the years, had made me feel like a housemaid dismissed for stealing. "I am to expect a letter from Lord Hyde's office, the Lord Chamberlain to the Household, within the week, revoking my lifetime right to live here gratis. We have three weeks to vacate . . ."

"But we knew the queen would be annoyed. I thought you were prepared for the worst."

"This is beyond the worst, George. I am being ostracized. Lady Airlie says the queen would never have said a word in anger against writing those articles if my name hadn't been plastered across the headlines. Every single magazine that bought the rights to this article, across the world, has my name and the words 'royal governess' on the front cover. Of course she is angry. I have done the one thing she specifically said I must not do."

I put both hands on top of my head in despair, and George took hold of them and held them in his. "She only made *thirteen* changes to the copy for the entire series when the Goulds sent it to her. She wasn't happy that I had taken the Goulds' offer instead of working with Mr. Morrah, but she was prepared to forgive. And now *this*!"

A firm shake of my hands in his. "For heaven's sake, Marion, calm yourself. She was not prepared to forgive. She is as mad as a scalded cat because *you* wrote it. She knew what was going to be printed because she was given every opportunity to edit it. And what did she do? She didn't touch a word you said about her children, but she certainly took the trouble to take out the bit about her resenting Mrs. Simpson and the king for abdicating. And even that was all insincere fakery. She loves being queen; she eats it up. It's not your fault, my love; it's really not your fault." He took me in his arms, outraged for my hurt. "My God, I don't think I have ever met a woman with such a lust for personal power as Elizabeth Windsor. The abdication shot her into the spotlight, where she could play the role of queen consort to perfection. And she still pretends that the Duke and Duchess of Windsor ruined her life."

"No, George. It's really not about my writing the article." I lifted my head from his chest. "It is the fact that the *Ladies' Home Journal* used my name: Marion Crawford—royal governess. I was so careful to explain that my name was not to appear. It was in the contract! Why didn't you check it?"

"I did—I read through every line, and there was no clause that stipulated your name was to be used. I particularly stressed this with Gould. And he told me that it was all agreed on in your first meeting with Mrs. Gould. I spent most of my time negotiating with the Goulds on world rights and then running back and forth between them and Macmillan, who wanted you to write the book. I had four days in New York, and most of it was spent on the subway or sitting in an office waiting for the contract to be rewritten." I drew away from him, but he pulled me back. "If there is one thing we can be sure of now, at least we understand the intricacies of a publishing contract!" He lifted my chin and two tired eyes looked down into mine. "Marion, you have to believe me, I do know about how to protect your financial interests. But you told me that the first thing you had all agreed on was not to use your name. And there was not a single line in the contract that said anything about what name should be used on the cover." And there it was. The unscrupulous Goulds had been careful not to stipulate that my name was not to be used—and had used it and my relationship to the princesses.

I woke after little sleep. Gray light filtered through the edges of the curtains. I heard George downstairs clattering about in the kitchen. The pain that had settled like a rock in the center of my chest as soon as I had woken made me want to stay in our warm bed and hide from the world.

I got up and swung my legs out of bed. The bathwater was tepid; I ran just enough to wash in and got dressed.

"You need a big breakfast, Marion. No, not just a cup of tea. When you have eaten something, it will not feel like the end of the world."

I watched my husband bustle about. There was a copy of the *Aberdeen Press* open on the table. His search for a house was underway, a house north of the border. After three years of Kensington Palace eccentricities and archaic rules—no washing on the clothesline after midday; only vetted palace personnel to clean our house;

a refusal to correct rising damp, which might ruin the appearance of the outside walls of the cottage; windows that did not fit properly but may not be replaced; and a boiler that sometimes produced scalding water in the middle of the day, but never in the morning or the evening—we were to leave the land of the Sassenachs, and George could hardly contain his delight.

We finished the washing-up, and George pulled the half-filled bucket of soapy water out from under the leaking sink to empty it in the garden. "Look who's walking up our path. That's right, Marion, it's Lilibet." He took me by the shoulders. "Come on now, sweetheart. Did you think she would desert you?"

There was a tentative knock on the door as my clumsy fingers fumbled at my apron strings. I glanced in the kitchen mirror, and a white face looked back at me.

Lilibet's face was just as pale, underneath her suntan, her bottom lip caught between her teeth. But those large, clear, honest eyes told me everything.

"How could you, Crawfie?" she said as she took off her headscarf and came into the house. "I only got back from Malta yesterday. I don't think I have ever seen Mummy quite so angry. She told me that she thought you had gone off your head. She's speechless with fury."

Hardly speechless, I thought, as I turned to go into the kitchen and make tea.

"No, no tea for me. I can't stay. I just came here to beg you to apologize to Mummy."

"But, Lilibet, I have. I have. As soon as I found out that my name had been used, as soon as Lady Airlie gave me the *Ladies' Home Journal*." I pointed at the wretched thing lying on a coffee table, and Lilibet averted her eyes as if it was the sort of smut only sailors bought in fly-ridden ports of call. "I wrote to her saying that the Goulds had been specifically told not to use my name. Her Majesty read the articles; she was invited to edit them . . . The Goulds worded the contract so that they could in fact use my name. I had no intention of them using it. But they did. You have to believe me."

Lilibet shook her head; she kept on shaking it as I walked toward her, my hands outstretched. "Mummy thinks you revealed your name on purpose, to give credence to the articles, to make money out of us. But if you go to her and tell her how distressed you are about how this all happened, she will surely find a way to forgive." Lilibet drew herself up. She glanced at her watch. So, this was not a visit to reconcile, to forgive me for our innocent misunderstanding of the contract.

"There has been a complete misunderstanding, Lilibet." I tried again. "Let me give you Her Majesty's letter to me where she actually gave me permission to work on these articles with Dermot Morrah . . . then perhaps you will understand."

Lilibet pulled her headscarf out of her pocket. "There is only one thing I can think of that might help this situation. Her Majesty is going to visit Princess Marina at Kensington Palace the day after tomorrow at three o'clock." Surely this couldn't be Lilibet speaking? She sounded like Michael Adeane reading through her appointment schedule. "That will be your chance to talk to her." In all the long years I had known her, Lilibet had never used formal titles with me. "I don't think you realize how serious this is," she continued with one of her best Girl Guide looks on her face, the kind she had used as a child when someone made a hash out of building the evening campfire. "You see, Crawfie, everyone who works for us, anyone who has had a connection with us, or who works for the household, might be tempted to reveal . . . to reveal our private lives to the press . . . for money."

"No, no, I am sure they won't." My throat felt tight; my head swam. *Surely Lilibet doesn't believe that I have revealed my name on purpose?*

"Oh, but they will. And I am afraid it is because of that." She lifted her arm and pointed to the woman in the red cardigan beaming at us from the cover of the *Ladies' Homes Journal.* "You see, the only thing we have of our own is our privacy, our right to privacy." She tied her headscarf under her chin and walked to the door. "I hope you can patch things up, Crawfie, I really do. Otherwise, I have a feeling that the queen will forbid us to see you."

I put on my shell-shaped navy blue felt hat and adjusted it so it sat straight on my head. I tucked the ends of my black-and-gray scarf into the collar of my navy wool coat and pulled on black suede gloves. I looked neat, subdued, and tidy in preparation for my unscheduled meeting with the queen. As I settled my hat more squarely on my head, I looked up and saw Lady Airlie's cold face through the window. I jumped with nerves.

"No, thank you, Mrs. Buthlay, I don't have time for tea. I have come from the queen. She has asked me to clarify a few points to you." I had no intention of giving her tea; I had to be on my way in five minutes.

Standing in the middle of my drawing room, her face puckered with concern, her handbag clutched tightly against her body as if I might snatch it from her, she enumerated every one of Her Majesty's grievances, and then, fixing her eyes somewhere off to my left, she ended with, "And on no account are you to write to or try to communicate in any way with Their Majesties or Their Royal Highnesses. I hope I have made myself clear, Mrs. Buthlay. Her Majesty could not have been more emphatic. You are to sever all ties to the family and her household. You may not attempt to make any contact." Her mouth softened, but she would not look me in the eye.

"I'm sure there has been a misunderstanding between you and these ghastly people from the *Ladies' Home Journal*. Some awful mistake. I have known you for many years, and I have always felt you to be a loyal and deeply caring member of the household."

I nodded to acknowledge I had heard, too stricken to speak, and horrified that I might break down. There must be no tears: a show of emotion was considered vulgar.

"Good afternoon, my dear." Lady Airlie reached out and squeezed my arm. "Please don't try to see Her Majesty. She is very angry."

"No, Marion, do not change your plans. You go and see the queen." George glanced at his watch. "It doesn't matter what Lady Airlie says. Lilibet told you it was the best thing to do, so trust her. If you set out now, you will be in time to catch her as she arrives. East Wing, don't forget." He ushered me to the door. "It doesn't matter if we have to leave here, but it does matter that you leave on your terms. Off you go, and remember Lilibet urged you to ask forgiveness. Trust her judgment."

Trust her? Of course I trusted Lilibet. In all my life I had never met her equal for honesty and above all her sound, reasoning head. Margaret might cry and make promises and then change her mind ten minutes later, but Lilibet was solid.

I walked up the gravel path to the front of Kensington Palace and its acres of gravel drive to the entrance of the Duchess of Kent's apartments. There wasn't a soul in sight, but I heard the queen's Daimler long before I saw it; it purred up behind me and came to a halt in a crunch of gravel. Mr. Hughes got out and walked back to the side of the car. He saw me, and for one hopeful moment, I thought that he would call out, or at least tip his cap. But he opened the door, and with his head carefully averted, so he would not meet my eye, he handed out the queen.

Had she seen me as I had walked across the drive from the gardens? Apparently not. She thanked Mr. Hughes, adjusted her handbag on her arm, and started toward the steps to the house.

"Ma'am?" I walked forward, my mouth as dry as parchment. "Your Majesty?"

Her head swiveled round. It had been well over a year since I had seen her. Her round, flat face held no expression. She continued on toward the steps of the palace.

"Please, ma'am." She was two steps ahead of me. "Please let me explain. They were not supposed to use my name . . . I had no . . ."

She hesitated, her right foot on the top step. She *would* listen to me! "It was absolutely agreed that Mr. and Mrs. Gould would not . . ." Her left arm came up and for a terrible moment I thought she was going to push me away.

"I thought I made myself clear." She tilted her head back toward me without actually looking at me. I could see the side of her face; her jaw was clenched. "You are not to approach anyone in my family again . . . ever." Her head turned to me: skin pale and powdery in the winter light, eyes as cold as glass. Her malevolence so palpable that I nearly tripped up as I backed away. "Now that you have heard this from me, would you do me the courtesy of obeying?" And then on she continued, as if she had all the time in the world, toward the open door and the footman holding it, leaving me there: a thoroughly chastised dog who had misbehaved so badly that it must be sent away.

The bare branches of the trees, the tidy flower beds planted with winter aconite and hellebore, the gravel of the drive, and the black Daimler with a blue uniform standing next to it blurred together. I groped in my pocket for my handkerchief. It was empty. I blinked, hard. As hard as I could. *Not here, hold it together. Not here.*

I started to walk back past the Daimler to the sanctuary of the cottage. My nose was running, and a corner of my scarf that had worked free of my collar in my anxiety trembled in the draft of my desperate breath.

A hand at my elbow and I froze. Now what could she possibly want? Was I to be arrested?

"Come along, now." The gentle voice of the man I had known since my arrival at Royal Lodge nearly nineteen years ago. Mr. Hughes had been so much younger then, with thick, wavy dark hair, carefully trimmed and combed. He had chauffeured us on that momentous drive from Windsor Castle back to London through the thousands of flag-waving, cheering crowds on VE Day. He had driven me down from Scotland along icy roads to Sandringham so I could comfort Lilibet and Margaret Rose when Alah died and had met me at the station countless times on my return to the palace from Scotland.

"Come along, now, Mrs. Buthlay. Best foot forward. It happens to all of us in time. We work for them all our lives, and then we out-live our usefulness. It was just a job." His quiet sympathy as he pressed a clean handkerchief into my hand was my undoing. The tears began to pour down my face.

He patted my hand. "They have a lot to be thankful for." He steered me down the path and back through the gardens to the cottages. "There, lass, no need for tears. I read your articles in the wife's *Woman's Own*. I think you did them a great service. It was nothing but the good you shared with the world."

He opened the door to Nottingham Cottage. "Major Buthlay?" he called out. "Put on the kettle, would you, sir? I think your missus needs a cuppa." He delivered me into George's arms. "And if you have a drop of Glen Avon, it wouldn't do nothing but good."

Dusty and disheveled, we faced each other across the empty drawing room with its bare walls and empty windows. "There now, sweetheart; that's the last of it. The men will be here any minute.

Got to feel sorry for them; they have to carry this lot all the way down to the service road, must be nearly half a mile."

I looked around our first home. The furniture we had bought and refurbished would be on its way to Scotland, to Dunfermline and my mother's cottage, as we looked for a house to buy in Aberdeen.

I put the cottage door key down on the draining board of the sink. "I've been thinking, George. When we get to Aberdeen, would you please write to Macmillan and accept their offer to publish *The Little Princesses*?"

He ran his hand back over his head. "You are sure now, are you?"

"Yes, I am quite sure. It was a wonderful job: I loved every minute of it, but that part of my life is over now. I wish it had ended differently, but it didn't."

"You don't regret the *Ladies' Home Journal*?"

I stood on the threshold of Nottingham Cottage and looked out at the serried ranks of winter cabbage and brussels sprouts that we would never prepare in the little kitchen with its leaky sink. "No, not now. Everything I wrote was true. I betrayed no secrets. I told the world what kind, good little girls they were." A group of men were walking toward us, pushing a handcart. "And please make sure when you write to Macmillan that they are clear that my name and that I was the princesses's governess appear on the front cover."

CHAPTER THIRTY-NINE

August 1977
The Road to Balmoral Castle, Scotland

O nly a madwoman would go out on an afternoon like this. A thick, heavy rain had set in as I washed the breakfast dishes and had continued all day. Summer in Scotland was unpredictable and brief—even in August—but I had promised myself I would go to the castle, and I never let myself off lightly from a thing promised. I pulled on my Wellington boots, took my mackintosh from the hall closet, and searched for George's old golf umbrella.

It took twenty-three minutes to drive from Ballater station to the gates of the castle. I'd done it often enough in the old days to know the exact time of their arrival, which gave me six to be there on time. I opened the front door and almost closed it again.

The rain bounced up off the lane and seethed in a muddy puddle around an overwhelmed drain. "It's only rain," I said to my saturated front garden. "It's bound to be over soon." A cold north wind blew up the garden path. "Why am I doing this?" I hesitated on the doorstep. "Her mother will never forgive me . . ." But it was not Lilibet's mother I wanted a reconciliation with. I stepped out into a wall of water and walked down the garden path into the narrow road that led to the castle. And, just like that, the downpour eased to a thin drizzle as I reached the castle gates. I took it as a good omen: I straightened my back and lifted my chin as I turned my head to look back the way I had come.

There they were! I could see headlights on the road coming toward me. I was so intent on watching their approach that I didn't at first see Mr. Frazer come out of his cottage to open the gates. The gates to the castle were beautiful: tall, elegantly wrought in iron, they swung open without a sound.

The lead car slowed to take the turn. I put down my umbrella and raised my hand in greeting. A head turned, and the round, flat face of the queen mother gazed implacably at and through me before turning away. She pretended she hadn't seen me, but I didn't care. The queen mother had always been an uncompromising woman, never mind her celebrated charm. She was always ready with a snub for those who had displeased her.

"I didn't come here to . . ." I bit down on hot words: there was no need to behave like a Glaswegian fishwife. The car splashed through a deep puddle, sending a wash of muddy water back over my feet. "You were always an unforgiving soul," I said to my swamped boots and stepped farther out into the road.

My heart pounded with the belief that the second Daimler would slow to a halt and a well-known and much-loved voice would call out: "Crawfie? Is that you?" The driver would be out of his seat in a second, parade-ground straight as he opened the back door of the car for me. "Be quick and jump in," Lilibet's bell-like voice sounded in my head. "It's far too wet to be out on a day like this!" A trickle of rain ran down my neck; it might have been sweat.

The car came into the turn, and I took another step forward. The driver saw me and slowed. I was so close I could have reached out and touched the side window. A face looked up at me, the expression startled. For a brief second, our eyes met, and I saw recognition in hers, a half smile as a hand raised in acknowledgment. Lilibet leaned forward, the Daimler accelerated, and the tall outline of the duke turned to look out at me through the back window as the car swept on through the open gates.

"Lilibet?" I said to the empty road. She couldn't have recognized me after all. Was I that changed?

I was left alone and wet through to the skin as the cars disappeared under the dripping trees that lined the drive to Balmoral. It was the first time I had seen her in years, except of course on the television at Christmas. I tried to remember our last conversation, but my memory, usually so reliable, refused to cooperate. I could see her standing in the drawing room at Nottingham Cottage quite clearly: her headscarf clasped in her hand, her eyes troubled as she struggled to understand what had happened, what her mother had told her that I had done. I had replayed what she had said so often it had become a meaningless string of words. I shook my head to clear it. "Not forgiven, then," I said. "Not even after all these years."

"Miss Crawford?" A touch on my arm. Mr. Frazer peered out at me from under his black umbrella. Tall, spare, slightly stooped, and lifting his right finger to his cap with the courteous concern that we Scots extended to those who were born here. "Surely it cannae be ye efter aw these years?"

"It *is* Mr. Frazer, isn't it?"

"Th' same. Will nae ye come in out ay th' wet?" His face was concerned as he lifted his hand and pointed to his cottage. The rain picked up: I could barely see him.

"Thank you, but I must be getting back." He nodded; his right finger touched his cap again in salute. He turned to go back to his cottage, to his tea and the warmth of his fireside. I imagined him shaking the rain off his jacket and patiently answering his inquisitive wife's questions.

"Who was tha?" Mrs. Frazer was younger than her husband, and she probably took more of an interest in the world outside Balmoral than he did.

"Miss Crawford." Like all Scots of his generation, he was a man of few words.

"Her that used to be their governess. An' they dinna stop?"

"Nay, they did not."

"Not tha' I'm surprised. Not after wha' she did." And she would bustle off to get his tea.

All the resolve I had felt that had driven me out into this wet afternoon evaporated. I was tired through and through. My mother would have scolded me. "What are you thinking, Marion? It's too wet to go for a walk. Come on, let's make a start on that new jigsaw puzzle." And I would have put away my raincoat, made a pot of tea as she banked up the fire, and we would have settled ourselves in the parlor for the afternoon.

But my mother had been dead these past twenty years, long before I came here to this lonely house on Balmoral Road with George. When I went home, it would be to an empty house. I stopped to gather my resolve to go forward through the rain. George had gone too. He had died in December. I had held his hand as he had faded away from me. The panic and pain I had felt still waited for me every morning that I woke alone in our bed.

"How old is she now? Elizabeth," I asked the slick tarmac as I trudged back down the road. "Fifty? Fifty-one?" Lilibet, Elizabeth—both beautiful names—was still a lovely woman: skin as smooth as cream, marvelously clear blue eyes.

I opened the front door and dripped water all over the hall carpet. I was shivering. My head felt hot, and my fingers trembled as I pried open the buttons on my mackintosh.

The fire had gone out in the parlor. "Tea!" I said to the empty kitchen, anything to break the silence in the house. We Scots drank good, strong tea as an antidote to shock. I put on the kettle and rubbed my wet hair dry with a tea towel.

"I *am* cold," I said in surprise as I backed through the parlor door from the kitchen with a tray laid with the Crown Derby tea service, a gift from Dowager Queen Mary, arranged on starched cutwork linen. I did all my own washing and ironing. No one in the royal household at Balmoral, Sandringham, Windsor, or even the palace would turn their nose up at *my* arrangements for teatime.

I coaxed the fire back to life and sat as close to it as I could get; it was comfort I needed more than warmth. My arms and legs felt as if they were made of wood, fingers so stiff I clumsily spilled milk into the saucer as I poured my tea. I hadn't eaten a thing since breakfast, hours ago. I took a bite of shortbread. It felt like chalk in my mouth, but the tea slid down my grateful throat in two long swallows.

Cup after cup I gulped down, until my nerves quietened and my hands were steady. I reached out and took down onto my lap a large, morocco leather–bound album. I carefully dusted away crumbs from my fingers and opened it.

The photographs, as I turned the pages, greeted me like the old friends they were. The rigid muscles in my neck and shoulders began to lose their tension. So silly of me to have gone out like that in this weather. They probably hadn't even seen me standing there in that heavy downpour. So much better to enjoy the comfort of the fireside in the company of pleasant memories. Wasn't that what old women did? Enjoy the mementos of happier times? I turned another page.

Princess Elizabeth, Lilibet, smiled up at me out of an old black-and-white photograph as if it were yesterday. Eighteen she had been then, wearing an evening gown that Bobo had made for her out of some silk they had found in a storage trunk. She was smiling: a smile that shone out of the old photograph with youthful joy. *Christmas 1944. Windsor Castle*, my even copperplate hand informed me.

"That was when he fell in love with her," I said as I stroked the film of the photo with my thumb. "When he came for Christmas in the last year of the war. He couldn't take his eyes off her—not for a moment."

Two issues were at the back of my mind when I made the decision to write *In Royal Service to the Queen*.

One was that of time and place: Britain from 1931 to 1950, which saw the end of the Great Depression, the start and the end of the Second World War, and the landslide victory of the Labour government in Britain, which was to bring about many laws and reforms for the benefit of the British working people. The other was the monarchy, which provided the backdrop to Marion Crawford's story as the royal governess who was the first servant to the Windsor family to kiss and tell. As I plowed through biographies of the Windsor family and the British aristocracy, I felt at times as if they had been living two hundred years earlier—separated from the reality of a world that was striding forward toward the end of a century of intense change and hopeful progress.

The upheaval in 1936, when King Edward VIII decided to choose love over duty so that he might marry Wallis Simpson, must have added to the immense burden Queen Elizabeth endured as she sought to establish herself as King George VI's queen consort and help rescue the monarchy from the shame of the abdication. Exiled to Paris, the ex-king left the monarchy and the British people tottering.

It was unfathomable in the Britain of that time that a king would abandon his country to marry a twice-divorced woman. And it was deeply disappointing that his younger brother Bertie, crowned King George VI, was hardly what kings were made of: small in stature, timid, with a speech impediment, the new king inspired pity rather than reverence—a man who would infinitely prefer to fade into the landscape and spend a quiet life with his family. But during the war years and particularly during the London Blitz, King George redeemed himself and displayed courage and endurance, remaining in London with his queen beside him during those dark and dangerous times.

They toured bomb sites together, offering encouragement and compassion to their fellow Londoners; observed strict rationing at the palace; and raised money for charity. Who would have guessed that this shy, stuttering man possessed such pluck and courage? And who would have known that his overdressed and apparently frivolous queen possessed such strength of character and a natural talent for public relations? Queen Elizabeth worked extraordinarily hard to put the monarchy she revered back on the path to respectability after the abdication crisis, so it is understandable that she was horrified by Lilibet's determination to marry a man she referred to as "the Hun," even if his royal lineage was far more elevated than her own.

Into the life of the overprivileged ruling class came Marion Crawford: a Presbyterian Scots girl of twenty-two, educated enough to teach the then Duke of York's two little girls: Princesses Elizabeth and Margaret Rose. Crawfie, as the girls called her, was woefully underpaid and extraordinarily impressionable, but she had a strong practical streak and was an enduring presence in the Windsor family through the worst of times. Her loyalty was unquestioning until fate in the shape of two American journalists intervened, and she became the first royal servant to lift the veil and reveal what life was like if you were born to privilege, wealth, and royal tradition.

When Crawfie retired on a meager pension after years of service, she accepted the Goulds' offer to write articles for the American publication the *Ladies' Home Journal* and followed the articles up with her book: *The Little Princesses*. The queen was so incensed at what she called Crawfie's disloyalty for this devotedly loving account of the princesses's childhood that Crawfie's grace-and-favor cottage was taken from her, and she was ostracized by the family for the rest of her life.

But was Crawfie guilty of disloyalty or mere disobedience?

The letter that the queen wrote to Crawfie to "advise" her on how to proceed with the Goulds' offer of "American dollars," is quoted, in this account, from the actual letter Queen Elizabeth wrote in response to Marion Crawford's request to write the Princess articles for *Ladies' Home Journal*.

The queen's letter came to light long after Crawfie died alone in a nursing home. It was among the many personal letters and mementos of her time as governess that she instructed her solicitor, Bruce Russell, to return to the Royal Family on her death. The letter is quite clear that the queen had no problem at all with articles about the princesses being flogged off to *Ladies' Home Journal*—but what she hedges about is who should actually write them. She patronizingly suggests that if Crawfie is short of money she should maybe take a teaching job or help Mr. Morrah (a man who had worked with the king on his speeches and was an expert in royal heraldry, and a candidate selected by the queen) in his article for *Ladies' Home Journal*.

If Crawfie was as disloyal as she was painted to be, wouldn't she have released the queen's letter to the press when the queen shunned her from any contact with her family and took away her rent-free cottage? Or was the compliant governess simply fed up with being used and decided to write her book? She certainly made a small fortune from both magazine articles and her book, enough to retire with her husband to Scotland in comfort for the rest of their years together.

In my opinion Crawfie did the Royal Family a colossal favor: her account of the little princesses—whom she presented as charming, unpretentious, and decent little girls—was hugely appreciated by the postwar reading public of the time. Exactly what the queen and the British Foreign Office had hoped for: a perfect exercise in public relations. But what irked the queen was that Crawfie was identified on the cover of the book: *The Little Princesses: The Story of the Queen's Childhood by Her Nanny, Marion Crawford.* This clearly advertised to everyone in the royal household that the family was fair game for future small fortunes to be made in publishing by generations of loyal servants to come.

Since the letter from the queen to Crawfie was not made available until very recently, at the time, there was considerable speculation in the royal household as to where the true fault lay. Many believed that Marion's husband, George Buthlay, exacted his revenge on a family that had deprived him of happy years he could have spent with Marion, since it was he who signed the contract with *Ladies' Home Journal* on Marion's behalf, leaving it wide open for the Goulds to publish under Crawfie's name, revealing that she was the princesses' governess and giving her articles verisimilitude.

Others thought that Crawfie had been treated poorly after years of selfless service. She was retired on a deplorably lean pension of three hundred pounds a year and awarded a Commander of the Royal Victorian Order—an honor bestowed on those with many years of royal service, rather than the queen's much-hinted-at carrot: Dame Commander of the Royal Victorian Order. Her grace-and-favor cottage might be rent-free and picturesque, but it was desperately in need of renovation.

The queen's reputation in the palace was that of a woman who had great charm and a will of iron who must not be crossed. It was also believed by the royal family that after all the sacrifices they made to serve their country, the very least their servants could do was work long hours for poor pay, and keep their silence. How dare a servant publish a book about the little girls who had been raised so carefully to erase the shame of the abdication!

Or was this entire episode one of misunderstanding between two women who, over the last years of Crawfie's employment, had grown to mistrust each other? Perhaps the queen resented Crawfie's close relationship with Princess Elizabeth, forged in the lonely war years at Windsor Castle—perhaps she resented the support the governess extended to her royal charge in pursuing her marriage to the man she loved.

I hope that in this recounting of Crawfie's life as the royal governess I have managed to touch on what life was like in Britain during those not-so-long-ago years, particularly in royal service, and that Crawfie's intentions, however misguided or misunderstood, were still honorable.

FOR FURTHER READING
ON THE HOUSE OF WINDSOR

George VI: The Dutiful King by Philip Ziegler

King Edward VIII by Philip Ziegler

Royal Sisters: Queen Elizabeth II and Princess Margaret by Anne Edwards

The Queen Mother: The Official Biography by William Shawcross

Prince Philip: The Turbulent Early Life of the Man Who Married Queen Elizabeth II by Philip Eade

Alice: Princess Andrew of Greece by Hugo Vickers

Princess Margaret: A Biography by Theo Aronson

Matriarch: Queen Mary and the House of Windsor by Anne Edwards

Elizabeth the Queen: The Life of a Modern Monarch by Sally Bedell Smith

The Little Princesses: The Story of the Queen's Childhood by Her Nanny, Marion Crawford by Marion Crawford

Our Hidden Lives: The Remarkable Diaries of Post-War Britain by Simon Garfield

ACKNOWLEDGMENTS

My first thanks must go to my mother, who told me the story of "Princess Elizabeth's governess scandal" in 1988. When Marion Crawford died alone in a nursing home in Scotland—still ostracized by the Royal Family—there was no talk of "the Royals" in those days!

Thank you always to my agent, Kevan Lyon. It was during a conversation with her in the spring of 2018 that she asked me if I was enjoying *The Crown*—and Marion Crawford popped into my head again. It was Kevan's enthusiasm for this little-known story that sent me digging around old biographies of the Windsors for more clues as to what had really happened between Queen Elizabeth and her daughters' governess of sixteen years.

Huge thanks to Michelle Vega at Berkley for her insights and encouragement in helping me to bring Marion Crawford's story to fruition. And of course to the delightful team at Berkley: Brittanie Black, Elisha Katz, Jennifer Snyder, and Vi-An Nguyen, who designed the beautiful cover.

But most of all, thank you to my husband—for his patience and his generosity. For his belief that, once again, I will triumph despite my terror of plots that might sink in the middle.

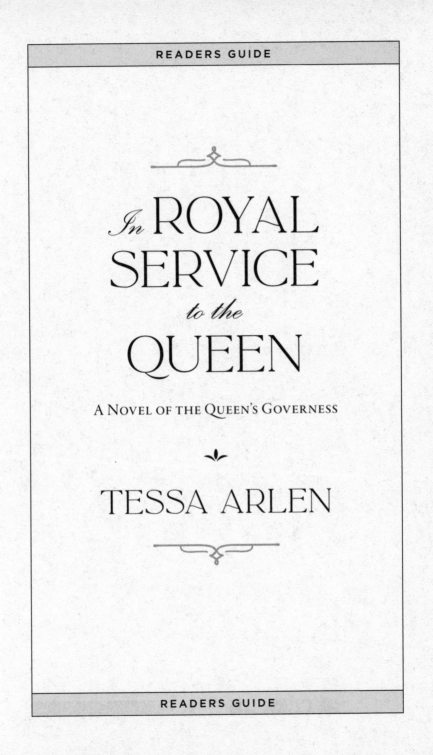

In ROYAL
SERVICE
to the
QUEEN

A NOVEL OF THE QUEEN'S GOVERNESS

TESSA ARLEN

Questions for Discussion

1. Had you heard of Marion Crawford before you read *In Royal Service to the Queen* and, if so, did you come to this book with any preconceptions about her relationship with the Windsor family? Or was Marion's life as the royal governess to princesses Lilibet and Margaret Rose new to you?

2. As portrayed in the novel, contrast Marion's relationship with her mother with the princesses Elizabeth and Margaret's relationship with their mother. Was Marion as dutiful to her mother as Princess Elizabeth was to hers? How much have children's relationships with their parents changed since the 1940s?

3. When Marion first meets the princesses, they are very young. How does this first meeting influence their relationship going forward?

4. In the late 1930s and throughout the war years, Marion sought to bring a sense of ordinariness to the princesses' lives. As portrayed in the novel, what sorts of things did she do with and expect from the princesses to offset palace formality and sycophancy?

5. In contrast to today's standards for female independence, do you consider Marion to be more independent than most women of her age and generation? What was Marion's greatest fear that may have convinced her to pursue marriage with George?

6. Lilibet is a rather serious and dutiful young woman, whereas her sister, Margaret, is outgoing and often outspoken. Which sister do you identify with? Do you believe that Marion had a favorite princess, and if she did, why?

7. As portrayed in the novel, Queen Elizabeth, as consort to King George VI, was described in her day as "a marshmallow made on a welding machine," by Cecil Beaton. Do you think this is an apt description of the queen?

8. Marion comes from a very humble background. How much influence do you think she had on the future Queen of England? Did she believe that her role as governess was to influence her charges or protect them? How did her relationship with the princesses change as they grew from childhood into adolescence and adulthood?

9. Do you believe Marion deserved to be ostracized by the Windsor family for writing the articles about the little princesses for *Ladies' Home Journal*?

10. Marion worked to help support her mother financially, and later, with her earnings from the princess articles, she provided for her and George's retirement. How does that contrast with societal expectations of women in post-WWII Britain and the United States?

11. As portrayed in the novel, how much do you think George Buthlay influenced Marion's decision to "go it alone" and write the articles about the princesses for *Ladies' Home Journal*?

12. Marion is described as the first royal servant to "kiss and tell." Did her book have any impact on the lives of royal servants in future years?

Photo by author

Tessa Arlen was born in Singapore, the daughter of a British diplomat; she has lived in Egypt, Germany, the Persian Gulf, China, and India. An Englishwoman married to an American, Tessa lives on the West Coast with her family and two corgis.